2495
SIGN

JUNIPER, GENTIAN, & ROSEMARY

Other Books by Pamela Dean

The Dubious Hills
The Secret Country
The Hidden Land
The Whim of the Dragon
Tam Lin

JUNIPER, GENTIAN, & ROSEMARY

PAMELA DEAN, P.J.F.

Pamela Dean

TOR®

A TOM DOHERTY ASSOCIATES BOOK
NEW YORK

JUNIPER, GENTIAN, AND ROSEMARY

Copyright © 1998 by Pamela Dean Dyer-Bennet

This book is printed on acid-free paper.

Edited by Terri Windling and Delia Sherman

A Tor Book
Published by Tom Doherty Associates, Inc.
175 Fifth Avenue
New York, NY 10010

Tor Books on the World Wide Web:
http://www.tor.com

Tor® is a registered trademark of Tom Doherty Associates, Inc.

Library of Congress Cataloging-in-Publication Data

Dean, Pamela.
    Juniper, Gentian, and Rosemary/Pamela Dean.—1st ed.
        p.   cm.
    "A Tom Doherty Associates book."
    ISBN 0-312-86004-8 (alk. paper)
    PS3554.E1729J86   1998   98-5520
    813'54—dc21   CIP

First Edition: June 1998

Printed in the United States of America

0 9 8 7 6 5 4 3 2 1

To David,
to Elise,
and to Raphael

ACKNOWLEDGMENTS

The author is much obliged to Laurie Campbell, David Dyer-Bennet, Lydia Nickerson, and Beth Friedman, for commentary;

to Jan Murphy and Richard Knowles, for the loan of their telescope books;

to Karen Uhrig, for advice on astronomical detail and psychology;

to Hilary Hertzoff, for recommended reading;

to Patricia Wrede, Elise Matthesen, and Caroline Stevermer, for support and patience;

and to Emma Bull, Steven Brust, Raphael Carter, Kara Dalkey, and Will Shetterly, for detailed and honest opinions.

JUNIPER, GENTIAN, & ROSEMARY

1

There was a new house next door to Gentian's. The lot it occupied had been vacant since before she was born. Little boys had played baseball there; Gentian and her older sister Juniper organized two girls' softball teams one year and played furiously for one entire summer; the next year Gentian's younger sister Rosemary built a dolls' castle out of cardboard boxes and defended it against all comers with rocks and mudballs. When Gentian became an astronomer, she had taken an old chaise lounge and her beginner's binoculars into the middle of the lot and found the Summer Triangle.

But for the past few years she and her sisters and the Zimmermans, the retired couple on the other side of the vacant lot, had planted gardens there. There had been some conflict about this, since the now-larger boys wanted to play soccer on the lot; but the Zimmermans, everybody said, had a way with teenagers, and they must have exercised it in this instance.

The Zimmermans put in an enormous garden, with squash and corn and watermelon and even potatoes. Gentian and Juniper and Rosemary had each a small plot. Junie's was the smallest because she hated sweaty work. She grew pink and white flowers: tulips, carnations, cosmos, bee balm. Rosemary grew only plants that came from very large seeds: nasturtiums, four-o'clocks, morning glories. Gentian grew so many tomatoes and so much basil that her father threatened to make her learn Italian. She also grew the blue flowers she was named after, mostly because it made Junie and Rosie jealous. Junie hated juniper bushes and rosemary wasn't hardy in Minnesota.

But in September of the year Gentian entered the eighth grade, before the Zimmermans had even dug their potatoes, whoever owned the land must have sold it, for a building firm that seemed to consist of two sullen sunburned teenage boys and a large middle-aged man in dirty white overalls dug a basement and built a house in almost no time.

On September 7, the first day of school, when Gentian dashed past the lot in a driving rain, the Zimmermans' garden was still blazing green and red and yellow. A week later the grass and wildflowers and gardens had vanished into a wilderness of mud and there was a huge pit in the middle of the lot. The week after that, when Gentian came home on Friday afternoon, the wooden frame of the house was up. She did not register this very precisely, because she was planning how to get up at five-thirty the next morning to watch Venus almost occlude Regulus. But when she took out the garbage on Saturday morning, still yawning, the frame had black tarry paper and a roof on it, and she remembered then that she had seen the frame the day before.

On Sunday morning, it had red vinyl siding and the mud was all smoothed and graded. On Monday morning, when she went to school, arborvitae shrubs had been planted to hide the cement-block foundations. By the following Friday morning, there was a bright green lawn. Her father had planted grass seed in the bare spots of their own lawn a week before, but none of that had come up yet.

At dinner that night she interrupted her parents' discussion of Junie's demand to quit band instantly and take driver's education instead.

"Didn't that house go up awfully fast?" she said.

"What house, darling?" said her mother.

"The one next *door*."

"Oh, they've been working on that half the summer."

"They started it the same day we started school," said Gentian, incensed.

"They were very quiet about it, though," said her mother, passing Rosemary the gravy. "I remember thinking that."

"It doesn't fit the neighborhood," said Gentian's father, giving her a look she knew the meaning of very well, though she didn't know what was behind it.

She kept her mouth shut, which was what the look meant, and thought about what her father had said. It was true. The neighborhood was composed of one or two large late-Victorian houses on every block, with the rest being stucco houses of varying size, most of them two-story, built in the 1920s and '30s. The new one next door was a ranch house with mean little windows and a front porch that was just a slab of concrete with a couple of pillars holding up the roof. It was the only red house for blocks around, too; there wasn't another one between here and the river.

"I like it," said Juniper, typically: she would often remark on a subject just as everybody assumed it had been dropped. In this case, Gentian could see, she had forestalled both her mother and Rosemary, each of whom had been about to say something.

"It's modern," added Juniper.

Their own house was one of the three-story Victorians; it had been built in 1901 and still had all its gas lighting fixtures, not to mention the telescope dome. Gentian loved it. Hearing Junie scorn it made her furious. But Junie got away with saying many awful things because she had red hair and people liked to joke about her temper.

"It's not, really," said their mother, reflectively. "It looks like all those little boxes in Richfield. Fifties or sixties stuff. Maybe some from the forties."

"Beats *this* dump," said Juniper, slicing viciously into a leaf of lettuce.

"If we lived in it," said Rosemary, "you'd have to share a room with Genny. It's about the same size as our garage." She favored Juniper with a brilliant smile. She was tiny and blonde and very fetching, and got away with saying a different sort of awful thing.

Not that Junie would ever let anybody, however fetching, get away with anything. Junie was not susceptible to being fetched. "No, *you'd* have to share with Genny," she said. "I'm the oldest, I'd get my own room."

"I'd rather share with Rosie any day," said Gentian. "She doesn't use hair spray."

"I'm pleased to hear," said their mother, very dryly, "that should we suffer a financial catastrophe and be forced into smaller living quarters, you'd be willing to settle things so amicably."

Their father began to laugh. Their mother called him a saturnine redhead, and in fact he didn't look as if he could laugh, so when he did one always felt either complimented or alarmed. In this case, Gentian understood that he was laughing because he was so fond of their mother, but both Juniper and Rosemary were affronted and excused themselves.

"Pumpkin pie for dessert!" yelled their mother after them.

"No, thank you!" Rosemary yelled back; the only response from Juniper was the resounding bang of her bedroom door.

"I know what's the matter with her," said her mother. "She's sixteen. But what's the matter with Rosie?"

"She's eleven," said Gentian.

She herself was the middle sister in all possible ways, including having gotten the freckles that ought to have belonged to Juniper and the miserable sensitive skin that was Rosemary's proper birthright. She had brown hair and boring, symmetrical features. She made up for these deficiencies as best she could by being clever. She knew that she wasn't as quick on the uptake as Rosemary or as good at mathematics as Juniper, but she read a great deal more than they ever bothered with, and could come out with peculiar facts or common-sense observations, as the situation warranted. Most people thought this was funny, but her father always thanked her gravely, and her mother often talked to her as if she were another adult, as long as cleaning the cat box was not the subject of their conversation.

Gentian added thoughtfully, "And she hates pumpkin."

"Eleven's usually a good age," said her mother. "Usually a lot better than fourteen."

"When I was eleven," said Gentian, "I wanted to be a fisherman like in *Captains Courageous.*"

"And what do you want to be now?" said her father.

Gentian was an astronomer, but she wasn't sure the universe knew this yet. She wasn't sure she wanted it to. "A linguist," she said, not quite at random; there had been an article about linguists in an old *New Yorker* that her father had left in the basement bathroom.

Her parents looked at her as if she were an exhibit in a museum. She looked back at them, thinking of the bust of the Duc de Guise in the Art Institute. But her nose wasn't sharp enough.

"Chomskian or what?" said her mother after a minute.

"What," said Gentian.

As she had hoped, this made them laugh, and her father got up and started to clear the table.

On the fourth of October, a family moved into the new house. Juniper and Gentian and Rosemary all crowded into the landing of the front stairway, whose window conveniently overlooked the driveway up which the unfortunate moving crew was carrying a lot of heavy-looking furniture. There were huge carved chairs in dark wood, with tapestry seats; there were carved chests sprouting mirrors; there were bookcases with glass doors, and large mirrors with melted-looking gold frames, and no fewer than three grandather clocks, and a huge number of boxes all of which made the people carrying them grunt and sweat and from time to time swear loudly.

Gentian heard two phrases she had never encountered before, not even among the senior boys who smoked during lunch hour. She made a quiet bet with herself concerning when Juniper would choose to bring them out. Then one of the two young men carrying a gigantic headboard with what looked like roosters' heads for posts tripped on the edge of the driveway. They staggered, swore, recovered, and bore the object in through the sliding glass door at the back of the house. But they had made

Gentian really look at them. They were the same sullen sunburned teenagers who had helped build the house. She looked
back at the truck, and out of it, lugging a peacock-blue wing
chair, came the older man, still in his dirty white overalls.

"It's grandparents," said Rosemary, in disgust. "That's all old
grownup stuff."

"Maybe they're just rich," said Juniper.

"They wouldn't be moving in next door to us if they were,"
said their mother from their own huge carved table, where she
was paying the bills, an operation that always made her speak as
if the entire family were shortly to end up on the street.

"If they are grandparents," said Gentian, "they might plant
a lot of rosebushes and give us cookies."

"I give you cookies," said Juniper, affronted.

"You burn them."

"I cook them. You should just eat the dough, you—"

"Mom," said Rosemary, "would our grandparents have done
that if we had any?"

"Given you cookies, probably," said their mother. "But no
rosebushes. Your grandmother could kill a plant faster than anybody I ever knew."

"What about Daddy's mother?"

"She had mathematical hedges and made cakes like geomet-
rical diagrams," said their father, coming in from the kitchen
with a cup of coffee.

He had filled it too full. Gentian bet with herself that he
would spill three sploshes on the polished floor and one on the
newly shampooed rug. He spilled two on the floor and missed the
carpet by moving so fast he slopped coffee on the table instead.
Gentian owed herself either a large box of chocolate (not to be
shared with her sisters) or a copy of *Bulfinch's Mythology*, depending on how her allowance was holding out, whether the
Martins needed a babysitter this weekend, and whether Jamie
Barrows smiled at her in English class again.

"Well, where *are* they?" said Rosemary, standing on Gentian's foot in an effort to see further.

"In the house directing the movers, stupid," said Juniper.

"I didn't see them go in," said Gentian, "and there's no car, just the van."

"You don't see *everything*, Genny," said Juniper, "even if you are as nosy as—"

"There isn't a car," said Gentian.

"Maybe they came in the van," said Rosemary, thoughtlessly. Gentian could see the precise moment in which she realized that she had been as stupid as Juniper said, and watched her forestall Juniper's scathing comment with a shrill giggle. "Maybe they're vampires and they came in their coffins!" said Rosemary.

"In those wooden chests," said Gentian, collaborating happily.

"Vampire grandparents," said Juniper, relenting. "Watch your kittens when their grandchildren come to visit."

They pressed their foreheads to the glass and watched for coffins. A hat rack, rolls and rolls of carpet, the drawers for all the objects that had gone in earlier, the footboard of the rooster bed. A fine, misty drizzle began. A swirl of wind drove a shower of red leaves from their maple tree, and when it had subsided they saw a boy climb out of the truck.

"There, Junie!" said Rosemary. "A vampire grandchild. It's a *boy,*" she added.

"Is he cute?" said their mother.

"His hair is black, his eyes are blue, his lips as red as wine," said their father, reflectively. "Or do his teeth brightly shine?"

"He's *got* black hair," said Juniper. "Oh, God, Mom, he's as tall as me."

"He's too old for you, then," said her mother.

"Why should his teeth shine?" said Gentian, turning around and addressing her father. If the boy was too old for Juniper, she might as well forget about him; and anyway he was probably like all the seniors.

"If he's a vampire," said her father.

Gentian rolled her eyes.

2

Once the moving van had departed, the new house might as well still have been empty. No lights shone from its windows at night. No flattened cardboard boxes, evidence of unpacking, were put out for the recyclers on the Thursday following the arrival of the moving van. The red and yellow leaves from other people's trees lay unraked on the lush green lawn. The black-haired boy did not go to Juniper and Gentian and Rosemary's school, nor did he appear at the bus stop with the group of kids who attended the larger downtown school, or across the street where local children caught the other bus to suburban magnet schools.

For three solid days after the new family moved in, Juniper pestered both of her parents to go over and welcome them. But their father was not sociable and their mother said she wasn't going to bother people who were busy settling in just because her daughters had an obsession about vampires.

Gentian was grumpy on October 7 because Venus was going to appear only six degrees away from Jupiter, and this allegedly spectacular pairing would be very hard for anybody in the Northern Hemisphere to see because of the planets' position relative to the sun. The sun caused a lot of trouble, one way or another. Entertained by Junie's defeat, but curious herself about the new family and feeling that everybody else might as well suffer annoyance if she had to, Gentian walked into the dining room where the rest of them were still eating their supper and read aloud from the opening of *Pride and Prejudice.*

" 'It is a truth universally acknowledged, that a single man in possession of a good fortune must be in want of a wife. However little known the feelings or views of such a man may be on his first entering a neighborhood, this truth is so well fixed in the minds of the surrounding families, that he is considered as the rightful property of some one or other of their daughters.' "

She received blank looks from her sisters and a rather sharp remark from her father, to the effect that he might be very like Mr. Bennet but she should thank her lucky stars that Mother was nothing like Mr. Bennet's wife.

"What's Mr. Bennet's wife like?" inquired Rosemary.

"She has nerves," said Gentian, "and she's not very smart."

"Oh, like Rosie," said Juniper.

"Just because I'm *sensitive,*" said Rosie, hotly.

"I am sensitive," intoned Gentian, reminded irresistibly of her Latin class, "you are nervy, she's nutty as a fruitcake."

Her mother cast up her eyes. Her father laughed.

"Behold the linguist," he said.

Rosemary laughed suddenly, having figured out that Gentian was probably making as much fun of Juniper as of anybody else.

"But don't you think it's weird they never go out?" said Juniper.

Her mother said dryly, "I go to work, your father holes up in his study most of the day, you girls go to school. They could cavort around the yard from ten to two every day and nobody would notice a thing."

"But they didn't put their recyclables out or anything."

"Vampires don't have recyclables," said Rosemary.

"They could read the newspaper," said Gentian.

"They don't get the newspaper," said Juniper. "I asked Marie and she said they don't subscribe."

"Unlike Mr. Bennet," said their father, almost as dryly as their mother, "I don't need to get my daughters off my hands by any means available. If you'd pay half as much attention to your social studies class, Junie, as you do to the neighbors, I wouldn't have to go talk to Mrs. Gruber on Monday."

Gentian got up quietly and went through the dining room and the butler's pantry and into the kitchen. The repeated mention of neighbors had reminded her of something. The green tomatoes she had snatched from her vines the day before the bulldozer smashed all the gardens were sitting in a paper sack in the bottom of the refrigerator, fat and bright red and, if the truth be told, a bit past their prime. She had a standing agreement with the Zimmermans that she would give them tomatoes and they would give her potatoes. Mrs. Zimmerman, who seemed to think gardening was vastly amusing, called it the Nightshade Treaty.

She went out the back way. It was dark already, and chilly. The stars stared at her like a host of censorious daisies. She walked through the soaking grass along the side of their house, rather than jumping the new retaining wall to land on the new driveway. She passed through the square of light from the stairway window, and heard her mother's reading-aloud voice. They had turned back to *Pride and Prejudice*. Gentian looked at the new house. It was altogether dark. Even the glass of its mean windows reflected no lamplight from her own house, no starlight from anywhere.

Ordinarily, she would have walked to the center of the vacant lot and located particular stars. She went on down the driveway and right into the middle of the street, where she tilted her head back and found Aldebaran, Capella, and the Pleiades. She used averted vision to look at the Pleiades, directing her gaze off to the east of them, but keeping her attention on them directly, which meant that the parts of her eye that were better at gathering dim light were trained on them. It was one step further from watching something out of the corner of your eye. She had had a lot of practice at this technique before she became an astronomer or knew it had a name. She had used it to observe Juniper while appearing to ignore her. Nobody ever recommended using averted vision on so easily visible an object as the Pleiades or one's sister, but she liked doing it. She thought the Pleiades deserved the attention. Juniper did not deserve it, but as a dangerous older sister, had compelled it.

The Pleiades were called the Seven Sisters. Gentian supposed bright Alcyone would be the dangerous older one. To Gentian's direct vision, only six of the sisters were visible; but with averted vision, on a good clear moonless night, the dimmer Pleione and Celaeno and sometimes even Asterope would creep out against the black night. She let them do this, grinning briefly at the thought that she and her sisters could have had even more awful names than they did, and thought about her work for the month.

In October this year, Venus would follow the sun down so closely that you could almost never find it. Mars and Jupiter would linger longer, sharing the same part of the sky but not coming too close, like cats who only stay together in the kitchen because the food is there. Next week the waxing moon would rise in the evenings with Saturn, grow round, and pass above it from the stars of Pisces into those of Aquarius. Saturn blazed in the southern sky every night. Beginning on the eleventh of the month, Mercury, so rare and elusive, would creep above the horizon an hour before sunrise, higher and higher each day. Between it and Saturn, Gentian would have trouble finding time to do her homework.

She had a lot of homework this year. She and her best friend Becky had remarked to one another just today that school got socially easier and intellectually harder as one grew older. This year was all right, socially. She and Becky and the rest of the Giant Ants had all been friends since the third grade, when Steph joined them. Becky and Gentian had known each other since nursery school, Alma had arrived in kindergarten, and Erin had come along in second grade. This year, finally, nobody had any classes from the teacher who picked on Erin, or the one who thought Claudius was the good guy in *Hamlet,* or the one who expected Gentian to be just like Juniper.

Gentian's neck was getting sore. She looked at the new house again.

It was the same from the front, as dark as dark could be, taking the light from her house's porch, and from the streetlight, and not giving it back. She went up the Zimmermans' driveway to the Zimmermans' back door, and the other side of the new house was just the same. Gentian banged the knocker. The knocker made a different noise now that there was a new house here. The strong white light from the fixture over the Zimmerman's back door, which had once stretched almost to Rosie's flower garden, stopped at the edge of the Zimmermans' lawn. The new house must be casting that black shadow.

Mr. Zimmerman answered the door after about a minute. He had a cadaverous face, a large belly, and a lot of gray hair. The Zimmermans' two white cats peered around his legs.

"Hi," said Gentian. "I brought your tomatoes. I'm sorry they're late."

"Hello, Genny," said Mr. Zimmerman, who was punctilious, Gentian's mother said, to a fault. "How nice to see you. Come in and say hello to Razzy and have some tea, and I'll find you some potatoes."

Mrs. Zimmerman's name was Rosemary Ann, but there wasn't much confusion with Gentian's baby sister, because most people called Mrs. Zimmerman Annie, and her husband called her by that peculiar nickname made up from her initials. Gentian would have hated it, but Mrs. Zimmerman had never said anything about it. Gentian came in, laid the string bag of tomatoes down gently on the kitchen table, and petted the nearest cat.

"I wasn't sure you'd have any," she said, "on account of the gardens getting plowed up."

"We didn't think you'd have any tomatoes," said Mr. Zimmerman. "Sit down, do please." He went to the head of the stairs and called, "Razzy! Gentian's here!"

"I picked all the green ones," said Gentian. "But they should be okay. These all had yellow bits already. Dad made the really green ones into relish."

"I'm surprised you even had any green ones," said Mr. Zimmerman, filling the big red kettle with water and plunking it down on the burner. "They started in on that house so early."

"Not till the first day of school," said Gentian, with a slight sinking sensation.

Mrs. Zimmerman came into the kitchen. Like her husband, she was tall and had a lot of gray hair. She, however, had a round face and a small belly.

"Oh, good," she said, taking the tomatoes out of the string bag and admiring them one by one. "Snatched from the jaws of destruction."

"Did you get any potatoes?" said Gentian.

"Well, they were all new ones, but we'll just think of it as an unearned luxury. I've got your bag all ready; I just haven't gotten around to bringing it over."

"It's that house," said Gentian. "It's in the way."

"That's true," said Mrs. Zimmerman, sitting down across the table from her. "And it went up too fast. There wasn't any time to get used to it."

"I didn't think it was fair," said Gentian cautiously, "that they started it the same day we went back to school."

"Yes, that must have made the whole process seem even faster, because you weren't home all day to watch it."

"They started it long before the first day of school," said Mr. Zimmerman, spooning tea into the blue pot. "July sometime."

Gentian looked at Mrs. Zimmerman, who shook her head.

On a foggy Sunday afternoon a week or so later, the vampire grandmother came to the back door and asked to borrow a snake. Rosemary, who answered the bell, was thrown into utter confusion by this request. Gentian, doing her homework at the kitchen table because they were reading Poe's stories and these scared her too silly to sit up in the attic by herself, looked up and saw a thin, gray-looking woman in blue clothes, squinting at the bewildered Rosemary.

"Is your drain clogged up?" said Gentian.

"I thought you used a fish for drains," said Rosemary.

"No, dummy, that's for electrical work. Ask her in, Rosie."

Rosemary, still looking bewildered, moved aside, and the woman came in, blinking in the fluorescent light as if she didn't much care for it. "I'm Mrs. Hardy," she said. "We moved in next door." She made this sound like a daring and unusual exploit.

"I'm Genny," said Gentian. She was embarrassed. She felt

they had been inhospitable not to have visited the newcomers by now. "This is Rosemary. Give her some coffee, Rosie, and I'll get Mom."

Mom, when gotten, managed to persuade Mrs. Hardy to sit down and drink her coffee, which was more than the dithering Rosemary had done. Rosemary's eyes were enormous. She had probably been remembering that vampires didn't eat or drink. Mrs. Hardy did drink her coffee, and swallow it, though she refused the spice cookies Juniper had made.

Gentian and Rosemary sat very quiet, eating the cookies themselves, while the two women talked about the neighborhood and the dreadfulness of drains and the worse dreadfulness of plumbers. Gentian noticed, with a feeling half of regret and half of relief, that Mrs. Hardy's fingers were of the usual length with regard to one another, and that her canine teeth were no more pointed than anybody else's. They didn't shine, either: she probably needed to go to the dentist.

Gentian thought her mother and Mrs. Hardy were so unalike that they might as well belong to different species. Mrs. Hardy was of an undistinguished height, and so thin she seemed almost like something made out of plywood. Gentian's mother was tall, taller than her father, but round; her forehead and cheeks and chin, her forearms and hips and waist, were all round. Mrs. Hardy was nondescript; you couldn't remember what color her hair or eyes were once you had looked away from her. Gentian's mother was vivid: she had rich brown hair with a lot of red in it, and startlingly green eyes, and a lot of pink in her skin. Mrs. Hardy's manner was dull. Her mother was not effusive, but her dryness had a definition about it.

The two of them had begun to talk about their families. Mr. Hardy was, it appeared, hopeless with plumbing, though he dealt well with furnaces and wood stoves and barbecue grills.

"What about your son?" said Gentian's mother.

Mrs. Hardy looked startled, and then began to laugh weakly. "Him? Oh, no," she said. She seemed to realize that this response lacked something, and added, looking at Gentian with her nondescript eyes, "I think he's about your age."

"He's tall for fourteen," said Gentian's mother.

"I'm wrong, then," said Mrs. Hardy, as if she were used to it. "He's fifteen."

"He's tall for that, too," said Gentian. "Tell him to watch out for my big sister."

Mrs. Hardy looked dubiously at Rosemary, who was trying not to laugh; and Gentian's mother changed the subject. Mrs. Hardy left after another five minutes. Gentian cleared away her coffee cup and examined it. No, she had really drunk that coffee.

"Why didn't you tell her her son could come over and meet us?" said Gentian to her mother.

"Because if I had, Juniper would have explained to me that having his mother tell him it was okay was the very best way of making him never come near any of you girls. And then she would say I had done it on purpose."

"Do I have to be like that when I'm sixteen?"

Her mother put the cups and saucers in the dishwasher, laughing. "I don't think there's a law that says you have to," she said. "Statistics, however, are very much against you." She leaned against the cabinet and pushed her hair out of her eyes. "From the other side," she went on thoughtfully, "it feels very different."

"But I don't want people discussing me in the kitchen."

"I'll remind you of that on your sixteenth birthday," said her mother.

She went off to root her husband out of his study and make him come for a walk, a process Gentian had admired so many times that she no longer needed to witness it to be amused. Juniper was over at her friend Sarah's house watching all Sarah's brother's tapes of "Red Dwarf," and Rosie was with her Girl Scout troop being shown the wonders of Lock and Dam Number One on the Mississippi. When the door had closed behind her parents and she had watched them to the end of the block, Gentian went up to the second floor and into Junie's room.

Junie had the room at the head of the stairs. It wasn't very large, but Gentian coveted it intensely because there was a sunporch attached to it and she had, since she was about six, wanted it herself for a library. Junie had painted it pale lavender and made lavender-and-green-striped cushions for the two old wicker chairs they had found there when they moved into the house. She had announced plans to paint the chairs too, as well as a long wicker table found in the garage; then she was going to make a rag rug for the floor and have her friends in to tea. The Portmeirion teapot and cups she had gotten for her birthday three years ago sat on the grimy gray table. In the corners were piles of clothes Junie hadn't gotten around to mending, baskets of rags for the rug, their mother's old sewing machine, stacks of old magazines Junie hadn't cut recipes out of yet, and a towering, precarious pile of yellowed newspapers. Junie had planned to make a scrapbook out of articles about the explosion of the space shuttle, but she hadn't cut those articles out yet either.

The wasteful use Junie made of this room filled Gentian with a combination of scorn and envy that almost made her feel sick. It was idiotic of her. She was obviously destined for the attic room, because it contained the dome the Victorian builder had put in for his telescope. Juniper's room was hopeless for astronomy. But Gentian coveted it just the same.

She unzipped the striped cover of the back cushion on the right-hand chair and pulled out Junie's diary, a fat blue leather book stamped with silver roses. Junie had been keeping it for two years, and had almost come to the end of it, although she wrote very small and sometimes skipped a week at a time.

Gentian sat down in the other chair and flipped through the diary backwards. She didn't manage to come up here very often in the summer, and the weather had been so good for stargazing that she had missed her usual mammoth catch-up session in September.

It was only during the summer that Junie was forced to admit in her diary that she had a family. During the school year she filled it up with accounts of lunch-table conversations and chance encounters with boys in the hallways and the long conversations she and Sarah had on Friday nights when they slept over with one another. The way Junie recorded these conversations drove Gentian to distraction. Junie would remember stuff about whether Sarah thought Denny liked her, and would write every last line down; but if they had an interesting discussion, like what Sarah thought about having sex, or whether this or that book was any good, Junie would just note it briefly.

Gentian found the beginning of summer vacation, marked with a double line of stickers in the shape of roses, and began to read. Her sister had spent several pages bemoaning the fact that she wouldn't see Denny all summer and had only one class with him next year. That took care of the month of June. She spent most of July writing poetry that didn't rhyme and was full of ellipses. Gentian skipped over that. She knew that Becky's poetry was much better.

In August Juniper became hugely excited about something she talked about in such cryptic terms that Gentian was mystified. It had to do with running into Denny in the library one weekend and finding out that Sarah had a crush on Denny too, but exactly how Juniper had determined this was uncertain. Juniper wrote a lot of poetry about it, but it wasn't very coherent.

In September Juniper rhapsodized about the Creative Writing class she (and Sarah) shared with Denny. She also wrote down a number of uncomplimentary remarks about both her younger sisters, but particularly Rosemary. Rosemary, she wrote, was a wimp and a coward and was likely to turn out even worse than Gentian. Juniper had dared Rosemary to knock on the door of the new house next door, and Rosemary had said she would, but she hadn't.

"And why couldn't you do it yourself, Junie?" said Gentian. The sound of her own voice made her jump. It was getting late.

Gentian put the diary back, zipped up the cushion cover, shook that cushion and the one she had been sitting on with great vigor, and went on up to her own domain on the third floor to do her homework.

3

entian liked her room. Juniper, predictably, hated it. Rosemary only liked it in the summer. Gentian always thought of this on first opening the door. She supposed Rosie meant the white walls and the green rugs. It was a perfect place for the telescope, especially in the winter, when she could make it as cold as she needed to for stargazing without any complaints from her family.

Gentian shut her white-painted door behind her. She walked around her room, turning all the lights on one by one, naming their names as she did so. Tau Ceti, Rigel, Betelgeuse, Epsilon Indi, Epsilon Eridani, Sirius, Alpha Centauri. They were electrical fixtures now, but they had once burned gas, as stars all did. This was not a scientific observation, but she thought it might pass as a poetic one. She had tried to put in colored bulbs, to match the colors of the stars, but the strange light had been impossible to read by. She had the colored bulbs in a drawer, and put them in once a year, on her birthday.

Maria Mitchell was curled up in the middle of Gentian's bed, with her tail wrapped around her nose. Gentian had named her five years ago, with the best intentions, but the name embarrassed her more every day. She had meant it as a tribute, but surely there were better tributes to the first woman astronomer than naming your cat after her. Luckily, Maria Mitchell had patches of brown and yellow and orange and white, so Gentian's family had been calling her M&M for years. Gentian called her Murr, but could not seem to stop thinking of her by her full name.

Gentian decided not to bother her, and walked to the window, stepping deftly over stacks of books and piles of folded T-shirts and tangles of yarn. She climbed the scuffed cherrywood steps to the little platform under the dome, opened the dome up, put her hands on either side of the telescope, and leaned to the eyepiece. It was not a particularly exciting night for astronomy, but keeping one's hand and eye in was a good thing. Besides, looking at the Pleiades with her eyes alone always made her want to find them through the telescope.

Something was blocking her view. Gentian made adjustments, blinked, and looked again.

It was the new house. It couldn't be. It was one story tall; she was at the top of a three-story house. But there the new house was, with its mean windows and red vinyl siding whose boards were too wide for its height and shape. Gentian sat on her stool, dumbfounded, and gazed at the telescope for a few moments. Then she opened the bottom drawer of her desk and took out its manual. She had memorized it when she got the telescope, but sometimes looking at the printed text would make the right information stand out.

There was nothing in the manual she hadn't thought of trying, and certainly no indication of how a telescope trained on the heavens from the third story could be blocked by a one-story house next door. It was a very simple mechanism.

Maybe Becky could come over for dinner sometime this week and help her figure things out. Becky didn't know much about telescopes, not half as much as Gentian did, but she had a way of looking at something that was broken and seeing what was wrong with it. Sometimes she could fiddle with it and fix it, always looking vague and pretending she didn't know what she was doing. This annoyed Gentian, and had done so since she first met Becky in preschool and Becky put the wheel back on

Gentian's truck for her. But Becky was a poet, and that was how she thought poets should behave. Gentian used to give her biographies of poets who behaved quite differently—which turned out to be most of them—but it never changed Becky in the least.

Gentian's father called Becky's talent "the laying on of hands." Becky had done it for his computer once in a while, and had also dealt with the big kitchen mixer and the microwave. She even put microwaves and computers in her poetry, which helped resign Gentian to the way she moped around.

Gentian patted the telescope, put the manual away, and sat down at the desk with her geometry homework. She hardly needed her mind for it: it was a repeat of last week's lessons because half the class had failed the pop quiz and, Mr. Schoenbaum said, a little more practice wouldn't hurt the rest of them. Gentian scribbled diligently and thought about Junie's diary.

It was odd. She would never dream of reading her mother's or her father's correspondence; and when Becky had left her alone in the room with Becky's diary because her grandmother had called from Canada unexpectedly, Gentian shoved it under the pillow so it wouldn't tempt her. She was just as curious about Becky, but she felt a moral obligation to her privacy that she didn't feel toward Junie's.

All's fair in love and war, she thought. It's not love, so it must be war. But if it is, what are we fighting for? Their father always used to ask them that, separating them when they were too young just to use words, and infuriating everybody, including their mother and probably the neighbors, by singing that stupid song.

They weren't fighting for anything, though. They weren't even fighting over anything, really. Becky, who had no sisters and adored her younger brother, had witnessed one stellar Gentian and Juniper fight in appalled silence, gone home, and called Gentian a few hours later to inform her that the two of them were like the fighting cocks in Plato, who fought only because the one would not give way to the other.

Gentian thought this missed the point. Juniper wanted things her way, all the time. Why should anybody give in to her?

She folded the finished geometry problems into her textbook and looked gloomily at her assignment list. Even putting it into a blank book with the Hertsprung-Russell diagram on the front and the Great Nebula in Andromeda on the back did not always compensate for the fact that it was full of things she had to do whether she wanted to do them or not. She was supposed to read about Alexander the Great, write a book report, and be prepared to discuss Act I of *Julius Caesar.*

Gentian picked up the Arden paperback of the play and ruffled through it. She liked her school, on the whole. The people who ran it believed that children learned better if they were not regimented too rigidly, if they were allowed to set their own schedules and learn at their own pace. You were spoken to if you skipped all your classes or never did any work, but there was none of the marking people tardy and taking attendance every hour and making a tremendous fuss about hall passes that ordinary high schools excelled in. You could take any semester's class over and over again until you had learned what you needed to. Gentian got science credit for her astronomical work, though they wanted so much detailed reporting of what she had looked at that it was sometimes more trouble than it was worth.

Gentian's mother said the school's basic attitude was more like that of a college. She also said that she doubted very much that all children could learn this way, but she was willing to let hers try. Since they didn't want to go to the regular school and be ordered around, they mostly went to school and mostly did their homework.

The one thing Gentian did not like about her school was the dreadful enthusiasm with which teachers were always trying out new things. She supposed it was only natural: if they hadn't been enthusiastic about having a new kind of school, they'd still be teaching in the old kind. But you never knew what wild idea they would come up with. You didn't have to go along with the ideas, but they looked sober and then coaxed if you didn't, and they were not above using moral pressure or peer pressure to make you join in.

This year they had decided to have study groups. Since each of the Giant Ants was in a separate one, Gentian suspected that the point of the exercise was to shake up whatever habits and cliques people had fallen into and force them to make new friends. Since the Giant Ants were among the best habits Gentian had, this was annoying. The Giant Ants had agreed when they went from being Gentian and Becky and Erin and Steph and Alma, or "those five troublemakers," or simply "Them," to being a deliberate group, that they would always stand by one another and never laugh at one another's ambitions. It was silly to try to keep them away from one another.

She supposed her study group was all right. It contained the best Latin scholar in probably the entire school, which was useful, and there were two good mathematicians and an artist and somebody who was good at biology. But none of them, not one except Gentian, could read aloud well, and the thought of reading Shakespeare with them, as Mrs. Peterson had suggested, made the back of Gentian's neck prickly with embarrassment. She had said she was busy for every meeting time they proposed—she really was for some of them, what with Mercury and Saturn—and they had gone ahead without her. But she would feel dumb when Mrs. Peterson started asking how reading *Julius Caesar* out loud made them think about it, if she had to say she hadn't read it.

Gentian shut the book and took it with her downstairs. Her parents were in the kitchen, her mother reading to her father while he washed the dishes that could not be put into the dishwasher. Gentian lingered in the doorway, listening in the hope of being able to guess the book and make a grand entrance.

" 'Ronay heard music then, for many voices,' " her mother read. She read flatly when it was narrative, but she was good at sounding different for each character.

" 'It was old music, written long ago, when the Moon had seemed a simple place; that didn't matter. "Four things." ' " Her mother gave him a low and mellow voice, like the one in which she talked to the cats but without the affectionate edge, and with no babytalk.

" 'He waved a finger toward the ceiling.' "Air and light." He picked up the glass of tea. "Water." He pointed at Matt. "And people." He sat on the arm of the chair, bringing himself a little lower than Matt. "With air and light and water, and people to work with them, we can make anything else we need." ' "

"Heinlein!" proclaimed Gentian, walking into the kitchen. Her parents adored Heinlein. He made her itchy; he made her feel as if she were sitting in a lecture hall and needed to sneeze.

"I can't tell which one, though," she added, as her mother looked up from the book.

"That's because it isn't Heinlein," said her father, and made a tremendous splash with the dishmop.

Her mother shut the book over one finger and showed Gentian the cover. *Growing up Weightless,* it said, in gray-brown letters edged with blue. Gentian stood perfectly still. The phrase affected her as certain lines of Keats or Swinburne or Sarah Teasdale had, as if it were full of ineluctable meaning. I'd like to do that, she thought, I'd like to grow up weightless. But what does it mean? She didn't ask. She was afraid the book would be nothing like the effect of its title, and if she asked any questions her parents would be after her to read it.

"I was wondering if you'd like to read some Shakespeare," she said. "We have to discuss the first act of *Julius Caesar* in English tomorrow."

"Not one of my favorites," said her father, letting the water out of the sink.

"Act One's short, isn't it?" said her mother, putting down her own book and taking the Shakespeare from Gentian.

"Yes, but if we read one act with her, we'll have to read them all. Ask Mrs. Peterson why you kids can't read *King Lear,* Genny."

"We get that after all the histories and comedies."

"Too long to wait," said her father. He dried his hands and turned around. "All right, we'll do it. But it's bedtime right after."

"Okay," said Gentian. She could read her history under the bedclothes by flashlight and write the book report on the bus. "Who's going to rouse out the Sisty Uglers?"

"You, if you go on talking like that," said her mother.

"I'll do it," said her father, "and you'll wash the dishes for me tomorrow or I'll know the reason why." He hung the dish towel on its hook and left the kitchen.

"So how is it?" said Gentian to her mother. "Is he as bossy as Heinlein?"

"No," said her mother. "In fact, he hardly deigns to tell you what's happening. I'm not sure I want you reading it, though: you might get ideas."

Gentian eyed her narrowly. It was probably a ploy to get her to read the book. Her mother just looked placid, a thing she was very well equipped to do, being so plump and round in the face. It was deeply deceptive, however: her mother was about as placid as a waterfall.

"What kind of ideas?"

"There's a group of kids in here that reminds me of you and your cronies, that's all. Smarter, though."

She grinned, and Gentian made a face at her.

Gentian's father called them from the living room, and they went in to join him and Juniper and Rosemary. Juniper looked sullen and Rosemary eager, which was normal. Gentian sat on the couch with her mother, since Rosie had snagged the rocking chair and Junie was glowering all over the loveseat. Her father sat on the floor and gave out the parts; it was his turn, thank goodness. Her sisters didn't fuss as much about his choices as about one another's.

He gave Juniper the part of Cassio, which annoyed Gentian since it was her favorite. Then he gave Gentian Brutus, and Juniper scowled and Rosemary said, "Oh, good name for her!" and her father turned around and presented her with the part of Caesar's wife and told her she had better start being above reproach. Rosemary pouted. Their mother received the part of Mark Antony with a quirk of her mouth; their father, having taken Caesar, briskly handed Flavius to Juniper, Marullus to Gentian, the carpenter to Rosemary, the cobbler to their mother, and the soothsayer to himself. Then he advised them to start, because bedtime waited for no man and for no girl neither. Shakespeare always made him talk like that.

They read Scene I well, Gentian thought. Juniper, as Flavius, scolded the carpenter and the cobbler for being out in their best clothes on a working day in much the same manner as she nagged at her sisters about leaving wet towels on the floor of the bathroom. Rosemary answered her saucily as the carpenter, and their mother produced, for the cobbler, a voice of bland innocence so like Juniper's that the rest of the family howled with laughter and Juniper sulked, which caused her line, "I'll about, and drive away the vulgar from the streets," to be uttered with particular force and meanness.

That was the end of the first scene. For Scene II, they stopped to read the notes about the foot race, part of the celebration called Lupercalia, during which women who could not have children stood where the runners, who were considered holy because the Lupercalia was a religious feast, could touch them and maybe cure them. Rosemary said that the whole family should celebrate the Lupercalia and all the runners could touch Mrs. Zimmerman. Their mother said very sharply that Mrs. Zimmerman did not need a plague of children at her age and already played grandmother to the entire block, and that if any child of hers ever said anything to Mrs. Zimmerman about the Lupercalia or being barren or anything similar, said child would be very sorry indeed.

"Huh," said Rosemary, quelled but not persuaded. "Mrs. Zimmerman has a sense of humor. Not like some people."

"The quarreling's for later," said their father. "Save your energy. And you are Caesar's wife, not carping Kate. Read."

"You read," said Rosemary. "Caesar's got the first line."

They read. Mark Antony, abjured to touch Calpurnia as he passed her in the race, said, "When Caesar says, do this, it is performed." Caesar's real-life daughters giggled, and Caesar frowned horribly at them. Then he changed into the soothsayer and, in thrilling accents, demanded Caesar's attention; Casca said, "Bid every noise be still," and their father, once more in Caesar's voice, said, "Would I could do so much in my own household."

"Caesar expected to do it to the world, and look what happened to him," said Gentian.

"Casca expected it for Caesar," said their mother. "Though you don't notice Caesar protesting."

"Get on with the play, for God's sake, or we'll be here until midnight," said Juniper.

"It's my homework," said Gentian, "and I like the—the—"

"Exegesis," said her mother, briskly. "But we can do that afterwards, and Junie can go to bed."

The soothsayer said, "Beware the Ides of March," turned into Caesar, and said, "He is a dreamer. Let us leave him. Pass on." Then Cassius and Brutus had a long conversation. Juniper, as Cassius, invited Gentian, as Brutus, to come along and watch the race in a tone about as friendly as the one she employed to tell Gentian it was Gentian's turn to take the kitchen scraps out to the compost pile. Gentian had no trouble saying, "I am not gamesome" in a weary voice.

Juniper answered, "You bear too stubborn and too strange a hand over your friend that loves you."

Gentian forgot she was speaking to her sister and gave Brutus's speech of excuse with what she hoped was great conviction. She ended, "Poor Brutus, with himself at war, forgets the show of love to other men." Brutus needs the Giant Ants, she thought, not these weirdos. She wondered what the Elizabethan would be for "Giant Ants," and had to work not to laugh.

Juniper answered, "Then, Brutus, I have much mistook your passion" convincingly enough that Rosemary did not giggle. They argued for a while; then the sound of a crowd cheering made Brutus say, "I do fear the people choose Caesar as their king," and they were off conspiring. Cassius, rather as Juniper might have described Rosemary's malingering of a Monday morning with her homework undone, explained how Caesar couldn't swim well and occasionally got sick and acted piteous, which meant he could not be a god and therefore was not fit to rule Rome.

Brutus noted another cheer from the crowd, but did not otherwise reply to Cassius. Gentian marked this technique down for future use with her actual elder sister.

Cassius, unaware of this subsidiary plot, began the famous

speech they always wanted you to learn in school; Juniper might indeed still, several years later, have it by heart. "The fault, dear Brutus, is not in our stars, but in ourselves, that we are under-lings." My fault certainly isn't in my stars, thought Gentian. Then came the temptation: " 'Brutus' will start a spirit as soon as 'Caesar,' " and more ranting against Caesar. When Cassius had done, Brutus allowed as how Cassius had a point, which Brutus had been thinking about already, and said they would talk about it later. It was a shifty speech, moving back and forth from agreement to hesitation, like Gentian's father when he brought in stray cats or dogs and had to agree that they would be a terrible nuisance, without ever planning to take them away again.

Caesar and his train then came back. Caesar said to Mark Antony, "Let me have men about me that are fat, sleek-headed men, and such as sleep a'nights. Yon Cassius hath a lean and hungry look. He thinks too much; such men are dangerous."

Gentian's mother read blithely, "Fear him not, Caesar; he's not dangerous. He is a noble Roman, and well founded." Her tone made Gentian realize how chilling this was, because Antony was wrong and Cassius was going to kill Caesar.

Caesar remained unpersuaded, and cited a long list of Cassius's faults: he was a keen observer, he loved no plays or music, he hardly ever smiled. This speech convulsed Rosemary with laughter, though it did not really line up with Juniper's numerous faults. Caesar then invited Mark Antony aside to tell him what Antony *really* thought of Cassius; and Brutus pounced on Casca and asked him what had happened to make Caesar and his train look so upset.

Casca was a scatterbrain, and Rosemary, who had far too much practice pretending to be stupider than she was, dealt with him admirably. Eventually Brutus and Cassius extracted from Casca the information that Mark Antony had offered Caesar a crown three times, and Caesar had refused it each time, but Casca thought Caesar would very much have liked to take the crown, just the same. Then, said Casca, at the third refusal the crowd had yelled so much, and had such bad breath, that Caesar fell down in a faint and foamed at the mouth.

" 'Tis very like," said Gentian as Brutus, "he hath the falling-sickness."

"No, Caesar hath it not," said Juniper-Cassius, in a morose and meaning tone, "but you, and I, and honest Casca, we have the falling-sickness."

"I know not what you mean by that," said Rosemary, giddily, "but I am sure Caesar fell down."

"And after that," read Gentian, "he came thus sad away?"

"Ay," said Rosemary.

"What said Cicero?" asked Juniper.

"He spoke Greek," said Rosemary, with a disgusted look that made her father choke.

"To what effect?" said Juniper, in exactly the tone she would have used to her sister in a similar situation.

Casca didn't know. Cassius invited Casca to dine with him on the morrow, and Casca accepted and departed.

"What a blunt fellow is this grown to be!" read Gentian, trying to remember which voice was for Brutus. "He was quick mettle when he went to school."

Juniper laughed unpleasantly, and then had to regroup for Cassius's speech. "So is he now," she said, "in execution of any bold or noble enterprise, however he puts on this tardy form. This rudeness is a sauce to his good wit, which gives men stomach to digest his words with better appetite. Don't," she continued in her own voice, "think you can use that as an excuse, Rosie."

Rosemary stuck out her tongue.

In Scene III, four characters whose names all began with C met in a thunderstorm. The first two were Cicero, whom Gentian's mother hastily assumed, and Casca. Casca was frightened by the storm, and by various strange happenings within it: fire dropping from the heavens, lions in the Capitol who went by without molesting the people, men all in fire walking up and down the streets. Cicero, in just the same calm tones with which Gentian's mother would discuss tales of how Juniper behaved in school, said that well, yes, it was strange, but there were many ways to interpret it all, and asked if Caesar was coming to the Capitol tomorrow. Casca said he was, and Cicero went home.

Cassius came in; Casca tried to get him to admit that the storm was frightening, and Cassius informed him that he, Cassius, had been going about exposing himself to the lightning with no ill effects whatever. Casca asked, in effect, what was the matter with him, and Cassius, in Junie's best scornful-sister voice, said, "You are dull, Casca, and those sparks of life that should be in a Roman you do want." She went on in considerable detail to explain that Cassius knew a man as monstrous and unnatural as the storm itself.

Obediently, Casca said, " 'Tis Caesar that you mean, is it not, Cassius?"

Cassius said it didn't matter whom he meant, the Romans were womanish. Juniper, who had been increasingly flushed during this conversation, slapped her book down and cried, "Foul!"

"Don't be such a knee-jerker," said Rosemary. "All the Romans were sexist."

"Shakespeare wasn't a Roman," said Juniper, furiously.

"Give the man a chance, Junie," said their father.

Cinna came by, was assumed by Gentian's father, and said Cassius should win Brutus to their party. Cassius said he would go to Brutus's house and talk to him again, and that they would all meet later.

"And so shall we," said Gentian's father, closing his book smartly. "To bed, to bed; the glowworm shows the matin to be nigh, and 'gins to pale his uneffectual fire."

Gentian kissed her parents, smiled at Rosie, and went back upstairs. Maria Mitchell was pacing about the upstairs hall, emitting sounds of profound disapproval. She could meow like an ordinary cat, but the noise she made when Gentian had forgotten to feed her more nearly resembled the creak of an ungreased bicycle.

"Oh, no," said Gentian, and went at a gallop into her bathroom, where the cat food lived under the sink in a galvanized metal pail with latches to the top. She tipped a generous amount of food into Murr's blue porcelain bowl, dumped yesterday's water down the tub, and filled the green porcelain water bowl again while Murr growled pleasurably over her meal. The plates had been her grandmother's; they had chipped gold rims and were painted with pansies.

Gentian sat down on the crumpled bath rug and watched Maria Mitchell eat. It was really unconscionable to forget to feed one's cat. How would you like it, she said to herself, as always. Not a bit, was the usual answer, but somehow it did not serve very well; once a week or so, she would always forget.

She went back to her desk, where the rest of the undone homework awaited her, and made a big sign with blue paper and a red marker: FEED CAT! She taped it to her door, and sat back down to her algebra. About halfway through the assignment, she went over and looked through her telescope again.

The dark side of the new house looked back at her. Maybe Becky would come over tomorrow after school.

4

Gentian overslept the next morning. Maria Mitchell, fed so copiously so late, did not awaken her. She opened her eyes suddenly on a shaft of sunlight she usually saw in that spot on a weekday only when she was sick. Murr was curled around her head, purring madly. The smells of bacon and coffee had come up the stairs and faded while she still slept. From Juniper's room, just below, came the irregular tapping of her sister's unskilled typing on the computer keyboard, unfairly fulfilling the morning requirements of her schooling by typing reams of stupid stuff on the local teens echo and pretending she was doing a sociological study by logging in as two different people, one male and one female.

"Why didn't anybody wake me *up!*" cried Gentian, trying to untangle herself from the quilt.

Maria Mitchell, wise in the ways of the household, sprang away from her head and landed neatly on the headboard of her bed between a precarious stack of the last ten issues of *Sky and Telescope* and a tangle of Mardi Gras beads that Steph's big sister had brought back from New Orleans two years ago.

Gentian sat up, rubbing her eyes, and said, "Way to go, tiger." Murr gazed blandly over her head. Gentian got up, patted the telescope, and rummaged in her second drawer for a T-shirt.

She was hungry, rumpled, and much disinclined to go to school, but if she wanted Becky to come over and look at the telescope, she would have to go.

There was a note for her on the kitchen table. "Don't bother Daddy, he's got a deadline he forgot about. Juniper, let Rosie use the computer for at least a hour this afternoon; Gentian, remember you said you would rake the yard."

Gentian gazed blearily around the kitchen: red countertops, red and white floor tiles, white cabinets, with the door to the one where they kept the cat treats a bit ajar; half a carafe of coffee keeping warm, or getting thick and bitter, depending on how you looked at it, for her father as he worked; Rosie's cereal bowl and Junie's toast plate, and their teacups, piled in the sink; the magnetic letters on the dishwasher that said CLEAN—WHOEVER PUTS THESE AWAY GETS FIRST CRACK AT THE NEW YORKER, which meant that it was her father trying to get out of the job, since nobody else would think first crack at *The New Yorker* was worth that much trouble; her own Peter Rabbit bowl and mug set out on the table with a blue napkin and the glass jar of granola.

The light was wrong. Not because of the hour; because of the house next door.

Pounce, her father's white cat, bounded into the kitchen and leapt up into Gentian's chair. He made a small chirp when he landed, like a slightly startled bird.

"Cat," said Gentian, "what day is it?"

She went over to the back door and consulted the Minnesota Weatherguide Calendar hanging there. It ought to be the eighteenth of October. She dug her assignment notebook out of her knapsack and looked at the last page. "Friday, October 15 (new moon) Act I JC (disc. Mon)." There were the history reading, the book report, the repeat of the geometry problems, right where they should be. She sat on the edge of the kitchen table and rubbed Pounce's spine. He purred. Yesterday was Sunday, surely. Mrs. Hardy had come, and her mother had been home. The day before that had been Saturday and Gentian had gotten up at 6:45 to look at Mercury and spent much of the rest of the day raking the lawn.

Gentian took her denim jacket out of the front-hall closet and went outside. There was a drift of red maple leaves in a corner of the porch, and a red butterfly clinging to the chain of the porch swing. Gentian looked at it thoughtfully. "Isn't it getting late for you?" she said. She jumped over all four wooden porch steps and landed jarringly on the sidewalk. There were leaves on the front lawn, certainly, because the trees were shedding like a cat in spring. But that lawn had been raked. There were the four bags of leaves she had gathered, lined up against the foundation of the porch.

Gentian ambled down the front walk, looking at the day. The new house squatted like a toad on her old garden. There were no leaves on its lawn now, and no sign that there ever had been any.

She went briskly down the steep concrete steps, also scattered with maple leaves, and began walking down the middle of the street, which pleased her because she could see the way the elms met in an arch in the middle of the sky. The black asphalt of the street was strewn with their yellow leaves, and a few stray ones from the maple. Gray porch boards, white cement steps, black street, all patterned with red and yellow leaves, like samples in a wallpaper book. The sky was brilliant. It was not a day to be inside. Maybe she could persuade Becky to leave school early. If it was Monday, their last period was a study hall; during the one before it, Gentian had Gym, which didn't matter, but Becky had Algebra. Becky alternated between saying poets didn't need to know mathematics and saying poets needed to know everything.

The city bus arrived on its weekday schedule, which was a slight relief. Gentian read her history assignment on the way downtown and bolted into the school building just in time to catch Becky as she came out of their shared English class.

Becky had resisted all blandishments of fashion since before she went off to kindergarten. When almost every other girl in the school, including both Gentian's sisters and even Alma and Steph in Gentian and Becky's own circle, had cut and curled her bangs and put her hair up in a ponytail with a great huge filmy bow on it, Becky went on wearing her straight brown hair brushed ruthlessly back from her freckled forehead and plaited into one braid down her back, which she decorated with a piece of yarn from whatever she was knitting at the time. It was red today. Her sweater was yellow, her pants blue, and her socks purple. Gentian regarded her with immense satisfaction. Nobody but Becky would tell Becky what to do.

"Where were you?" said Becky.

"Mom thought it was Sunday."

"Your *Mom?*"

"Well, maybe Daddy did and she believed him."

"Yeah, right."

"Anyway, can we leave early? There's something the matter with my telescope. We'll feed you macaroni and cheese for supper and we can do our homework together."

"I'm supposed to have supper with Steph."

"Okay. Is tomorrow Tuesday?"

"Last time I checked."

"Can you come over then?"

"It's Jeremy's birthday," said Becky. Speaking of her younger brother, she did not pull the kind of face anybody else would have.

Gentian considered. Wednesday, Rosemary's Girl Scout troop would be there; Thursday, she had to do a lot of reading for a history test on Friday; Saturday, her parents were going out and refused to let teenaged girls reach critical mass in their absence.

"Can you come over on Friday?"

"I could come spend the night. I have to rake leaves and clean my room after school. I could come after supper, maybe around eight."

"Okay. If I don't call you, it's all right with Mom."

"Sarah's not coming to stay with Junie, is she?"

"I don't think so. I think it's Junie's turn to go over there. Why?"

"I found the giggling very distracting last time," said Becky, with a primness that made Gentian, not much prone to such things, giggle herself, as Becky had meant her to.

"We'll be as solemn as judges," she said, "engaged in the desperate work of repairing the telescope before the giant meteor hits us."

"You read too much fantasy," said Becky. "Giant meteor indeed."

"Only somebody who didn't read any would think that's where I would get such terminology."

"Giant is not a scientific term."

"Red giant. White dwarf."

"A hit," said Becky, "a hit, I do confess it. Do I have to buy you lunch?"

"It'd be nice if you did. I forgot my wallet. Can we go to the Golden Dragon?"

"Well, I don't know; it'll make us late for Biology."

"Oh, right. I forgot it was Monday."

"I guess you did," said Becky, eyeing her sidelong as if she were a broken toaster.

"It's that new house," said Gentian.

"Let's go to Burger King, all right? It's better than gluey spaghetti. What new house?"

"The one they built on our vacant lot."

"When did they do that? You never told me."

They walked out of the school building and went down to the corner to cross the street. Gentian, left to herself, would have jaywalked, but Becky refused to do so, and it was irritating to dart across the street and then wait for Becky to come around by the light.

The Burger King had a little concrete courtyard with concrete benches and tables, plants in concrete boxes, some tattered umbrellas, and a large collection of interested sparrows. Gentian always got an extra hamburger so she could crumble the bun up and give it to them. Becky often brought birdseed.

They took their lunch to a table in the corner. Mercifully, their classmates had gone mostly elsewhere today, and besides themselves and the sparrows the courtyard held only a young woman with two toddlers and an elderly gentleman reading a copy of the collected poems of William Butler Yeats. It was the same red-covered paperback Gentian's father had had in college.

Rosie had been hoarding it in her room for several months now.

"When did they build the new house?" repeated Becky.

"A couple of weeks ago," said Gentian vaguely.

"They can build a house in a few weeks?"

"Apparently."

"Has it got a basement and a foundation and everything?"

"Yes. Well, I don't know about everything, but yes to the first two; and it looks like a house, not a shack or a summer cabin or anything. I don't know what it's like on the inside, of course."

"Maybe when somebody moves in you'll find out."

"Somebody has moved in."

Becky paused with an onion ring halfway to her mouth, and gave Gentian the broken-toaster look again. "When?"

"Right after the house was finished."

"What date?"

"End of September?"

"Don't ask *me*."

"I don't remember. It's not as if I didn't have anything else to think about."

"What's the new family like?"

"We only saw the mother," said Gentian, bending her mind backwards. "She was undistinguished. She came to borrow a snake."

"Did you just happen to have a boa in the basement?"

Gentian laughed. "I'd like to see anybody trying to get a boa to clear out the plumbing."

"And how do you know she's a mother?"

"Oh," said Gentian, jolted. "Because there's a kid, too. And she said he was her son."

"Maybe you can babysit."

"He's fifteen."

"Gentian Meriweather—"

"No, really, that's not why I didn't tell you. Come on, Becky. I might ask you not to tell Steph, but I'd tell you."

"Well," said Becky, "tell me, then."

"His hair is black, his eyes are blue, his lips as red as wine," said Gentian.

"Genny."

"No, really, they are. Well, we weren't close enough to see his eyes. But he's taller than Junie. And we haven't seen hide nor hair *nor* tooth of him since the day they moved in."

"Which was when?"

Gentian concentrated. Becky would keep asking, for months if necessary, until she got an answer. "All right," she said. "They started building the house on the first day of school. And it took about three weeks, I think; and then they moved in."

"Gentian Meriweather, you have seen me every day at school and spent the night at my house two times in that interval, and you never said a word about it."

"I forgot," said Gentian, holding Becky's eyes. She had, in fact.

"I want to see this house," said Becky, looking back at her steadily. She did not seem disbelieving; nor was she wearing the broken-toaster expression. This was something less clinical. If Gentian had ever seen Becky look worried in the ten years they had known one another, she might have thought this look was worried.

She said reasonably, "Well, come over on Friday and you will."

"I want to see it now."

"And miss Biology?"

"Yes."

"Well, all right." Gentian shook the crumbs off her tray onto the pavement, and there was a rush of sparrows. "I don't usually skip a whole day of school."

"Well, we can get back by sixth period, I think. If we hurry."

"The house will be there tomorrow, you know," said Gentian, standing up nevertheless and scattering the sparrows.

"That's just what I don't know," said Becky, flinging her remaining onion rings smartly over the table. The hovering sparrows settled. Gentian held her tongue. Steph had given them her french fries last time, and Gentian's objection had begun a discussion, which still burst out occasionally, of whether birds had problems with their cholesterol. Nobody ever had bothered to go look it up, though Becky had asked their biology teacher.

They tipped their trash into the receptacle provided, stacked their trays, and caught a bus. Gentian's stop was across the street from Memorial Park, a huge expanse of close green lawn, cunningly dotted with clumps of crabapple trees, sweeping steeply upwards to the limestone arch that gave it its name. Although she knew what lay on the other side of the arch—formal rose gardens, a pine grove, a playground, and a little stream—in the benign autumn sunlight it looked, to Gentian, immeasurably tempting, like the entrance to Elfland, or some English garden complete with talking toad or psammead or the ghosts of Elizabethan children, going about their daily business. She touched Becky's shoulder. "Let's go for a walk."

Becky looked at her, and shrugged. "All right."

They trudged up the winding sidewalk, kicking at the narrow red crabapple leaves that lay on it in neat overlapping lines, as Gentian's father would arrange crackers on a tray for a party. Gentian could feel Becky looking at her, and then looking away. It occurred to her that such a request, which she had made out of sheer exuberance at the weather, and out of the restlessness autumn always produced in her, had probably made Becky think Gentian had something important to tell her. She cast about for something.

They reached the top of the hill, panting slightly, and passed under the cool damp shadow of the arch. The shrieks of children on the swings of the playground came to them on the breeze, with a mingled odor of pine and water.

"Remember that boy with the red hat?" said Becky.

Gentian assembled her mind. "In fifth grade?"

"Uh-huh."

"Yes, I do. You yelled at him for chasing butterflies." Becky had chased him down that very hill and into the stream, yelling blue murder, and come back with the butterfly net, which she had tried to break over her knee and eventually had to go fling on the railroad track where, in younger and less opinionated days, she and Gentian had laid pennies to be flattened. Gentian and Alma had tried to persuade her that it was dangerous to the train to make it run over a butterfly net, but Becky had been unmoved.

"He asked me to go to a movie," said Becky.

"Which one?"

"Just a movie."

"When?"

"Sometime," said Becky, smiling with one side of her mouth in the way that brought out her much-detested dimple.

"Has he," demanded Gentian, sitting down on the nearest wooden bench, "said one word to you in the entire intervening time?"

"No," said Becky.

"So are you going?"

"If I can think of a movie. We were going to see *Roan Innish* with Steph, weren't we, and you wanted to see *Much Ado About Nothing.*"

"Make him take you to see *Frankenstein,*" said Gentian, who had refused to see any movie made from a book she had read ever since she first watched, with horrified disbelief, *The Wizard of Oz* on television.

"He wouldn't like it," said Becky. "Anyway, Alma wants to see it."

"How do you know he wouldn't like it?"

"He thinks scientists are always the good guys."

"How in the world do you know that?"

"I could tell," said Becky, "when I yelled at him about the butterflies."

"That's a long time ago," said Gentian, cautiously.

"Do you want to have kids?"

"What? No."

"Do you think it's a vast injustice that your moods should be dictated by a bunch of chemicals?"

"Yes, and you know it. What—"

"You thought all that in fifth grade."

"Oh." Gentian considered. "Well, look, then, *Frankenstein* would be good for him, wouldn't it?"

"Well, probably, but if I'm going to do him good I should be the one to take him. Maybe next time."

"There hasn't even been a this time yet."

"Well, it can't be *Frankenstein* this time if there is a this time."

"Do you think he'd let you?"

"What? Take him to a movie?"

"I know," said Gentian. "If he doesn't, he can forget about you."

"What are you laughing about?"

"You felt like that in the fifth grade, too."

"What does growing up mean, then?"

"Forgetting all the good parts," said Gentian, with finality.

"When I am an old woman," said Becky, "I shall still wear purple."

"Well, you're different."

"We're all different. Maybe that's what we forget."

"What's his name?" said Gentian.

"Micky."

"Huh."

"Yeah, I know. Micky and Becky. Blech."

"Has he got a middle name?" Becky's middle name was Letitia. Micky and Letitia, thought Gentian, and swallowed a giggle. Her own middle name was every bit as bad.

"Should it become an issue," said Becky, stretching her legs out in front of her, "I'll ask him."

"I always thought Steph would be the first."

"Yes, me too. Or maybe Alma—she's so unpredictable."

"Are you going, then?"

"Maybe."

"*Henry V*'s at the Riverside. You wanted to see that again. And it hasn't got any embarrassing parts—or at least, they're all in French."

"Now that," said Becky, "is a thought." She sat up and jammed her hat more firmly onto her head. "I want to see that house, and I could look at your telescope at least briefly."

They walked to Gentian's street, kicking at the leaves to make them rustle. The tall Victorian houses stood benignly in their brilliant yards, set about with juniper and elm and late zinnias and a dozen kinds of chrysanthemum.

"There," said Gentian, pointing at the new house.

Becky eyed it from under her hat. "It looks as if a tornado just set it down there by accident." She took her hat off and looked at the house some more. "You'd expect it to look a bit cowed, somehow," she said, "like those little tiny houses on Summit Avenue next to all the mansions. But it doesn't."

"No," said Gentian, arrested. "It looks smug." This anthropomorphic remark bothered her; she added, "It must be the position of the windows."

"Mmmm," said Becky. She went on gazing at the house, and turning her hat around in her hands. "I want to see all around it."

"Well, come on; they never come out, and if they did that'd be interesting, even if they yelled at us."

They walked up the new side of the driveway. Becky looked at the house, and Gentian looked at Becky. "It's remarkably ugly," said Becky.

"Junie likes it."

"Because it's modern?"

"Yep."

"Well, that's not why I think it's ugly. I think there's something wrong with the proportions. And the siding's an awful color. It's hard to look at. It makes my eyes water."

They reached the top of the driveway, and without further consultation turned onto the little walkway that led to the new house's back door. The concrete was glaring white, the lawn was glaring green, without a dandelion or a bit of mullein in it anywhere. Gentian wondered what they had used on it, and whether it would mess up her mother's wildflowers. Under that lawn were Rosie's crocuses and Juniper's pink tulip bulbs and some yellow flag iris that Gentian had put in last spring. She hoped they would come up and break the sidewalk.

The walk split when it got to the back door, and led around to both sides of the house. Becky and Gentian, again without consulting one another, turned right to walk towards the Zimmermans'. There was a flower bed between the sidewalk and the back of the house. It had been filled with polished black stones. In the long narrow windows above it the shades were drawn down to the windowsills.

"It's not very big when you look right at it," breathed Becky as they rounded the corner, "but it looms out of the corner of your eye."

She did not correct this potentially ambiguous statement, and Gentian did not feel inclined to laugh at it. They walked on, between the new house and the Zimmermans' house, on bright clean concrete, in a cold dark shade. The side of the house looked almost black. The windows on this side were also covered with drawn shades. They came out past the house and the dark evergreens that hid its foundation in front, and with one sudden accord bolted across the bright green lawn to the good, cracked, grayish public sidewalk with its covering of leaves. They looked at the house again. It was small and crouched and red.

"Let's go look at that telescope," said Becky.

That telescope, looked at, proved to have nothing wrong with it whatsoever. Becky could not, even by depressing it to the utmost, make the house next door appear through it—which was just what Gentian would have expected, if anybody had asked her.

They stood in Gentian's room with Maria Mitchell winding around their feet and scolding them, gazing at one another, Becky with pensive speculation and Gentian with a hopeless bafflement.

"If you were Steph," said Becky at last.

"It's not a practical joke. What would be the point?"

"I know."

"Maybe now you're curing things just by deciding to come look at them."

"Tell all the AIDS cases to line up below," said Becky, in a voice of utter desolation, and sat down on Gentian's bed.

"You know I meant fix."

"You didn't say it."

Not saying what you meant was the mortal sin in Becky's calendar: the only sin, Gentian sometimes thought; chasing butterflies fell into some other category altogether.

"I'm sorry. I was just joking."

"What would be the point?" said Becky, still desolately. She fell over backwards on the bed and put the nearest pillow over her face.

"Don't be depressed, Becky. I can't stand it right now."

"Why right now especially?" said Becky from under the pillow.

That, thought Gentian, was a very good question. "It's fall," she said at last.

Becky threw the pillow at her and sat up. She was laughing; but it seemed like polite laughter, as if Gentian were an aunt who had told her a joke.

5

Becky declined to stay for dinner, and Gentian was obscurely relieved. She felt as she had the day after Steph's thirteenth birthday. Erin had hosted a slumber party to celebrate. They all stayed up until eight in the morning, when Erin's father cooked them pancakes. Then they slept until noon, when Erin's little sister burst into the nice dark basement rec room with a demand to watch television.

Gentian had then walked home in bright October sunlight, rather like today's; negotiated a stay of execution on her Saturday chores; and before the puzzled gaze of Maria Mitchell, fallen into bed in her best blue jeans and the oversized pintucked white shirt that took so long to iron, and slept for seven hours, after which she gloomed around all evening, picked a fight with Junie, and went to bed at ten. That Sunday then felt like Saturday, because she did her Saturday chores. Monday felt like Sunday, which made going off to school feel most unjust.

This was even worse. Today felt like Sunday, and Saturday, and a day she had missed school, all jumbled up. She didn't even know what her homework was.

Well, there. Say it was a day she'd been sick. She would, on such days, call Becky, Steph, and Alma, and that would get her all the assignments except Latin. Nobody she liked was in her

Latin class. Nobody else in the Giant Ants was taking Latin at all, though Gentian had tried to persuade them repeatedly. Alma and Steph, who did everything together, were taking Spanish so they could read *Don Quixote* and decide whether it was better than *Man of la Mancha*. Becky was taking French so she could read *Cyrano de Bergerac*. Erin was taking Russian because she wanted to be an astronaut and she thought making all the cosmonauts speak English was unfair.

Gentian called Alma first. She loved every voice in that family except that of Alma's mother. The rest were dark, furry, complicated voices, but Mrs. Jackson sounded like a hammer hitting tacks into a plaster wall: flat, flat, flat, thud. She said, "Well, hello, Genny," in just that way, and fetched Alma, who demanded, without greeting or preface, "Are you sick?"

"No, truant disposed."

"I would not hear your enemy say so," said Alma, elongating the vowels of Hamlet's line and blurring the r's almost to nothing, "but I believe you. I missed Geometry today, but I got it from Steph. Problems eleven to nineteen in Chapter Two and the odd-numbered ones in Chapter Three, except seventeen. English is Act Two. Creative Writing is write a sonnet or else an essay about why not."

"Why not what?" said Gentian, scribbling.

"Why not write a sonnet."

"How long?"

"Fourteen lines," said Alma, and cackled.

"Alma."

"One page, both sides."

"Thanks."

"You plan to be truant *next* Monday?"

"I didn't plan, it just happened. Why?"

"It's Steph's birthday. We could take her out for lunch."

"Okay. What does she want?"

"Makeup."

"Uck."

"It's not your birthday."

"I'll give her a Dayton's gift certificate. Maybe she'll buy something else with it."

"Reformer."

"I am *not*. I'd just get her the wrong color, anyhow."

"Steph thinks you can wear makeup and still find Narnia."

"Well, so do I, but why make things harder?"

"Because she's *Steph.*"

Gentian admitted the justice of this remark, thanked Alma, hung up, and called Steph, who answered the phone on the first ring. She had a low but rather hesitant voice, with just the ghost of a stutter.

"It's only me," said Gentian.

"Better than Caitlin's E-mail buddies. Were you sick today?"

"Truant."

"I almost was too," said Steph. "It was a gorgeous day, and I was thinking about painting the sumac with Alfalfa lying in it. But then I wouldn't have seen Randy again until next Friday."

Gentian had never understood why anybody should want to see Randy at all: she considered him sarcastic without being witty, and he was redheaded as well. Far too much like Junie. But Steph didn't have to live with Junie.

Gentian made a noncommittal noise, and Steph told her the history assignment.

"Thanks," said Gentian. "Did Randy smile at you today?"

"He looked at me over his glasses," said Steph, "with his beautiful blue eyes. Oh, and *Genny*—Micky Adomaitis talked to Becky in the hall."

"He probably wanted his butterfly net back."

"That was *his* butterfly net?" said Steph, who had joined the magic circle in third grade but missed having fifth with the rest of them because the school district got divided that year and she lived on the wrong side of the highway.

"The very one."

"He's cute," said Steph judiciously, "but the stuff he wrote for *Tesseract* was awful."

"He doesn't write poetry too, does he?" said Gentian. The notion of Becky's taking up with a fellow poet was alarming.

"No, it was short stories."

"Oh, okay."

They said good-bye, and Gentian ran through the list of people in her Latin class. The study-group Latinist was two semesters ahead of her, so she was no use. She supposed she could try Randy. Then she could tell Steph all about it, especially if she managed to mention Steph and got a good response to report. But Randy would be so wearing; and then, too, he might say something mean about Steph, whereupon Gentian would have to find some suitable rebuke and then not tell Steph about it.

She called the quietest member of the class and gratefully received her stammered explanation of the assignment.

It was dark by now. The weather forecast had said the night would be clear. Mars would not rise until almost midnight, and Jupiter was still hiding near the sun; but Saturn would be up and bright. Gentian climbed the stairs, opened the dome, and looked through her telescope.

The dull red side of the new house smote her eye like a bonfire. Gentian jumped back from the telescope and stepped on Maria Mitchell's tail. Murr yelped and vanished under the bed.

"I'll bring you some shrimp," Gentian told her, still eyeing the telescope. She got out its manual again, and then dug into the closet and found all the books she had used while she was researching buying one, and all the ones she had used when she thought she was going to build her own. She stacked them all on her desk and went downstairs.

Her mother was making salad. Her father was frying shrimp. Junie was beating batter with a wooden spoon and complaining bitterly about her parents' presence in the kitchen. Gentian decided against stealing a fingerful of dough from her, and took a radish from her mother's cutting board instead.

"You always take whatever I'm short of," said her mother, petulantly for her. "Have a carrot, if you must scavenge."

"And stay the hell away from me," said Juniper.

Gentian stabbed a finger into the batter and fled, followed by imprecations from Juniper and a mild, "Genny, you cannot resist temptation," from her mother; but by no actual thrown objects. She went out onto the front porch, licking her finger. Spice cookies.

The autumn night smelled of them already: damp, sweet, crisp all at once. Moths still darted and fluttered around the porch light. Gentian sat on the swing and addressed them. "Gather ye rosebuds while ye may," she said. She felt, all of a sudden, profoundly mournful.

Why had Becky gone after Micky and his butterfly net, anyway? The butterflies hardly lived at all: what did cutting their lives short signify in a scheme of things that had started four billion years ago in an explosion so grandiose as to make every one since look like a cap pistol?

Becky would say that that was why, of course: If they had so little you mustn't take any of it away from them. "Unto every one that hath," said Gentian, who had attended Alma's church with Alma for a year to see if the heavens really did declare the glory of God's handiwork, "shall be given, and he shall have in abundance: but from him that hath not shall be taken away even that which he hath."

The moths were not impressed. Gentian looked at them carefully. It seemed suddenly important to appreciate them before the frost got them. They were not very easy to appreciate. They were handsome enough in a somber way, being triangular with mottled gray and brown markings, like a faded Oriental carpet designed by an aesthete. But Gentian knew, because when her mother sat on the porch with anybody she always said it, that these were the moths of the cutworm caterpillar that would ooze along below the surface of the soil and nip off the stems of young seedlings. After they had slaughtered the innocents, they turned themselves into moths and hung around porch lights to inspire adolescent angst. Gentian grinned suddenly.

At dinner, she said, "We need to read Act Two before next Monday."

"Let's do it tonight, then," said Rosemary. "I've got a Girl Scout hike on Sunday."

"You're going to make us read the whole play?" said Juniper.

Gentian noted the pause where her sister had almost added

what their father called an adverse qualifier before the word "play."

"We always do," she said.

"Well, I'm tired of it," said Juniper.

She got tired of something about once a week. Gentian, who was tired of Juniper's tiredness, did not offer the usual panacea.

"And," said Juniper, after an expectant pause during which Gentian carefully did not look at their mother, "I don't *want* you to iron all my shirts."

"Oh, for heaven's sake," said their mother.

"Two faces spited," said their father, nodding at her.

Gentian liked it when they did this in a benevolent atmosphere, but she hated it to be directed at her.

"You never iron *my* shirts," said Rosemary.

Gentian gazed at her in hurt disbelief, even as her mouth said automatically, "T-shirts big enough for four of you that you're just going to throw under your bed don't need ironing."

"I do *not*—"

"Girls," said their mother. "Stop it at once. Somebody is going to shoot Francis Ferdinand any moment now, and then there'll be no turning back."

"Wrong war," said Juniper, for some reason now allied with their parents and no longer angry.

"They're all wrong," said her father.

"In any case," said their mother, "Gentian will help to iron Juniper's shirts and, as always, help Rosie clean her closet, and Juniper and Rosemary will help her read Act Two of *Julius Caesar* after supper."

Gentian was strongly tempted to let out a howl of outrage, but instead looked in mute appeal at her father, who took the cue for once and said, "It has never seemed to me that these are equitable bargains. One's opportunities to show off and to painlessly absorb Western culture are curiously absent from ironing and cleaning closets and abundantly present in the reading aloud of Shakespeare."

"However," said Gentian's mother, "the opportunities to keep this household running smoothly are equivalent."

Gentian opened her mouth, and her father shook his head at her. Gentian said bitterly to her mother, "I thought you were a feminist."

"Being a feminist doesn't mean you can neglect the household," said her mother, sharply for her. Then she added, "I don't have any boys to give the ironing to while you mow the lawn, Genny. It's all girls hereabouts."

"Like a utopian science fiction novel," said her father helpfully.

They were doing it again. Fundamentally, they were always with one another. You could not divide and conquer.

"Besides," said her mother, "you seem rather too attached to the parts of feminism that say you needn't do things women traditionally do, and rather too unattached to the parts that say those things are worthy."

"I don't care if they're worthy," said Gentian, "they're *boring.*"

"So's Shakespeare," said Juniper.

"So are you," said Rosemary, to Juniper.

"Was that the Zimmerman telegram?" said their father, to their mother.

"Very like," she answered wearily.

Gentian, watching her parents commiserate over their offspring, kept quiet, with an effort she supposed nobody would ever credit her with. She watched Junie, and when Junie had thought out whatever she was going to say, Gentian spoke first. "Something's the matter with my telescope," she said.

Juniper got up and left the room, not without dignity.

"Can I have her dessert?" said Rosemary.

"No," said their mother, still looking at their father. She had laid down her fork and put her hands on the edge of the table, as if about to get up, but after a moment their father got up instead, and went after Juniper.

"If she wants to talk to Daddy," said Rosemary, taking the cornbread from Juniper's plate and buttering it, "all she has to do is ask."

"Rosemary," said their mother, "a little less spite masquerading as precocious perspicacity, if you please."

"I am not spiteful!"

"Just fed up," said Gentian.

"Fine," said their mother, standing up after all. "You may sympathize with one another while you clear the table and clean up the kitchen. Gentian, the last time you gave your cat shrimp she threw it up on the bathroom floor and your father stepped in it at four in the morning."

"That was a hairball. The shrimp was coincidental."

"And when did you last give her any Petromalt?" Her mother left without waiting for an answer, which was both deeply unfair and a profound relief, given that the answer would have to be, "sometime last month."

Gentian looked at Rosemary. "What *is* dessert?" she said.

"Ice cream," said Rosemary. She wrinkled her delicate nose and added, "And Junie's spice cookies, if you think they're not poisoned."

"I," said Gentian, "shall be thy taster, small sister. If by the time the dishes are done my taste of the dough hath not killed me, you may safely eat."

They cleared the table, scraped the dishes, and loaded the dishwasher in amiable silence. Juniper was accustomed to being very fussy about how things were put into the dishwasher. When Rosemary put the big plastic strainer into the top rack, thus displacing several mugs to the bottom and ousting the cheese grater entirely, Gentian just smiled and washed the grater by hand. In her present mood, she rather liked the way it shredded the sponge.

"Genny," said Rosemary as they were wiping down the counters.

Gentian, occupied with wondering whether she should make her parents' after-dinner coffee, since they seemed to have forgotten it, jumped slightly and said, "What?"

"Nothing," said Rosemary, scrubbing away at a grape-juice stain that had been there since she was about ten months old.

"Oh, please," said Gentian. "That's a Junie trick."

"So's that."

"*What,* then?"

"Should I go out on a date?"

"Who with?"

"Just should I?"

"You're *eleven.*"

"That's what Mom said."

"Well, so why are you asking me?"

"Well, *Mom,*" said Rosemary, abandoning the juice stain and rubbing away at the gray spot on the refrigerator where Junie had once put up a bumper sticker backed with very durable glue, "didn't have a date at *all* until she was eighteen."

Gentian had never thought about their mother's first date. The information made her vaguely uneasy. "Look, Rosie," she said. "Even Juliet was thirteen."

"Mom said that, too."

"Then *why* are you—"

"How old'll *you* be when—"

"Thirty-five," said Gentian, flinging the grater-chewed sponge into the soap dish and smearing her hands with the cream her mother used after gardening.

"Don't you like anybody?"

"Sure," said Gentian. She opened the freezer, and four boxes of film fell out. She caught the cascade of square plastic containers of tomato sauce that threatened to follow them and peered inside for the ice cream. "I like Becky, and Steph, and Erin, and Alma. Sometimes I even like you."

Rosemary was bright red and had wound most of her hair around her wrist, but she met Gentian's eyes squarely. "You know what I mean. Do you?"

"I'll tell if you will."

Rosemary looked wistful, but said nothing.

"And *not a word* to Junie," said Gentian. It was both a threat and a promise.

"You go first."

"Let's get ice cream and take it out on the porch."

The moths were still circling. It was too cold to eat ice cream out of doors. Gentian took a mouthful anyway. Rosemary clutched her bowl in both hands and eyed Gentian as she used to when Gentian would come home from school and read stories to her.

Gentian swallowed. The ice cream made a track of cold right down the center of her.

"All right," she said. "There's a boy called Jamie Barrows."

"And he almost deserved it," said Rosemary.

"Hush. We didn't get him until sixth grade. He has an English accent and he uses words like—like Mom does when she's mad and Dad does all the time. The first thing I ever heard him say was, 'No, Mrs. Logan, I think the problem with "Young Goodman Brown" is that Hawthorne was concentrating on the accidental rather than the essential aspects of fiction.' "

Rosemary looked baffled but respectful. "So he's smart."

"Very. And smart the way I like best. Like Becky."

"So did you ever talk to him?"

"Mmmmmm. Well, once."

"Well tell me."

"In the library the summer after fifth grade."

"Well *tell* me!"

"I was embarrassed," said Gentian. "Because I was doing summer reading and I had an enormous stack of Goosebumps books."

"So what happened?"

"So he said he read them too and we talked about why we liked them when they're so awful."

"So that was good?"

". . . Yes."

"You sound like something wasn't good."

"I don't know," said Gentian. "I never quite figured it out. He kept—he kept—he kept sounding like Daddy."

"What's wrong with that?"

"He's not my father."

"Oh. *That* kind of sounding like Daddy."

"Mmmm-hmm."

"I thought you just meant he talked like him."

"He kept laying down the law."

"So what then?"

"So I thought about it a lot."

"Did you talk to him any more?"

"A couple of times. There's not much chance at school unless you want everybody to think you have a crush."

"Who cares what they think?"

"I don't care what they think," said Gentian, quoting Erin, "but I don't choose to come to their attention."

Rosemary looked at her over the bowl of ice cream. "But you're one of the big kids."

"I don't mean they'd beat me up, Rosie. I don't want them thinking about me." Rosemary opened her mouth. "It's like the way sometimes you don't want Junie thinking about you," said Gentian. "She isn't going to hit you. But she'll say things."

"Oh," said Rosemary, looking absorptive.

"Now," said Gentian, who was beginning to experience the slightly hollow feeling of somebody who has talked too much, "it's your turn."

"Well," said Rosemary. She turned her head completely away from Gentian, tugged fiercely at her hair, and said, "I don't *like* boys."

Gentian considered her. She considered and rejected a number of responses, notably, "Well, you don't *have* to." Her mother could represent that viewpoint all too well. Finally she got caught up in the intellectual interest of the problem. "Well, I don't know," she said.

Rosemary unzipped the green cotton cover of the nearest cushion and then zipped it up again.

"Because," said Gentian, thinking back to sixth grade, "if you don't like them now I'm not sure if you ever will, because as far as I can tell they just get worse. It's all downhill after they're eleven."

"It's all downhill after everybody's eleven, as far as *I* can tell," said Rosemary. While she had been known to make similar remarks in a pointed fashion to annoy her older sisters, she seemed serious and unconscious enough that Gentian did not protest this time.

When she was sure Rosemary was not going to expand her

observations, Gentian said, "Maybe it is, but we must get worse in different ways. Because I'm still friends with Becky and Steph and Erin and Alma. But we used to play with Micky and Aaron and—oh, what was his name, the kid with red hair—some Greek hero, we had it in English class and he hated it—"

"Orestes?"

"No, that's Micky's big brother; he was a pill, we never played with him. Jason, that's it."

"He was a pill too."

"No, he wasn't. He had a splendiferous rock collection, and he showed me how to test for different minerals."

"He threw rocks at Ariel and me."

"When?" demanded Gentian.

"Last summer."

"See? That proves it. We weren't playing with him by then. He was twelve. Anyway—we used to play with boys but they all got weird in a way that made us not want to play with them any more. But the girls all stuck together. Maybe it's not because we're girls. Maybe it's just the Giant Ants. But we never deserted one another, even when some of us got breasts and some didn't, and some of us have really easy periods and some have awful cramps."

"When *are* you going to get breasts?" said Rosemary.

"Will you *quit* being a bratty little sister long enough to have a decent conversation?"

"I *am* having a decent conversation!"

"Twitting people about their tits is not decent."

"I wasn't *twitting*. I want to know. I'm more like you than I am like Junie, and I want to know how long I've got left to be a kid."

Gentian looked at her. She was zipping up the cushion cover again. She was not smiling secretively as she would when teasing a sister. She probably meant it.

"You'll be the first to know," Gentian said, a little helplessly.

"When you were playing with those boys," said Rosemary, "did you like them the way you like Jamie Barrows?"

"No," said Gentian. "Steph did, and so did Erin. Alma and I thought they were crazy."

"So maybe I'll like boys when I'm older," said Rosemary. She gave the cushion a vicious punch and added, "Even if they all turn into jerks on their twelfth birthdays."

"Well, lots of girls like boys, jerks or not."

"But not you?"

"Well—is Jamie Barrows a jerk?" said Gentian, as much to herself as to her sister.

"If I say yes you'll hit me."

"You don't even know him."

"You said he laid down the law. If he lays down the law, he's a jerk."

"You have no concept of jerkdom if you think that makes him a jerk."

Rosemary sighed heavily. "Maybe I'll be a nun," she said. "Chanting cold hymms to the pale fruitless moon. Why *should* there be fruit on the moon, anyway?"

"You aren't a Catholic. And nuns can be jerky too."

"I'll be a Buddhist nun."

"You aren't—"

"I'll convert!" yelled Rosemary, and flung the pillow over the porch railing.

Gentian looked at her. "I've got a book about Buddhism," she said. "You want to borrow it?"

"Fine!"

"You're acting like Junie."

"Junie would never read a book about Buddhism."

"Never mind."

Rosemary sat sulkily eating her half-melted ice cream.

Gentian stirred hers around and around in the bowl. Finally she said, "Fruitless means barren."

Rosemary scowled. Then she smiled. "So this is barren ice cream?" she said.

"Extremely," said Gentian, and began to eat hers.

They sat silently, shivering a little in the autumn breeze. Gentian did not want to suggest going in. Somebody might still say something interesting. Finally their mother opened the front door, letting out the smell of brewing coffee, and said, "Drama calls, girls."

They got up, without looking at one another, and went inside to read the second act of *Julius Caesar*. Gentian found herself feeling grateful that it was not *Romeo and Juliet*.

6

It was almost midnight when they finished. Saturn would be setting; not long after, Mars would rise. Gentian went upstairs and set her alarm clock for seven, thinking she should really go to bed, thinking that she could always skip the whole morning's school, thinking she should save doing that for some more truly spectacular astronomical event.

Maria Mitchell sat on Gentian's pillow, watching the alarm-setting process narrowly. She always seemed both ingenuous and calculating, because of the markings on her face. Her muzzle was white, with a harmless-looking pale pink nose; but above that her face was half orange and half black, with judgmental green eyes and a rakish look to the ears. Gentian rubbed the back of her neck, and Murr fell over sideways—dropping, as Gentian's father liked to observe, as if she had been shot, which might be striking but was not a very pleasant simile—and purred loudly.

Gentian looked at the telescope. This was, really, a good time for Saturn; she ought to just try it. She went up the scuffed cherry steps, thinking, I should really refinish those soon. She opened the dome. For no reason she could think of, in the ashamed knowledge that she was behaving ritualistically rather than scientifically, she shut her eyes, fitted her face to the telescope, and adjusted it by feel. She opened her eyes.

One of the mean little windows in the new house was lit up, and on the drawn shade was the silhouette of a woman sitting at a dressing table, gazing into its oval mirror. Gentian stared at her, using every technique she had learned for looking at the sky. She didn't see how that delicate, curled, elegant profile with its coiled hair could possibly be Mrs. Hardy. Well, maybe they had a house guest who never went out either. Come and see us for a week; I promise we'll never go anywhere. After all, Erin had moods when such an offer would seem like heaven.

The woman put a long hand up to her head and smoothed back a hair or two. Then she sat still again, gazing. Her blouse— her dress, almost surely—had a stiff frill of lace that stood up under her chin and ran down the low opening. *Her* little sister would not ask her indecent questions.

Gentian shut her eyes and turned her head from the telescope. What on earth was she doing? She was a scientist, not a spy. It had never once before occurred to her that one could use the telescope to look at things far closer than any planet, closer even than the moon. It was like reading Junie's diary, except that there was no excuse for it.

The telescope would obviously be useless until Becky had time to really diagnose and fix it. Gentian shut the dome, put on the lens cap, got into bed, and turned out the light. Maria Mitchell came and sat on her pillow, purring, just out of reach.

The next evening after she had done her homework, she sat looking at the telescope. Everyone had said it was a good model. She had originally meant to make her own, and still had the half-ground mirror somewhere, but it took too long and made her twitchy, and her parents kept pointing out that there was no manufacturer's warranty on an instrument you made yourself. This had not impressed Gentian much, but the fact that the longer making the telescope took, the more unique astronomical events she would miss, did impress her. And now she was in the same situation. She could take up working on the homemade one again, she supposed.

What had she done before she discovered astronomy? That was a long time ago; she would have been about Rosie's age. She had done a lot of things, but there was no center to her life then. Astronomy to her was what poetry had always been to Becky.

"I," said Gentian to her cat, "am going to go live in the desert and discover comets like your namesake."

Becky would, if presented with that sentence, ask how a comet could be like anybody's namesake, let alone like a shy mathematician from Nantucket.

And who, Gentian thought, would lay hands on her tele-scopes if she lived in the desert? The Giant Ants had already had several arguments about whether all of them could possibly go to the same college and at the same time properly fulfill their ex-tremely varied destinies. Steph and Alma would probably change their minds about said destinies five or six times between now and college time, but Becky, Erin, and Gentian were steadier. Even the difficulty of finding in one place both good star-gazing conditions and a decent creative writing program, leaving Erin and her need for the space program out of it entirely, had pro-duced several agonizing four-in-the-morning conversations. Gen-tian was afraid they were due for another one, if Becky should take it into her head to add Micky to the equation.

"Nonsense," she said to the cat. "No romance for us, not even little Victorian notes from consumptive intellectuals to keep in scrimshaw boxes. Romance interferes with real life."

Maria Mitchell, prevented in her youth from having an opin-ion on this subject, rolled over on her back and required to have her belly rubbed. Gentian did this, meanwhile subjecting what she had just said to a Rebeccan analysis and laughing wildly at the notion of keeping consumptive intellectuals in scrimshaw boxes.

She looked at the telescope again. She was almost tempted to put it away somewhere, but that would be admitting defeat. She reached into the deep shelf under her bedside table, pulled up the antenna on the weather radio, and turned it on. "Serving east central Minnesota and west central Wisconsin," said a rather surly voice, "in cooperation with Minnesota's Division of Emer-gency Management and the Department of Transportation. The forecast for the Twin Cities metropolitan area: tonight, clear until late, then partly cloudy, with northeast winds fifteen to twenty-five miles per hour. Partly cloudy tomorrow with increasing clouds by evening. Chance of rain or snow, sixty percent. The low tonight—"

Gentian turned the radio off and approached the telescope firmly, like a cat she intended to take to the vet. Maria Mitchell, being both observant and cautious, went under the bed.

The woman with the elegant profile was sitting at the window with her chin in her hand, gazing straight at Gentian. Gentian lifted her forehead from the rest with extreme deliberation, thinking furiously, get out of my telescope, damn you. She peered around the telescope. There was nobody in the window, which was dark. Probably the woman had gone to call Gentian's parents and complain. Gentian sat by the telephone for some time, though she would not know until it actually rang if she would pick it up hastily and impersonate her mother. It did not ring.

On Wednesday and Thursday she kept away from the telescope; this had to be accomplished by staying downstairs until she was too sleepy to keep her eyes open. Her sisters made snide comments; her father asked her if she was feeling all right, and felt her forehead; her mother asked if the heat was working properly upstairs. Gentian responded vaguely and did her geometry at the kitchen table. On Thursday evening her father served dinner in the dining room, displacing a Girl Scout project of Rosemary's and eliciting a shower of scornful comment from Juniper. Gentian smiled at him and decided to do some chore of his over the weekend.

After dinner Rosemary, grumbling, took her project upstairs to the guest room, and Juniper, sneering, went out onto the front porch to wait for Sarah, with whom she was going ice-skating. Gentian sat at the kitchen table, making Christmas lists and counting her money and cursing the purchase of Bulfinch's *Mythology*, which had given her a series of unpleasant dreams and set her back financially.

Somebody knocked at the back door, briskly. Gentian got up; it was probably Mrs. Zimmerman with some late pumpkins. She pulled aside the blue curtain over the glass in the door and peered out. The boy from next door looked back at her. She had to look up at him: he was taller than Junie. She gaped foolishly for a moment. In the brilliant blare of the security light he looked like somebody on a stage, about to summon spirits like Prospero. He held up the snake his mother had borrowed, as if it were a sceptre. He had a round glittering cookie tin in his other hand, like a crown.

Gentian unbolted the door and opened it. His hair was black, and his eyes were dark blue or perhaps black, and his lips were as red as wine, though that was probably from the cold. He was beautiful. He might be taller than Junie, but Junie was out.

He smiled at her. His teeth shone, but were no more pointed than anyone else's. "I'm Dominic Hardy," he said. His voice had changed already; it was middling deep and clear. "Here's your snake, and my mother sent some cookies."

He was wearing a white shirt—no sweater, no jacket, no hat. The brisk northeast wind of a Minnesota October lifted the hair on his forehead.

"Come in; you'll freeze," said Gentian, intelligently, and banged the door behind him so that somebody would hear and come help her out. The guest room was right above the back porch; maybe Rosemary would hear. She was too young and shy to constitute competition, and perhaps Dominic would think she was funny.

"Do sit down," said Gentian, removing the snake from his grasp and sliding it in between the refrigerator and the wall. "I was just going to make some fudge."

She had never made it in her life, but she had hung around plaguing Junie when Junie made it. There were cookies and divinity and fruitcake already, but Juniper had made all those and Gentian would have to say so. There were Dominic's cookies, but you couldn't feed people things they had brought themselves, could you?

"You could wait and take some back with you." You've come such a long way, she thought, and almost snickered at herself. It would repay him for the cookies, at least.

Dominic either had good manners or didn't want to go home. "Thank you," he said, and sat down.

He was not very conversational. Gentian tried him on as-tronomy, mathematics, Shakespeare, Robert Heinlein, modern poetry, a couple of Junie's favorite bands, a couple of Junie's tele-vision shows, and finally, as a mad stab in the dark, Elizabethan music. His responses were mostly quotations. When she said she had a telescope, he said lazily, "Then felt I like some watcher of the skies, when a new planet swims into his ken." Gentian knew that this was from a sonnet by Keats. Steph had made her a poster of it in somewhat shaky calligraphy the summer after sixth grade, and it was hanging over her desk at this moment. But something prevented her from letting Dominic know this. She felt odd that he should quote one of the Giant Ants' own special fa-vorite poems.

"These days you're lucky to see a new comet," she said, and pulled the canister of sugar from under the overhang of the upper cabinets.

His remark about mathematics was, "Euclid alone has looked on beauty bare." Gentian had studied that one in school, didn't like it, and felt justified because Becky didn't either, even though Becky was wild about some of Edna St. Vincent Millay's other poems. She made a noncommittal noise and got out the choco-late.

For Shakespeare, he said, "Nature's child, warbling his native wood-notes wild." Gentian was not familiar with this quotation, if it was one, but it sounded unlikely to her. She took the milk from the refrigerator.

For Heinlein, he said, quoting from *Glory Road,* "Women and Cats. Men and Dogs."

"That's what I don't like about Heinlein, all right," said Gen-tian. "Some of his books are awfully good, though."

"Specialization is for insects," said Dominic, quoting from a Heinleinian passage her mother used to deride, from a novel Gentian had not read yet because her parents had suggested she wait until she was sixteen or so.

It was odd that he should have read so many of the things her family and friends had. And this was a discussion she might at more leisure have found fruitful, but by now she was hunting for the fudge recipe and wondering if she could remember it. She could just say she couldn't find it, and offer him something of Junie's. On the other hand, it was useful to have something to occupy her; sitting at the table with him would be much more embarrassing. Poking about in the dusty disarray of her father's recipe box, she said, "Do you like modern poetry?"

"Tennis without a net," said Dominic, definitively.

"That's not true at all," said Gentian. "It's just got a different sort of structure."

Come to think of it, the fudge recipe wasn't on a card, it was in a cookbook. Junie had spilt milk on that page, so if she looked at the page-edges of each cookbook, there should be a bulgy wrinkle in about the right spot. "It was okay for Robert Frost to say that," she added, shoving Betty Crocker back into place and yanking Fanny Farmer out. "He was talking about how he felt about writing it. But reading it with that attitude is like going to a hockey game and getting mad because it's not tennis." All of this was Becky's opinion, more or less verbatim. Gentian liked the modern poetry that Becky read to her, and otherwise had no relationship with it.

"But they call it tennis," said Dominic; for the very first time, he sounded about half interested.

"No, they don't. They call it a game. People just assume it must be the same one they're used to."

"What bass is our viol for tragic tones?" said Dominic.

"I beg your pardon?" There was the recipe. Gentian propped the book against the tea canister and began assembling pots and measuring spoons.

Dominic did not answer her.

"I've heard recorder music coming from your house," said Gentian, rather desperately. "Do you play?"

"Do you think I am easier to be played upon than a pipe?" said Dominic.

He did not, despite quoting Hamlet in a fury, sound offended, but Gentian at this point gave up on him and concentrated on the fudge, which was giving her difficulties.

She had burned her tongue for the sixth time, and the fudge was still refusing to form a ball in the cold water, when Junie came back. She banged the back door behind her, dropped her skates on the floor of the porch, and shot the bolt, which Gentian always forgot to do. The sound made Dominic jump, which was some satisfaction. Juniper came into the kitchen, pulled off her green beret, shook out all her long red hair, and said, "What are you burning?"

"None of your business," said Gentian, stirring idly. "Say hello to Dominic."

Juniper didn't even blink. "Hello, Dominic," she said. "I'm Junie."

Gentian turned around from the stove, moving the spoon randomly in the uncooperative fudge; she had to see this.

Dominic studied Juniper for several seconds as if she were a kind of food he had never seen before, and then smiled at her. Gentian saw Junie melt, and made a bet with herself about how long it would be before they went out together. He was better than the smoking seniors, anyway; if Mom ever found out about *them* she was liable to ground all three girls until they were twenty.

Rosemary, who must have been having her bath when she should have been listening to Gentian bang the back door, came slouching into the kitchen in Juniper's green flannel bathrobe, which she liked because it was too long for her and she could sweep the skirts around the floor, gathering cat hair and playing at being a princess. Junie's melting process reversed itself suddenly, but she couldn't launch into a tirade because Dominic was there.

While Juniper was thinking how to be politely scathing, a thing Gentian knew to be almost impossible for her, Rosemary stared at Dominic as if he were a food she recognized and didn't like. He smiled at her, too. Gentian fully expected Rosemary to turn red and run away, which was her usual method of dealing with strangers who were nice to her.

But Rosemary spoke to him. "You've got the broken chair," she said. "You need the cushion."

And she swept Juniper's bathrobe around and exited without tripping on it, to return bearing the fat gold-and-black-and-white

Hmong pillow that they had given their mother for her birthday. Gentian supposed that it had had to happen sometime. Rosie would probably appreciate somebody who had no conversation; it would save her having to make any. She could get pregnant and be the family statistic.

A horrible smell of burnt sugar and chocolate smote her nose, and as she recoiled from that she felt herself recoiling also at the thoughts she had just had. It was all right to think that way about Juniper; Juniper was acting like an idiot and had been for years now. But Rosie was all right.

"Get away from that pan!" shouted Juniper.

Gentian got out of her way and yielded up the wooden spoon cheerfully, and went to sit at the table and watch Rosie be worshipful and Dominic see Juniper in a temper.

Dominic said, not very loudly, "What is the difference between an angry girl and a mad bull?"

Gentian froze.

"What?" said Rosie.

"You can reason with the bull."

Rosie giggled. Gentian wanted to, because he had so perfectly characterized Juniper. If he had asked what was the difference between Junie in a temper and a mad bull, she would have fallen off her chair laughing and repeated it to be sure Junie, now immersed in clouds of steam at the sink, had heard.

She said, "How many feminists does it take to change a light bulb?"

"I beg your pardon?" said Dominic.

Gentian looked at him dubiously, but Rosie said at once, *"That's not funny!"* and collapsed over the table in a fit of giggles.

Dominic looked at Gentian across the table. His eyes were extremely blue. "Ah," he said. It was what her mother called a "diagnostic ah." She didn't know what he had diagnosed—rightly, that she was a feminist, wrongly, that she had no sense of humor, or simply that she had not thought his original joke a good one. She looked back at him, as if he were something she saw through the telescope. Rosie stopped laughing and sat up.

"I have a project that I need help with," said Dominic, impartially to both of them. Gentian stared; he had actually volunteered a piece of information. She wondered if Rosemary's attitude was responsible. She tried to look encouraging, and Dominic explained further. "I want to build a time machine."

Rosemary looked stunned. Gentian said, "What for?"

"Well," said Dominic, "I'll tell you if you'll tell me, what is the maid without a tress?"

"Bald," said Rosemary.

Dominic grinned at her. "No," he said.

"Junie didn't have any hair until she was almost three," said Gentian meanly.

Juniper, stirring an entirely new batch of fudge, ignored this feeble thrust, but Dominic leaned back against the Hmong cushion and looked carefully at her. "Well, we'd better have Junie, then," he said.

Gentian, feeling conspired against, said, "Well, what do you want to build a time machine for?"

Dominic said, "What was the tower without a crest?"

"Topless," said Rosemary, and then giggled and turned red.

"Rosie, for heaven's sake. Ilium had topless towers," said Juniper.

"They didn't finish the Tower of Babel," said Gentian.

Dominic leaned his elbows on the table and stared at her until she felt herself turning redder than Rosemary, and she hadn't even made a dirty remark. "We'll have you, too," said Dominic.

"You still haven't said why you want to—"

"Which is the water without any sand?"

He was like their father, thought Gentian, a curious collection of nonsequiturs.

"Tears," said Rosemary, who loved riddles and was obviously recovering her equanimity.

"We'll have Rosie, too," said Dominic.

"Why do you want to?" said Gentian.

"You think about those riddles," said Dominic, "and you'll know. Have you a chamber here where we could build it?"

"The attic," said Juniper, now furiously beating the fudge.

"That's *mine*," said Gentian.

"You don't need all that space."

"You should have entire control over when we may use it, Genny," said Dominic.

Gentian felt a most peculiar shiver up her spine when he used her name. She was not altogether sure she liked it.

"Well, in that case," she said.

"Excellent," said Dominic. He got up. "I will requite you," he said, bestowed a particular smile upon Gentian, and let himself out the back door.

Juniper turned around from pouring the fudge onto a sheet of waxed paper. "It'll be cool enough to eat in just a minute," she said.

The back door shut firmly.

"What did you *say* to him?" demanded Juniper, and banged her empty saucepan into the sink.

"Nothing!" said Rosemary hotly, answering the spirit of her inquiry.

"I said we could use the attic to build the time machine," said Gentian, answering the letter.

Juniper regarded them with equal ill favor and stamped out. Her feet thundered up the steps, and her bedroom door banged resoundingly.

"Well, we can eat all the fudge, anyway," said Gentian.

After they had eaten a great deal of it, she got ready for Becky's arrival. This entailed putting the green sheets on the bed, because Becky thought the white ones with the red pattern looked like something out of a cheap horror movie. It also entailed making a batch of tuna-fish-and-cashew sandwiches, a batch of cheese-and-jelly sandwiches, a batch of hummus-and-pickle sandwiches, and an apple-and-celery salad. She stole some of Junie's spice cookies and legitimately acquired from her mother bags of pretzels and corn chips as well as a large jug of cranberry juice and a six-pack of lemon soda. She put the perishable parts of this feast into the cooler Rosemary took when she went camping with the Girl Scouts.

She got out four fat beeswax candles, her grandmother's lace tablecloth, and the plates from the set of dishes Murr's bowls belonged to. She swept the clutter of notebooks, rulers, Rick Brant books, graph paper, and gardening texts from the top of her cedar chest, spread the cloth where they had been, and set two places.

Murr lay down in the middle of the lace cloth and tucked her feet in all around.

"Becky's coming," Gentian told her. "You can steal corn chips."

Maria Mitchell gazed at her distantly, like somebody scanning past a familiar object in search of the unfamiliar. Did cats use averted vision? Were their eyes even structured the same way? Gentian rubbed Murr behind the ears and put the items she had removed from the chest into the boxes designated for them in the closet.

As an afterthought, she dusted both bedside tables and swept the floor. Murr chased the broom, sneezing. Gentian brushed her vigorously, and then picked the tricolored hairs from the lace tablecloth. Her father said that gracious living was impossible if one had animals, but this was disingenuous. Gentian knew that in the first place he had no desire for gracious living and in the second he was merely pretending that he understood how a constant stream of strays might be troublesome to some people, notably her mother.

Or possibly Junie. Her mother *was* gracious, but gracious living was more up Junie's alley. Murr didn't like the strays very much either. Gentian thought it was because she was solitary by nature; Juniper said it was because the strays were uniformly ill-behaved; Rosemary said Murr would like them fine if anybody gave her a chance.

"Would you?" said Gentian to Murr, pausing in the act of putting her broom away. "Or would you eat them up, like Lessingham's daughter?"

Murr blinked, benignly. Her namesake had been solitary, after all.

Friday morning was warm and sunny and striped with long

clouds. Gentian got to school in time for assembly, earning an ex-
travagantly raised eyebrow from Erin and a giggle from Steph.

A series of students read announcements about various clubs
and activities. They all sang "Turn the World Around," though
it was almost as unsuitable as "The Star-Spangled Banner" for
large untrained groups to sing. Then the principal came to address them, as she did every few weeks. Most of her addresses
dealt with internal school matters and were very funny, but this
one did not and was not. A junior at the other downtown high
school, she said, had been attacked in the parking lot of that
school on the previous evening, as she left after attending a meeting of the chess club. The assailant was another student at that
school, and had been caught already; but the incident had crys-
tallized a lot of people's anxieties about how freely students of
the open school came and went at all hours and wandered
around downtown in between.

She laid down a series of new rules. Since she said at the beginning that the rules would be printed up and distributed to the
students, Gentian ceased to listen at this point, except to notice
the groans and outcries and mutters of her fellow students as restriction followed restriction in the list.

"They'll never enforce that," said Steph in Gentian's ear. "If
we wanted to live like that, we'd go to Roosevelt. And look what
good that did *her.*"

"Why don't they restrict the boys?" said Gentian, almost idly.
"I mean, if it's the boys who they think are going to do the dam-
age, why make the girls creep around like Chuchundra the
Muskrat, as if we were the guilty ones?"

"Most of the boys aren't guilty."

"None of the girls are." Gentian considered this statement,
and added scrupulously, "Not of raping other girls in parking
lots, anyway."

"Where would I fit in?" said Erin. "Is it time to get that big
G tattooed on my forehead?"

"Then you'd have to live with it forever," said Gentian.

"Besides," said Steph, "they worry about the boys getting
beaten up or mugged and told them to travel in pairs too."

"In passing," said Gentian.

"Let's see what it looks like on the printed list, okay?"

Gentian desisted, less because of Steph's request than because of Erin's question.

Everybody said Erin looked like a boy. Erin said cheerfully that this suited her. Superficially, Erin looked a lot like Gentian. She was middling tall, and long-limbed and pale, with brown hair, a little lighter and straighter than Gentian's, and medium blue eyes, and a face with all the features in the right place and more or less the right size, neither cramped nor expansive nor breathtaking. But even when Gentian was four and had hair a quarter-inch long because Junie had cut chunks out of it with a pair of plastic scissors, nobody ever mistook her for a boy.

After years of intermittent consideration of the issue, beginning on the day Erin showed up for kindergarten and Mr. Johnson called her Eric, Gentian had decided that Erin made the question of what one meant by looking like a girl or looking like a boy completely meaningless.

This decision was alternately intriguing and very annoying. Along with the biography of Maria Mitchell that had set Gentian on the path leading to the telescope and, eventually, a desert, an observatory, and comets, she had been given biographies of Clara Barton, Susan B. Anthony, Elizabeth Blackwell, Elizabeth Cady Stanton. The horrors of nineteenth-century sexism in all its glory, even as recounted in books intended for children, and books moreover whose essential point was that everything was all better now, had moved Gentian to the greatest fury she had ever known. She had figured out that this was because her righteous indignation at injustice, at idiocy, at pompous cruelty, at unthinking insult, at intellectual waste and spiritual blight, was colored by the personal, by the thought that she could have been one of those girls, one of those struggling women; could have been one even in today's world, in some other country, in the wrong family.

Gentian had hated men, including her father, for about six months. She realized one day that, in the absence of specific insults to herself, she did not have the emotional fiber to keep up such a hot white vigorous fire; this was distressing for a while, but then, perhaps, evidence of a cool scientific temperament, though of course an even cooler one would not have taken things quite so personally to begin with. Then again, you couldn't leave the personal out. Even Maria Mitchell couldn't. Scientists were human too, perhaps unfortunately.

During the time that she was hating men, Erin made her uneasy. She and Erin had always been at opposite sides of the arc formed by the Giant Ants: Gentian was friends with Becky, Alma, Steph, and Erin, in that order. But she and Erin shared a few things the others did not: a passion for *A Girl of the Limberlost,* a liking for Lock and Dam Number One quite in excess of the interest to be got from the guided tours; a fondness for anchovies on pizza; a propensity for walking in the rain.

Erin derived an enormous delight from being taken for a boy. Gentian had never seen such a reaction in anybody else. One of her cousins was always being taken for a girl, and he beat up anybody who teased him; Rosie had gone through a stage of being thin, active, plain, and short-haired, but when she was taken for a boy she put on pink shirts and stuck barrettes in her hair. But Erin loved the mistake; she looked bland, she dressed confusingly, she egged them on.

Now Gentian looked at Erin, as they stood up and waited for the crowd to disperse so they could go off to class, and said, not sarcastically, since she hated skirts herself, "If you couldn't get a tattoo, you'd have to dress like a girl."

"Whatever that means," said Erin, predictably.

"Don't start," moaned Steph, herding them ahead of her towards the doors. "Don't start on skirts. And Gentian, you have got to stop talking as if there is No Difference Between Boys and Girls."

"I never said that. There's just not much. And people are very stupid about what there is. Like now. Why *don't* they make all the boys pay for statistical aggressiveness, size, and anatomical advantage? Instead of making all the girls pay? Don't we pay enough when the prevention fails, without having the prevention be a punishment all by itself? What's the matter with them?"

Steph shrugged. "Ask them."

"They *are* them," said Gentian, mostly to make Becky laugh when she told her about it later, but also because it was true.

"No," said Erin, "we are Them."

"Giant Ants," they chorused, "from White Sands."

Jamie Barrows went by, casting upon them an odd, rueful, maybe wistful glance. Gentian felt herself blush. Her immediate instinct was to disassociate herself from her friends, go after him, ask him something, anything; to make herself pleasant. She took Steph's arm instead. Love me, love my ants, she thought, and giggled, and looked mysterious when Erin asked her what was so funny all of a sudden.

She and Steph were going to the same part of the building as Jamie, and when she saw his curly head and blue denim shirt as he paused at his locker, she thought suddenly, "He is them. He really is."

They walked past him, going fast now because Ms. Ogden made sarcastic remarks when you were late. Gentian nodded at him. He smiled back. He hardly seemed big enough to be the enemy. And what had he done to her, anyway, to make her think of him that way? Laid down the law. Rosie said that made him a jerk; Gentian had found herself thinking it made him the enemy; it did, maybe, make him suspect. You couldn't trust him to understand important things. Then again, you couldn't trust most people to understand anything at all. That was why the Giant Ants were so important.

Steph caught her elbow as she walked right past the door of their classroom.

"Thanks," said Gentian, following her in.

"Dreaming of Jamie Barrows?" said Steph.

Gentian felt herself blush again, which of course made Steph smile. They sat down in the back of the room, Gentian behind Steph since she was the taller. "More like a nightmare," said Gentian.

Steph turned sideways in her seat and cast on Gentian a familiar, mildly exasperated look. She had a delicate face that she had forbidden everybody to call "elfin," and big dark eyes with long lashes. It was not a face that could really look as exasperated as Gentian knew Steph often felt. "Think less, dream more," Steph said, and turned smartly around again before Gentian could answer. Her permed dark hair and straight thin shoulders were as unresponsive as a statue's.

Gentian wrote her a long indignant note instead, started to tear it up, and then saved it to show to Becky.

7

On Friday evening Juniper electrified her family by announcing, in the interval between dinner and dessert, that she was going out on a date: not this weekend, which was booked, but next weekend, with somebody she knew from the teen chat echo.

"Who does he think he's going out with?" said Gentian.

"Me," said Juniper, coldly.

"Which one?"

"All," said Juniper, slightly less coldly. "He guessed. That's the only reason I'd even think about going out with him."

"What's his name?"

"Never you mind."

"You're going to have to tell me, at least," said her mother.

"I know, but don't tell *them*."

Rosemary's not a Giant Ant, thought Gentian, and giggled. Juniper glared at her.

"What about telling me?" said their father.

Juniper considered him. "Okay, but you can't speechify."

"I certainly can. I speechify very well indeed."

Rosemary and Gentian laughed. Juniper said between her teeth, "You *may* not speechify."

"I think it's pretty likely, in fact," said their mother.

"Why?" said their father. "Is he too old? Mad, bad, and dangerous to know?"

For some reason this question made Juniper, who had shown every sign of bursting into temper, smile demurely.

"I'll try to rein in his propensity to lecture," said their mother, "but I think he'll have to be in on the secret."

"I'm glad I'm the youngest," said Rosemary.

"Why?" said their mother.

"Because if I ever go on a date they'll be too old to care."

After dinner Juniper went off to research a history paper at the library with Sarah, and Gentian asked for permission to use the computer in Juniper's room.

"You should have asked before your sister left," said her mother, who seemed to be in rather a sour mood. "If she's got anything obviously private sitting out, don't look at it, and don't sit on the bed if she's got a pattern laid out, all right?"

"It's not fair the computer should be in her room."

"It's there because she has two rooms; there's no space for it elsewhere."

"It's not fair she should have two rooms."

"Rosemary likes to be snug and you need to be high enough for your telescope."

Gentian considered pointing out that when the present room allotment had been made, she had been five years old and had not had a telescope, but she decided not to press the issue.

Juniper's diary was where it always was, not left sitting out. Her bed was covered with rejected clothing; most of it was clean, and she had just put it on, exclaimed in horror, and taken it off again. She was not usually quite so picky about what she wore to go to the library with Sarah, so she must be hoping to encounter some boy or other there. Maybe Denny; maybe the person from the chat echo. She wondered if Juniper had found out what he looked like before agreeing to meet him. She wondered if she herself would do the same.

Gentian held Juniper's diary in her hand for a moment and then stuffed it unopened back into the chair cover. She could look at it later if what she wanted to know was not in the mes-

sages on the chat group. She would rather, if it were possible, de-
duce the identity of Juniper's date from available evidence. She
removed a stack of old newspapers from the chair and sat down
cautiously at the computer. As a scientist she should be comfortable with such devices, should view them as extensions of herself,
tendrils of her own mind reaching out to the universe. That was
how she felt about the telescope.

But the computers at school were too battered and cranky,
and this one, while intended for all the children of the family, was
too much Juniper's. Gentian, fingers poised above the keys,
thought about trying to use her father's computer instead. Somehow she felt that Juniper would know if her sister read her chat
groups from her own machine. This was irrational. Besides, her
father was in his office, using his computer and listening to Laurie Anderson sing about angels.

Gentian sighed and logged on. She called the BBS so seldom
that every time she came back her account had expired. For this
occasion she called herself Laurie March and used "Scrabble" as
her password.

Within five messages she remembered why she didn't do this
more often. Nobody could spell, punctuate, or write a sentence
longer than five words unless they did it by leaving out the period
and sailing gaily on to the next five-word sentence.

And they flirted, with an ineptitude so profound that Gentian, who found the whole process despicable and tried to know
nothing about it, could not help recognizing it. At least when
Steph or Alma flirted, you might initially think they were just
having a conversation with somebody who happened to be male,
until you thought twice, or Becky pointed out that Steph had a
special voice for flirting and Alma always put her hand on the
arm of the object of her affections. Gentian was sorely tempted
to send several pairs of these flirters private mail with advice in
it, especially the ones who said they wanted "intelligent females"
and demonstrated the intelligence of a large rock.

She quit reading and looked at the list of messages to see
what threads Juniper was involved in. Juniper had three presences: herself, Juniper Meriweather; an older girl called Crystal

Gold whom Gentian found even more insufferable than Juniper herself; and the fifteen-year-old boy she had made up for her school project, who was called Jason Breedlove, pronounced, as Jason reminded everybody repeatedly, more like "breadloaf."

Gentian could tell at once which subject headers Juniper had written herself. Wanted: Jane Fairfax. Television tuned to a dead channel. Are You Just Drawn That Way? Keep those cards and letters. Anything Except Star Trek. Ride in Triumph Through Persepolis. And, exasperatedly, You Keep Using That Word. When she wasn't talking to her family, Juniper could be interesting.

She was also involved, sometimes extensively, in threads named Fear Rules, Beam me up Snotty, Is their anybody there, and Hot Dud sees you.

Gentian knew Juniper's own on-line personality, of course, of old, and was also wearily familiar with Crystal, who made occasional appearances when Juniper was vying with Rosemary for the bathroom they were supposed to share. But Gentian had not logged on since Jason made his appearance.

Her first conclusion was that with the addition of Jason to the cast, Juniper no longer needed to talk to anybody except herself. Her second was that Jason sounded much more like the Juniper her sisters knew than did either of the other two. Her third, as she leaned back fascinated from a long furious exchange of messages in which Crystal berated Jason for being a sexist, Jason defended himself coolly, and several other girls came eagerly to Jason's defense, was that Jason was Juniper with the unreasonableness left out, but he was still a jerk. How odd of Juniper to think boys were more reasonable than girls.

Jason's opinions were idiotic, of course; Juniper had apparently just inverted the sensible half of her own dearly held maxims to create his philosophy, if you could call it that. But he wasn't impetuous, fanatical, insistent, involved—you could almost say he wasn't interested in his own opinions, except that somebody who wasn't would not in fact argue them, even so coolly.

Paging idly through a discussion of several Disney movies, some bands she had never heard of and never planned to, and a couple of British television shows she had similar intentions about, Gentian found the word she was looking for. "There's no need to be shrill," Jason said to a massed opposition composed of Crystal, Juniper, Hot Dud—who just might be what her father referred to as a conscious comedian, rather than an illiterate silly-boy—and the only other participant with a female name who agreed with them that Jason was being a sexist. That was what Jason wasn't, all right. Shrill. And by not being shrill, he had put the rest of them into a position where they could hardly be anything else.

Gentian leaned back in the chair, regarding Juniper's calendar, which was still on its June page, a photograph of the bluebells in Kew Gardens.

"Wow," she said.

Did Juniper know what she was doing, or was she just stumbling around? And would anybody else in this odd group, this improbable medium, catch on, or would they either nod sagely or throw metaphorical rocks, depending on whether they agreed with Jason or not? She was tempted to post a message of her own, just to make things clearer. Good grief, if she had met Juniper this way and were not by experience with Juniper or someone like her so put off by histrionics, she might even like Juniper. She would certainly like her better than Jason.

But why? she thought, drumming her thumb on the wrist-rest. He acts scientific, doesn't he? He's detached? No. Or well, yes, he *acts* scientific but he isn't in fact scientific; he has the attitude but not the essence. He gives detachment a bad name.

She bit off one corner of her thumbnail, and sighed. Steph would notice that on Monday and give her a lecture. Maybe it would be entertaining to tell her that one of Gentian's criteria for a boyfriend was that he *like* bitten nails. That might shut her up. Which was more than you could say for Jason: Gentian couldn't think of anything that might shut him up. I wonder if anybody could really get that way, she thought, having those awful opinions and yet not being involved with them, not taking things personally; I wonder if that makes sense. Nobody else has noticed that it might not, but they're only kids.

She looked at her watch. There was plenty of time yet. The

echo she had looked at first was theoretically for the discussion and, she supposed, promulgation of teen romance. There was another one for "teen culture," or something like that. She selected it from the menu and looked at the list of messages.

Juniper was posting there under her own name, as was somebody called Peter Pan, who was Juniper's early try at a male alias. People seemed to be able to spell their subject headers better in this group. Gentian took a look at it. Junie was, of course, in the middle of an argument.

Her chief opponent appeared to be somebody whose handle was The Light Prince. They had a prolonged fight going about George MacDonald, especially the Curdie books. Since Gentian had found *At the Back of the North Wind* so cloying that she refused even to look at anything else its author had written, she could not make much of the discussion. Juniper got considerably more heated than The Light Prince did.

About ten messages along, Juniper's alias had joined in. Gentian thought that if calling herself Peter Pan and pretending to be a twelve-year-old boy had so little effect on Junie's basic personality, she might as well not bother. Surely anybody could tell they were the same person? When they used not only the same arguments but the same kinds of sentences?

It was true that Juniper could spell and Peter Pan couldn't. Gentian had to admire her sister. Peter Pan had trouble with double consonants—he never knew where they belonged and where they didn't. He had a bit of trouble with double vowels, too. But was that really enough to throw people off the track?

Apparently it was. Not only that, but Peter's misspelled arguments got more credit than Junie's correct ones. Peter Pan had written, "It's dumb to sugest that taking the fantasy ellements out of *At the Back of the North Wind* would make it beter. You wouldn't have a storry at all if you did that. You'd have a borring morral treetise."

Juniper had written, as herself, "It's foolish to suggest taking the fantastical elements out of a fantasy. It's like saying *Romeo and Juliet* would be better without the romance or *Hamlet* without the ghost. You wouldn't have any story at all—just a sermon."

To Juniper, The Light Prince had written, "But surely the definition of a fantasy is that you can't take the fantastical elements out without the story's falling apart. But AT THE BACK OF THE NORTH WIND would still have the same story if it were not a fantasy."

That was bad enough, but somebody else called Mutant Boy had agreed cordially, if semiliterately, with Peter and then spent three incoherent, unparagraphed, unpunctuated screens yelling at Juniper for being an intellectual snob and a show-off because she had mentioned Shakespeare.

No wonder Junie was so bad-tempered, thought Gentian, her fingers twitching over the keyboard. Of course, Junie had been bad-tempered long before there was a computer in the house. But still, this was enough to make anybody wild.

"Besides," she said aloud to Mutant Boy's tagline, "if you were so all-fired anti-intellectual and *modern,* you moron, you wouldn't be reading George MacDonald in the first place. You wouldn't be reading *anything.* Little creep."

She read on, past several incoherent messages, and one ill-spelled but possibly insightful discussion of Curdie's godmother and the ways in which she differed from similar figures in folk tales, until she arrived at an argument between Peter Pan and Juniper.

Juniper had written, "Has anybody read Patrice Kindl's *Owl in Love?* I think it's brilliant." Mutant Boy had merely inquired nastily if Juniper ever went to the movies or watched television. Gentian, knowing her sister's addiction to no fewer than four television shows despite her parents' rules about how much television could be watched in a given week, was momentarily puzzled until she saw a follow-up message from Peter Pan, recommending the shows Juniper already watched as "stuff even an intellectual like you might like."

Gentian thought this highly uncharacteristic of Peter Pan, who was at least as intellectual as Juniper even if he used somewhat shorter words and couldn't spell all of them. But the conference as a whole seemed to applaud this remark. The Light Prince was one of the few who did not. He—if it was he, thought Gentian; what else, after all, was Juniper trying to point out?—

began a lengthy discussion of what exactly constituted being an intellectual, and concluded that Juniper was not one.

Gentian was delighted and wanted to see how Juniper had taken this insult to the core of her identity, but she had reached the end of the messages. Juniper had not yet responded. It would be a beauty when she did.

She still had half an hour before Becky's arrival, and everything had been ready for hours. She tapped her fingers on the edge of the keyboard. She was still sorely tempted to swat Mutant Boy, and she also wanted to take up the definition of "intellectual" with The Light Prince. That would take most of her half hour. She backed herself out of the layers of menu, provided herself with an alias, and came back in as Betony. At least the jokes would be different, assuming anybody even realized it was a plant or bothered to look it up.

It was only after she had saved the messages and logged off that she realized who would recognize her middle name.

"Genny," said Rosemary, putting her head around the door, "Becky's here. What are *you* doing on the computer?"

"Looking at the U's library catalog," said Gentian. She got up. Well, Juniper would just have to lump it. It wasn't her own personal discussion area.

As she shut the door of Juniper's room behind her, it occurred to her that she had never looked in Juniper's diary to find out who it was from the chat echo that she was going out with. It couldn't be anybody whose messages she had seen. It must be someone who lurked and then sent Juniper private mail.

Becky was wearing a long emerald-green wrap skirt with a long royal-blue tunic belted over it by means of a bright red scarf in a pattern of yellow and purple flowers. She had on red sneakers, but they were a different red. She was carrying a small overnight case and a huge shopping bag overflowing with books, notebooks, compact disks, and tapes. Gentian's mother said neither of them ever ventured into the other's house without enough supplies for a month-long stay. In fact, for such a stay, either of them would almost immediately have run out of underwear, but never come close to running out of entertainment.

"What in the world were you doing on the computer?" she demanded, toiling up the attic stairs after Gentian.

"Well, in default of the telescope—"

"Uh-huh." Becky dropped her bag of books heavily into the basket chair and shut Gentian's door behind them.

"I was checking up on Junie's project, and I got so mad at somebody I decided to leave a message. He said Junie wasn't an intellectual."

"I suppose the Pope's not Catholic, either," said Becky, bending to greet Maria Mitchell, who had materialized from the direction of the closet.

"When I have time to print the message I'll show it to you."

"What's that other person's definition of an intellectual?"

"He kept talking about Wittgenstein. He thinks an intellectual is exactly the same as a philosopher, only untrained."

"Wittgenstein?"

"No, this kid. The Light Prince," said Gentian, curling her lip and watching Becky roll her eyes briefly ceilingward. "I mean," said Gentian, "Wittgenstein might think that too; I don't know. But The Light Prince definitely thinks that."

"Even so," said Becky, sitting down on the bed, "why doesn't Junie qualify?"

"Because she watches television and prefers fiction to non-fiction."

"I should think it wouldn't depend on what she did, it would depend on—on the spirit in which she did it."

"Well, that makes sense. But The Light Prince says that Wittgenstein only dined in the Great Hall at Cambridge once, because he found the conversation dull, so therefore Junie's not an intellectual." Gentian shrugged. "You know, not one person said anything about how silly it is to compare the Great Hall at Cambridge with watching television."

"Cambridge?" said Becky. "When?"

"I don't know. I never heard of him before."

Becky got up and made for her bag of books, whence she extracted the battered biographical dictionary. "C. S. Lewis was at Cambridge," she said, paging through rapidly. "I think it would be hilarious if he missed out on talking to Lewis. No, wait, he died in 1951 and I don't think Lewis went to Cambridge till later." She paged through again. "No, he didn't—not until 1954. Oh, well. Maybe there really wasn't anybody decent to talk to."

"Maybe they didn't want to have philosophical discussions at dinnertime," said Gentian. "I wouldn't."

"Just goes to show you're not an intellectual," said Becky.

Gentian threw a pillow at her. Becky put the dictionary away and came back and sat on the bed again. Maria Mitchell went over and sniffed at the pillow, delicately, with the tips of her whiskers, as if it might suddenly fly off again.

"Gen," said Becky, "do you think this person might be defending Junie?"

"What?"

"Well, you said she was *accused* of being an intellectual, as if those morons in the chat group thought it was an insult. So if he's giving reasons why she isn't one, he's defending her."

"Huh," said Gentian.

"If it is a he," added Becky.

"Whether it is or not," said Gentian, "it won't do whoever any good with Junie. *Junie* thinks she's an intellectual and the rest of them are just that, morons, and she's not going to agree with him. Besides, they won't like her no matter what anybody says, because they *are* morons."

"You don't like her either," said Becky.

"She doesn't treat them the way she treats her family," said Gentian. "At least, part of her doesn't. If I didn't know who she was I'd like her a lot. But they think all her good traits are bad ones."

"Maybe they're nicer in person," said Becky, "the way Junie is nastier."

"I wouldn't hold my breath," said Gentian.

"I shouldn't have used the word 'moron,' " said Becky. "People can't help being stupid, they can only help being stupider than they need to be."

"These people are much stupider than anybody needs to be."

"Well," said Becky, stretching, "feed me something, and then let's have a look at this telescope."

They sat on the bed and ate sandwiches—the table setting was for the midnight feast, not incidental snacking—and then Becky went up the cherry steps and stood leaning on the carved railing of the platform, looking speculative.

"I know you're a scientist," she said, "but really, on reflection, I'd say it was bewitched." She looked thoughtful, as she did when replaying something she had just said, and grinned. "Sorry. I didn't mean to make a pun."

"What does bewitched mean?"

"Well, lots of things, depending on your belief system."

"My belief system is rational."

"Yes, I know," said Becky, as if Gentian had said, "I have allergies." She sat down on Gentian's stool. "Is the dome open? Okay." She adjusted the stool to her height and fitted her face to the eyepiece. "All right," she said after a moment. "Maybe we can be rational about this. We'll call it the observer effect. Come and tell me what you see when you look into it."

"It's a telescope, not a crystal ball," said Gentian, irritably; but she did as she was told. Becky stood behind her, exuding a slight smell of sandalwood. She must have been borrowing her mother's soap again.

The rain-drenched evening sky rewarded her gaze. "Great," said Gentian. "I can see the sky, and it's cloudy."

"It was perfectly clear earlier," said Becky.

Gentian turned the stool around. Becky was looking at her watch. Gentian handed her the pad and pen she kept by the telescope, and Becky wrote down the time.

"All right," she said. "I'm going to leave the room, and you look again."

She did, and Gentian did. "Sky," said Gentian.

Becky put her head around the door. I'll go right down into the basement, all right?" she said.

"Sure," said Gentian over her shoulder. "Should I come get you?"

"No, just keep looking through the telescope."

Gentian did so, listening to Becky's sneakers thud down the stairs, and the snick of the door shutting at the entrance to the second floor, and the drip of the rain, and Maria Mitchell washing herself, and the small occasional tick of the bedside lamp heating up and expanding its metal shade. The sky was a uniform flat gray, dyed slightly rosy by city light. Her back began to hurt, because the stool and telescope were adjusted for Becky, who was shorter.

The stairway door opened and Becky came up the stairs and into the room and shut the bedroom door behind her.

"Well?"

"Sky."

"Huh. All right, we'll try it again when I go home tomorrow. I wish we had walkie-talkies or something."

"Alma's brothers had some, if they haven't broken them already."

Becky sat down on the bed, pried off each sneaker with the other foot, not bothering to untie them, and tucked her feet up. Her socks were the same red as her sneakers.

"Your socks match your shoes," said Gentian.

"Yeah, well, Jeremy gave them to me when I had the green shoes, and he gets fractious if I don't wear them sometimes."

"Well, if it's Jeremy."

Becky's little brother was everything Gentian's sisters were not. "I had the weirdest conversation with Rosie," said Gentian, reminded.

Becky looked receptive. Gentian hauled out the corn chips. "I can't tell you details, I promised. But it was weird. She might turn into somebody."

"What else happened this week?"

Gentian thought. The earlier part of the week seemed infinitely far away. "You go first," she said. "My brain's not very collected."

"Telescope withdrawal," said Becky. She ate a corn chip. "Well, I wrote four sonnets, but I don't think they're much good. You can see them later. Steph made me go for a walk and listen to her quarterly lecture about the way I dress."

"She's early," said Gentian.

"It's because she's worried about you. She thinks I'm a bad example."

"Yeah, right," said Gentian. Steph's preoccupation with wearing just exactly the right cool clothes and Becky's with never wearing matching colors seemed, on one level, exactly the same kind of thing to her; she could not imagine taking so much trouble over one's appearance. She liked Becky's trouble better because it was revolutionary, but it was still trouble.

She did wonder what Dominic liked girls to wear, but because it seemed likely to involve something black and slinky, she wasn't going to waste a lot of time fretting over it. She looked thoughtfully at Becky. "What exactly is she worried about? That the Cool People will laugh at me? That I'll never have a boyfriend?"

"Both."

"Well, I'd feel I was doing something wrong if the Cool People didn't laugh at me, and you can't captivate anybody if you feel like an idiot, which I would if I dressed the way Steph thinks I should."

"Steph knows that," said Becky, "but she doesn't understand it."

"She keeps thinking that I'll hit some magical age when I agree with everything she wants," said Gentian. She added thoughtfully, "She's just like most people's mothers."

"Mine, certainly," said Becky, and ate another corn chip with a gloomy gesture.

Gentian crammed her own mouth with a stray quarter-sandwich. She could hardly imagine a better daughter than Becky, and Becky's mother's obvious dissatisfaction in the matter made Gentian want to spit. She swallowed and said, "And what's so tragic about not having a boyfriend, anyway?"

"Don't preach to the choir," said Becky.

"Are you going to a movie with Micky?"

"Even if I am, it's not to avoid the tragedy of my single life." She ate another corn chip. "What's single about it, anyway? I've got difficult parents and a really great brother and the Giant Ants and three pen-pals and *Tesseract*. And the whole inside of my head. I'm about as single as an acorn on a hundred-year-old oak."

"But more singular," said Gentian.

"Yes," said Becky. "There's always that."

"How can Steph be so smart and so conventional?"

"Protective coloration," said Becky. "To protect her from her family."

"Morons."

"No, let's save that for Junie's chat buddies. Boneheads, that's what I think Steph's family is." She paused. "Are. They are boneheads. Steph's family is boneheaded. Steph's family is composed of boneheads."

Gentian laughed. But while an evening with Becky would never be complete without an excursion into language, dividing stupidity into finer and finer shades was depressing. She cast about for another topic of conversation. What had she been doing, anyway? Not astronomy: not only had she been unable to use the telescope, she had not done her reading, her research. All that homework, *Julius Caesar,* all full of astrology instead. The fault, dear Brutus, lies not in our stars, but in ourselves, that we are underlings.

Becky's study group wasn't reading *Julius Caesar.* They had gotten *Romeo and Juliet.* Gentian wouldn't have liked that any better, but some of her group would. The rest of the kids who would have liked *Romeo and Juliet* were stuck with *A Comedy of Errors.* Gentian suspected malice aforethought on the part of their teacher, who was far too astute for comfort.

"Speaking of boneheads, how's *Romeo and Juliet?*" she said.

Becky smiled. "I got Mercutio."

"Your *hooouuusssess,*" carolled Gentian, imitating an unfortunate senior production of the play that they had been made to see when they were in sixth grade.

"Micky remembers that, too," said Becky. "But I beat him to the part."

"Are you *doing* it that way?"

"No, certainly not. I was afraid he would, though."

"How *are* you doing it?"

"Like Erin," said Becky.

Gentian was momentarily nonplussed; then she understood. "The onlooker," she said.

"Who sees most of the game," said Becky.

"For all the good it did him," said Gentian.

"That's because he was careless in dangerous times," said Becky. Her round face looked austere, not a usual expression.

Gentian considered this remark. "Well, I don't know," she said. "He was just being a little—a little fantastical, just having fun. And covering up how bad he felt by being silly. Just like lots of people."

"Yes, but it's not safe," said Becky. "Not if you're in Shakespeare, anyway."

"Well, sometimes it is. It depends on the play, doesn't it?"

"No, it's never safe. Sometimes it turns out all right, but it's never safe."

Becky had taken a course in Shakespeare's comedies last summer, at the university, which had been having a program for junior-high students—presumably, Gentian's father said, because they were alarmed by the quality of the freshmen they were admitting and wanted to get at the local population before the high schools ruined it. Gentian had thought of taking the course too, but she had never found Shakespeare's comedies very funny, and summer was the prime stargazing season. She was therefore ill-equipped for argument.

"What if you're not in Shakespeare?" she said.

"Well, then it would depend, wouldn't it?"

"On what, then?"

"On how dangerous the times were," said Becky, patiently.

"I'm not sure people can tell. I think they get used to whatever's going on."

"Well, maybe up to a point. But being used to it means taking a lot of precautions, it doesn't mean taking a lot of unnecessary risks."

"Maybe it depends on your temperament."

"Mercutio's got that, sure enough."

"Is that why he's named that?"

"Oh," said Becky, looking delighted. "I never thought. I'll ask in class next week, shall I?"

"Sure. Nobody makes fun of his name, though, the way they do of Tibault's."

"The way *he* does of Tibault's," said Becky.

"Why do I always like the play better when I talk to you than I do when I see it?"

"I have no idea. I can't believe you hated the Zeffirelli."

"It was gooey."

"What romantic stuff *do* you like, for pity's sake?"

Gentian looked at her carefully. That was a Stephian question, but Becky seemed quite earnest. "It probably hasn't been invented yet," said Gentian.

Becky, to her relief, laughed. Then she said, "Weren't *any* great woman astronomers romantic?"

"There's such a lot to choose from," said Gentian, dryly. "Caroline Herschel wasn't either."

"Poets have a wider range of role models," said Becky.

So you did pay attention to those biographies, thought Gentian. She said, "I think you should emulate Emily Dickinson and put your stuff in the teapot for posterity."

Becky lunged at her, laughing, and upset the bag of corn chips onto the floor. Gentian defended herself with her Hmong pillow for some seconds, but was eventually pinned by Becky, who was twenty pounds heavier than she, and tickled until she cried, "I give, I give! She did *not* put her poems in the teapot, that's a vile patriarchial lie," which made Becky laugh so much that Gentian was able to squirm away from her and thump her on the head with the pillow.

"We'd better stop," said Becky, "Maria Mitchell is eating all the corn chips."

"Leave her the broken bits. Let's pick the rest up and have some reading."

Becky stepped over the crunching Maria Mitchell and rummaged in her bag of books. Gentian, shaking cat hair from the corn chips and laying them on a convenient issue of *Sky and Telescope,* in case Becky should be having a fastidious day, hoped it would be either Becky's own poetry or prose.

"I found this just for you," said Becky, sitting down on the bed again, in her hands a book whose edges bristled with scraps of paper marking everything in it she had found worthy of mention. She opened it to the only purple scrap, and read aloud.

"His heatless room the watcher of the skies
Nightly inhabits when the night is clear;
Propping his mattress on the turning sphere,
Saturn his rings or Jupiter his bars
He follows, or the fleeing moons of Mars,
Til from his ticking lens they disappear. . . .
Whereat he sighs, and yawns, and on his ear
The busy chirp of Earth remotely jars.
Peace at the void's heart through the wordless night,
A lamb cropping the awful grasses, grazed;
Earthward the trouble lies, where strikes his light
At dawn industrious Man, and unamazed
Goes forth to plow, flinging a ribald stone
At all endeavour alien to his own."

"Who's that?"

"Edna St. Vincent Millay."

"Really! I thought she only did gushy stuff."

Becky sighed.

"The last one you read me was all full of roses."

"That doesn't mean it was gushy."

"All right, all right, it wasn't gushy the way you mean it. But it was romantic."

"Undeniably."

"I like this one a lot. I like 'earthward the trouble lies.' Can I have a copy?"

She could tell that Becky saw right through this transparent attempt to placate her; but since Gentian really did want a copy of the poem and Becky really was pleased, she was in fact placated. Gentian said, before the argument should start again, "What else have you got?"

"That sonnet," said Becky, "is from a whole set of them called 'Epitaph for the Race of Man.' They're mostly pretty grim."

"Are you going to read me all of them?"

"No. I just thought you should know."

"All right, now I do."

"Now, you read me something."

"I'll read you a little bit," said Gentian, "but then I'll show you something."

"Without the telescope?"

"Yes; for heaven's sake." She pulled her history of the telescope out of the nightstand drawer. It fell open to the passage she wanted.

> "My brother began his series of sweeps [Caroline wrote] when the instrument was yet in a very unfinished state, and my feelings were not very comfortable when every moment I was alarmed by a crack or fall, knowing him to be elevated fifteen feet or more on a temporary crossbeam instead of a safe gallery. The ladders had not even their braces at the bottom; and one night, in a very high wind, he had hardly touched the ground before the whole apparatus came down."

"That's Caroline Herschel?"

"Yes. And so is this." She turned back a few pages and held the book out; they leaned their heads together over it. The drawing of Caroline Herschel, in black and white, showed a woman leaning on a pillow, regarding the viewer with a steady and not very encouraging gaze. She wore a sort of knitted cap with white fringe; a ruff under her chin like those you could see in illustrations of Elizabethan dress; a shiny-looking dark dress that was probably satin but reminded Gentian, partly because of its lines of stitching, of an aviator's leather jacket; and a pair of spectacles around her neck on a strap. She had big eyes, a long nose, and a straight mouth. Gentian had never been able to decide if she was thinking of the eight comets she had discovered or of how her back hurt her.

"Wow," said Becky. "Now that's a face."

"But listen to this," said Gentian. She read the caption aloud. "Of this drawing, which shows Caroline Herschel in 1847 at the age of ninety-seven, her friend Miss Beckedorff wrote that it does not 'do justice to her intelligent countenance; the features are too strong, not feminine enough, and the expression too fierce.' "

Becky snorted.

"Daddy says Caroline Herschel's in one of those historical novels he reads."

"Are you going to read it?"

"No; he says she doesn't actually show up, she's just mentioned as helping the hero with making his telescope, and the hero's wife is jealous of her, even though she's sixty at the time."

Becky snorted again, more lengthily.

"No, it was cool," said Gentian. She considered. "Well, Dad thought it was cool. Because the writer knew that she was a real astronomer and really interested in making telescopes, not just her brother's housekeeper."

"No, I meant about being sixty."

"Caroline Herschel was sixty, not the hero's wife."

"Whichever."

"Well, all right," said Gentian. "The reason she didn't need to be jealous was that Caroline Herschel was just interested in the telescopes, not in the hero."

"That's the most reasonable thing to *be* jealous about," said Becky.

"Telescopes?" said Gentian, who very rarely got to tease Becky about saying something ambiguous.

Becky rolled her eyes, shook a corn chip carefully, and ate it.

"What, though?"

"Shared obsessions. Like telescopes. I think telescopes are interesting and I like astronomy, but I don't feel about it the way you do."

"No, you feel that way about poetry."

"Right. But I might feel a little strange if you met somebody who was just as interested in astronomy as you are." Becky tapped another corn chip on the magazine and ate it whole.

Gentian sat still. "But I don't want to," she said at last.

"I wondered why you never joined the Astronomy Club at school," said Becky. "Or read the astronomy groups on Fidonet or the Internet. Or anything."

"It's private," said Gentian. "I don't want to talk to anybody else about it. Except you."

"Well, it's going to be a little difficult to study it that way, you know."

"But don't you feel that way about poetry?" Gentian remembered, suddenly, finding out that Micky had written for *Tesseract* and her alarm that Becky might take up with another poet.

Becky shook her head. "I don't show it to people I think won't get it, but I'd love to find more people who do get it. I like the *Tesseract* crew, even if some of them are clueless. They understand what it's like to have written a poem."

Gentian took a corn chip and put it into her mouth, not because she wanted it but to give herself an excuse for not saying anything. Having chewed, she said slowly, "But you don't all write the same kind of poetry, and you don't write it for the same reasons. Does anybody write it for the same reasons you do?"

"No, nobody I've met."

"Well, I don't think anybody else does astronomy for the reason I do it, and I don't want to talk to other astronomers, because they'll ask. Do the people in *Tesseract* ask you why you write poems?"

"No," said Becky, and grinned. "They assume that I write poems for the same reasons that *they* write poems, and I just keep quiet."

Gentian immediately felt better. "I don't want to have to worry about it," she said.

"I don't worry; it amuses me. But I can see that you would."

"So," said Gentian, "you don't have to worry that I'll meet somebody who cares as much about astronomy as I do, because I'd run in the opposite direction, fast. But if you met somebody who wrote poetry for the same reason you do, then what?"

"Well," said Becky, wrinkling her brow. "It's not the same thing. I'd like to find somebody like that, but we wouldn't be writing poetry together like you might be doing astronomy with somebody else." She considered for a moment. "Unless we collaborated on an epic poem."

"You don't write epic poetry."

"I know, that's why it'd have to be a collaboration."

Gentian shook a corn chip briefly and ate it slowly. She could tell that Becky was still thinking, and in time Becky said, "Do you remember when Steph was so taken with Mary Beth Jenkins?"

Gentian did. "Fourth grade." Mary Beth Jenkins, who had moved to Arizona the summer after sixth grade, had been a lot like Steph: extremely pretty, almost aggressively ordinary in her interests and her clothes, a straight-A student and a good soccer player, much given to pronouncements about what was ladylike.

"Well," said Becky, "we weathered that."

Gentian regarded her dubiously. She could not see that Steph's delight in discussing feminine frippery with a regimented-games type was comparable to Becky's delight if she ever found a fellow poet or Gentian's if she ever found a fellow astronomer whom she cared to talk to, but Becky's tone had had a certain finality in it that Gentian did not feel up to contesting.

She contented herself with saying, "Well, yes—we did weather *that.*"

"What are you reading this week?" said Becky.

Gentian thought. It was hard to recall this week at all. "Homework, mostly, I guess," she said. "Oh, and Bulfinch's *Mythology.*"

"How is it?"

"Mmmm, I'm not sure. The introduction was awfully funny."

"Funny?"

"It starts out, 'The religions of ancient Greece and Rome are extinct.' "

"Well, he didn't know there'd be neo-Pagans."

"He also says that the Greeks and Romans didn't have the information *we* have 'from the pages of Scripture.' "

Becky gurgled. "Well, I'm sure he thought of it that way."

" 'Information,' " said Gentian. "As if it were a scientific text."

"You don't laugh at Jane Austen for thinking Sunday traveling a very serious problem."

"Where?"

"I can't remember if it's *Emma* or *Mansfield Park.* Frank

Churchill or Henry Crawford. I think it must be *Mansfield Park*.
It feels like Fanny."

"Yes, I remember now. It's Fanny worrying about Henry
Crawford."

"You don't laugh at that, do you?"

"But that's Fanny thinking just what Fanny would think,"
said Gentian.

"Well, isn't the introduction to Bulfinch's *Mythology* Bulfinch
thinking just what Bulfinch would think?"

Becky was prone to these disconcerting dissections. Gentian,
struggling with a profound feeling that the difference was perfectly obvious and Becky just refused to see it, was suddenly reminded of her conversation in the porch swing with Rosemary.
She said, "Yes, I guess, but—Fanny's just worrying. Bulfinch is
laying down the law."

"Would Jane Austen have read Bulfinch?"

"I don't know," said Gentian, who had difficulty attaching
dates even to the history of astronomy; she knew the order in
which things had happened, but could never relate any of the
things to any other event, at least not reliably. She knew Maria
Mitchell had helped with navigational mathematics for sailing
ships, of course, but not when sailing ships had gone out. Jane
Austen had no astronomical information at all to anchor her in
time.

Becky went for the biographical dictionary again. "Nope,"
she said. "She died in 1817 and *Age of Fable* wasn't published
until 1855."

"Why did you want to know?"

"I just wondered what she'd have had to say about his tone
of voice, that's all."

"Something snarky," said Gentian.

"Well, probably."

"Even if she was religious."

"So what else about Bulfinch?"

"He quotes a lot," said Gentian. "Like Dominic."

"Who?"

Oh, good grief, thought Gentian. She had forgotten about

meeting Dominic. No, it wasn't that at all; she had absorbed his existence somehow, so that she assumed everybody knew about him. Or, maybe, she didn't want anybody to know about him. But it was unconscionable to keep things like this from Becky.

"Dominic's the boy next door," she said. "He came over to return the snake his mother borrowed—" Becky laughed, and Gentian acknowledged it by casting her eyes at the ceiling, "—and I tried to make fudge but I burned it, and he quoted the whole time."

"You tried to make fudge?"

"Junie wasn't home."

"You wouldn't even make fudge for Steph's birthday."

"Well, I didn't make it for him, either. I burned it and Junie had to make another batch, and then he left without eating any."

"Was Junie much enamored?"

"Probably; she always is. But listen, so was Rosie."

"Rosie came *out?*"

"Just so."

"What did he quote?"

"Heinlein. Shakespeare. That dumb poem about Euclid. Keats—*our* sonnet. A lot of things I didn't recognize but I could tell they were quotations because they didn't make normal sense otherwise."

"Did you like him?"

"I don't know," said Gentian, slowly. "He was interesting."

"So's a rattlesnake," said Becky.

"I don't think he's a rattlesnake, but he might be kind of clueless."

"Better leave him to Junie."

"*He* might not be enamored even if she is."

"Did he seem to be?"

"I couldn't tell. He just quoted."

"Is that the big news of the week, then?"

"I guess it is," said Gentian. She added, with no idea of whether she was telling the truth or not, "The problem with the telescope kind of pushed it out of my head."

"You aren't yourself when you can't do astronomy," said

Becky, nodding. She sat forward suddenly. "Wait—didn't you use to do stargazing with binoculars?"

"Sure, to learn my way around the sky before we spent a lot of money on a telescope."

"Have you still got them?"

"Sure."

"We should check and see if they work, too. And if they do, maybe you could use them until we figure out what's wrong with the telescope."

"That's an idea. It's not the best time of year for it; I'd have to go outside. But it would be better than nothing. If it ever stops raining."

"We'll check periodically," said Becky. "Did Dominic say anything about seeing you again?"

"You make it sound as if we'd had a date," said Gentian, irritably. She took a deep breath. "He said something about having us help him with a project of his, a science project, and no, it is not astronomy, and I wouldn't do it if it were."

"Well, what is it?"

"I'm not exactly certain. Something to do with time, maybe relativity." It was odd: she and her sisters had not laughed at the thought of a time machine, but she shied from mentioning it to Becky.

"Who's us?"

"All three of us."

"*That'll* be a treat," said Becky.

"Such a *nice* way to get to know your neighbors, dear," said Gentian.

Becky chortled. "Well, let me know what it's all about," she said.

"When I find out. Were you going to read me some of *your* poetry?"

Becky propped herself up on Gentian's pillows and read to her. The first poem was called "Clowns and Puppets." She had taken its theme from a quotation that Gentian's father had had pasted above his computer for some years: "I will not be the toy of irresponsible events." Her father said it was from a comedy, but Becky's poem was very serious, except for the puns. She

punned on "be" and "bee," on "pawn" and "pun" and "upon,"
on "responsible" and "responsive," if that was a pun. The poem
was about being helpless, or maybe about refusing to be helpless
even when you couldn't do anything about the universe.

The second poem was called "Both Your Houses." Gentian
did not understand it, but she loved it. It was full of bright leaves,
cold winds, swords, stars, and defiance.

The third one was called "The Butterfly Hat," and it was
about the day Becky took Micky's butterfly net away from him.
The octave was accurate, but in the sestet she said she had put the
butterfly net over his head and his hair had all come out in butterflies that stuck themselves onto his scalp with little pins, as
though he were a card to display them on. It was gruesome and
cheerful.

The last one was called "On the Snow in April." Becky read
it with particular care.

> *"It's enough to make one turn to pagan rites,*
> *Burn incense with sly purpose, promise anything,*
> *To bring to these obediently shortening nights*
> *Some herald of the obstinate spring.*
> *Dear Heaven, has it not been cold long enough?*
> *Remember that the regular is beautiful.*
> *Things stretched past their due time are not the stuff*
> *Of loveliness, and all chaos is dull.*
> *What shivering sad time is this for Easter?*
> *There are not even natural miracles.*
> *Is it that through this gaunt delay there pulls*
> *The gleeful string of that essential jester?*
> *They say, let spring bring Christ to mind; this year,*
> *Christ must persuade there will be violets here."*

Gentian was floored. She tried not to be. As she herself had
gone to Alma's church for a year to see if the heavens declared the
glory of God's handiwork, Becky had gone to Steph's church for
six months to see what poetic roots were in the Christian religion.

Becky's father was, he said, an unobservant Jew, a phrase

that continued to delight the Giant Ants disproportionately long after it had been explained to them; her mother was, she herself said, a recovering Mormon, a phrase that also delighted the Ants but less enormously; neither of them, despite a distaste for the religions they had been born into, had anything good to say about Christianity either. Erin said that in a broad sense, a worldwide, cultural sense, all three religions had a lot in common and it wasn't surprising that anybody who wanted to reject one utterly would toss out the other two as well. Becky said her father's attitude was not utter rejection but rather the kind of "Who, me?" attitude you see in a cat you are trying to get to come indoors at evening. Her mother, now, was utterly rejecting.

Becky had come back from her six churchly months in a depressed state. "It's like sexism," she said. "It's just *everywhere.*"

Becky was looking at her now. Gentian said, "I wish you hadn't. You make C. S. Lewis sound right."

C. S. Lewis, in his autobiography, had said that when he was an atheist, he had been troubled by the perception that the best authors were either Christian or, if they were too early for that, anticipated Christian views. "Christians are wrong," he had said, "but all the rest are bores."

"I know it's the best one, technically," said Becky, in a discouraged tone, "but that's because I've been picking at it longer and polishing it up longer."

"When did you write it?"

"Spring before last."

"And you wrote all the others just this week?"

"Mmm-hmm."

"Oh."

"My one comfort," said Becky, "is that I sent it to a lot of religious magazines and they all rejected it. They said they wanted something more *uplifting.*"

"You sent it out?"

"I had to."

"You could put it in *Tesseract.*"

"I'd never live it down."

"Read it to me again," said Gentian.

Becky obliged her.

"It's really kind of creepy," said Gentian. "I mean, if there were a God you'd like it to have a sense of humor, but you don't really want it to be the sort who plays practical jokes. It would make you wonder if you *were* one."

"It's been suggested," said Becky, grimly.

"I like the ending," said Gentian. "I don't think that's very religious. Well, it's not very typical, I mean. Demanding that Christ persuade you of anything. You think that's what the magazines didn't like?"

"I hope so," said Becky.

"Anyway," said Gentian, "all the rest *aren't* bores. I like 'The Butterfly Hat' best and I think 'Both Your Houses' is extremely cool."

"What about 'Clowns and Puppets'?"

Gentian considered. "I like it," she said, "but I might like it even if it weren't very good, because I know what you mean."

Becky groaned. "Typical adolescent angst, you mean?"

"We're *allowed*," said Gentian.

"Yes, but it's so boring."

"Having your poems makes it less boring."

Becky laughed. "You're supposed to say they make it all worthwhile."

"I suppose that's what Steph says."

"Yep."

"Steph doesn't understand the meaning of degrees."

"She does mean it, though."

"I know," said Gentian, nettled. The thought of Steph was making her particularly twitchy just at the moment. "Look," she said, "don't tell the rest of them about Dominic, okay?"

"You mean don't tell Steph."

"Yes, I do, but that's easier if we just don't tell anybody."

Becky looked dubious. She drew her knees up under the long skirt, folded her arms on them, rested her chin on her arms, and looked at Gentian. "I don't know," she said, in the muffled tone this posture created.

"You do understand why I don't want to tell Steph?"

"Yes, but I don't like having secrets from everybody. We used to be much more a group; now we're pairing off."

"An odd number of people can't pair off."

"Well, we are. Erin just varies who she pairs with." Becky sighed gustily. "Maybe it's because we're teenagers and we're evolving our romantic instincts for later."

"I want mine to devolve, thank you," said Gentian, more or less automatically. She ate the rest of the corn chips.

"But when's the last time you did something just with Erin?"

Gentian said, "I thought you didn't want us to pair off?"

"Not *exclusively.*"

Gentian found this inconsistent, but it was easier to answer the question and see what argument Becky was trying to develop. "It has been a while," she conceded.

"Didn't you guys use to sew a lot?"

"Yes, but then Eileen got divorced and moved back in with the baby and we couldn't use their basement any more."

"Couldn't you do it over here?"

"I guess."

"I don't mean you have to sew," said Becky. "It's just that I think maintaining all sorts of contact is important."

"All sorts of—?"

"All directions." Becky considered this. "All variations. All possible combinations."

"You gonna make Alma and Erin go to a movie together?"

"Some things," said Becky, "are beyond even my passion for togetherness."

"Well, that's a relief."

Gentian got out the next set of sandwiches, and they ate several. Gentian thought about "The Butterfly Hat" with growing delight, and finally asked, "Have you talked to Micky any more?"

"Just in passing," said Becky. "I was thinking of showing him the poem. I figure if he can take that, he's definitely worth going to a movie with. But then I wonder if it's really fair. Maybe he'd take it better from somebody who had been civil enough to go to a movie with him first."

"I don't think your affections can be very much engaged," said Gentian, borrowing a phrase her mother had used on Junie when Junie was about ten and had a terrible crush on Kenneth Branagh. "I mean, you sound like me. Calculating," she explained, borrowing a term her father had used about her when she was first deciding whether to have Becky or a now-vanished Jessica Lindholm as her best friend.

"I'm trying to be sensible before the hormones strike."

Gentian looked at her with some alarm. The only person whom she had watched the hormones strike was Junie, and Junie had never been sensible since the day she was born.

"It's such a silly arrangement," she said.

"That essential Jester," said Becky, sourly.

"Let *him* try it and see how he likes it, that's all."

"Well, the Christians say he did."

"He tried being a man. Big deal."

"So it does make a difference?"

"*I never said it didn't,*" said Gentian between her teeth. "I said it never makes the kind of difference they *say* it does. And they ignore the real differences. They don't test drugs on women as well as men, and they don't build bigger restrooms for women even though we take longer, and they don't pay any attention to real differences unless they want an excuse to tell us we can't do something."

"Hormones strike boys, too," said Becky, thoughtfully.

This meant that she did not concede the point but could not think of an argument, or perhaps simply didn't want to bother. Gentian leaned over and turned on the weather radio.

"At midnight in the Twin Cities, we have clear skies and forty-one degrees, with a southeast wind at five to ten miles per hour."

"That was fast," said Gentian. She could still hear the rain dripping. She bounced off the bed, stepped over Maria Mitchell, and peered out the window. Yes, it was clear in that direction, but it might start raining again. It would be easier to try the binoculars than to worry about opening and closing the telescope dome.

She got the binoculars in their battered case from the very

back of her closet, with some unnecessary assistance from Maria Mitchell, whose obligations as a cat included jumping up onto the shelf as soon as Gentian had removed her suitcase from it, and also sniffing and rubbing her face on every other item on the shelf.

They went out into the hallway, discouraging Maria Mitchell from accompanying them. She insisted on leaving the bedroom, but then ran into the bathroom and jumped into the tub. Gentian tossed her a ping-pong ball, and they went quickly past the two small doors that led into storage space under the eaves. Just beyond these, ending the hall, was a short wide door with a padlock. Gentian unlocked the lock and pulled the door open. In this damp weather, it stuck; it also, of course, creaked. Gentian felt around on the left and found the light switch and shoved it upward. It was an old, thick, heavy switch that made a click as though it were turning on the power for some large, complicated, 1930s factory. The light produced this way was anticlimactic: one forty-watt bulb high in the roof went on, dustily.

Gentian led Becky along the broad dusty boards in the middle of the unfinished attic. There were two finished rooms up here, somewhat lost in the corners. Rosemary had lived in one for several months when she was angry with her entire family. Gentian could never have done it. Her own room was cozy; this part of the attic was cavernous. It was here that they would have to help Dominic build his time machine, supposing he had meant a word he said. They would need a lot more lights.

At the very front of the house was another short wide door with a padlock on it. Gentian unlocked this one too, and dragged it open. A huge breath of night came in. Gentian ushered Becky out onto the little balcony, and wrenched the door shut again. The balcony floor was covered in shingles, which gave it the impression of being a misplaced piece of roof. It had a decorative railing of wrought iron, already dry after the rain. This structure had been reinforced by Gentian's father a few years ago with a network of two-by-fours that Mrs. Zimmerman had pronounced adequate and safe, but was mercifully hard to see in the dark.

The lounge chair Gentian had used was still folded up against the wall, but it would be wet and possibly mildewed. She took the binoculars from the case, looped the strap around her neck, and leaned her elbows on the two-by-four.

"This should work," said Becky. "We're not facing that house at all."

Gentian had forgotten to take the lens caps off the binoculars. She unscrewed them with increasingly cold fingers and slid them into the pocket of her sweater. Then she pressed her eyes into the eyepieces. Mars sprang out of the southeastern sky at her, a tiny disk, like the ghost of red. She settled her elbows and looked for Orion. There it was, still low; there was Rigel, and Betelgeuse, and Aldebaran.

"Well, that's a relief," said Becky.

Gentian turned and brought into her view the sky above the new house next door. It was all there as it ought to be. She feasted her eyes on her stars, picking out particular favorites. It was not the best time to be doing this: good stargazing in mid-October mostly happened earlier in the evening, and October and November formed a largely unspectacular pause between the glories of the Summer Triangle and the lovely cold abundance of Orion and the stars of winter. Becky sometimes talked of the odd omissions in the subjects used for poetry, and had occasionally said she thought of making a specialty of one or the other of them; Gentian had similarly thought of making her own study of the night sky from mid-November to early January. She would bet there was more there than people thought.

"Gen," said Becky. "Gen."

Gentian said, "What?" She had the impression that Becky had been saying her name for some time, over and over. Normally you would tap someone so preoccupied on the shoulder or something, but Becky had done that to Gentian once in the early days of the binoculars, and been snapped at. Gentian knew her way around the sky much better by now and would not have been much annoyed even if Becky did jog the binoculars, but Becky didn't know that. Gentian was pleased to be considered, even if she didn't need it.

"I'm getting cold," said Becky.

"There's a sweater in my room."

"Is there another pair of binoculars?"

"What? No."

"I think I'll pass, then. I'll go read. Come in when you get hungry."

"I'll only be a moment," said Gentian.

As her family had done when they spent a weekend in New York, she thought, what must I see, what can't I possibly miss, as though she might never have the chance again. What had been exciting when she first used the binoculars? Oh, of course.

She lowered the binoculars and walked along the balcony to its northern side, and found the Little Dipper lying crooked not far above the northern horizon. Curved around it were the stars of Draco. There was Thuban, there Eltanin—there. She lifted the binoculars, and where there had been one point of light, two minute distinct stars like a pair of headlights shone at her. She went back to Polaris, in the handle of the Little Dipper, and found the Big Dipper from that. Moving back between them she pounced on the tiny spirals, one flat and round to view and the other showing only its edge, of the galaxies M81 and M82, eleven million light-years away, showing her light that was new when the Himalayas were emerging and *Ramapithecus* was finding trees uncongenial and moving onto the savannah. There were angiosperms and insects and mammals, but no people. No industrious man, flinging a ribald stone at any occupation not his own; though it was probably not to be supposed that anybody's hominid ancestors had been very interested in abstract learning, either.

She moved on and found bright Vega, and then the Northern Cross with Deneb crowning it.

As one star set, she found another, and another, as the whole sky wheeled by her and moved behind the far roofs of the city and into some other astronomer's sky. Her right elbow hurt. She shifted to the left one, which hurt too. She straightened up, and almost yelped; her back hurt, and so did her knees. Her hands did not hurt, but were so cold she was afraid to try to move them lest she drop the binoculars. She shoved the door open with knee and elbow and forehead, shut it with her hip, and stood shivering in the relative warmth of the attic until she could unclose her fingers and put the binoculars back in their case. While she was waiting, she looked at her watch. Three-thirty. She and Becky usually stayed up until six or seven, so that should be all right.

When she got back to her room, still shivering, Becky was in bed, in the patchwork nightgown Erin had made her, her bristling poetry book open face down on her chest, apparently asleep.

Gentian climbed out of her cold clothes, hurried into her sweatpants and sweatshirt, and dived under the covers. "Hey. You aren't asleep, are you?"

"Certainly not," said Becky, without opening her eyes. "Why would I be?"

"His heatless room the watcher of the skies," said Gentian, apologetically.

"Nightly inhabits when the sky is clear," said Becky. "You're just like me with reading; the longer since you haven't done it, the longer you end up doing it to make up."

Gentian objected on principle to giggling at inadvertent salaciousness, but she giggled nonetheless.

"Now you know how sleepy I am," said Becky.

"We always stay up much later than this."

"Sure, but we're talking. And usually drinking something with caffeine in it."

"You could have had some; it's right there in the cooler. Or you could have come and gotten me."

"No, I don't think so," said Becky. She finally opened her eyes, saw the position of her book, and hastily closed it, smoothing the spine with her fingers.

"Are you mad?" said Gentian cautiously.

"More bemused."

"Can I bring you something?"

"Not yet. Tell me what you saw."

Gentian did not actually feel her mouth dry up, but she was as speechless as if it had, and on reflection wished it would. "I can't talk about it," she said. "I could show you. I've showed you before, mostly. We split Nu Draconis, remember?"

"Don't most astronomers take pictures?" said Becky.

"Yes, but I'm not that advanced yet. It's not the same, any-way."

"You'd better get that telescope fixed," said Becky.

"I guess I'll ask Dad if we can take it in to the store," said Gentian, gloomily.

"Maybe they'll rent you a replacement, like they do with cars."

"I guess they might for a working astronomer, but not for a kid."

"Well, ask them. You'll be impossible until you get it back."

"You are mad."

"No, I'm not. I've just found out something new about you. I didn't know there was anything."

"Maybe it's really new. I mean, maybe it wasn't here last year. Don't people change when they grow up?"

There was a long pause. Finally Becky said, "For the first time ever I understand Peter Pan."

8

entian and Becky woke up at eleven in the morning, which felt decidedly odd, and ate all the remaining food for breakfast. Then they tried to have the kind of conversation they ordinarily had at six in the morning, but this proved impossible. The smells of coffee and pancakes from downstairs, the sounds of Juniper playing all her mother's Peter, Paul and Mary CDs on random selection and of Rosie practicing karate in her bedroom, were distracting; so was the strong sunlight coming in through the windows and the skylight. They both grew embarrassed, which had hardly happened to them since they were five.

"How very odd," said Becky at last. "One might make a poem out of this."

"We'll try again next week," said Gentian, feeling acutely guilty.

"In the meantime," said Becky, "I'd better go home and do my homework."

She put on her clothes and stuffed the patchwork nightgown into her bag of books, along with the collection of poetry and her own poems. Gentian saw her downstairs.

"What are you doing up?" demanded Juniper over the sound of Peter, Paul and Mary going on and on about how this train didn't carry no gamblers, this train.

"Is it dinnertime already?" said Rosie.

In the front hall, Gentian's mother said, "Is one of you ill?"

"No, we just went to bed early," said Gentian. She and Becky rolled their eyes at one another, which made her feel better.

They escaped out the front door, crossed the porch safely, and were caught by Gentian's father, who was planting bulbs in the front lawn. His usual reaction to their appearances was to say, "Ah, youth," in a melancholy fashion. This time he said, "What emergency could bring you out before sunset?"

"Gentian's telescope is broken," said Becky, crisply.

They went down the steep steps to the sidewalk. It was a glorious sunny day, abnormally warm, with all the red and yellow leaves as precise as stained glass. Gentian's mother's chrysanthemums shone like huge stars, dark red, pale red, yellow, white, orange.

"Well," said Becky. "I'll see you at school."

Gentian was reluctant to let her go, without being able to think of anything to say that would keep her. Becky seemed to feel something similar; at any rate, she said, "I'll call you," before she turned and walked away, her lumpy bag bumping on her shoulder and the green skirt billowing in the warm southern breeze.

Gentian went back up the steps and found her way blocked by her father, standing muddily in the middle of the sidewalk and looking perplexed. "You broke that telescope?" he said.

"No," said Gentian, "but it won't work. It's out of adjustment somehow, and Becky can't fix it."

"It must certainly be out of adjustment, then," said her father.

"Can we get it fixed?"

"Well, we can get it diagnosed and get an estimate on what it will take to fix it, anyway."

"When?"

Her father looked over his shoulder at the bulb planter, the hose, and the dozens of little mesh bags of bulbs piled by the shrubbery. "Right now," he said, "if you help me plant bulbs when we get back."

Gentian glowered at him, but it was mostly for form's sake.

They climbed all the stairs to her attic and removed the telescope from its careful installation. "You look as if somebody were taking out your liver without anesthesia," her father remarked at one point. "We'll put it back."

Gentian felt too hollow to answer. They swaddled the telescope tenderly in bubble-wrap and Styrofoam, wound tape around the resulting bundle, and carried it down all the stairs, snapping at one another to be careful and scraping their knuckles on the plaster walls.

"Did you find a body in the attic, or what?" shrieked Juniper, over a loud rendition of "Don't Think Twice, It's All Right."

"Can I come too?" cried Rosemary, just as if she were still five years old.

"Is that your telescope?" demanded her mother as they carried it through the kitchen. "Is that what all the thumping I heard last night was about?"

"Yes. No," said Gentian, and banged the back door shut with the bottom of her foot.

The telescope store was a rather makeshift affair across the street from the vet they always took Maria Mitchell and Pounce to; it had originally been a Middle Eastern restaurant and still had a small green-and-gold half-dome over its door. The sleek shining instruments displayed in its windows looked out of place. It had its own cat as well, a large black-and-white beast called Lowell. Lowell was not allowed in the display windows, and all the merchandise was in glass cases, to keep out the cat hair.

The young woman who had sold them the telescope was not there, and the middle-aged one behind the counter did not seem to know what she was doing. She had great difficulty understanding Gentian's description of the problem, and even once or twice looked at Gentian's father as if she did not really believe Gentian at all. The third time she did this, Gentian's father said, "She's the expert. And she isn't a practical joker."

"Well," said the woman, "I'll look at it this afternoon, and if I can't see anything wrong, either Josh or Janice will look at it on Monday."

She took their address and telephone number from Gentian's father. "If we can't fix it, we can ship it back to the manufacturer," she said.

Gentian was cheered, until she realized that this would mean quite a lot of time without the telescope; her father looked glum, which probably indicated it would also mean a lot of money.

They went out into the sunny, windy day, blinking.

"Why don't we sneak out for lunch before going back to an afternoon of hard labor?" said her father.

"I won't go to that Middle Eastern place," said Gentian.

"Fine, and I won't go to any pizza place whatsoever."

They went to a Chinese restaurant and ate shrimp lo mein and curried squid. This made them very pleased with one another, since nobody else in the family would touch squid and everybody else in the family resisted having shrimp in restaurants because they had it every Friday—Catholic theology, their mother remarked, being far less durable than Catholic menus.

"So," said her father about halfway through, "Juniper is of the opinion that you and your sister drove a potential swain away?"

"What? Who?"

"The young man from next door?"

"Junie's crazy," said Gentian. "He just went home. Nobody drove him. You'd think he was a flock of sheep. He wants us to help him with a science project." She looked at her father, content and mellow with shrimp, and risked it. "We thought we might use the attic."

"What kind of project?"

"I think it's some kind of relativity experiment."

Her father put down his chopsticks. "In the attic? Most relativity projects I can think of are either strictly thought experiments or require very large things like particle accelerators. Unless he wants to do Michelson-Morley. That's pretty tricky, and I don't think you could get everything up those stairs."

Gentian knew that if she were going to be an astronomer she would have to learn physics, but so far, with the exception of the optical theory necessary to understand her telescope, she had avoided doing so. You couldn't take physics in school until you had gotten through biology and chemistry, anyway. She said, "If we can get stuff up the stairs, can we use the attic?"

"Well, let's check with your mother to make sure she hasn't decided to make it into a computer room or a pool hall or a conservatory."

Gentian laughed.

"And the lease will have to have a comparatively short date. You can't leave stuff strewn around up there for months."

"If it's a school project it'll be due at the end of the year."

"You mean by next spring."

"Yeah."

"When do you propose to begin?"

"I don't know. He only just mentioned it. It might be for next semester."

"Well, let's lay the proposal before your mother."

"What's the wiring like up there?"

"The wiring is adequate—your mother did it before we moved in, and gave the attic two circuits all its own, just in case she did decide to have a conservatory—but there isn't a great plenitude of light fixtures, and she didn't finish wiring all the outlets. Just what power requirements are you anticipating?"

"I don't know, really; but you can hardly even see up there, as it is."

"Well, your mother's been panting for an electrical apprentice for years."

"Why can't you do it?"

"Because I drop things," said her father, and cracked open his fortune cookie. He looked blank for a moment and then extremely sardonic. " 'The cautious man misses many opportunities,' " he read.

"Oh," said Gentian, "a platitude cookie."

"What does yours say?"

Gentian broke hers open, gave the bits to her father to eat, and unfolded the fortune. " 'The morning and the evening star will smile on you.' "

"Well, at least it's a fortune," said her father. "Even fairly apposite. Perhaps they'll fix that telescope of yours in a timely manner."

They didn't, though. They called late the same afternoon, when Gentian and her father had just come in from planting bulbs, to say that nothing obvious was wrong and they had cleaned and adjusted the instrument on general principles, but really Gentian should wait until Josh got over the flu so he could look at it, though of course she could come get it at any time if she liked.

Gentian consented with very ill grace to her father's suggestion that they let Josh have a crack at it when he could, with the provision that there was a lunar eclipse on the twenty-eighth of November and she wanted the telescope back by then regardless.

The time without a telescope had to be got through somehow. Sunday was like Saturday, warm and sunny and windy. Gentian went with her mother and sisters to fly kites in Memorial Park. They came home and had a picnic in the back yard, since, her mother said, this weather could not last much longer.

"Doesn't matter if it does or not," said Rosemary, casting a baleful glance at Dominic's house. "We don't have any gardening work to do."

"I have a great deal," said her mother. "You can help me."

"It's not the same thing at all."

On Monday, in accordance with her mother's prediction, it was still windy but very much colder, brilliantly sunny and clear. At lunch that day Gentian asked if any of the Giant Ants would come over that evening and help her make a red corduroy jumper to wear to all the holiday parties. She knew that her taking an interest in clothes would please Steph; she also knew that her asking for help would please Becky, no matter who volunteered or even if nobody did. In the event, Alma did.

In this way Alma became the first of the Giant Ants to actually lay eyes on Dominic. Theoretically, Gentian would of course have liked this honor to be bestowed upon Becky, but in fact she could hardly conceive of those two as existing in the same universe—it would be as though Arthur Ussher met Elizabeth Bennet. Theoretically, also, she wanted to keep Steph away from

Dominic, but while the consequences to Gentian's own ac-knowledged but not considered plans might have been dire, the spectacle of their meeting would have been almost as good as a play.

Erin would probably have been Gentian's first choice. She would not have shown Dominic that she was impressed, but she would have talked about him afterwards to the others in a calm tone that would convey better than anybody else's gushing just how impressed she was. But Erin was busy that evening, baby-sitting her niece.

Gentian's mother had taught her how to run the sewing ma-chine when she was ten, and had given her a number of peculiar tips designed to overcome difficulties Gentian did not suffer from, but she resolutely refused actually to touch any project of Gentian's.

"It'd be the kiss of death, sweetie," she had said, laughing. "King Sadim's own touch. Your father had to make his own wed-ding cravat." Gentian hunted King Sadim through every refer-ence book in the library until Steph, apprised of her frustration, looked at the name and pointed out that it was "Midas" spelled backwards.

After Gentian and Alma had cut out the pattern and stitched the major pieces together, with Alma making the interfacing be-have, they went outside and took turns tossing Juniper's soccer ball through the basketball hoop attached to the garage.

Alma had just made a spectacular shot from halfway down the driveway when Dominic appeared under the last red leaves of the apple tree. Appeared was exactly the word for it. Gentian had not heard the back door of the new house bang—not that she ever had—nor the rustling of his feet through the drying grass. But there he was.

Gentian managed not to gape at him. She waved instead and tried to look insouciant.

Dominic walked across the grass to where Alma stood ad-miring her shot. The cold fall afternoon that had put Gentian into sweatshirt and leggings and made Alma get out her denim jacket blew around Dominic's black T-shirt and thin billowy trousers like the balmiest breeze of April. It lifted the black hair delicately off his white brow. Gentian couldn't decide if he looked like a rock star, Hamlet, or a person with a wasting disease.

His big dark eyes conveyed interest and curiosity and something else that made Gentian's spine shiver, in a sensation, like going downhill on a roller-coaster, that was thrilling and pleasurable even though when you examined its component parts in careful abstraction no single one of them seemed anything but unpleasant.

"A good shot," said Dominic to Alma. His voice made Gentian's stomach jump.

"I didn't expect to get it from here, the way the driveway slopes," said Alma, in her slightly breathless way. Steph had once said that Alma should be an actress because she could make anything sound exciting. She looked like somebody constructed to be Dominic's opposite: dark where he was pale, round where he was angular, as tall as he was but strong where he was delicate, with her hair, as black as his, braided all over her head and covered in blue beads while his fell disarranged and straight.

Gentian kicked the soccer ball back along the driveway to announce her intention of joining the conversation. Dominic picked it up, sent her a grin that made her knees feel odd, and, examining the ball with momentary puzzlement, looked vastly entertained and said to Alma, "Should you like to use this in its intended game for a little?"

"There isn't really enough room," said Gentian, arriving. "I know the yard looks big, but a lot of it's Mom's creeping thymes."

"We can play in the street," said Dominic. "There will be no cars."

He dribbled the ball down the driveway, through the deep shadow of his mean little house.

"Fine," said Gentian to Alma, who was tying her shoe. "Wait'll Woody honks at him and calls him a damn kid."

"I wonder what he'll say back," said Alma, pleasedly, and stood up.

She was destined to go on wondering, because Woody did not drive down the street at his usual time.

There were, in fact, no cars. In the cold autumn evening under the streetlights they kicked the ball over the leaf-strewn asphalt, laughing and shouting. Alma and Gentian were understood, without any arrangement except that possible between people who have known each other since the first grade, to be members of opposite teams. Gentian's goal was the roots of a huge maple tree that had buckled the asphalt in front of the Careys' house, and Alma's was the manhole cover at the other end of the block.

Dominic was either a third team with no goal, or else a kind of Lord Gro of the soccer field who changed sides whenever the one he was on seemed to be winning.

The white segments of the ball, Dominic's white face, the white hem of Alma's T-shirt hanging below the hem of her jacket, dipped and floated in the darkening air. Gentian kicked the ball over a luminous pattern of pale leaves that seemed laid across a void as deep as the sky above the street, where one by one, without any fuss, the stars were coming in.

They dodged and leapt and laughed, dizzy and breathless, until in full darkness on the long-empty street they collapsed panting onto Gentian's goal. Gentian and Alma leaned on one another, still laughing. Dominic sat with his legs drawn up, on a different root a little distance away, dandling the ball on his knees.

"Where is no dust in all the road?" he said.

Gentian looked at Alma; they both looked at the city street, scattered with leaves and the occasional cigarette pack or Styrofoam cup; they both looked at Dominic. Gentian looked at the street again. It had lost dimensions since they sat down. She gazed at her sky instead. It was as always, infinite distances of black strewn and scattered and sewn with stars, before and behind and around one another. A luminous density, a powdering like spilled talcum on a velvet dress, announced the Milky Way.

"The galaxy," said Gentian, lazily.

"Clever child," said Dominic to the soccer ball.

Gentian felt Alma looking at her; she smiled slightly and shook her head, to admit that she had guessed the riddle by accident, and Alma smiled back and started to sing.

"I gave my love a cherry
That had no stone;
I gave my love a chicken
That had no bone;
I gave my love a story
That had no end;
I gave my love a baby
With no crying."

Dominic's red, precise mouth smiled. "How can there be a cherry that has no stone?" he said, sounding like Hamlet, or Romeo, or Mark Antony declaiming to Rome's citizens. "How can there be a chicken that has no bone: how can there be a story that has no end: how can there be a baby with no crying?"

Gentian did not even have to look at Alma. Together they carolled,

"A maraschino cherry, it has no stone;
A chicken à la king, it has no bone;
A story in soap opera, it has no end;
A baby that is strangled has no crying."

Alma collapsed laughing again—the soap opera line was hers, since they had forgotten that line of the parody, and it always did her in—but Gentian felt uneasy. She looked at Dominic. He was looking at her. His head was cocked a little. He was thoughtful, speculative, as though he were about to ask her to help assassinate Caesar. Between the acting of a dreadful thing and the first motion, all the interim is like a phantasm and a hideous dream. She had read that line as Brutus, and it had stuck with her.

Gentian felt that she did not want to hear what Dominic had to say. She poked the giggling Alma and began to sing another song.

"Tell me why the stars do shine;
Tell me why the ivy twines;
Tell me why the sky's so blue;
And I will tell you just why I love you."

They had learned it in Girl Scouts, but even the religious Alma and the conventional Steph had found the original answers soppy. " 'Because God made' is always a copout," Steph said. "No it isn't," said Alma, "but it's cheating in a riddle song."

Dominic dropped the soccer ball; he looked distinctly annoyed.

"Nuclear fusion," sang Gentian, "makes the stars to shine." She always got to sing that line, of course.

"Cellular osmosis," Alma sang, "makes the ivy twine."

"Molecular diffusion makes the sky so blue—" Erin got that when she was present, but Gentian took it for her, since it was still science.

"Glandular hormones are why I love you." And that was Steph's line, but Alma picked it up for her.

Dominic retrieved the soccer ball; he still looked rather fractious, but also relieved somehow. Gentian concluded that he didn't like his riddles being made fun of, but liked religious songs even less.

"I should be heading home, Gen," said Alma, regretfully.

"I'll walk you," said Gentian. "It's pretty dark."

"I'll walk you both," said Dominic, imitating her tone precisely, "so you needn't come home in the dark."

"Let me go tell Mom," said Gentian. She sprinted up the driveway and plunged onto the back porch and into the kitchen. Her mother was sitting at the kitchen table, replacing the switch on the coffeemaker. It had been defunct for at least two years; you turned the machine on by plugging it in and turned it off by unplugging it again.

"I need to walk Alma home," said Gentian.

"Well, take one of your sisters, then."

"Dominic says he'll come with us."

Her mother laid down the screwdriver and looked at her. "He does, does he?"

"We were playing soccer with him."

"That's wholesome enough, I suppose. All right, but I want you back in twenty minutes. That's plenty of time."

"For what?" said Gentian, nastily, and plunged outside again.

Dominic and Alma were standing at the bottom of the driveway, talking in low voices. Dominic sounded intense and Alma dubious. Gentian resisted the urge to tread softly and overhear them. She stomped a little. They stopped talking. Alma came to meet her, very promptly, and put an arm through hers. They walked sedately down the driveway. Dominic fell in with them next to Alma, and they went just as sedately along the sidewalk, scuffing up the dry leaves. Gentian wished they had brought the soccer ball. She could not think of a single thing to say.

Alma lived six blocks away. They came to the end of the first block and crossed two streets at once on a neat diagonal. Gentian looked up at the sky. It was dazzlingly clear. There was a brisk wind, from the west, with no ice in it. I want my telescope, she thought.

Two blocks. Three. Four. Gentian had to clear her throat, but she said firmly to Alma, "Thanks for helping me. That lining was awfully slippery."

"That's the idea," said Alma. She had to clear her voice too. "So you can wear things under it. But it can be a bitch to sew."

Gentian saw Dominic's head turn when Alma said "bitch." He said nothing. She suppressed an urge to giggle and another to see what else might shock him. She said, in a voice that came out slightly stifled, "The soccer was fun too."

"Yeah," said Alma. She leaned a little so she could see Dominic. "Thanks for playing with us. We should get Steph and Erin next time."

Becky hated sports, but Alma and Steph were always trying to get her to play anyway. Gentian wondered if Alma also thought Becky and Dominic hardly belonged in the same universe.

"What about Becky?" she said.

"I think what we were doing needs an odd number of players," said Alma.

They stopped before Alma's house. Alma dug in the pocket of her jacket for her keys, said, "Thanks for the company; see you in school, Gen," and ran up the sidewalk. Gentian and Dominic watched her unlock the door and go inside. The door shut. Gentian and Dominic stood there.

"You are bold to consort with her," said Dominic.

Gentian turned and started back home. "Why?" she said.

"She has the fierceness of her race."

"She what?"

Dominic was silent. Gentian looked at him as they walked under the streetlight at the end of Alma's block. He looked disbelieving, a little pitying, a little mocking. He looked superior.

Gentian suddenly understood him. "Wouldn't you say she's the bold one?" she said scornfully. "We've got her outnumbered four to one, after all." She sounded like Junie in a temper. She was in a temper. She wished she weren't. Dominic had made her say, "we" and "her" as if the difference he was being insinuating about mattered one whit. That was all losing your temper got you; you played into the hands of idiots. "Where are you *from?*" she said furiously.

"Oh," said Dominic, "south of here."

I just bet, thought Gentian. She could not think of a way to express her feelings that did not sound sanctimonious, priggish, self-righteous—or no way other than smacking him in the face, which would be satisfying, but only briefly. Besides, then she would have done in her escort, which would upset her mother. This struck her as funny, and she vented her furious feelings in an explosion of giggles.

Dominic looked vaguely alarmed. Gentian got herself under control, and said, "Alma *is* fierce, but no more than my sister Junie, or our friend Erin."

"Though she be little, yet she is fierce," said Dominic.

Gentian walked faster. He had met Juniper, and Juniper was no littler than Alma; neither was Erin. She wondered if he were perhaps a bit crazy in some way, or if he indulged in inappropriate quotations so she would correct him and there would, thus, be conversation, since conversation was so clearly something he was not very good at. His remarks were as irritating as her father's, and they did not, somehow, carry the same conviction that they would make sense if you wanted to bother thinking about them.

Two blocks. Three. Four. Dominic was not keeping especially close to her, but in the chilly autumn night she could locate him by warmth alone. He'd be all right if he never spoke, she thought.

"The female of the species," remarked Dominic, "is more deadly than the male."

"*Which* species?" said Gentian instantly.

"How beastly the bourgeois is, especially the male of the species," said Dominic.

Steph's father was a Marxist, but he did not talk like that. Dominic went on, as if he were continuing a rationally connected series of ideas, "I describe not men, but manners; not an individual, but a species."

"Women are ruder than men?" hazarded Gentian. Any meaning at all would be preferable to nonsense.

Dominic did not answer. They reached the bottom of her front steps. Does he care if I say anything? she thought.

"Thank you for the company," she said.

"I'll have cause to thank you for yours," said Dominic, "once we come to build our time machine."

He had meant that, then.

"When do you want to start?" said Gentian. If he made any racist remarks to Junie, Junie would skin him alive, although all her own friends were white. That might be interesting.

"I'll call on you soon," said Dominic. He made a courtly gesture and ushered her up the steps to the porch. When she had the door open, he said, "Farewell for the moment."

Gentian turned to say something else, she hardly knew what, but he was gone.

It was very warm and bright inside. From the front sunroom came the sounds of one of Junie's television shows. Her mother had built a fire in the fireplace and was lying on the hearthrug with Pounce, reading Shirley Jackson's *Raising Demons,* not for the first time. Her father was curled up in an armchair with *Benet's Reader's Encyclopedia,* looking distracted. Rosemary was sprawled on the sofa reading *Little Women,* also not for the first time; the fact that she was doing so downstairs meant she was getting close to what she would call the sad part and Gentian would call the sentimental soppy part. Gentian much preferred Louisa May Alcott's adventure stories, and she had never forgiven Alcott, Jo, or Professor Bhaer for making Jo stop writing them.

"I'm back," she said.

"Is your homework done?" said her mother, without looking up.

"Yes."

"Have you had something to eat?"

"Yes, we ate that leftover spaghetti. Can I use the computer?"

"Use mine," said her father, also not looking up. "Junie needs the other one as soon as her benighted show is over."

"Thanks," said Gentian, and went through the family room and the breakfast room to his office.

He had left the door shut, and when she opened it she saw why. There was a new cat, mostly black and white, crouched under the radiator. It hissed at her.

"Yes, I know," said Gentian, quickly shutting the door again. She sat down at the computer. It was possible that they had forgotten to tell her, and equally possible that he had not yet gotten around to confessing. Nobody came in here without permission, especially when the door was shut.

She called the BBS. The line was busy. Gentian let the program go on trying while she thought, and kept half an eye on the new cat. When she shifted in the chair, it growled; otherwise, its white-tipped black tail twitched from under the radiator and back again every few seconds, flicking out with it a growing collection of dust and cat hair.

"Nice job sweeping," said Gentian.

The cat hissed.

The terminal chimed to tell her that she was connected to the BBS, and the cat growled. Gentian logged on, after a pause to remember who she was, and looked at the teen romance echo first.

Jason had posted a short, pungent message that accused Juniper and Crystal of being the same person. Gentian thought this was dangerous. But, of course, it was near the end of the semester, and Junie would want to bring her project to some spectacular close.

Why was she giving Jason the job, though? Why not have Crystal accuse Juniper and Jason? It was terribly tempting to post a message that would somehow address this point without giving Junie away; but contaminating your sister's sociology project, however satisfying, was really beyond the pale.

Gentian sighed, and looked at the teen culture echo. Juniper had posted eight messages since the last time Gentian read it, but she had not addressed The Light Prince's contention that she was not an intellectual, and she had not taken any notice, either, of Gentian's message posted under the name of Betony. Hot Dud had called her Bethany and made a joke on one of her typos. Mutant Boy addressed to her a long diatribe on the obsolescence of literature, and added a few insults based on the fact that she could spell. Someone called Silk who, she said, had never entered a message before, remarked that if more people in the group could spell she might join in the conversation. The Light Prince welcomed Gentian to the group without addressing anything she had said.

Gentian decided not to answer any of the messages right now, but she did mark them unread, in case she needed them later. Then she went upstairs, thinking of the dazzling clarity of the sky tonight. She looked at the spot where the telescope had been, and did her homework. The moon was waxing, anyway, and it had risen at 3:50 in the afternoon and would not set until almost three in the morning. And clouds were coming in. And Mercury and Mars were too close to the sun to be seen just now.

On Tuesday it snowed in northern Minnesota and was cloudy everywhere. Gentian retired early and reread her biography of Maria Mitchell for comfort.

On Wednesday it cleared up, and Gentian got out the binoculars again, but the relief of being able to do some astronomy, any astronomy, was beginning to wear off. There was not much to look at except Saturn, anyway, which was much better through the telescope.

Thursday it snowed in central Minnesota, though not very hard. Gentian was already feeling gloomy on her way to school, when Alma pounced on her as she climbed the steps and said, even more breathlessly than usual, "Can I talk to you? Without anybody else?"

"Sure," said Gentian, considering her with some alarm. Becky always said that Alma had cheerful bones, and it was true that her resting expression even during essay exams in English, her weakest subject, was merely alert and interested; but she looked far from cheerful at the moment. "What disposable classes have you got?"

"Oh, all of 'em. When're yours?"

"Second period. Where?"

"Oh, the library, I guess."

"Okay." They went up the steps and headed for assembly. "Are things okay at home?" said Gentian cautiously.

"What? Oh, yeah, fine. This is just personal."

"Are you mad at Steph?"

"What? *No.* You want me to get a note from her?"

"Has Becky been talking to you?"

"What?"

"She thinks the Giant Ants are not cohering as we should."

"We what—oh, never mind. Just wait till I can *tell* you, all right?"

"All right, all right," said Gentian.

The library was one of Gentian's favorite places in the school, probably second only to the art room. It was not like her idea of a library, being sunny and airy and full of steel shelving, but it had tables, chairs, cushions, and a great many books, as well as a librarian who put a shelf of banned books right at the entrance with notices exhorting one to read them.

Gentian paused to see if there were any new ones. She found the Newbery Award a better guide to what was good to read; as Becky said, some banned books were boring, some were absurd, and some were contemptible, but she didn't see why somebody else should decide any of those things. But if a book had won a Newbery and had also been challenged or banned, it was almost always worth a look.

Alma came hurrying in, her earrings dancing, and beckoned

Gentian into a far corner full of cushions. They sank down and regarded one another.

"Is Dominic a good friend of yours?" said Alma.

"He only moved in in September," said Gentian, "and I've only talked to him once or twice."

"Do you want him to be a good friend of yours?"

Yes, thought Gentian. "How can I tell until I know him better?"

"There's something the matter with him," said Alma.

Gentian thought wildly of diabetes, heart conditions, leukemia. "What?" she said.

"I don't know. I don't know if he's stupid or if he's crazy or if he's a troublemaker."

"What did he say to you?"

"He never *said* it, but he talked like you guys only put up with me—"

"What?"

"—because it made you feel so liberal."

"Did you tell him who founded the Giant Ants, for God's sake?"

"Nope. I'm not telling him anything. I don't want him to know anything about us."

"But if it was just a misunderstanding—"

"He didn't misunderstand, he *assumed*. And then he *sympathized*. And then he—he never said anything right out, do you get that, he hinted around—he *gave me to understand,*" said Alma, precisely, "that he had experienced racial prejudice himself and that therefore we had a lot in common."

"Well, I guess he might have. I don't know where he's—oh. He said he was from the South."

"Uh-huh."

"Well—he said south of here, anyway."

"I don't care if he was raised by penguins and they pitied him because he didn't have a tuxedo," said Alma.

Gentian laughed, despite the mix of awful sensations warring in her middle.

"You know what was worst?" said Alma. "He was being

nice. He just knew he was being nice to me and of course I'd love to hear all about it. If you hadn't come down the driveway I'd have—"

"Alma. How'd he know about us? You're the only one he's met."

"No kidding? I don't know. I didn't tell him anything."

"That's very weird."

"*He's* very weird," said Alma.

"I thought weird was good," said Gentian, quoting a maxim of the Giant Ants from the fourth grade, when one of Steph's ordinary friends had asked her why she liked to talk to weird people like Alma and Erin. Gentian thought that was when Steph and Alma's firm friendship dated from, but she wasn't sure.

" 'There's nothing either good nor bad but thinking makes it so.' "

"You said that was a pernicious doctrine."

"Well, it is. I just meant we're using two different meanings of 'weird.' "

"Well, yeah, I guess we are."

"It's something like the difference between nonconformist and spooky. Dominic is spooky."

"Thank you for telling me," said Gentian.

"Sure. Oh, and I should warn you: Steph has a Plan."

"Uh-oh. Did she tell you what it is?"

"No; she said she'd tell us sometime before Thanksgiving."

"Is it a winter plan?"

"Dunno. She's not dropping hints this time."

"Wow."

"I trust the rest of you all to sit on her if necessary."

"Okay, I'll alert the troops."

Alma went away to catch the last part of her math class, and Gentian sat on in the sun, musing on what it meant to be weird, and what it meant to be spooky. Maybe I'm attracted to spooky boys, she thought. Who else is spooky? Well, I don't like vampires. She brooded. Do I like Dominic? The way I like Jamie? Yes and no, she decided. Much better to stick to astronomy.

Friday it snowed, in a desultory and absent way, as if it might forget to stop, ever. Gentian's father had called the telescope store in the afternoon, and greeted Gentian when she got home from school with the news that Josh was over his flu and was looking at the telescope, but was very puzzled about it.

Becky called after supper while Gentian was worrying, and asked her to spend the night on Saturday. Gentian agreed, and then complained at length about the telescope. "There's a conjunction of Venus and Jupiter on November eighth and one of Mercury and Venus with Jupiter very nearby on the fourteenth and there's a lunar eclipse on the twenty-ninth and I have got to have a telescope."

"What about the binoculars?"

"They're better than nothing but they're not the same at all."

"You know what you could do," said Becky, "if they continue to be stymied. You could get the telescope back and bring it over here and see how it works here."

"Oh, that's an idea. Except—oh, hell, they're all in the southeast and you've got that hill."

"Oh. Right. Sorry. Well, you know, taking the telescope somewhere and seeing if it works better there is still a good idea."

"And soon," said Gentian, "so I don't get out in the middle of nowhere the night of the first conjunction and find out it still doesn't work. I wish I could *drive.*"

"What planets is it again?"

"Venus and Jupiter first and then Mercury and Venus with Jupiter pretty close."

"That's interesting."

"Well, it's not spectacularly rare, but it's unusual."

"I meant mythologically," said Becky. She giggled suddenly. "You should call Erin."

"Why? She's right down in a valley, you can't see anything from her house at all."

"Well, I always thought, if men are from Mars and women are from Venus—"

"That's a *stupid* book."

"—then Erin must be from Mercury."

"We're all from right here," said Gentian, "unfortunately.

But she'd probably like to be from Mercury. You call her; it's your joke."

"You call her," said Becky. "I bet you haven't yet, have you?"

"Well, no."

"I promise I won't mention it again," said Becky. "But I wish you would."

"I don't have anything against it," said Gentian, irritably. "I'll see you tomorrow around seven." She tapped her finger sharply on the hook and, getting the dial tone, dialed Erin's number.

Eileen answered; Gentian could hear the baby yelling in the background. She asked for Erin. Eileen said she would get her; in the meantime, Erica, Erin's younger sister, said, "Hello?" and engaged Gentian in a long monologue about how Erin would not lend Erica a particular red jacket that they had previously agreed would be shared equally between them. Erin's mother interrupted this to tell Erica to go change the baby, Eileen came back to say Erin would be right there, and finally Erin said temperately, "Yes?" Her voice was a register lower than anybody else's in the family, and she seemed generally to live at a much slower tempo. Gentian had seen this exasperate the rest of them almost to tears, but she mostly found it soothing.

"Hi," she said, "it's me."

"Oh, gosh, you beat me to it," said Erin.

"I did?"

"Becky has been at work."

"Oh, good grief."

"Yes, well. Do you want to go to the Planetarium?"

"Oh, that's an idea. When?"

"I thought the Friday after Thanksgiving. I'll need to get out of this menagerie," said Erin, raising her voice against renewed childish shrieks.

"I'll need to get out of mine, too. Do you want to spend the night afterwards? We can hide upstairs."

"I'll ask Mom and get back to you."

"Oh, and make a note on your calendar for November fourteenth, if it's clear in the morning, to look at the southeastern sky at about six-fifteen. There's a conjunction of Venus and Mercury, with Jupiter close by."

"Don't they get along as a rule?" said Erin.

Gentian sighed.

"Hey, count your blessings. Becky would have asked you something grammatical."

"Actually, she didn't."

"No? Oh, well. Okay, I'll look; and I'll call you back when I've talked to Mom."

Gentian hung up, filled with virtue, and turned on the weather radio again, just in case they should have decided to say there was a one hundred percent chance of clear skies on Saturday. They temporized, as usual. It really didn't matter; the moon was almost full, which made finding anything else problematic, especially with binoculars; but she couldn't help checking.

Gentian thought she would go have another look at the attic. She took her flashlight from the drawer of her bedside table and went out into the hall. Maria Mitchell leapt up the steps, bounded between Gentian's legs, and sat down before the door to the attic, looking expectant.

"Oh, all right," said Gentian. She turned on the hall light, unlocked the square door, and left the door open.

It was certainly a huge space. Well, it covered the whole front half of the house, except for the sunrooms. Gentian shone the flashlight on the walls on either side, which were finished up to the point where they met the roof. Her father was right. Her mother had put in the wiring for a grounded outlet every three feet, although she had only put in four or five of the outlets themselves. Gentian remembered running in and out of the attic while her mother was doing the work, occasionally bringing her a Coke or feeding a wire down inside the wall for her, if her father was busy. They could certainly do any reasonable science project here, even if Dominic wanted to bring in a computer. How likely any science project of Dominic's was to be reasonable was a separate question.

Depending on how large a space he needed, one of the two finished rooms might be better. They had overhead lights already.

Gentian went along to the first of these, which was halfway to the front of the house on her left. This was the one Rosie had lived in when she was angry, and the things she had drawn on the wall were still there. Maria Mitchell came tearing in from the hallway, ran up to Rosie's drawing of her, and rubbed her whiskers against it.

"Clever cat," said Gentian, and went to look at the other room. This was where she and Junie had hidden from Rosie when Rosie was a toddler. They had brought their dollhouses and the model train and the castle and the lead soldiers up here, and the books they didn't want Rosie to tear up, and the art projects they didn't want her to spoil. Gentian had done watercolor paintings of spaceships, supernovae, the galactic core, the moons of Jupiter, comets hitting the Sun, Maria Mitchell (the astronomer) discovering comets with her two-inch telescope, the Big Bang, and Susan B. Anthony hitting politicians in top hats over the head with signs saying RESISTANCE TO TYRANNY IS OBEDIENCE TO GOD and NO TAXATION WITHOUT REPRESENTATION.

Juniper would sit across the old painted kitchen table from her and write and write and write. If they were mad at their parents or annoyed with Rosie, she would write the incidents up and read aloud to Gentian what she had written.

"Huh," said Gentian.

Maria Mitchell came trotting into the room with something in her mouth. Gentian dived for her, missed, hurriedly shut the door, and lay down on the floor to get a better look. It was a grimy calico mouse, not a real one. Murr was acting as if the catnip in it still had some zing, which was improbable. Gentian sat on the dusty boards, watching Murr roll around and rub the mouse against her cheek, and wondered when she and Junie had stopped having any friendly relations. They had always argued furiously. They didn't really do that much any more; it was more like an automated program, with little real content.

Gentian didn't think it had been her fault. Junie had started shutting herself up in her room all the time. Their parents had had several irritable conversations during which one or the other of them would recite or read from some book or article the signs of impending teenage suicide, and the other would snap that these were virtually indistinguishable from the simple signs of teenage existence. Then they would draw straws for who went to talk to Junie, and whoever lost would emerge in fifteen minutes or so looking harried.

All this had happened before Gentian got the telescope, when she was trying to make her own. By the time she had given that up and decided to use all her savings and all her potential Christmas presents to buy one, Juniper had emerged from her chrysalis of despair the cranky, touchy, energetic, clothing-obsessed, sister-hating creature she was today.

"Huh," said Gentian. "Wow." She listened to herself, and laughed. "When Daddy talks to himself," she informed her cat, "he at least uses complete sentences."

The cranky Juniper had always existed, she decided; it was just that in the past three years or so, that one had taken over Juniper's life at home. The teen echo could have that one, as far as Gentian was concerned; but no, it got the good one.

Gentian picked up Maria Mitchell in one hand and the damp catnip mouse in the other and went back to her part of the attic. Here she leafed morosely through several copies of *Sky and Telescope*. There was a great deal to being an astronomer besides using a telescope, but somehow she could not get around the lack of one.

9

Saturday was cold. Sunday, which was Halloween, was forecast to be even colder, in the teens, a temperature that one welcomed gratefully in February after a bout of daily high temperatures below zero, but that in October caused an escalating series of arguments between Juniper and Rosemary and their mother about the suitability of their Halloween costumes.

The Giant Ants did not go trick-or-treating, except early in the evening with any sibling under the age of five whom one or the other might be saddled with. The Giant Ants had costume parties at which they ate exactly the kind of candy they liked and played charades. Sometimes they invited other people, but mostly they didn't. This year the party was at Gentian's, and Gentian's mother kept trying to persuade Juniper and Rosemary that they would just as soon stay home and join Gentian's friends as go traipsing around in freezing winds dressed, respectively, as Hamlet with his doublet all unbraced and Mary Lou Retton.

"Mom," said Gentian, cornering her mother in the kitchen at a moment when Juniper was appealing to their father in his study and Rosemary was sulking upstairs, "I don't want them at the Giant Ants' party. We won't be able to talk about anything important if they're there."

Her mother was emptying the dishwasher so fast that Gentian

didn't dare help for fear of being stepped on. She said, "You know, for the past two or three years all my parenting energy has gone into keeping you girls out of one another's way and protecting you from the terrors of one another's presence. I'm about out of patience with it."

"They don't want to come to our party anyway."

"I'm aware of that," said her mother, dryly. "You would probably get more points for pretending you'd love to have them and heaving a surreptitious sigh of relief when I am utterly unable to persuade them to stay home."

"I hate duplicity," said Gentian.

"It's the lubrication of social discourse."

"Ugh."

"Yes, well."

"Didn't Mary Lou Retton have a warm-up suit?"

"Yes, and if it hadn't had Olympic patches on it it would have made her look like any other little girl out on her paper route on a cold evening. The conclusion is left as an exercise for the student."

"And Hamlet had a cloak."

"Hamlet's cloak didn't show off his chest."

"What chest?" said Gentian, nastily, and stamped upstairs to clean her room up. She would be at Becky's tonight and probably well into tomorrow, so the work had to be done now. She picked up her dirty clothes from the floor and fed them down the laundry chute in the hall. She made her bed. She put a small collection of crumby plates and ringed mugs and glasses on a tray and set it at the head of the stairs. Then she looked around, blinking a little. Not being an astronomer seemed to be making her much tidier. Her reference books were all still on their shelf; *Sky and Telescope* was stacked neatly on its shelf, unread; no scribbled notes and diagrams dotted the floor. She put the biography of Maria Mitchell back in its place of honor in the headboard of the bed and shoved her homework, textbooks, and school notebooks into their drawer; and that was all, she was ready to dust and sweep.

So she did, fuming. Having Rosemary at the party wouldn't

be disastrous, but having Juniper would. The Giant Ants knew about siblings; there wasn't an only child among them. But none of them had anybody quite so irritable and condescending as Junie. She would be bored, but she wouldn't go away decently and do something she liked; she would just make snide remarks.

"I wish *I* were an only child," said Gentian to Maria Mitchell. Maria Mitchell was engaged in murdering a bit of carpet that she had detached from her scratching post, and paid no attention.

Gentian packed her suitcase to go to Becky's. Cotton nightgown—Becky's room was overheated, in Gentian's opinion, and her usual sweats were much too warm there—clean underwear, socks, T-shirt. Toothbrush, hairbrush. The biography of Maria Mitchell. Her current notebook. *Pride and Prejudice, Julius Caesar, Owl in Love, The Princess and Curdie,* the last four issues of *Sky and Telescope,* Carl Sagan's *Comet,* and *The Space Child's Mother Goose.* Several pens, a protractor, a stylus. The binoculars in their case. Her ephemeris. Her father's CD of Laurie Anderson's "Strange Angels." Her own CD of Holst's "The Planets." Some stray chocolate-chip cookies from Junie's last batch. The suitcase was full. Gentian considered it, and crammed a set of astronomical postcards down into one side pocket. This late in the year, there was a danger of being snowed in. There had been Halloween blizzards before.

Maria Mitchell leapt into the suitcase just as she was about to close it.

"I'd take you if I could," Gentian told her. "You know you'd just yowl. And Jeremy's allergic to you."

Maria Mitchell kneaded the CD boxes with both front paws and purred.

"And no, you can't have any cookies. Chocolate is bad for cats."

Maria Mitchell sprang out of the suitcase and hurried into the bathroom, whence she could be heard making annoyed sounds. Gentian followed her, to find the food bowl empty. She filled it halfway, then full, then put another half cup on top of it all. Halloween blizzards cut two ways, after all.

She highlighted the FEED CAT! sign with fluorescent pink marker, petted the crunching Murr for several minutes, and took her suitcase downstairs. Her mother and Rosemary had emptied the contents of the rag bag and the sewing chest all over the living-room sofa. Her mother had put on music and turned it up quite high. "Next, I'll grow into your arms a toad but an eel; had me fast, let me not gang, if you do love me leel."

"Oh, *Mom,*" said Gentian under her breath. "What is this, psychological warfare?"

"Did you feed your cat?" shouted her mother.

"Yes!"

"Say hello to Becky!"

"All right!"

"Bring Jeremy to your party!" shrieked Rosemary.

Gentian lugged her suitcase to the front door without answering. She wondered what Rosemary wanted Jeremy for. He was only eight. Possibly to demonstrate a decent sibling relationship to Juniper.

She opened the front door and recoiled. It really was cold out there, enough to make her eyes water. She put a poncho on over her sweatshirt and grabbed the nearest pair of gloves. She grasped the suitcase firmly and went outside.

Mrs. Zimmerman was planting bulbs in front of her house, on the strip of land between the sidewalk and the street.

"Are you running away?" she said as Gentian came into her field of view.

"Yes, I can't stand my sisters any longer and I'm going to Antarctica to seek my fortune."

"Good timing," said Mrs. Zimmerman. She jerked a plug of soil out of the ground with her bulb planter and popped a scaling lily bulb into the hole. "I think it's spring in those latitudes."

"I always think ahead," said Gentian solemnly. They both laughed. "Actually, I'm going to spend the night with Becky."

"Give her my regards," said Mrs. Zimmerman, dumping half a cup of organic fertilizer on top of the bulb. Its sour, complex smell tickled Gentian's nose. Her father had used it too, on all those hundreds of bulbs he had made her help plant in exchange for taking the telescope to people who didn't know what they were doing.

Mrs. Zimmerman said, "Are you insects having your usual Halloween celebration?"

"Yes, it's at my house."

"Perhaps Ira and I will go to Antarctica instead."

"You'd better. Mom wants me to let Junie and Rosie come too. She thinks their costumes aren't warm enough."

"What is everybody dressing up as?"

"I haven't decided. The Giant Ants always keep it a secret, anyway. But I think everybody's sort of at loose ends this year. We've all *been* everybody we like. Well, Steph always has some new obsession, but last year everybody said they didn't know what they'd do next, and I still don't."

"Marie Curie?"

"I did her in first grade."

"Ah. What are your sisters dressing as?"

"Rosie wants to be Mary Lou Retton and Junie wants to be Hamlet."

Mrs. Zimmerman laughed and tamped the plug of soil back into the ground. "Have you been a telescope?" she said.

"Mmmm, no. If I went trick-or-treating it'd be okay, but if I have to be at a party where I want to sit down, it would present problems."

"Do you think your young neighbor goes trick-or-treating?"

"Wow," said Gentian, putting her suitcase down. "I don't know. He could be all sorts of things."

"I take it he's not invited to your party."

"Well, gosh, no, it's usually just us. I'd invite you first if we decided to expand."

"I saw you and Alma playing ball with him, and wondered if you had expanded your circle."

"It takes more than playing soccer to do that."

"I see."

"I don't think Alma likes him very much, anyway."

"I'm not sure anybody does," said Mrs. Zimmerman, pulling

out another plug of soil and dropping in another lily bulb. "That evening was the only time I've ever seen him with anybody."

"Do you see him much? I hardly ever see him at all."

"He walks around late at night."

"Really? How late?"

"Two, three, four in the morning."

"What does he do?"

"Just walks up and down, and to and fro."

"Huh."

Mrs. Zimmerman obliterated the hole she was working on and made another. Gentian picked up the suitcase. "I'd better go or I'll be late." Becky's mother was fussy about dinner's starting on time. "Have a nice Halloween."

"You, too," said Mrs. Zimmerman. "Have you ever come *as* giant ants?"

Gentian laughed and went on her way. The elms had lost most of their leaves during the rain, and assumed their winter tracery against the blue icy sky. The maples were still turning; some of them had green leaves here and there. The feathery locusts, Becky's favorite tree, were vivid yellow. The wind was violent. She walked faster.

Becky was sitting on the front steps of her house, bundled in a yellow down jacket, a teal-green hat, and black mittens. Her nose was red and her eyes wet. Gentian leapt up the steps. "What's *wrong?*"

"No, it's just the cold," said Becky. "I'm trying to get winter into my blood so I can write a new poem."

"Wouldn't it go in faster if you sat out here in a swimming suit?"

"No, part of winter is wearing too many clothes."

"Well, I'm freezing. Can we go in?"

"I guess so. It's dinnertime, anyway."

Gentian found Becky's mother both alarming and exasperating, but she seemed to be in a good mood tonight. She fed them chicken with almonds and eggplant in garlic sauce and asked civilly after their Halloween costumes. Jeremy, it transpired, wanted to be Marco Polo and carry a box of vermicelli to indicate that he had brought noodles back from China. Becky's father asked if he should follow Jeremy in a chef's costume to indicate historical influence. Gentian liked him better than she liked Becky's mother, but he seldom said very much.

They escaped upstairs in good time. Becky, like Gentian, had the attic room. It was much larger and lower, being the entire upper floor of a much smaller house. Becky had her desk and bed in the middle of the room and other shorter things against the half-sized walls. She had painted it in dazzling white enamel to make it look lighter and bigger. There was red vinyl tile on the floor. Steph said it looked like a kitchen, but Gentian liked it. One of Becky's mother's amiable traits was that she did patchwork, and Becky had a quilt on her bed and another on a slanting portion of ceiling, and patchwork pillows in all sizes, and window-sized quilts that could be rolled up, instead of blinds.

They sat on the bed and ate salted cashews. "What did you write this week?" asked Gentian.

"I'm terribly afraid it's going to be a short story," said Becky. "I thought it was a poem, but first it had a plot and then it started being free verse and then it grew dialogue and finally there just didn't seem to be any reason for it to be poetry."

"What's it about?"

"A girl with no friends who finds a magic tree."

"Oh."

"Well, I can't help it."

"I'll like it fine when it's done."

"You can hate it if you want to," said Becky, irritably. "You aren't obliged to like everything I write."

"I always do like it, though," said Gentian, startled.

"Yes, I know, but you don't have to. Sorry."

"What's the matter?"

"I don't like it when my poems turn around like that. And I don't know what to do about Halloween. I just don't look like Sappho."

"Mrs. Zimmerman asked if we had ever all dressed as giant ants."

Becky chortled. "Well, maybe next year. Erin and Steph are

awfully smug about whatever they're going to be, and I don't think there's time to make all those costumes anyway. What are you going to be?"

"I don't know. Mrs. Zimmerman suggested a telescope."

Becky collapsed across the bed, laughing.

"Ha, ha," said Gentian. "And you can be a poem. It's about as practical."

Becky sat up. "But I could. I could go as a poem."

"You could?"

"Yes. Just let me ponder it. Maybe you can help me later. Now, what have you been doing?"

"What *can* I do? No telescope. I'm getting it back Monday no matter what they say. Boneheads."

"Yes, then you'll have time to try it in other locations before November eighth. But come on, what have you been doing with all your spare time? Research?"

"No, I haven't got the heart for it." Gentian considered. "Alma and I made that jumper."

"It's too bad Erin couldn't help."

"That's okay, Alma's good at sewing too. And Erin and I are going to the Planetarium the day after Thanksgiving *and* she's going to spend the night afterwards. I guess you'd better ask if you can come on Saturday that weekend. I need to be at home for astronomical purposes."

Becky beamed upon her. "There, that's better."

"It won't be, if we can't get the telescope to work."

"Maybe you need a new one."

"Too expensive."

"An early Christmas present?"

"Well, I could ask."

"You'd better. You're just mooning around wasting time."

"Thanks a lot."

"Are you doing your homework?"

"For heaven's sake. Yes."

"Well, you can't let something like a malfunctioning telescope set your whole career back."

"All *right,* I get the point. What about your career? Have you got anything to read me?"

"No. The short story isn't done yet. Well, all right. I have a really, really bad poem, but I'll read it to you if you want me to."

"I do."

Becky dragged a dog-eared sheet, much marked and erased, out of the drawer of her bedside table, and read.

"Fill your head with rubbish,
Fill your soul with dreams,
Better than from hashish
Or from flying machines:
From it all come creeping
Out the mangled shapes that seem
More the province of a sleeping
Than an open-eyed regime.
Fill your head full up with learning,
And your soul, reality:
Ignorance will stream out, pouring
Shapes of mindless fantasy.
What the eyes regard the mind
Will take and tangle to a skein
The very fates could not unravel
Nor the god of plots disdain.
Plainness turns to Turkish carpet,
Parthenon to Taj Mahal,
And the gold of every target
Covers red, and blue, and all."

"I like the way it sounds, but it makes no sense whatsoever."

"Well, that's the point."

"Oh. Okay."

"No, it's not okay," said Becky, "but never mind." She grinned. "I showed Micky 'The Butterfly Hat.' "

"Good grief." Gentian felt peculiarly jolted. "What did he say?"

Becky grinned again, the most evil grin possible on such a face as hers. "He said it was really creepy, and then he asked me if I were a vegetarian."

"What did you say?"

"I said there was a difference between fair use and copyright infringement."

Gentian laughed. "Did he get it?"

"Oh, yes, and then we had a long argument."

"Is he a vegetarian?"

"No. He just thinks that anybody who believes in kindness to animals ought to be."

"Why on earth?"

"He thinks Asimov wasn't a real scientist because he quit medical school rather than get a dog from the Humane Society and kill it. He thinks *he's* going to be a real scientist." She said this with particular emphasis. Gentian looked at her carefully and decided to pursue the emotional rather than the philosophical path.

"Are you going to a movie with him?"

"Yes, the Friday after Thanksgiving."

"Good, you can tell me about it on Saturday."

"I will, too. Have you got anything to read to me?"

"I have music." Gentian opened her suitcase and got out the Laurie Anderson disk. "It's my dad's. He likes it because of the song about the day the devil comes to get you."

"He does?"

"It's funny. It says the devil's a rusty truck with only twenty miles, he's got bad brakes, he's got loose teeth, he's a long way from home."

"I'll take your word for it."

"He likes the strange angels song, too, and so do I."

"Is this a religious record?"

"No, no, no. It's got a song about icy comets whizzing by, too, and kerjillions of stars. He played me that one first, to soften me up for the other ones."

"Kerjillions?"

"Kerjillions."

"Okay."

"And the one I brought for you is called 'Beautiful Red Dress,' and I think it's got to be about menstruation. That's not exactly common."

"No, it's not, and there's a reason for that."

"Becky. What the hell is the matter?"

"Go ahead, play the song."

Gentian got off the bed, turned Becky's CD player on, put the disk in, and started to select the song. Then she thought about it. "Let's play the whole album," she said. "I think the song is better that way."

"Whatever," said Becky.

All through the first song she maintained a deadpan expression that made Gentian perfectly sure that something was, in fact, the matter. It was not like Becky to refuse to enter into one's enthusiasms. The second song, about stopping by the body shop and asking to have a stereo put in her teeth and high-heeled feet installed, made her smile briefly, and when the requests were followed by a reference to "The Monkey's Paw," which was one of her favorite stories, Becky looked at Gentian and nodded. The third song, not one of Gentian's favorites in any case, got the deadpan treatment again. Gentian waited it out. The fourth song was called "Ramon," but Gentian always thought of it as the Angels Like Lawn Mowers song, and she was fairly certain that Becky would find it irresistible. It had a number of goofy moments and others reminiscent of Ophelia's remark, after she went mad, "Lord, we know what we are, but know not what we may be," which had been known to reduce Becky to tears, even when read badly.

The song began,

"Last night I saw a host of angels,
And they were all singing different songs,
And it sounded like a lot of lawn mowers,
Mowing down my lawn."

Becky burst into delighted laughter. Gentian liked the song because it had the speed of light and the speed of sound in it, mixed in with more common elements of poetry, and it made her feel that she and the singer were members of the same human race, rather than the usual human race everybody was always blathering about.

Becky looked almost herself at the end of that. The fifth song began, "I don't know about your brain, but mine is really bossy," and that made her laugh too.

The next song was the one Gentian had brought the record for. It was called "Beautiful Red Dress." Becky got up at the line, "Cause the moon is full and look out baby, I'm at high tide" and went over and turned the sound up and remained standing in the middle of her braided rug for the rest of the song, looking blank and almost altogether absent, as though she had no sense left but hearing. When it was over, she punched the skip button so that it played again. She played it five times before she let it go on to the song about the devil.

Gentian thought of pausing that song, since it was perfectly obvious that Becky was not going to listen to it, but she decided that she might as well have something to listen to while Becky was cogitating.

"*The day the devil comes to getcha*
He's got a smile like a scar.
He knows the way to your house.
He's got the keys to your car.
And when he sells you his sportcoat
You say: Funny! That's my size . . .
Give me back my innocence.
Get me a brand new suit.
Give back my innocence.
Oh Lord! Cut me down to size."

Gentian giggled; it was so deliciously ironic. Becky didn't move. The Devil song went on, and ended; the next one began.

"*Hansel and Gretel are alive and well*
And they're living in Berlin."

Gentian should have liked this song, but it always irritated her. She got up and paused the disk.

"Think of something else I'd be good at," said Becky as Gentian passed her on her way back. "I'm giving up poetry."

Gentian looked at her. The last poet who had made her say

that was Emily Dickinson, and the one before that was Tolkien. She did not altogether see how Laurie Anderson fit into this progression. "Songs are different," she said.

"But that's the kind of thing I want to do," said Becky. She reflected. "Well, one of them."

"What is?"

"That song. It's got images that add up to something and it's funny and it's serious and it's snarky and it's about important things."

"Well, so does your stuff."

"Not like that."

"Well, you're just starting out."

"I'll never be able to do anything like that."

"Well, you'll do something different that's just as good, then."

Becky shook her head mournfully and climbed into bed, where she sat staring into space. Gentian sighed and started the CD player again. She might as well enjoy the rest of the record. Becky had not had an attack of the Poetics like this for some time. Gentian got her telescope book out of the suitcase and sat reading it and listening to the music. She tried to think of an astronomer who would make her think, "I'll never be able to do anything like that." Certainly she was unlikely to do the equivalent of inventing differential calculus or a new kind of telescope, but she was perfectly confident about being able to find interesting things and have insights about them.

"I think I'm obsessed," said Becky suddenly.

Gentian put the book down. "With what?"

"Whom."

"*Micky?*"

Becky nodded. She looked miserable. "I keep thinking how much more fun the Giant Ants' party would be if he were there too."

"Good grief."

"And it probably wouldn't. I know he doesn't appreciate Steph and he thinks Alma's weird for not having any black friends."

"And what does he think of Erin?"

"He thinks she's cool."

"That's something."

There was a pause. Becky chewed on the end of one braid, which she had not done since she was eight. I won't ask, thought Gentian; then she thought, if I can't ask, what's the point of anything; then she thought, but it's all right for some things to remain unsaid; and finally she thought, but this is what's wrong.

"And what does he think of me?" She tried not to sound aggressive or demanding.

"He knows you're my best friend," said Becky, "so he doesn't express an opinion."

"But?"

"He thinks we're cliquish and snobbish and unwelcoming."

"We're not a social club, for God's sake."

"He says most of us would like to have other friends too but you won't let us."

"How did you get onto this from scientists and the philosophy of vegetarianism?"

"Oh, we didn't. We talked on the phone another time."

"And," said Gentian, exasperated beyond prudence, "I'd like to see me not let you guys do anything you wanted to do. It's like herding cats. And it was *Alma's idea* to be a group and have a name. And what's wrong with it anyway? Is my family cliquish and snobbish and unwelcoming because we don't ask all the neighbors to move in with us? And everybody *has* other friends. You have the *Tesseract* crew and Steph's got Glee Club and Alma's got soccer."

"What about Erin?"

"Erin is solitary."

"What about you?"

"I'm an astronomer."

Becky grinned briefly but said nothing.

"Do you *agree* with him?"

"No, I think he exaggerates and simplifies, like Mr. Rothman says you have to do to draw a caricature."

"But you think there's an underlying truth?" said Gentian, going on with their art teacher's definition. "You recognize the resemblance?"

"I don't know," said Becky. "I'm confused and I don't like it."

They sat gloomily while the last Laurie Anderson song on the disk ran out. It was an odd amalgam of Longfellow's "Hiawatha" and other bits and pieces, including a chorus about how they were going to hang some new stars in the heavens tonight, and Gentian had meant to bring it to Becky's attention. Instead she found herself saying suddenly, "You know, even if he thinks all those things about us, why did he say them to you?"

"We agreed we'd be honest with each other."

"What? Just like that? With somebody you just started talking to?"

"We didn't agree we'd tell each other everything," snapped Becky. "Just that what we did say would be the truth."

"I don't think that explains it."

"I'm not sure it does either," said Becky. "It's awfully strange. I don't know if I'm not suited for any other acquaintance because I've been in the Giant Ants so long, or if there's something odd about him. I get paranoid, I find myself wondering if he's been mad at us for years for some reason and he just put up this front of wanting to get to know me and have an honest relationship right from the beginning so he could tell me what he thought of us."

"What did we ever do to him?"

"I don't know, but he's obviously thought about us a lot."

"That's spooky."

"Oh, I don't think so. There are a lot of us and we're often kind of loud. Is it spooky when Laurie sees the March girls having fun and thinks about how nice it looks?"

"Everything in *Little Women* is spooky," said Gentian, automatically applying the insult of the moment to that despised work.

"Oh, for heaven's sake. It is not."

"All right, no, you're right. It's soppy, but it's not spooky."

"So maybe Micky's being soppy too."

"No, he isn't, because he doesn't approve of us."

"Well, he isn't being soppy in the same way as Laurie, certainly."

There was a meditative silence. Gentian thought of Dominic.

She had used the same word about Micky as Alma had used about Dominic. She considered telling Becky something about all that. But it's different, she thought, Dominic and I don't have a relationship, I'd never say "we" about Dominic and me, there isn't any such entity. Thinking "Dominic and me" even while denying the validity of such a construction made her feel a profound pleasure.

"Read to me from the history of the telescope," said Becky. "Read me something really, really technical. I think it will be soothing."

Gentian picked up the book again and found an early chapter detailing the nature of armillary spheres, quadrants, the torquetum, and the astrolabe. These descriptions were intertwined with remarks on the Ptolemaic theory of the solar system and the refinements made to it, which Gentian found considerably more complicated than Newtonian theory; she trusted Becky would too. She read on through the advent of Tycho Brahe, who thought a conjunction of Saturn and Jupiter had precipitated the great plague of 1563 and who caused to be built a nineteen-foot quadrant, the better to observe future conjunctions. Not satisfied with this, he added transversals. He finally built an equatorial armillary, meanwhile rejecting the Copernican theory for an earth-centered one in which the other planets revolved around the sun, which revolved around the earth. Less by this theory than by his fiery disposition, he made enemies among the Danish nobles so that eventually his income was curtailed and his observatory fell into ruin.

Gentian cleared her throat.

"Read another chapter, please," said Becky.

Gentian read to her about the history of optics. She had to stop near the end of the chapter because her throat was so dry.

"I'm sorry," said Becky, "I'll get the repast."

She went downstairs and came back with a large insulated jug of grape juice and a tin of samosas and another of date-and-almond bars. Her mother, besides making patchwork, was a splendiferous cook. Gentian wondered why she couldn't combine these domestic virtues with a different disposition. It was odd.

Junie was a good cook, and she was irritable and opinionated too.

"Do you want the rest of the chapter?" she said when Becky had rejoined her on the bed and she had drunk a glass of juice.

"I don't know. How soon do we get to Galileo?"

"That's the next chapter."

"Maybe later, then."

"Did it help?"

"Yeah, it did."

"What do you want to do now?"

"Let's play Scrabble."

"Where's the *OED?*"

"We can use the *Shorter Oxford* for now; I don't feel like messing with the magnifying glass."

They sat in the middle of the rag rug with the board and the dictionary between them, playing Wide-Open Scrabble, which allowed proper names, archaic terms, hyphenated compounds, trade names, and all manner of slang. Alma had refused to play the ordinary kind of Scrabble ever since she discovered that the official dictionary did not contain the terms "sixte" and "carte," from fencing, and she had rapidly addicted the rest of the Giant Ants to the new version.

Alma and Steph were cutthroat players, much engaged with triple word scores and piling words atop other words and filling the board tightly. Erin liked finding elegant solutions. Becky and Gentian liked making interesting words. Becky's triumph this evening was "Timbuktoo," and Gentian's was "Hertzsprung." She did get a triple word score on that one, and won the game.

They finished the samosas and took the cookies to bed with them, and lay crunching cookies and reading in a desultory and interruptable fashion.

"I forgot to tell you," said Gentian. "Mom is trying to persuade Juniper and Rosemary that they would rather come to our party than go trick-or-treating in the cold."

"Rosie might, but I can't imagine that Junie would give us the time of day."

"She might enjoy sneering."

"Good luck to her," said Becky. "I think we're a match for her. We had to have Eileen one year, remember, the year before she got married, and she was much more supercilious than Junie."

This led to a series of reminiscences about all the Giant Ants' past Halloween parties. Gentian thought of suggesting that Becky write a poem about them, but decided it might be too soon. They trailed off into sleep at about five in the morning.

10

⌒

Early Sunday afternoon Gentian hurried home in the cold, lugged her suitcase upstairs, dumped it on the bed, petted her cat, and ran downstairs again to see if her father had remembered to take her party list to the grocery store. Sitting on the kitchen table was a brown paper bag labeled "Genny" in big green letters. Investigation showed that he had probably forgotten to bring the actual list but remembered almost everything on it. The omissions were unfortunate: both salted nut rolls and peppermint creams were traditional items, and it was especially necessary to have the nut rolls because Steph was allergic to chocolate.

Gentian hunted her mother down in the basement, where she was patching a hole in the floor; extracted a ten-dollar bill from her; and ran up the stairs and out the side door.

It was bright, still, and icy out. Gentian blinked a few times, turned to go down the driveway, and saw Dominic standing at the bottom of it. He had his back to her. He was not dressed for the weather any more than he ever had been. He was all in black. Gentian stood stock still, clutching her father's string grocery bag. She could not just walk up behind him, and she didn't think she could speak. She had just decided to go back into the house and come out the front door, so that he might hear her and so that in any case she would be approaching him from the side, when he turned around.

"Hello," called Gentian, hurrying down the driveway.

"A damnable doughnut, that," said Dominic, amiably.

Another riddle, lovely. "Happy Halloween," said Gentian.

"When graveyards yawn, and hell breathes forth contagion to this world?"

"My mother says it's the Time of Masks, and we like it that way."

"What path do you follow, then?"

Gentian was not sure what he was asking, but in case it should be mystical, she said firmly, "I'm a scientist."

"We murder to dissect," said Dominic.

Gentian suppressed a mad urge to ask him if he were a vegetarian, and said, "I have to go to the store, and I'm in a hurry, but you could walk along with me if you like."

The moment she said it she felt her entire face go hot. And what if he asked her what she was buying the candy for? She couldn't ask him to the party, not when she didn't want Micky. Besides, she would have to check with everybody first. She couldn't help foisting her sisters off on them, but Dominic was an avoidable evil.

She added, "We could talk about your time machine. Is it a school project? When is it due?"

Dominic fell into step beside her as she turned away from him in the direction of the little corner store. "Time," he said gravely, "is the school in which I learn. I am my own school."

Gentian's parents had considered home-schooling, until they found out about the open school. She wasn't sure that was what Dominic meant, and in any case it was a side issue. "When do you need to start?" she said.

"The beauty of a time machine is that it renders time irrelevant," said Dominic.

His tone was still amiable, but Gentian felt thoroughly snubbed. She was glad that the store was only two blocks away. She scuffed through the fallen leaves, thinking of the color temperatures of stars and wishing Dominic were inside one of them, preferably a Type O.

He walked beside her serenely, as far as she could tell from looking at him through her hair, which she had not had time to brush back or secure with its usual headband. She thought of asking his advice about her Halloween costume, but that came too close to talking about the party, and anyway he might snub her again. She contented herself with looking at him, since he was gazing far ahead and a little upwards, as if he were either thinking deeply or hoping to see a flock of exotic birds. He had an exceedingly pure, pale profile; even the sharp wind did not make his cheeks red. His lips, as her father said, were red as wine. His hair is like a raven's wing, thought Gentian, and then had to stifle a snort. She had never seen a raven's wing. Hair like a grackle's wing, she thought, and snickered; hair like a pigeon's behind, she thought, and giggled.

Dominic immediately gave her a courteous-looking attention.

"Sorry," said Gentian. "I was just woolgathering."

"And can you tell which is the upper and which the under end of your wool?"

"No," said Gentian, cheerfully.

He shook his head a little and said nothing further. They came to the store. Gentian went in first, to avoid awkwardness should he try to open the door for her. She collected her candy and an extra carton of heavy cream, just in case they wanted to whip it and put it in their cocoa, and had paid for all of this before she realized Dominic had not come in with her. When she came out, he was standing on the sidewalk examining a crabapple tree and being scolded by a crow. Gentian decided not to look at the crow's wing.

He turned as the door of the store banged, and came up to her. "It's not a day to be within doors," he said.

"It feels like a lovely one to spend by a nice fire to me," said Gentian.

"I have fire with me," said Dominic.

"I guess you do, if you walk around without a coat in this weather."

They crossed the street at the light and walked down the first of the two blocks back to their own. They were going briskly, but the silence felt much heavier to Gentian.

"Do you knit?" she asked him desperately. "Is that why you asked me about telling the wool?"

"No," said Dominic. "I don't knit. I unravel."

"Oh, like Penelope?"

Dominic laughed. Gentian jumped; it was the most unexpected sound she could remember hearing in her entire life. She had said what she did because everything in Bulfinch's *Mythology* was still rattling around in her head. She had not thought it would produce a reaction from him, any more than most of the other things she said. You never knew what would make an impression on Dominic. Maybe she should read more mythology.

"No, oh no," said Dominic. "And yet I am faithful, in my fashion."

They had reached the foot of their shared driveway, and Gentian was thankful. Sustaining any kind of interaction with Dominic was wearing. One reason having him at the party would have been pleasant was that all four of the other Ants could have helped her elicit reactions, including, she was very sure, some she could not discover on her own if she talked to Dominic until Doomsday. But it would be more relaxing without him.

"Well," she said, "I've got a lot to do. It was nice to see you. Let me know when you want to get started on the time machine. We'll have to do a little work in the attic first."

"The whirligig of time brings in his revenges," said Dominic, quite as though he were making some commonplace farewell; and he went up the driveway and into his house and shut the door.

Gentian collected herself and went up her own front steps. The Halloween battle was still raging inside. Gentian fled to her room, sat down with her cat in her lap, and applied herself to the problem of her own costume. "I could go as you," she said to Murr. "A double disguise—a cat named for a famous astronomer." She had been the astronomer Maria Mitchell when she was in the fourth grade, and had decided that that was the only Victorian person she would ever be in her life. The clothes were terribly heavy and cumbersome, and that year Halloween had been warm.

She could certainly go as a cat. Rosemary, who tended to be aggressively ordinary in her Halloween plans, possibly in rebellion against her older sisters, had been a pumpkin complete with orange face paint one year, and a black cat with stiffly wired plush tail the next; and Rosemary never threw anything away. The face paint might be dried up, though.

"I could be an angel with a lawn mower, but nobody'd get it except Daddy and Becky. I could have a beautiful red dress and go as menstruation. Yuck. I could go as a constellation." She had in her youth dressed up as several different planets, but like the telescope costume these posed the problem that one could not easily sit down in them. "I could go as Elizabeth Bennet." No, those clothes were almost as nasty as the Victorian ones. And the men's clothes were worse, so Darcy was out as well.

"I really think, Murr," she said, "that I'll have to go as you."

Erin arrived first. She took off her hooded red wool coat with the elephants embroidered on it and stood there in khakis and heavy boots. She had brushed her hair straight back, fastened it in a ponytail, and powdered it gray. She had a notebook under her arm.

"Stanley?" said Gentian, hanging up the coat. "Livingston?"

"Guess again," said Erin.

"You guess me while I think."

"Junie's dressed up as the gingham dog and you're going to eat each other up."

"Half right."

"Oh," said Erin. She smiled. "Oh. Maria Mitchell. Oh, very nice."

Gentian was pleased. "Margaret Mead?" she said.

"She often wore dresses in the field."

"Is she closer than Stanley?"

"Well, you got the gender right."

"Are the elephants on your coat a clue?"

"Distantly."

The doorbell rang. Gentian opened the door and was faced with a distorted mirror image of her own costume—orange cat ears, whiskers, tail draped over the arm. This one had painted her face in tiger stripes and put on a tiger nose. She bounced suddenly forward, almost upsetting Gentian, thus revealing herself to be Alma. She was shivering. Gentian shut the door behind her and pointed her in the direction of the fireplace.

Alma went over in large bouncing steps. She had orange boots anyway, and she had put black stripes on them.

Erin laughed. "But whatever his weight in pounds, shillings and ounces, he always seems bigger because of his bounces."

"I thought," said Alma, turning her tiger nose in Gentian's direction, "that I was the only one there was."

"You are," said Gentian. "I am an astronomer."

Alma burst out laughing as only she could. The doorbell rang. Gentian opened the door again and was confronted by Steph with her dark hair frizzled all over her forehead and screwed up in back under a large straw hat. The rest of her was wearing what looked like a very full knee-length kimono over harem pants.

"Ah," said Gentian. "Ms. Bloomer, I presume."

"Ms. Bloomer did not live in this climate," said Steph.

Gentian let her in, and she joined Tigger at the fire. They both began trying to guess who Erin was. Gentian went into the kitchen and brought out the tray of sandwiches.

"Ooh, all the things Tiggers like best," said Alma.

"You know," said Erin, "I almost came as Tonstant Weader."

"Oh, so did I!" cried Steph. "I was going to be Dorothy Parker and Alma was going to be Edmund Wilson, and I was going to fwow up and she was going to say, 'Oo, those awful Orcs,' over and over until you got the point. But she didn't like the way he dressed, so we didn't."

"It wasn't only that," said Alma. "It was Dominic."

Everybody looked at her.

"Gentian's new next-door neighbor."

Everybody looked at Gentian.

"Alma's probably had more conversation with him than I have," said Gentian. "He's very elusive, but he did come out and play soccer with us after we made my red jumper."

"Yes, but who is he?" said Erin. "And how did he make you dress up as Tigger?"

The doorbell rang. Gentian got up and answered it. Becky was standing on the porch, almost unrecognizable because she was dressed all in white, in a kind of caftanlike garment that looked as if it had started life as a sheet. No, it wasn't all white, it had lines and circles of black on it.

It had writing on it.

"Come in, for heaven's sake, so I can read you," said Gentian.

Becky was cold too; she came in readily, and stood next to the radiator under the hanging lamp so Gentian could examine her costume. Gentian read, "And I replied to her in these words: 'Go with a light heart, and with memories of me, for you know how we cherished you."

"No, start farther up," said Becky, "on the left shoulder."

Gentian backed up a little and started over.

"It seems to start in the middle—"

"Yes," said Becky. She stretched the sheet a little flatter. It read:

"and honestly I want to die"
—so sobbing, many times, she left me
and she said this [to me]:
"My god! what awful things are happening to us;
Sappho, I swear I am leaving you against my will."
And I replied to her in these words:
"Go with a light heart, and with memories
of me, for you know how we cherished you.
And if not, then I want to
remind you

At which point there was a rent in the white cloth, so that the black leotard Becky wore underneath showed through, instead of black words.

"What's that for?" said Gentian, touching the edge of the rip with her finger.

"It's a lacuna," said Becky.

There was another rip at the beginning of the next line, and
then:

> *and we had good times*
> *For ma[ny] garlands of violets*
> *and roses [another rip] together*
> *and [   ] you put on beside me*
> *And many garlands*
> *woven from flowers about your soft neck*
> *[   ] fashioned*
> *And with m[uch] myrrh*
> *from rich flowers [   ]*
> *and royal you rubbed your skin*
> *And on soft beds*
> *tender [   ]*
> *you would satisfy desire [   ]*
> *And there was no [   ] nothing*
> *holy nor [   ]*
> *from which [we] kept away*
> *No grove [   ]*
> *[   ] sound*

This was followed by a long series of tatters.

They were all gathered around Becky by now, reading aloud
and murmuring and exclaiming. Becky was looking at Gentian.

"That's horrible," said Gentian. "It just seems to disappear;
it looks as if somebody had ripped bits out of it in a fury."

"They probably didn't," said Becky, "the manuscript was just
awfully old. But it makes you think, doesn't it?"

Then she looked over Gentian's shoulder at Erin and cried,
"Erin! You're Jane Goodall!"

"A touch, I do confess it," said Erin gravely, but anybody
could tell she was pleased.

"It's the ponytail that does it," said Becky. "I don't think your
face is much like hers, but the ponytail and the khakis really
work. And your posture."

"She's the only reason I grew my hair this summer," said Erin. "I'm getting it cut on Monday."

Then they all milled about admiring one another and letting Becky guess Alma and Steph, which she did easily. Gentian stood back from the crowd a little, smiling to herself and waiting. Her mother came in with a pot of hot cider and a little spirit lamp to keep it warm, and some pumpkin cookies that Juniper had made. She was followed shortly by Juniper herself, in her disheveled-Hamlet costume. She did have a cloak over one shoulder, and in addition she had put on a beige leotard and tights under her costume, which would not only help keep her warm but allowed her to have her doublet, left over from a college production of her father's, well unbraced, and her stockings truly down around her ankles. She had tucked her long red hair up under a black beret. She looked more imperious than mad, more like somebody who had become disarranged while riding than somebody who had rent her garments in despair. Possibly this was how she interpreted Hamlet's character.

After her came Rosemary, in a red, white, and blue warm-up suit and a serious case of the sulks. They were each carrying one of the big canvas bags that their father used for groceries.

Gentian felt a sudden lightening of the spirits. Her sisters were going trick-or-treating. She could be with the family of her heart, with the ones she had chosen.

There was a brief mingling of both families, as Becky quickly made it clear that Rosemary was perfectly recognizable as a famous gymnast, and everybody else took up the pretence. Juniper spoke briefly to Steph, whose influence on Gentian she had often wished loudly were greater, and to Alma, probably because she still had a weakness for the Pooh books. Both her sisters departed in a flurry of admonitions from Gentian's mother, who then put on a jacket, took a space heater under one arm and a huge sack of candy under the other, and went to sit on the porch, where Gentian's father was already handing out lollipops to the younger applicants.

The Giant Ants had the use of the house for the next two hours.

"Isn't it kind of cold for your parents to sit on the porch?" said Steph.

"They sat on the porch during the Halloween blizzard," said Gentian, piling candy into bowls.

"Well, they were younger then."

"Well, *we* were younger then. I think they were just the same."

"Your dad's getting gray in his hair."

"Fine, that means he's old enough to make his own choices."

Steph desisted, biting her lip. Gentian was sorry she had been snappish. She tried to think of a peacemaking remark—"I got you salted nut rolls," or "That's a great hat"—but the first seemed self-serving and the second was so blatantly unlike her that Steph would almost certainly answer sarcastically.

"Really, they like it," she said. "You can try to talk them out of it if you want, though. We can use my room for the party. I cleaned it up in case we wanted to keep going late."

Alma put her arm through Steph's. "C'mon, let's go try. Gentian's dad is cute."

They went outside and shut the front door.

Becky said to Gentian, "I thought you didn't like T. S. Eliot?"

"I don't," said Gentian, at a loss.

"But then what—oh. Oh! Oh, unfair, you know we agreed never to repeat a costume. Oh, dear, it's an awful visual pun." Becky sat down in the nearest chair, creasing several lines of poetry into temporary lacunae, and giggled quietly to herself.

"I think Erin wins," said Gentian, "because you're the only one who guessed her."

"Did anybody guess me?"

"Actually, no, I don't think anybody did. I mean, I guess you're a poem, but I don't know whose."

"It says so right in the poem, actually."

"I'm not sure what constitutes winning, anyway," said Erin. "Maybe doing something everybody can recognize shows more skill."

"I don't know if recognition has anything to do with it at all," said Becky. "What about effort, or originality?"

"Have you got a prize?" said Erin to Gentian.

"Oh, gosh, no, I forgot all about it." She had meant to go out one day during lunch hour and find something Antlike, but somehow she had never gotten around to it.

"Well, we'd better not have a competition, then."

"Oh, I don't know. The winner could be Queen for the Night and we could all do her bidding."

"I think I'd rather not," said Erin.

"Which, be Queen or do somebody's bidding?"

"Either one."

"Well, maybe I wouldn't either, come to think of it."

"I'd rather have something friendlier, I think," said Erin, perching on the dining-room radiator. "We're all a little porcupine-like lately."

"It's puberty, I suppose," said Becky, gloomily.

Steph and Alma came back inside, shivering and giggling, and made for the fireplace. Gentian joined them, and put another log on the fire. Erin and Becky stayed in the dining room for a few moments, talking in low voices.

"Well," said Steph, looking over her shoulder at Gentian, the firelight outlining her big hat, "you were right. We couldn't budge them. Your mom recognized my costume, though."

"She tried to get Junie to dress as Amelia Bloomer a couple of years ago, when Junie was a raging feminist and it made her feel guilty about her clothes."

"Isn't she a raging feminist now?" said Alma.

"Yes, but that was when she'd just started being one. Even Junie can't rage all the time."

"Was Amelia Bloomer a raging feminist?" said Steph, settling down on the hearth rug with her tunic, the infamous short skirt that had so upset the Victorians, spread all around her and reaching to her outstretched calves.

"I think she was more cheerful than raging," said Gentian, trying to remember the biographies she had devoured in the fifth and sixth grades. "She was a suffragist, and she edited a feminist newspaper, and she delivered lectures, but she didn't rage like Elizabeth Cady Stanton raged."

"They all raged, though, as far as everybody else was concerned," said Alma.

"Well, yes, I guess so," said Steph. "The way I don't care if something has a tablespoon of cocoa in it or is solid chocolate; it's all chocolate to me. I bet feminism was all raging to them."

Becky and Erin came into the living room. Erin sat in the large armchair and Becky folded herself down next to Gentian on the loveseat. They all looked at the fire. Pounce came out of the sunroom, stretching in all directions, walked around them several times as if he were choosing a Christmas tree, and got into Becky's lap.

The silence felt peaceful and contented, but Gentian, as the host, was made twitchy by it. She wanted to leap up and make everybody eat something, or play a game, or listen to music. She wanted at least to start a scintillating conversation. She wriggled deeper into the cushions and kept quiet. If Steph or Alma got bored, they would suggest something to do.

The fire crackled.

"So," said Steph, "tell us about this Dominic."

"He lives next door," said Gentian, "we almost never see him, or anybody else either; he came out when Alma and I were shooting baskets with the soccer ball, and asked if we wanted to play soccer, so we did for a while, and then we walked Alma home." What he had said to Alma was Alma's story to tell if she wanted to, and what he had said to Gentian was nobody's business.

"What's he like?"

"Totally gorgeous," said Alma, "and maybe a few fries short of a Happy Meal."

"What do you mean?"

"Gentian knows what I mean."

Gentian looked at Alma, but with the Tigger makeup her face was unreadable. "He can't really have a normal conversation," she said cautiously. "Sometimes what he says doesn't seem very connected."

"Sounds like a lot of people I know," said Steph, "including some of the ones in this room, sometimes. Maybe he's shy. Tell us about the gorgeous part."

"Oh, you know," said Alma, "your basic haunted heroic vampire, all pale with black, black hair and a profile to die for. And he is not shy, he says what he thinks, you just don't know why he should say it when he does."

"Hasn't Junie snapped him up yet?" said Steph.

"She hasn't had a chance," said Gentian. "Really, we just about never see him."

"You could have asked him to the party."

There was a chorus of groans; Steph said that about some boy every year. Gentian glanced at Becky, who had not groaned. Becky looked blank, which just meant she didn't intend that anybody should think she had an opinion.

"Well, I did think about it," said Gentian incautiously.

"Oh, oh, Gentian's smitten!" cried Steph.

Denying that kind of accusation was futile. "I just thought we could all have a go at making his conversation make sense. But it wouldn't be a Giant Ants Halloween party if we did that."

"We could have a new kind of party another time," said Steph. "We could all invite anybody we had our eye on."

"You can have my share," said Erin tranquilly.

"Don't give me that, I've seen you talking to Brent."

"And, of course, I'd never, ever talk to anybody I didn't have my eye on."

Everybody laughed. "That's closer to true for you than for a lot of people," said Alma.

"Brent talks to me because he thinks he's not a real boy and I'm not a real girl. It's not romantic."

"It sounds terribly romantic to me," said Steph.

"That's because you believe in soulmates."

"I guess Jane Goodall wasn't a real girl either," said Gentian.

"Define your terms," said Becky, sitting up suddenly.

Everybody groaned again.

"No, I mean it."

"You always mean it," said Erin.

"What I meant," said Gentian, "was that story you told me about how she disappeared for a whole day when she was six, because somebody had told her eggs came from hens, and she didn't know where on a hen was an opening big enough for an egg to come out, so she just sat in the henhouse and watched until a hen laid an egg, and then she knew. Most girls wouldn't do that. Of course," she added, and finished in chorus with Erin's impatient, "most *people* wouldn't do that."

"Yes, exactly," said Becky. "It's the scientific temperament, that's all, and most people haven't got it."

"What I like about that story," said Alma, "is her mother. She didn't yell at her, she told her she was smart."

There was a pause, in which a number of conversations about everybody's mother's shortcomings hung in the air, but nobody felt obliged to repeat any of them. Gentian thought about her own mother, who valued intelligence, individuality, interest of almost any kind in almost anything. The best of the bunch, certainly. Which didn't mean she couldn't be terribly exasperating.

"Let's sing rounds," said Alma.

They did, and when they ran out of the ones they knew Alma taught them some new ones her study group was working with. Gentian's favorites were "Rose, rose, rose, rose, will I ever see thee wed, I will marry at thy will, sir, at thy will," even though she deplored its sentiments, and Julian of Norwich's, which ended, "All shall be well again, I know."

Gentian's parents came inside again when they were all getting silly with the tune to Frère Jacques. Steph had just made them sing, "Are you eating, are you eating, Brother John, Brother John? Pancakes in the oven, pancakes in the oven, all dried up, all dried up."

"Quite a nest of singing birds," said Gentian's father, hanging his coat up in the entry closet.

"And one croaking one," said Gentian, who was not musical.

"Oh, you make a nice background sound, like the drone on a bagpipe."

"She's perfectly fine when she doesn't let herself get distracted," said Steph indignantly.

"So are we all," said Gentian's father. "Genny, given how cold it is, I think we'd better give everybody a ride home. You've got about an hour."

Everybody protested; Gentian's mother said, "It's a school night, even if nobody at school cares what time you get there."

"Let's go up to Gentian's room and tell ghost stories," said Alma.

"Hey, I have to sleep there afterwards," said Gentian.

"You can tell them down here," said Gentian's mother. "We ancients of days will retire to the TV room."

"Well, and you have to live down here," said Alma to Gentian after her parents had taken Pounce into the sunroom and shut the door. "Would you rather do something else?"

"Let's have a seance," said Steph.

Gentian and Becky looked at each other. The question was always whether to indulge Steph in these mundane ambitions, or not. Gentian still felt guilty for snapping earlier, and Steph was her guest, after all. She knew perfectly well that the movement of the planchette was caused by the people whose hands were resting on it, caused unconsciously or consciously depending on what anybody had in mind at the time. She had moved it herself on occasion, and she and Becky had engineered a session a few years ago so successful that Rosemary still believed they had spoken to the ghost of Elizabeth Blackwell. Becky and Gentian had intended to dissuade her of the notion that the ouija board worked at all, but Rosemary refused to believe them. The thought made Gentian a little queasy now, but she could always just not make any attempt to direct matters and see what happened.

"What do you guys think?" she said.

"I guess ghosts are better than ghost stories," said Alma.

"Sure," said Erin; Becky nodded.

Gentian got the board out of the cupboard beside the fireplace, patting the Scrabble box regretfully as she did so.

They cleared all the art books, photography books, comic books, Christmas catalogs, cat-food coupons, old bus passes, stray buttons, pens, crayons, home-repair books, computer manuals, scouting manuals, and one stray ice skate off the big marble coffee table, and put the board in the middle of it. It was low enough that they could all sit around it and reach the planchette easily. Gentian built the fire up and then turned most of the lights off.

Gentian had never understood how Alma and Steph could do

this kind of thing. She had tried to discuss it with them once, and they had kindly informed her that it was a good thing she was not religious, because if she were she would be a fundamentalist and they would find her hard to put up with. Gentian was somewhat disappointed that they did not find atheism and skepticism hard to put up with, but on the whole it was just as well.

"All right," said Steph when they were all settled and had determined that Erin would write down what was spelled out to them, if anything. "Shut your eyes, clear your minds, think sensible thoughts."

Gentian smiled and tucked the smile back in before it became a laugh. Steph's brand of mysticism was wholesome, like Steph. She caught Becky's eye, but Becky did not look amused.

It was tricky to keep your fingertips lightly on the planchette, so it could move around the board easily; it made your arm hurt. Gentian was just going to suggest that they take a break to stretch when a log in the fire cracked and fell in a flurry of sparks, and the planchette jerked under their hands and began moving with such force that they all gasped.

"Geez, you guys," said Gentian under her breath.

Steph was calling out letters and Erin was writing them down. Gentian concentrated on discovering who was moving the planchette; she was not even trying to move it herself. She could not make it out; the force seemed to come now from one direction, now from another, and Steph, Alma, and Becky all continued to look startled whenever it veered suddenly and headed for the next letter.

It went on for what seemed like a very long time. The room got colder and colder, and Gentian began to feel as if the walls of the house were dense and prickling with presences that could not get in. She did not like it; it did not even make sense under the hypothesis that something supernatural was moving the planchette, because in that case, something *had* got in.

There was a tiny, distinct crack, and the planchette broke under her fingers and showered in a handful of plastic shards over the alphabet of the ouija board. Nobody said anything; they all looked at each other. The fire had died to a dim muttering glow. Gentian stood up carefully, got the poker, stirred up the fire, and piled on more wood. While she was doing that, Erin got up and turned on every light she could find.

"Good thing that wasn't glass," said Alma, shaking her fingers.

"What on earth did it say?" said Becky.

Erin sat back down in the armchair and gathered up her notes. The pages rattled a little, but her voice was firm. "I think I got the hang of it after a while," she said. "It did little pauses between words and longer ones between phrases, but sometimes it got in a hurry. Here's how I think it's divided up. It doesn't make a lot of sense, but you could probably publish it in *Tesseract*. Midday chiron."

"What?" said Alma.

"Chiron's a centaur," said Gentian.

"Oh." Alma thought. "I think my remark stands," she said. "But go on, Erin."

"Dim hydra icon."

"Ditto," said Alma.

"A hydra's a —"

"I know what a hydra is, Genny, I'm not a total illiterate."

"Sorry."

"Damn icy rid cry hid domain."

"Wow, a verb!" said Becky.

"Monarchy did I."

"Another one!"

"Day choir mind. Ro did my chain."

"It rhymes," said Becky. "It even kind of scans."

"As I said," said Erin. *"Tesseract."*

Everybody except Steph laughed. Gentian looked at her. She was as pale as somebody so olive of complexion could get, and she had tears in her eyes. "I want to apologize," she said. "This was a really bad idea."

Alma put her arm around her.

"Why?" said Erin.

"None of us moved that planchette, and certainly none of us *broke* it. And it got so cold. Didn't the rest of you feel *anything?*"

"It got cold because the fire was low," said Gentian. "But I did feel something, something, I don't know—"

"Crowded," said Becky. "As if the air were full of people, you just couldn't see them."

"I wouldn't mind if it were people," said Steph, and burst into tears.

Alma patted her on the back and everybody else looked helpless. Gentian got up after a moment, went into the kitchen, poured some tea into Steph's favorite cup with the roses, and brought it to Alma. Steph was blowing her nose by then, and she smiled when she saw the tea. "When in doubt, make tea," she said. She took the cup from Alma and drank some. "Sorry, everybody."

"I know what you mean," said Gentian, "but it just didn't take me that way."

"It felt evil," said Steph.

"It felt cold and dark," said Alma.

"So's my room when I do astronomy," said Gentian. "And the room was cold, but the feeling wasn't."

"I just felt the crowding," said Becky. "It was urgent, yes, but I don't know about evil."

Everybody looked at Erin.

"I was writing," said Erin.

"I think I want to go home," said Steph.

Gentian went and told her parents that Steph wasn't feeling well—"Did you girls give her chocolate again?" said Gentian's mother—and her father packed them all into the van and drove them away. Gentian patted Steph's shoulder as they all went out the front door, but her eyes were for Becky.

"I'll call you," said Becky.

The door shut. Gentian turned back into the living room, where every light blazed, the fire burned hugely, and Amelia Bloomer's straw hat lay forgotten on the hearth.

11

Gentian often skipped morning school on a Monday, but the day after the seance she got up early, partly to try to find Mercury with the binoculars—no luck, there was a haze on the horizon—and partly because she wanted to make sure Steph was all right. Steph was at assembly, looking much as usual, though subdued, with Alma hovering over her like an anxious guardian angel. Alma had a bit of orange Tigger paint in her hair, and Steph's hair was still frizzed and tied back. Gentian caught her afterwards in the hall and said, "Are you okay?"

"Much better," said Steph. "I'd say we have to talk, but I don't think you'd listen."

"If you want to tell me not to do any more seances, I don't think I'd object."

"Well, that's a start."

Gentian made a serious effort and managed not to point out that the whole thing had been Steph's idea. She said, "I'm sorry the party ended that way."

"It'll give us something to talk about when we're old and sedate," said Alma.

Gentian, Becky, and Erin had lunch together; Alma needed to buy her mother a birthday present and Steph's study group was going to walk the Mississippi Mile and learn about river travel.

The three of them sat inside the Burger King—it was too cold to use the courtyard—and discussed the seance.

"Has Steph been at you yet?" asked Erin, who shared a study period with Steph in the morning.

"She said she didn't see any use in talking to me," said Gentian, and realized that she sounded smug.

"She thinks we really did call up an evil presence and now we need to banish it."

"That's not how it felt," said Becky. "Erin, what *did* you feel?"

"I really was concentrating on writing stuff down, you know," said Erin, "but I had to watch Steph, to catch what she said, and what it looked like to me was a kind of pressure from all sides, as if something was trying to get in and something else was trying to keep it out."

"As if something were trying to keep the planchette from moving?"

"No, not exactly. I can't describe it any better and I might have imagined it anyway."

"I wonder what happened," said Becky. "I know Gentian and I have faked messages before, but truly, I didn't do anything."

"Neither did I," said Gentian.

"Well, I didn't have a chance to," said Erin.

"It's not Alma's style at all," said Becky, "and Steph was scared out of her wits."

"The Giant Ants have a powerful subconscious mind," said Gentian.

When Gentian got home from school, her telescope was back where it belonged. Gentian flung her books on the floor and ran to it. She did not quite hug it. She picked up the sleepy, purring Maria Mitchell from off the bed and hugged her instead. Then she sat down, crunching Murr up in her lap, and looked through the telescope, before she could think. The rosy sky of the late autumn afternoon greeted her. Not a shingle or corner of the house next door obtruded itself. Gentian danced around the room with Maria Mitchell until Murr became annoyed and hissed at her. She put her down and lay across the bed, calculating.

It got dark much earlier now than it had when the telescope was taken away, but that didn't help much because the most interesting stars rose when they rose, not because it had gotten dark, and with the buildings on the western horizon, that was still effectually at about nine in the evening. Saturn would rise in the south, where because of a park there was mostly flat open country, an hour after sunset; that was something. She had better try to get the temperature equalized in the meantime.

She turned off the radiator and opened all the windows. The wind was from the south but brisk and cold just the same. Murr leapt into the smallest window, crouched for a few minutes, and came down again, shaking her head vigorously.

"I know," Gentian told her, piling her books on her desk with an eye to starting her homework so she could devote herself to the telescope later. "Astronomers should really have long-haired cats or live in more temperate climes. We'll go to the desert one day. Or to the moon."

She took a moment to unearth the electric blanket from the back of her closet, spread it on the bed, and switch it on. Murr settled down in the middle of it, looking not much mollified.

Gentian went back to the closet, extracted her fingerless gloves, put them on, and did her homework fast before the room chilled too much. Then she turned out all the lights and left. Maria Mitchell followed her and took up residence under the bathroom radiator, and Gentian went downstairs to see if anybody had cooked supper tonight.

Everybody was off somewhere. Gentian's mother had left a note detailing who was where and when they would all be back. Her father had left a bowl of tuna salad, a bowl of hummus, and a bowl of curried rice, which interested her much more. She put together a plate and ate in the dining room with her nose in *Julius Caesar*, which her study group was still struggling through. English literature was not their strong point; then again, if she really needed help with English literature, she had Becky, so it didn't much matter.

She finished Antony's vow to let slip the dogs of war and the last of the tuna salad at the same time, and sat for a while playing with leftover grains of rice and pondering the play. It was history, so she supposed it must have happened more or less like that, but it seemed a dim-witted way to go on. All these people could talk about Rome all they liked, but they clearly had personal ends in view, and yet they did not settle things personally, they dragged a lot of other people in. Antony was supposed to be so noble, such a great character, but when he wanted to avenge his friend he said that domestic fury and fierce civil strife should cumber all the parts of Italy, and blood and destruction should be so familiar that mothers would only smile to see their babies quartered, all pity choked with custom of fell deeds.

"Bah," said Gentian, left the book lying on the table, and banged her dishes into the dishwasher. "Get a life, Antony."

As she turned to put the leftover rice away, the note caught her eye again, and she looked to see when Junie would be home. Ten o'clock. There would be time to look in Junie's diary and maybe to visit the teen romance and culture echoes and see if her own message had garnered any more notice, or any at all from her sister.

She went upstairs, accompanied by Pounce. Junie's door was shut. Gentian knocked lengthily and vigorously, just in case Junie had suffered a fit of pique and decided to stay home. Nobody answered, or moved, or threw anything at the door, so she opened it and went in, turning on the overhead light as she did so. Behind her Pounce hissed, and from under the bed somebody else made a noise halfway between a scream and a growl.

Gentian shoved the bristling Pounce gently back into the hall and shut the door. Then she got Junie's flashlight out of the drawer of the bedside table and looked under the bed. The black-and-white cat she had last seen in her father's office opened its pink mouth and made a noise that would not have disgraced a cobra.

"Sorry, kitty," said Gentian. She pulled a length of the bedspread over the place she had been looking, and stood up. The cat hissed again, somewhat less dreadfully. Gentian put the flashlight back and went into the sunroom to find the diary.

Juniper's entries were somewhat hurried and erratic. She did write almost four pages about her date with the person from the chat echo, but to Gentian's disappointment she referred to him throughout as Mr. X. Juniper was breathlessly taken with how good-looking he was, and erudite, and how gentlemanly and courtly. They had gone to a coffeehouse, eaten soup and sandwiches and scones, and heard a local folk band play. Then they had walked home slowly in the moonlight. Junie rhapsodized about the moonlight and the leaves and the wind for several, paragraphs. They had talked about *The Princess and Curdie* and about other people on the chat echo, and about how some of the conversations were going. From a couple of amusing and snarky remarks of Mr. X's recorded verbatim by Juniper, Gentian deduced that Juniper's date was not Mutant Boy or Hot Dud. It really must be somebody who didn't post many messages but read them all; that would demonstrate his good sense, certainly.

Mr. X had kissed Juniper good night at the foot of the terrace steps, in the shadow of the honeysuckle bush. Gentian knew from the diary that this was not Juniper's first kiss, but it seemed to have impressed her more than the others.

The last line of the entry was, "And then I showed him that I am an intellectual after all."

Gentian stared at this with intense frustration, and turned over several leaves to make sure the entry was not somewhere continued. Then she read rapidly through all the other entries. Juniper mooned over Mr. X. a great deal, but she never wrote down how she had shown him that she was an intellectual. It didn't matter, though. Her date was almost certainly The Light Prince.

They had another date over Thanksgiving weekend.

Gentian closed the diary and put it back into the chair cover. She shut off the light in the sunroom and came slowly back into the bedroom, tripping over cushions and dirty laundry and recovering herself absently. She sat in the desk chair and looked at the computer. Juniper must have agreed to go out with him just to prove him wrong. It didn't seem like her. She was always blathering on and on about soulmates and perfect agreement being the only basis for a romantic attachment—which, of course, didn't make much sense when you thought about it, because she loved to argue so much.

Gentian turned the computer on, got it to call the BBS, and logged on. She remembered that her password was "SCRAB-BLE," and it was still good.

On the chat echo, the discussion of whether Juniper and Crystal were the same person was still raging. Juniper had not said anything in her own person or in Crystal's; she had to write for Jason, of course, since it was he who had made the accusation. Gentian, skimming a number of uninspired messages, thought that Juniper had truly missed a bet. If anybody had accused either Juniper and Jason or Crystal and Jason of being the same person, the argument would have been much more interesting and much more germane to Juniper's alleged inquiry, because people would certainly have begun explaining why Jason could not be female or Juniper male.

Hot Dud had run Juniper and Crystal's messages through a style checker and come out with different indexes for each. He said he offered this for what it might be worth.

Gentian got out of there and looked at the culture echo. The conversation about whether Junie was an intellectual was still going on, but without the benefit of either Juniper or The Light Prince. They were engaged in a furious and not very pleasant argument about whether women should be allowed in combat. Juniper's feminism, though raging, was not of the same sort as Gentian's: Juniper believed women were different from, but either just as good as or better than men, depending on the context. The Light Prince believed women were different, but at the same time he thought they were terribly impressive for having children and completely unimpressive at much of anything else. If Junie ever brings him home, I'll have to kill him, thought Gentian. And if he thinks Junie would make a good mother, he's out of his mind. She'd have a fit if her daughter spent eight hours in the henhouse waiting for an egg.

The argument was so far advanced, and The Light Prince was making so many assumptions at once, that it would be hours of work to catch up with and dismantle all of them. Juniper could get at most of them, anyway, if she would calm down long enough to think about it.

Gentian couldn't bear it, though. She finally posted a brief message, still as Betony, recommending *The Mismeasure of Woman* "to everybody on either side of this controversy." She hoped this would make the people on the wrong side more likely to read it, if she did not say outright that it could be used to demolish their arguments; but then again, the title itself might tell them too much.

Gentian left them to it and went upstairs. I wonder how much credit that kiss is good for, she thought; I wonder if she'll still go out with him in a month if he keeps this up.

Her room was beautifully cold. Maria Mitchell hopped out of the bathtub when Gentian opened the bedroom door, walked halfway across the wooden floor picking her feet up and shaking them as if she were walking in water, and finally bolted back into the bathroom, muttering.

Gentian put on a wool sweater and her fingerless gloves, and sat down with her telescope. Saturn was up. When she had finished doting on it, she took a farewell look at the Summer Triangle, pondering Deneb, Vega, and Altair as if she had never seen them before. Since she was there, she looked long and happily at Epsilon Lyrae, which was one star to the naked eye but two to the telescope, and had the further valuable trait of being an actual binary, two stars that orbited each other, as opposed to two stars that simply seemed very close together from where the Earth happened to be. Then she teased out Zeta Lyrae, another true binary but a much tighter pair—like Becky and me, she thought, while Epsilon is more like Erin and me. Zeta Lyrae benefited from the use of averted vision to bring its fainter component better into view. That wasn't like Gentian and Becky, though; you had only to look right at them to see that they were best friends.

She moved away from the neighborhood of Vega and found, between Deneb and Altair, the third true binary in this bit of sky. Sixty-one Cygni, hanging against the powdering of the Milky Way, was two fine clear stars. Finally she looked at Albireo, at the foot of the Northern Cross: a bright yellow star with a dimmer blue one behind it. This was not a confirmed binary, but she liked it anyway.

Gentian yawned and then shivered. It was only ten o'clock,

and she would have liked to revisit the North American Nebula and the Dumbbell Nebula, but the moon was full; and, frail, faint, gray as they were on even the darkest night, with the most averted of vision, they would not be visible. Besides, she still had some homework to do. She shut away the telescope, closed the windows, and turned the radiator back on.

On Tuesday it rained. November was a notoriously cloudy month, and Gentian had never been resigned to it, even before she became an astronomer. She asked her mother at dinner about putting in some of those outlets she had done the wiring for in the attic, in preparation for helping Dominic with his science project.

"I don't think he ever is going to do it," said Rosemary. "We've never even seen him since."

"I saw him on Halloween," said Gentian, "and he said he still meant to do it, but he didn't seem to have a schedule."

Juniper dropped her fork, but when she picked it up again she was smiling. Gentian supposed she had designs on Dominic still and planned to commandeer the project.

"I've got a lot of Girl Scout stuff right up until Christmas," said Rosemary, "and I'm going winter camping in January."

"I'm very busy until Christmas too," said their mother, "but if somebody with slightly more manual dexterity than a jar of peanut butter," and she smiled across the table at their father, who rolled his eyes at her, "would like to help me, we can put in a half-dozen outlets in pretty short order next weekend."

"I can help you," said Gentian, "as long as it's not dark outside."

"I'd prefer to do it during daylight myself; it's cold in that attic."

"We astronomers get used to that," said Gentian loftily.

Rosemary laughed; Juniper sneered.

On Wednesday it was warm and hazy. On Thursday it rained. That evening the rain changed to snow, and it snowed all day on Friday. It stopped snowing on Saturday, but it was still cloudy. Gentian helped her mother put in outlets and thought about looking Dominic up in the phone book. She certainly knew his address. She called Becky instead and on Sunday afternoon they went with Steph, at Becky's suggestion, to the Art Institute and looked at jade. Steph told Gentian that if she ever wanted to talk about the seance she must call Steph at once, even in the middle of the night. Gentian was able to say truthfully that if she ever did change her mind she would certainly let Steph know right away.

On Monday afternoon while Gentian was reading Act IV of *Julius Caesar* with her study group, their teacher having decreed that if they could not schedule time out of class to get together, they must read it in class, the sun came out, but by sunset clouds were oozing over the horizon again. On Monday, when she got up at 6:15 to look at Venus and Jupiter, the sky was gray; and then after all that upper atmosphere preparation, it only sprinkled lightly in the afternoon. On Tuesday there were no clouds, but an amazing number of thick contrails created exactly the same effect. Gentian cursed Minnesota weather and any technology more modern than that necessary to make a good telescope, and pored moodily over a map of Arizona.

On Tuesday the sky was a determined dark gray. Gentian came home from school and loitered about in the front yard, looking at the grass plugs in the lawn and at the bare flower beds, both of which hid bulbs, and tried to think about spring. When those bulbs first came up, there would not be much in the way of planetary doings, but she would see the Milky Way curved along the western sky, overlaid by Perseus and Betelgeuse, with Orion and Sirius and Aldebaran and the Pleiades all between it and the horizon; and overhead would be the Big Dipper and Regulus and the Coma Berenices. She still remembered how excited she had been when she read Heinlein's short story about the blind singer Rhysling and realized that one of Rhysling's songs, "Berenice's Hair," which she had thought was just more soppy romance, might actually refer to that constellation.

When the flowers bloomed, in May, there would be not only the most dramatic partial eclipse of the sun available to watchers in these latitudes until sometime in 2017, there would also be a partial lunar eclipse later in the month. Besides that, Mercury would be visible to the naked eye, making a short backwards loop in the west-northwest between the middle of May and the middle of June. Venus and Jupiter would both be evening stars as well, and she would be able to study the constellation of Hercules, with the globular cluster M13 hiding in its keystone. When you turned the binoculars on that seeming single star, it became a small patch of fuzz; but when you gave it to the telescope it flowered into a brilliant patchy blue-and-white center surrounded by fine distinct points of light. Averted vision brought out more and finer points still.

Gentian sighed heavily. If only her parents would move to Arizona. If only they would send *her* to Arizona. Why was there no astronomical boarding school for hopeful beginners?

"Why so pale and wan, fond lover?" said Dominic just beside her.

Gentian was so startled that she didn't even jump. She simply froze. Then, as her mind processed what he had said, she blushed. I wish I were like Erin, she thought; if he said that to her she would just feel sardonic.

"It's the weather," she said.

"Very seasonable for the time of year."

"Yeah, right, and when a fellow's hungry, what he wants is some victuals," said Gentian, automatically, this being the Giant Ants' response to any statement of the extremely obvious.

Dominic had apparently not read the Narnia books, since he looked blank.

"Did you have a nice Halloween?" said Gentian; she could talk to him about it now that the party was past.

"Oh, indeed, I did such bitter business as the day would quake to look on." His cool tone was more animated than usual, enough that Gentian found herself wondering when she had last seen Mrs. Hardy. She caught herself up quickly. Dominic quoted *Hamlet* all the time; it was not to be supposed he meant to be literal about it.

"Junie went as Hamlet," she said, "with his doublet all unbraced, you know. What did you go as?"

"Myself, as I am," said Dominic.

"You look a little like Hamlet anyway, I guess."

"I am what I am."

Who isn't, thought Gentian irritably. Or maybe he was quoting Popeye. It was awfully uphill work talking to him, really; he seemed to be better at doing. She did not feel she could bring the time machine up again so soon, though, after having been snubbed the last time.

"Do you want to go see if Alma wants to play soccer?" she said desperately. She remembered in the next moment that Alma disliked Dominic, as she had every reason to do.

"Hide fox, and all after?"

"I don't know that game."

"Many are called, but few are chosen."

"It sounds like a telemarketing scheme," said Gentian, and giggled.

Dominic looked blank again. This was some small revenge for the way he usually made her feel, but she still wanted to make the most of this encounter. She could suggest they call Erin and arrange to meet her in the park, but Erin didn't like him either.

"If I got my sisters to come out," she said, "would you like to play soccer with us?"

"They have pinned the door with a silver pin and put soft pillows under my head," said Dominic, "but truly he seems to me to be equal to a god, who sitting opposite you gazes at you and hears you sweetly laughing."

Gentian was simultaneously flattered, amused, and stymied. This was not exactly what she had wanted to make of this encounter; what she wanted was to be sure of their continuing to see one another. Anybody could, she supposed, spout sweet phrases when he happened to run across her. For all she knew it was very tiring to feel equal to a god and he wouldn't want to do it often. Not to mention that people who felt equal to a god would probably be laying down the law, sooner or later. She didn't want to be sweetly laughing all the time, anyway.

"Come sit on the porch," she said, boldly, "and I'll tell you something strange that happened on Halloween."

"To hear is to obey," said Dominic, and followed her up the steps.

It was really too cold to sit on the porch, but the wisteria had not yet dropped all its leaves, which helped stop the wind, and her mother hadn't gotten around to taking in the cushions. Dominic sat very straight in one corner of the swing. Gentian curled herself into the other corner with her feet tucked under her and told him the story of the seance.

His face, however beautiful, was not very expressive, and she could not tell what he made of what she was saying. When she had finished, he still sat silent. Gentian was goaded into becoming philosophical. "I don't believe in the supernatural," she said, "but I think it's a very interesting study in psychology, that nobody moved that planchette and we all felt something strange, but not exactly the same thing. I'm not surprised Steph felt something evil, she believes in it."

"But it does move," said Dominic.

He was quoting Galileo, which made Gentian beam on him. "You mean the planchette?"

"Virtue never will be moved."

"Do you agree with Steph, then?"

"When you have eliminated the impossible, whatever remains, however improbable, must be the truth."

"You don't agree with Steph, then." Gentian stared at him. "You think one of us moved it?" She remembered the conversation at lunch. It was *not* Alma's style, she was honest and straightforward almost to a fault. Steph might, on another evening in a very different emotional atmosphere, have done it to get attention, but she had been happy with the party and genuinely horrified and frightened by the moving planchette. Becky said she hadn't moved it, so that was that; Erin couldn't have; Gentian knew she herself had not exerted any pressure on the planchette. If anybody had consciously done it, it had to be Alma.

That meant that nobody had consciously done it.

"There is a dark inscrutable workmanship," said Dominic.

Gentian almost ordered him off her porch, except that she had invited him onto it and while she knew he was accusing Alma, he had merely, on the surface, uttered another poetic non sequitur.

"I don't think so," she said.

"You are fortunate."

"No, I just have some common sense."

When he spoke, she mouthed the words along with him. "Common sense is not so common."

"I should go in soon," said Gentian, feeling that what her father called her courteous reserves were in danger of exhaustion.

"My science project still awaits," said Dominic.

"Well—we're still ready to help, I guess. When do you want to start?"

"When the days are darker," said Dominic. "Give you good night," and he stood up, bowed to her, and walked down the steps.

Gentian sat holding her knees. She had wanted him to go, but it was maddening of him to do so before she had dismissed him. He might well be a terrible pain to work with. A time machine would be very interesting, or his theory of it would; she wasn't persuaded he could really build one. But as for Dominic, she thought, Junie could have him.

Then again, it wasn't Junie he had said made him feel the equal of a god.

"Bah," said Gentian, and went inside.

12

November continued cloudy. Gentian did manage to read all her back issues of *Sky and Telescope* and to continue her ongoing study in all the miscellaneous astronomy textbooks she had been collecting from used bookstores and the university bookstores for several years. When she got to a part she didn't understand, she would either skip it or go read another book for a while and come back to the hard book later. If the other book had hard parts too, she might have to start a third. She had once been reading eight at the same time, but that was when she was only eleven and, according to the child psychology books her mother sometimes read, had not yet developed her reasoning faculty. Gentian was pretty sure she had developed a reasoning faculty at about the age of five, but she didn't say so.

On November 14 was the conjunction of Mercury, Venus, and Jupiter at 6:15 in the morning. Gentian got up for it in spite of the weather forecast. The windowpanes were wet, and when she pulled up the shade and turned her lamp on so it would shine outside, she saw flakes of snow turning in the gray air like dust motes. The house next door was dark and there was no snow on its roof. They must have installed something to heat the roof and make the snow melt. Or maybe it was just poorly insulated. That would figure. You would never be able to do astronomy from the top of that house; and now that they were heating it, her own astronomy would probably suffer from the wavering air created by that warmth.

Gentian pulled the shade down and sat on the edge of the bed. Maria Mitchell, who had curled up in the warm spot Gentian left when she got up, set up a steady purring, just in case Gentian should not have noticed that there was a cat within petting distance. Gentian rubbed her under the chin and wished she could run away to an observatory, as children used to run away to join the circus.

Since she was up, she took a bath, aided by Maria Mitchell, who sat precariously on the edge of the tub and made occasional swipes at her hair. When she was a kitten, Murr had fallen into the bath water about once a week, but she never did now.

Gentian got dressed, went halfway downstairs, came back and fed Murr, who was sitting on the damp bathroom rug looking quizzical, and went downstairs again. She put the kettle on for tea and went into the living room, where one light was on. Her father never got up early voluntarily, but sometimes he had insomnia and would get up and read for a while and then sleep until noon. The light was the one over his armchair, but the person in it was Rosemary, in a tattered white T-shirt and pink leggings, her fair hair fetchingly tangled over her brow. When Gentian stepped on the creaky board, Rosemary jumped and dropped her book.

"What's the matter?" said Gentian.

"Nothing, only you scared me."

"No, I mean what are you doing up?"

"I'm studying for my badge."

"I thought you had to do things, not study."

"You have to do things *and* study. What are *you* doing up?"

"Guess."

"Well, astronomy, only you knew it was going to be cloudy."

"Sometimes they lie."

"Genny."

"What?"

"Do you talk to Dominic a lot?"

"No, hardly ever."

"Is he going to come build a time machine in our attic?"

"Are we going to build a time machine in our attic with him. I don't know, but every time I give up on him he says something about it."

"I think he's a drug dealer."

"You what?"

"Well, I do. He doesn't go to school and he's walking around really late at night and he talked to me about drugs."

Gentian sank down onto the sofa. "When?"

"Last week when I was coming home from Girl Scouts."

"Rosemary. Did he offer to sell you something?"

"Well, no."

"Or give you something?"

"He didn't say he'd give me anything, but he talked about dull opiates and nepenthe."

Gentian started to laugh and stopped hastily; if Rosemary got affronted she would never say another word. "Rosie, I think he was just quoting poetry. He does that a lot. Did he say anything about hemlock?"

"Yes, I think so."

"Okay, look, I think that's Keats." She got her father's battered paperback of Volume II of *The Norton Anthology of English Literature* from the shelf beside the fireplace and found "Ode to a Nightingale" in it. "See, here. 'As if of hemlock I had drunk, or emptied some dull opiate to the drains.' Is that what he said?"

"I remember the drains; I thought it was weird for a drug dealer to talk about drains."

"I don't think he's a drug dealer. He's maybe not all there."

"But what about the nepenthe?"

"That's in Bulfinch's *Mythology*. It means something that'll make you forget all your cares. It is a drug, but it's in the *Odyssey*; people don't sell it on the street. It's a mythological allusion."

"Okay," said Rosemary dubiously, and then in a rush, "I was so worried!"

"Rosie, if you really think people are trying to sell you drugs on the street you should tell Mom and Dad."

"But then they wouldn't let him build the time machine and you and Junie would be mad."

"We don't want drug dealers building time machines in our attic, Rosie, honest. Or murderers or burglars either, so if you think he's any of those, just say so and we won't let him, all right?"

"You're so weird about boys," said Rosemary.

"Well, we aren't that weird."

"I think Junie is."

"Well, you shouldn't indulge her in it."

"Oh."

"Did he say anything else?"

"Um. He said rosemary is for remembrance, which I already know, and he said I had laid soft pillows under his head, which I *didn't,* they were under his butt, he sat on them, and anyway there was only one."

"Did you tell him that?"

"Yes, and he said the very hairs of my head were numbered. So I said I had to go in, and I did."

"Do you like him?"

"I don't know. He doesn't throw rocks."

"Well, that's something."

The kettle whistled, and Gentian went to make her tea.

When Erin and Gentian arrived at the Planetarium, the doors were shut and locked, and there was a sign on them that said, "Closed for repairs."

"Boneheads," said Erin. "The recording didn't say anything about that."

"Well, let's go into the library, anyway."

When they had exhausted the charms of the library, they had to find fabric for Gentian's jumper. They wandered through the fabric store, fingering everything and concocting fabulous costumes. "This'd make a cloak—really weird leggings—a broomstick skirt—a pair of particolored hose—a smoking jacket." They separated gradually, Gentian heading for the cottons and Erin going to look for buttons.

"Genny," called Erin, "come look at this."

Gentian crossed the store to her. She had a roll of fabric from the sale table. It was dazzling white, with a fluid drape and a look, too, like water.

"It's silk," said Erin. "It's cheaper than some of those cottons. We could make your blouse out of it. We could make something dashing and piratical that you could wear with jeans, too."

"I've never sewn with silk," said Gentian, fingering it. "I'd be scared to cut it."

"It's on sale," said Erin. "I'll cut it. If I mess up I'll buy you enough muslin for a shirt."

"Why is it on sale?"

"I don't know. I don't see any stains. Maybe everybody was afraid to cut it."

"Well," said Gentian, "far be it from me to refuse an adventure."

"You want to watch that tendency," said Erin as they went to find somebody to cut a length of the fabric for them. "What if it had been polka-dotted?"

"The tendency?"

"The fabric, you Becky."

"Polka-dot fabric isn't an adventure, it's a misadventure."

"I don't believe that addresses my point," said Erin, as austerely as only she could. They both laughed, but Gentian knew an answer was also required.

"I choose my friends wisely," she said, "and they don't offer me polka dots."

"Never?" said Erin.

"Well, hardly ever."

"My point exactly."

They had come to the counter, and handed the bolt over to a young woman who was sorting ribbons.

"Three yards, please," said Erin.

When they had paid for the cloth and were walking to their bus stop, Gentian said, "If you're trying to warn me about something, I wish you'd just come out and say it."

"Be careful how you choose your friends," said Erin, with a very slight curl of her lip.

Gentian, stung because she knew that Erin thought she was obtuse, said sharply, "Which friend?"

"Just watch out for polka dots," said Erin. "That's all I have to say."

Gentian caught herself sulking on the bus, and made herself stop it. In the first place Erin would take no notice whatsoever, and in the second Becky wouldn't like it, and in the third it was a special trick of Juniper's and she did not want to emulate it. She exerted herself to talk to Erin, and finally remembered that Alma had told her Steph had a Plan, to be revealed around Thanksgiving, and that she had promised to alert the troops.

"Oh, what now?" said Erin, and they had a comfortable talk about Steph and how they liked her so much but found her so exasperating.

The snow had stopped when they got off the bus. The sky was still gray, but everything glittered subtly. The air felt colder than it had while the snow was coming down. The snowy outlines of tree and roof and traffic sign looked set, as though they might endure until spring.

Gentian and Erin hurried inside and set to sewing. Gentian had never had a silk shirt before, but she liked the way the material felt. They had cut out the pattern and put the larger pieces together when the sun came out.

"Let's go outside," said Erin, standing up. "We've spent the morning in a cave and the afternoon in a sweatshop."

All the snow was gone from the treeless lawn next door, and from the roof of the house.

"Is that where Dominic lives?" said Erin.

"Yes."

"Poor him."

"Yes, isn't it an awful house?"

They ambled around the back yard, took turns pushing one another in the tire swing, and admired the lines of snow, like brushstrokes of white paint, along the windward side of every tree trunk.

"Has Steph talked to you?" said Erin.

"Not really. I mean, I see her at school and we say hello and commiserate about school stuff, but I've been kind of avoiding talking to her privately. I'm afraid she wants to sermonize at me about the seance. I do ask her about her Plan once a week or so so she won't think I'm mad at her."

"She thinks we called something awful into your house and we have to get it out again."

"And just what does her church have to say about that?"

"Not much, I'd think. Methodists, right?"

"So she's being superstitious rather than religious?"

"There's a difference?"

"Well, not from where I stand, or you either." Erin was an agnostic; Gentian was an atheist. "But—I guess I think of stuff like astrology as superstition rather than as religion. And going off the deep end like this about a ouija board, when she and Alma spent an hour telling me that only fundamentalists believe that things like that, or tarot, or whatever, work at all, let alone that they're of the Devil—if that's not superstition, what is it?"

"Fright, I'd say," said Erin.

"Do you think it was anything except us?"

"No," said Erin, "but is it any more superstitious to talk about our collective unconscious's actually moving a planchette than it is to say we called up an evil spirit?"

"I see what you mean—but yes, it is more superstitious to talk about calling up an evil spirit, because it didn't feel evil."

"It did to Steph."

"But not to Alma, and she's really more religious than Steph is."

"Yes, I know, that's weird."

Gentian remembered her conversation on the porch with Dominic. She looked towards his house, and the back door opened and he came out. He was hatless, in a billowy white shirt and black trousers, with a black leather jacket slung over his shoulders. The wind blew his hair back. He came across his lawn and across the driveway and across Gentian's back yard, without calling or waving, but making straight for them.

When he got there, he didn't speak; he did look at Gentian.

"Erin," said Gentian, "this is Dominic Hardy. Dominic, this is my friend Erin Kerr."

Neither of them acknowledged the introduction.

Erin stood looking at Dominic, her hands in the pockets of her pink denim jacket, the tail of her oversized blue T-shirt hanging down to where the knees of her jeans would have been before she cut them out with Steph's pinking shears, her nice cap of straight brown hair unruffled in the light autumn breeze. She never slouched. Steph, who still sometimes did, accused her of secretly walking about all night with the Compact Edition of the *Oxford English Dictionary* on her head. "It would explain the circles under your eyes," she said.

Uncannily, Dominic looked with interest at Erin's sharp face and said, "You've been burning the midnight oil again, I see," as if he had known her for years and meant something secretly embarrassing by the term, "burning."

Gentian gazed at him. He had never spoken to her or her sisters like that.

Erin didn't like it. She took two or three casual steps backward, as though she found the crack in the driveway uncomfortable to stand on, and looked at Gentian.

"We've been sewing," Gentian said to Dominic.

"Cambric shirts?" said Dominic.

"What *is* cambric?" said Erin, to Gentian. "I keep forgetting to look it up."

"Shirts with milk in them?" said Gentian.

Erin laughed. "That does make me think it might be muslin or something else thin and white or off-white, just like tea that's mostly milk. Let's go look it up."

Gentian had contemplated asking Dominic in for cocoa, but Erin didn't want her to. Why didn't he ever come out when she was by herself?

Dominic said to Erin, "Make me a cambric shirt, without any seams or needlework."

It was his riddle-voice. Erin said, "In some songs, it's a shirt of nettles."

"Ms. Scattergood says you *can* make cloth of nettles," said Gentian, "though I don't know why you'd want to."

"Someone might ask you to," said Dominic. He was still looking at Erin, but he flicked the end of his glance at Gentian, rather as Junie, mixing dough, would check to see that she had remembered to get the eggs out. Would averted vision show him what sort of a double they were? When nobody said anything, he looked at the ground.

Erin shifted her feet. "Well—"

Gentian was profoundly reluctant to end this encounter. She might not see Dominic again until spring. She had almost given up on the science project.

"Well," said Erin, "it's getting cold."

Dominic put a hand to the collar of his leather jacket. Oh, save it for Steph, thought Gentian. She was more lightly dressed than Erin was. It was in fact the imagined sensation of that jacket, warm from Dominic, settling over her back and shoulders that made her say, "And we still have to do all the handwork. We'd better go in."

She was afraid, for a moment, that Dominic would offer to help them. Then she hoped he would—it would put the rudeness on his side, and he looked as if he might even be good at sewing.

But he only stepped back from Erin, very much as she had stepped back from him, and produced a gesture somewhere between a nod and a bow.

It made Gentian weak in the knees, but Erin said coolly, "Nice to have met you," and walked towards the back door.

Gentian looked at Dominic. She wanted to blame Erin. Sorry I can't ask you in, but she's my guest. Sorry she was rude. Sorry you won't look at me like that.

"Don't be a stranger," she said, and before the phrase was out of her mouth she cringed at it.

Dominic looked as if he had never heard anything like it.

"Oh, I'm not," he said. "You know me." He gave her a little bow, much more like a bow than the gesture he had made for Erin, and strode back to his mean red house.

Gentian watched him, a dark, upright figure against the brilliant green of his lawn, the vile red of his house. He put his hand on the handle of the back door. Let him be locked out, she thought. She could hear the small click of the latch over the sound of the wind. He opened the door and went in. The door snicked shut behind him. The cold wind rose in the old maple tree, gathered its last few yellow leaves, and with a sudden lunge drove them past Gentian and down the driveway. Behind them the air on her neck was bitter. A sifting of snow slid down inside the collar of her sweater. Winter had come.

Gentian went back inside and shut the door. The warm, untidy red-and-white kitchen shocked her like the blast of hot air that came out of the oven when it was set at 450 degrees for piecrust. Erin was sitting at the table. She had taken off her pink jacket and laid it on top of the scattered sheets of the Sunday paper. Pounce was curled up on it, looking smug.

Erin said, "How long has *he* lived here?"

Forever, thought Gentian. "Since September," she said. She took the glass saucepan out of the dishwasher, examined it narrowly for stray corn kernels or bits of onion, and thumped it down onto the right front burner.

"Good thing he doesn't go to school," said Erin.

Gentian got the milk out of the refrigerator, considered measuring it, shrugged, and poured it into the saucepan until the level looked right. "Well, not to our school."

"That's what I meant. He can deprecate some private school all he wants. I'm just glad he's not near Steph."

So am I, thought Gentian. She opened the corner cupboard and took out the glass canister of cocoa and sugar, mixed with great ceremony by her father every Halloween. She supposed she really ought to measure this part, but since she didn't know how much milk she had, it hardly seemed sensible. She was doing this all backwards, anyway: you were supposed to put the sugar and cocoa into the pan with a little water, mix it smooth, and boil it for one minute. Then you put in the milk.

"Has anybody besides Alma met him?" said Erin. She was accustomed to saying almost everything in a pleasant and unemphatic tone, but now she spoke austerely in a manner usually reserved for adults and television.

"No, not yet," said Gentian. She found the copper saucepan

with the ounce markings where Rosemary always wrongly put it, amongst the measuring cups, and spooned the cocoa mixture into it. "You're the second," she added. She should have put the water in first. She got out a metal measuring cup and ran a quarter cup of water into it.

"Becky hasn't met him? She's over here much oftener than I am."

"He's not around much," said Gentian. She located the copper whisk that went with the saucepan; her father had put it in with the mixer attachments. She poured the water onto the cocoa and sugar and began beating them together. The rich dusty smell of the wetted cocoa made her realize how short her replies were being.

"And we don't really know him," she said.

"He acted as if he knew you," said Erin.

Gentian turned on the burner under the saucepan of milk. "Yes, I know. He does that."

"Steph would say that means he's interested."

This had occurred to Gentian also, but while she was sometimes good at fooling herself, being dishonest with Erin or Becky was not worth the comfort of self-foolery.

"He's interested in everything and everybody, then," she said. She put the pan of cocoa paste on the left front burner and turned on the flame, stirring briskly.

"The world's his oyster?" said Erin.

"And he's just waiting for the pearl to get big enough."

"Don't you like him?"

"You don't," said Gentian, stirring.

"He treated me like a girl."

"You are a girl."

"Yes?" said Erin. "So what's your point?"

The milk was steaming. Erin didn't care if it boiled, but Gentian disliked the way boiled milk behaved. She kept an eye on it. If Steph were here, she thought, I wouldn't have to say this. "Sometimes," she said, "I think you guys take feminism too far."

"Excuse me?" said Erin.

Gentian picked up the saucepan of milk, put it down hastily,

13

~

ecky called on Saturday afternoon to find out if Gentian
would mind her asking Erin to have dinner and spend the
evening with them.

"Sure," said Gentian. "We could just ask her to spend the
night, too—I don't have any super-private news."

"I thought of that, but her mother doesn't want her gone two
nights in a row."

"Okay, whatever."

"When's your lunar eclipse?"

"Sunday night. Well, Monday morning. Midnight-twenty-
six."

"Too bad it's not tonight."

"I know, it's supposed to be clear as clear and very cold. Perfect conditions."

"I meant you could bring the telescope over."

"Well, it's kind of cumbersome. And the moon'll be in the
south. I think there's a house in the way. You could have come
over here, if it was tonight."

"It'd just be a pity if it suddenly stopped working for the
eclipse."

"I know, but it's been fine."

"Well, I'll see you this evening."

Erin was already there when Gentian arrived at Becky's. Becky's parents were going out, so the three of them got to have their supper on trays in Becky's room, a great relief. Jeremy had to come eat with them—his baby-sitter wasn't there yet—but he was, if less wonderful than Becky thought him, at least a perfectly reasonable child. He wanted to recite long passages of Dr. Seuss, but Erin could match him, so they had a pleasant enough time.

"Thanks for letting me crash your party," Erin said to Gentian, when Becky had taken the trays and her brother downstairs, to keep him company until the baby-sitter arrived.

"It's okay. Is something the matter?"

"Not exactly. I did want to talk to you guys."

"You talked to me all day yesterday."

"Yes, but I wanted to talk to both of you."

"Is this Giant Ant business?"

"Yes," said Erin, in a tone that did not encourage further questions.

"Tell me what you've been reading," said Gentian.

Erin had been reading *The Origin of Species, Rock 'n' Roll Summer, Weetzie Bat, The Night Gift, The Giver, The Wonderful Flight to the Mushroom Planet,* and *Morphogenesis.*

Gentian inquired respectfully after all the ones she had not read. Before she became an astronomer, she too had read as copiously and voraciously as Erin. She had even looked in astronomical catalogs for the special filter that, according to the Mushroom Planet books, would allow her to see Basidium through a telescope. She should remember how much there was to read, the next time she was balked by the weather. The alternative seemed to be to get seriously to work on mathematics— Maria Mitchell had been a brilliant mathematician—and she did not want to face that just now. Besides, there were computers these days, which ought to make some sort of difference. She had to learn to use a camera with the telescope, too, and it seemed standard for astronomers to develop their own pictures. Well, nineteenth-century ones, anyway. Professional ones today didn't necessarily do that.

"You're woolgathering again," said Erin.

"Sorry. Is *The Night Gift* as good as *Moonflash*?"

Becky came back, having handed Jeremy over to the baby-sitter, and put in the middle of the bed a tin of chocolate-chip cookies, one of Chinese sausage rolls, and one of pancakes stuffed with spinach, potatoes, and cauliflower.

"Now," she said to Erin, "what's up?"

"Alma thinks you're avoiding her."

"Alma?" said Gentian. "I thought you were going to say Steph thought so."

"Steph knows you are and figures everything will be fine when she unveils her Plan, whatever it is."

"I'm not avoiding Alma, truly."

"She says she knows you think she moved the planchette, because you're a materialist, and if it moved one of us must have moved it, and she's the obvious candidate."

Gentian snorted. "Only Alma would think she's the obvious candidate. She doesn't know the meaning of stealth."

"She says your friend says you think she did it."

"What friend?"

"Come on, Genny."

"I'm sorry, I really don't get it."

"She said you'd know, and after yesterday I know too."

"*Dominic?*" said Gentian. "I'll kill him. I never told him anything of the sort—and I bet he didn't say anything straight out to Alma, either, he wouldn't know how. He just made her think that was what he meant."

"Is that somehow better?" said Erin.

"Not if he did it on purpose, but I don't know if he did." Of course he did, and why was she defending him?

"Does she think I think so too?" said Becky.

"She thinks you're avoiding her out of loyalty to Genny."

"I bet Dominic insinuated that, too," said Gentian. She jumped off the bed. "I'd better call Alma, right now. Can I use the phone?"

"She's at Steph's."

"Oh, great, the chance of getting through is about like the chance of discovering a comet with binoculars."

"What would a comet want with binoculars?" said Becky.

Gentian stuck out her tongue and dialed Steph's number. Sure enough, the line was busy.

"Just as well," said Gentian, returning to the bed and taking a handful of cookies. "She's so stubborn, we'll need a plan."

"I'm upset with Alma," said Becky. "Why did she believe Dominic, and why didn't she talk to us?"

"Because it's a scientific issue, or a religious one, I think," said Erin, appropriating the tin of sausage rolls. "She thinks her defense is something you won't believe in, so she's screwed."

"She's a bonehead, is what she is," said Gentian. "Her defense is that she's honest and we know it."

"But what happened on Halloween, then?"

"How should I know? I keep an open mind. I haven't got a hypothesis."

"I think you'd better, before you talk to Alma."

"Well, I haven't, what am I supposed to do, make one up?"

"I think you'd better."

"No, wait, that's silly," said Becky. "Let's just test Alma's hypothesis. No, I mean, let's test what she thinks Gentian's hypothesis is."

"What?" said Erin.

"Yes!" said Gentian. "We'll have another seance without Alma and see what happens. If the planchette goes crazy—oh, gosh, I'll have to get another one, that one's just about disintegrated—then we'll have proved she didn't have anything to do with it."

"What if nothing happens?" said Erin.

"Then we'll have to wait for next Halloween when the conditions are similar and maybe by then she won't be such a bonehead."

"I guess it's worth a try," said Erin, dubiously.

"It's not a proper controlled experiment," said Gentian, "but it will—it will—demonstrate our confidence in her, don't you think? And I bet the four of us will find something just as weird happening. I really don't have a hypothesis, but I bet it's just us, because we've been together so long and know how one another think. Thinks? What's wrong with that sentence?"

"Steph won't stand for it," said Becky, not only refusing the grammatical question but perpetrating an ambiguous response.

Gentian was sure that Becky was aware of this, and while she couldn't help smiling, she decided not to say anything about it. "Well," she said, answering what Becky meant rather than what she said, as Becky was always being asked to do by other people, "nobody thinks Steph did it, so she doesn't have to be there."

"I'm not sure that's a very scientific assertion," said Erin.

"I don't care about being scientific, I don't see how you can be about something like a ouija board anyway. I just want to make Alma stop thinking we think she did it."

"Put a big red mark on the calendar," said Erin to Becky. "Gentian has just said that she doesn't care about being scientific."

"To be accurate," said Gentian, "I don't think it applies to the situation." Her mother had said that the year her father took in a pregnant dog and offered to build a kennel in the back yard.

Gentian called Steph's house again, and got a busy signal again. They settled down to play Scrabble, trying Steph's number again between games. Erin won two, and they had to outlaw two-letter words and speak to her very sternly, but she finally entered into the spirit of things in the third and produced "androgyne," while Becky triumphed with "Alexandria." Gentian managed, even in her distraction, to uphold her dignity by spelling "Xanthippe" in the fourth game, where the best Becky could do was "settlement" and Erin tried to make "prestidigitation" and left out two syllables.

By then they had decided not to call Alma at Steph's after all because it would mean they could not conceal from Steph the plan to have another seance. Possibly Alma would not agree to concealment anyway, but she could not be expected to take a long, agitated telephone call at Steph's house and not tell her what it was all about. Gentian would call Alma tomorrow when she woke up.

Becky's parents came back, and gave Erin a ride home when they took the baby-sitter. Gentian and Becky sat and looked at one another over the Scrabble board and the empty tins.

"I think you'd better tell me about Dominic," said Becky.

Gentian had been expecting the question, and had even framed several answers. She found it remarkably hard to begin. It was like revealing something you had promised to keep a secret. She had to eat two cookies and drink half a glass of milk before she could manage. Becky sat watching her with a vaguely anxious expression.

"All right. Well. He doesn't say things straight out," said Gentian. "He uses a lot of quotations and he is the absolute king of the non sequitur. He makes my father look like the most linear thinker in the entire universe. So it's not exactly easy to figure out what he's getting at. He insinuates things, or you think he might be; and if you ask him what he means, he just quotes something else or changes the subject again."

"I can't imagine why anybody puts up with him."

He's beautiful, thought Gentian. But it wasn't just that. If he were stupid or banal rather than perplexing, he might be nice to look at but she would not continually want to talk to him. "Well," she said. "It's a little like a computer game, maybe. No, that's not what I mean. Like a puzzle. No, not that either."

"Erin's met him?"

"Yes."

"I'll ask her."

"She didn't like him."

"Do you?"

"I don't know."

"At least I know I like Micky."

"Oh, gosh, yes, you went to a movie yesterday. How was it?"

"Mixed," said Becky. "Definitely mixed. We did go see *Henry V,* and he just hated it."

"Why?"

"Well, he doesn't really like Shakespeare at all, but he thought, if you had to do Shakespeare, you shouldn't do it that way."

"I don't see what right he has to an opinion of how to stage something he doesn't like."

"Well, there is that."

"So what was the good part?"

"Well, some of that was. We had a good argument. And I liked trying to figure out how he thought. And he does have a sense of humor, and he likes Emily Dickinson, so he's not totally devoid of literary taste."

"It's the same thing," said Gentian. "It's the same reason I keep talking to Dominic. It's a puzzle. You want to know how somebody can think like that."

"That's how I feel about Steph," said Becky. "Except that we've known her longer and we know she's smart and sensitive and thoughtful and laughs when you don't expect it."

"And she won't let you down," said Gentian.

They looked at each other.

"Yes, that's what we don't know yet about Micky and Dominic."

"What else did you do?"

"We went to Lac Vien and argued about food, and then we walked along the river and argued about nature, and then we went to the movie, and my dad picked us up and we argued about how to get to Micky's house."

"Wow. I didn't know you liked to argue so much."

"I don't know if I'd like it all the time."

"Do you guys agree about anything except Emily Dickinson?"

"That we like to argue."

"Great."

"It beats never saying anything right out and upsetting Alma."

"It's not the same thing. I'm not going out with Dominic."

"Would you, if he asked?"

"How would I know he was asking?" said Gentian, and they dissolved into giggles. But as they sprawled on the bed later, listening to the soundtrack of *Henry V*, she knew that while Becky had first instituted the comparison between Micky and Dominic, she had perpetuated it, and that denying its validity was dishonest.

When they got up, she called Alma's house, but Alma was still at Steph's. Gentian packed up her belongings and went home. It was bright and extremely cold outside. People were still shoveling their walks, and some, perhaps having gone away for Thanksgiving, had not done it yet. Gentian plowed happily along, and sometimes when she struck a patch of cleared, salted pavement, she walked in the piled-up snow instead. It scattered in dense sunny sparkles, like stars in light instead of darkness. Maybe the core of the galaxy was like that.

When she got home, their half of the driveway had been shoveled and her mother was working on the front porch. The sidewalk was still pristine.

"When icicles hang by the wall," Gentian's mother sang, from inside a cloud of fine snow. It was her snow-shoveling song.

Rosemary didn't like it. She thought "Then nightly sings the staring owl" was creepy and "While greasy Joan doth keel the pot" was gross. "Well, that's why we didn't name any of you Joan," her mother would say cheerfully. "Or Marian, come to that. No sense in being teased about your nose all winter."

Gentian, having climbed the unshoveled steps, stood thinking of this and regarding her mother with the sense of disbelief and resignation her parents regularly inspired in her. Only they could possibly believe that having a name from an obscure song in Shakespeare would subject a child to more teasing than being called after a bunch of plants—especially plants nobody else was named after.

"Oh, hello," said her mother breathlessly. "I didn't see you. If you'll finish the steps and shovel the walk, I'll make tea and cinnamon toast."

"Let Daddy make it," said Gentian, taking the shovel and handing her mother her suitcase. "You always burn it."

"That's just my shorthand," said her mother. "Good Lord, what is in this, neutronium? When I say I'm going to cook something, I almost always mean I am going to ask your father to do so."

She went inside, whistling the tune of her song, and Gentian started shoveling. It was one of her most hated tasks, but she hoped to see Dominic. She thought of singing something herself, so he would know it was she out there, and not her mother, but her singing voice was not one of her more admirable attributes. She couldn't think of a suitable song, anyway.

It clouded over and began to snow again while she was working, small constant flakes from a sky the color of Mrs. Zimmerman's hair. That ought to mean she would have company soon, even if it wasn't Dominic. The Meriweathers and the Zimmermans had always shared the shoveling of the vacant lot's sidewalk, and Mrs. Zimmerman didn't believe in putting off unpleasant tasks.

Gentian shoveled her way down the remaining porch steps, the short flat walk, the long flight of terrace steps, in a glow of virtue and a cloud of small sparkles. When she got to the bottom of the steps and paused for breath she found Mrs. Zimmerman standing, shovel in hand, regarding the clean bare sidewalk in front of the new house.

"You did all of it!" cried Gentian.

"No," said Mrs. Zimmerman, consideringly.

"They did it?"

"No. Look at it, Gentian."

Gentian looked. From the far side of the driveway the Meriweathers now shared with the Hardys to the place where Mrs. Zimmerman's sedums brushed the sidewalk, the concrete in front of the new house was not only clear of snow, but dry.

"Eugh," said Gentian. "Did they spread some new awful chemical on it?"

"They didn't do anything," said Mrs. Zimmerman. "I've been out here, or in the yard, all day."

Gentian stood and squinted at the falling snow. The flakes were so tiny that it was hard to follow a single one to its resting place. She half expected many things: to see the snow all deflected from the sidewalk to the grass on either side; to see the flakes land and sizzle instantly like water on a griddle; to see the snow blown aside. She saw none of these. The snow fell, but it did not reach the sidewalk.

"That's very weird," she said.

"I'd give a year's good compost," said Mrs. Zimmerman, "to know that woman's first name."

"*Would* you?" said Gentian, whose compost piles never

heated up, so that she had to wait three years for anybody else's one-year compost. Then, with a jolt, she thought, But I haven't got a garden any more. There's nowhere to put the compost. She glared at the Hardys' snow-covered lawn. No tomatoes, no basil, no bitter-juiced gentian, bluer than anybody's eyes; no snow-drops and no chrysanthemums. Why didn't it bother me before, she thought, what was I paying attention to instead? Astronomy, sure, but they always fit together. The thing closest to hand and the thing farthest away, Mom said. Stay up all night stargazing, weed before it gets hot, go to bed.

Dominic, I've been paying attention to Dominic. Only he's a lot more like a star than like a plant. She grinned, saw that Mrs. Zimmerman was looking at her curiously, and said hastily, "Because I think I can find out. I mean, if you don't want to just ask her."

"I don't, and neither do you," said Mrs. Zimmerman.

Gentian thought of the drab medium-sized woman in the shapeless clothes, her hesitancies, her conventionalities. She looked at Mrs. Zimmerman, all six foot four of her, in a long red down coat and a black scarf, her dark gray hair spangled with snow.

"Don't you?"

"No compost for just asking her," said Mrs. Zimmerman. "Now, let's finish your walk, shall we?"

Gentian went on thinking on how Dominic could have distracted her from the disappearance of her garden. A daytime star, she thought, like a supernova. Maybe I should try looking at him with averted vision. Only why, when he's so bright? She tossed a shovelful of snow onto the growing pile and giggled. Why, because he might be associated with dim companions, or with a nebulosity. His mother was dim enough, his father less noticeable than the nebulae.

When they had finished shoveling, Gentian invited Mrs. Zimmerman in for the promised tea and cinnamon toast. Her mother was nowhere to be seen. Junie was making rum balls in the kitchen, and glared ferociously. She would require careful handling. Gentian was still choosing both her words and her overall strategy, while Mrs. Zimmerman took her boots off, when her father came into the kitchen.

"That was fast," he said.

"The Hardy's walk didn't need shoveling," said Mrs. Zimmerman, shaking snow off her braid onto the rag rug that Rosemary had made in Girl Scouts.

"Didn't it?" said her father.

Gentian watched their eyes meet.

"Look," said Juniper, with suppressed violence. "I'm trying to work in here."

"Come into my parlor," said Gentian's father to Gentian. "We can make Rosemary some cocoa in the microwave." He always called Mrs. Zimmerman Rosemary, which caused a lot of confusion and made his daughter Rosemary mopey.

Gentian was annoyed that Juniper could drive away three people, two of whom were grownups, a different two of whom had just done some real work outside, but she followed obediently. She hoped her father and Mrs. Zimmerman would go on talking about the Hardys' sidewalk.

Her father's office was a sunroom originally intended as a breakfast room. It had four windows overlooking the back yard and another two facing the sharp drop into the Mallorys' side yard. It was painted bright yellow, with dazzling white trim, somewhat marred by fingerprints and some smudges where Pounce periodically rubbed his whiskers.

Her father had two filing cabinets, two black metal bookcases, another of Rosie's rag rugs, an old chrome-and-formica kitchen table with a computer on it, and a spindly, improbable-looking, insanely comfortable office chair. He gave this to Mrs. Zimmerman. Gentian, as usual, sat on the rug. It was red, green, yellow, black, and white, and she liked to find shapes in it.

Her father busied himself with the cocoa. Pounce slid out from under the computer table and climbed onto Gentian's lap. Mrs. Zimmerman took her father's copy of Strunk and White from his desk and opened it seemingly at random.

"Well, R. A.," said Gentian's father, shutting the door of the microwave on the cocoa and starting the oven humming, "how goes the neighborhood?"

"Still abuzz," said Mrs. Zimmerman. "*Is* there a Mr. Hardy? Well, you never see him. She's so closed, don't you think? And always borrowing strange tools."

"Well, that last makes sense," said Gentian's father, sitting on one of his filing cabinets. "They have ordinary tools; they just need to borrow the odd ones."

"Nobody with a brand-new house should need a snake, a fish, and a punch-down tool all within three months."

"It's an ill-built brand-new house," said Gentian's father.

The microwave chimed, and he took the mugs out one by one, peered at them, stirred each with an old red enameled chopstick, and handed them around.

"Well," said Mrs. Zimmerman, "what can you expect from something that went up so fast?"

Gentian's father lifted his head from blowing on his cocoa. He looked like Maria Mitchell about to pounce on a dustball.

"No," said Mrs. Zimmerman, just as if he had spoken. "Ira doesn't think so either."

"No," said Gentian's father. "Neither does Kate."

"Odd," said Mrs. Zimmerman.

"Only if it were a matter of perception."

"It *is* a matter of perception."

Gentian had been looking at Pounce's ears when the shape of the conversation changed. Now she had to go on looking at Pounce, lest they remember she was there and change the subject.

Pounce's ears were very pink and clean on the inside and covered with short dense white fur on the outside. Her father had found him hiding in the empty rabbit hutch on a cold day in February, so they had named him after Junie's first rabbit, an ill-tempered and ill-fated creature who challenged a German shepherd to a duel with horrible, if predictable, results. Junie had seemed largely unperturbed, but Rosie, who was four at the time, still had nightmares about it.

Pounce began to purr. Neither adult in the room had said anything more. Gentian did not think it was because they had suddenly remembered her presence. She could feel them arguing without arguing. Her parents did that sometimes too. Rosie was very good at it. Junie never did it; Junie was an overt arguer par excellence.

"Well," said Mrs. Zimmerman at last.

If her mother had said that, it would have meant something like, This is too pleasant a setting for an argument, I'll get back to you later, which Rosemary had in fact once heard her say not to their father but to her visiting roommate from college.

When Mrs. Zimmerman said it, it seemed to mean something more like, Yes, all right, the situation is more complicated than I make it sound. Steph said that a lot. She had to, because she was so fond of sweeping pronouncements that nobody would let her get away with.

Gentian's father said peaceably, "There's perception and perception."

"Kate's," said Mrs. Zimmerman, "is more like interception."

Gentian blinked at her; why make peace and then insult her mother for no reason? Her father, however, laughed, and asked Gentian if her cocoa was bitter enough.

"It's fine," said Gentian. She fixed Mrs. Zimmerman with the glare she used on Steph. "Tell him about the sidewalk."

"He saw it, Gentian," said Mrs. Zimmerman.

Gentian looked at her in disbelief. She sounded as parental as any parent, much worse than either of Gentian's own, a lot more like Steph's. That utterly dismissive use of one's name was almost more pedagogical than parental—the way teachers at her other schools had talked to her before she got into the open school, where they assumed you were human even after you filled the counselor's office with balloons.

Mrs. Zimmerman's tone of voice was, in short, odious, and completely unlike anything in their long friendship.

Mrs. Zimmerman seemed oblivious to this, but Gentian's father looked as though he might have noticed. "I saw that the sidewalk was dry," he said to Gentian, "but not what happened to the snow."

"Nothing happened to it," said Gentian. "It just wasn't there."

"Maxwell's demon," said Gentian's father.

"Pity they can't patent it," said Mrs. Zimmerman.

"It would cost too much," said Gentian's father.

Gentian knew how much a patent search would cost because Erin had investigated the matter when she thought she had invented a new kind of bicycle pump; but she did not think her father was talking about money.

After she had drunk her cocoa and ascertained that the two adults were going to talk about politics, Gentian went into the kitchen and made cinnamon toast. She had planned to do so whether Junie was there or not, but Junie had departed, leaving a smell of rum and spices and four large tins with threatening notes stuck to them. Gentian took her toast upstairs and called Alma's number, and after she had gone through two furry-voiced brothers, one of whom regaled her with the news that his hamster had just had babies and the other of whom yelled, "Alma! Telephone! It's Gentian!" with the regularity of a foghorn while apparently standing right next to the owner of the hamster, Alma shooed them away and said, "Genny?"

"Yes, it's me."

"You aren't mad?"

"Yes, I am, you dodo, I'm mad you thought for a moment we'd believe you moved the planchette."

"But nothing else could have happened that you'd believe."

"I believe I don't *know* what happened!"

"Do you?"

"What the hell has your church been telling you about scientists *now?*"

"Nothing, and don't swear at me. It was Dominic."

"And what did *he* say?"

"Praised you to the skies," said Alma, with an unaccustomed note of irony. "Said how you were so objective and clear-minded and logical and so good at eliminating wrong answers."

Gentian felt slightly winded. She bit her lip hard on an impulse to say, "He *did?*" so as to make Alma say it all over again, or say more. "So," she said, and had to clear her throat, "so, he didn't say I thought you did it, you just deduced he meant that?"

"He also said," said Alma, more ironically, "that you were so

fucking honest yourself you couldn't forgive dishonesty in anybody else, even in your very dearest friends."

"He didn't say *fucking.*"

"Nope. Too much of a gentleman, I'm sure."

"But, well, so what? Why did you believe him?"

"Come on, Gentian. You know what he's like. What he gave
me to understand was that you had talked to him about it all and
he was providing a friendly warning."

"Well, I didn't, and I wasn't. Well, I mean, I did tell him about
it, but I didn't say you did it, because you didn't."

"Oh, that's real logical."

"Listen, God damn it."

"Don't blaspheme at me."

"Then don't be an idiot. Look. Becky and Erin and I are going
to do a control experiment. We're going to have another seance
without you."

"And without Steph."

"Well, yeah, she wouldn't come, and it'd be nice if you didn't
tell her."

"I don't know if I can promise that."

"Well, think about it."

"What good will another seance do, anyway?"

"I think," said Gentian, goaded into claiming a hypothesis
despite herself, "that it was just the mental influence of the Giant
Ants that moved the planchette, so the three of us having another
seance should make it happen again, and you won't be there,
and then you'll be cleared. Not that we think you need clearing,
but it's the only way to persuade you."

"It might work better than swearing at me."

"I take it that means, not very well."

"I didn't feel what Steph felt," said Alma, "but I don't think
seances are an especially hot idea. I don't mean anything supernatural even. But look how much trouble this one's caused."

"Only because you're a dodo."

"Yeah, right."

"Okay, I'm sorry. Only because Dominic said a lot of ambiguous things to you and you acted like a dodo about it." Only,

she thought suddenly, because I talked to Dominic and gave him something to talk to Alma about. "When did he talk to you, anyway?"

"I was putting salt on the sidewalk Thanksgiving Day and he just walked up to me."

"Huh."

"I wish you wouldn't talk to him about me," said Alma. "If you have to talk to him."

"Okay, I won't. But don't you listen to him that way, either. I don't think he could have made you think we were accusing you if you weren't already worried."

"See, that's just it, he made me worried, when he talked to me before."

"But *why?* Who is he anyway? Why do you care what he thinks?"

"I think he's crazy," said Alma.

When she had hung up the phone, Gentian tried to settle down to her homework, while keeping a wary eye on the weather. She dispatched her history and her algebra and then sat looking at *Julius Caesar.* She could ask her family to read Act IV, but they might not like having missed Act III. Her study group would read it tomorrow, laboring and stumbling and, for a change, giggling; but she wanted to look at it by herself first.

She had a bit of Act III left, having quit in disgust when Antony became so bloodthirsty. She found the place and read on. At the beginning of Act IV, the Plebians—people like me, thought Gentian, moodily, who are going to have to work for a living—demanded to be satisfied about Caesar's death. Brutus and Cassius both agreed to speak to them. Brutus made a very pretty speech; Gentian made a note to show it to Becky, for its sentences if not for its sentiment. Its sentiment seemed to be that Caesar was wonderful but too dangerous to live.

Gentian sat thinking about it. If I hadn't gotten so mad at Antony for *his* last speech, about the dogs of war, she thought, I'd like this a lot. It's very reasonable. On the surface it's not a bit like Antony. But this last part, who is so base that would be a bondman, who is so vile, that would not love his country—

implying that if you think they shouldn't have killed Caesar, you must be a bondman and not love your country—that's stirring them up too, just like Antony wanted to. Well, not just like; Brutus doesn't want them rampaging all over the place murdering people's babies. But still.

Brutus ended, "As I slew my best lover for the good of Rome, I have the same dagger for myself, when it shall please my country to need my death."

This sat a little better with Gentian. The Plebians liked it a lot, yelling that Brutus should live, and be brought with triumph home, and be given a statue with his ancestors, and be proclaimed Caesar.

"Whew," said Gentian.

Brutus persuaded them to let him go home alone, and to stay and listen to Antony. They let him go, and grumbled about how it was certain that Caesar was a tyrant, and that they were well rid of him, and that Antony had better not speak any harm of Brutus.

Antony then gave his famous speech. Gentian was familiar with bits and pieces of it, and had heard people in speech class declaim the entire thing. In context, it was really wicked. He did point out a few facts: that Caesar had brought home captives to fill Rome's coffers (and who cares how they felt about it? thought Gentian), that he had wept when the poor cried (and a fat lot of good that did them, thought Gentian), and that he had refused the crown thrice. Now, that was true, it had happened earlier in the play. Antony added, after each fact, "But Brutus says that Caesar was ambitious; and Brutus is an honorable man."

It impressed the Plebians tremendously. They decided that Caesar had not been ambitious after all, and that Antony was the noblest man in Rome.

The crowd demanded that he read them Caesar's will. He explained that he couldn't because it would inflame them. They demanded again. Antony said he feared he had wronged the honorable men who slew Caesar, and the crowd cried that those men were traitors and demanded again to hear the will. Antony did not read the will, but gave a long speech about Caesar's mantle and whose dagger had stabbed where and how what really killed Caesar was not the knives but the knowledge that Brutus had betrayed him.

> *"Oh, what a fall was there, my countrymen! Then I, and you, and all of us fell down, Whilst bloody treason flourished over us."*

"Wow," said Gentian. She remembered reading Act I with her family, and Cassius saying, "No, Caesar hath it not, but you and I, and honest Casca, we have the falling-sickness."

Caesar had had it, though, in both senses. I bet everybody in this play has it, thought Gentian. I don't think I want to read the rest of this.

She had better finish Act IV, at least, or she wouldn't understand it when they read it tomorrow. The study group's reading aloud did not, as a rule, aid understanding; it was more likely to cloud it. She read on. Antony ended his speech by whipping the mantle away and showing the body of Caesar. The crowd moved from, "Oh piteous spectacle!" to "We will be revenged!" in short order, and yelled, "Seek! Burn! Fire! Kill! Slay!" The dogs of war, thought Gentian.

Antony told them not to let him stir them up to mutiny, and added that he couldn't do it, anyway, because he was not eloquent as Brutus was, but that if he were Brutus, he would certainly move the very stones of Rome to rise and mutiny.

Gentian sat back for a moment, feeling slightly dizzy. What a hypocrite, she thought. The crowd, of course, said it would mutiny, and just to make sure he read them Caesar's will after all. They scattered shouting about burning and tearing things up, and Antony said, "Now let it work."

In the last scene, a crowd killed Cinna the poet because he had the same name as one of the conspirators.

"Bleah," said Gentian, in heartfelt tones, and shut the book smartly. Maybe *Romeo and Juliet* would have been better after all.

By evening a pall of low cloud had settled over everything and was emitting a maddening mist of light snow. Gentian stayed up just in case, and might have seen a dull glow behind the clouds where the moon was, but it was hopeless.

"I *am* going to live on the moon," she said to Maria Mitchell. Then she laughed, because of course you could not study an eclipse of the moon while you were on the moon itself.

14

December began gloomily. On the first, there was freezing drizzle, cheating Gentian out of Saturn and a good look at the Winter Triangle. She and Steph agreed to cancel their shopping trip and try again later in the week. On the second, it grew very cold and perfectly calm, fine stargazing weather had it not been accompanied by an invasion of cloud that grew lower and denser day by day. On the third of December, Gentian and Steph had an argument at lunch about whether to brave the weather and shop downtown, or go to the Mall of America, generally referred to by Gentian's father and all the Giant Ants as the Mall of Anomie.

"There's lots of cool stuff there," said Steph, "and it's warm and it's easy to get to on the bus."

"I hate it," said Gentian. "It gives me a kind of gigantic claustrophobia. It's too big. What if there were a fire or an earthquake?"

"I'll take care of you," said Step comfortingly.

Gentian hated being humored, but she decided to get the shopping over with. They met in the awful, towering, echoing mall at eleven on Saturday morning—it was still cloudy—outside the Pottery Barn, since Steph knew of several things she wanted to buy there.

Gentian had forgotten to bathe again, and was only reminded of the fact when she began nervously twisting her hair around one finger and realized how greasy the hair was and how grimy the finger. She did not often find herself alone with Steph, and now she was going to have to feel grubby too. When Steph showed up with her hair shining and curling all down her back, in white corduroy pants and a huge red sweater and red half-boots, for heaven's sake, Gentian felt not only grubby but resentful.

"Now show me your list," said Steph, "in case I become inspired."

"I haven't got one," said Gentian. "It's just my family and the Giant Ants." She wondered what Dominic would do if she gave him a present. Since she had no idea what he might like, it hardly mattered.

She trailed Steph into the store, ducking glittering ribbons and shying away from precarious displays of fragile glassware and transparent Christmas-tree ornaments. Gentian had a very steady hand for a telescope, but in a store she became like her father. She dropped things, sometimes without even picking them up first. She cast a revolted glance at three simpering tissue-paper angels hung by their heads from a green-and-gold rope, and followed Steph into the back of the store.

Steph was having a saleswoman show her a set of little golden spoons with handles shaped like crooked twigs. "These are for my aunt," she said. "I wondered if Juniper might like them."

"She probably would; they could go with the tea set she never uses. But I'm not sure I like her enough to get her a set."

"You could just get her two, or go in with Rosemary."

"I'll get her two. The only person she ever has to tea is Sarah, and anyway it'll give her something to complain about."

"Now," said Steph, "here's the other reason I thought we should come here." She showed Gentian a set of bins full of assorted wooden and papier-mâché Christmas-tree ornaments. Many of them were standard: Santa Claus, angel, wrapped present, so-called star, camel, candy cane. But there were also small sailing ships; bright houses and castles; books closed and opened, including one with tiny but readable writing, which, when Gentian read it, regrettably turned out to be a verse from "Rudolph the Red-Nosed Reindeer"; rolltop desks, quill pens, typewriters; and, as Steph demonstrated, diving to the bottom of the last bin and emerging triumphant, telescopes.

"Oh," said Gentian, and then, "but I can't get something for myself."

"I thought you could give one to each of us, to remind us of you," said Steph.

"You won't be very surprised then, will you?"

"I don't care."

"I'd get you all something else, too, anyway," said Gentian after a moment. "I don't know, Steph, it seems a little egoistic."

"Well, think about it," said Steph. "There are lots more stores. And I have to get Caitlin some napkins." She wandered away towards the middle of the store, and Gentian went on sifting absently through the ornaments.

"For loveliness," said a familiar voice next to her, "needs not the foreign aid of ornament, but is when unadorned adorned the most."

Gentian dropped the ship she was looking at and turned. Yes, it was Dominic, in black for a change. In her unkempt condition, any remark about loveliness and adornment sat particularly ill with her.

"I can just see telling my mother that when she wants us to help trim the tree," she said. "Are you Christmas shopping?" Oh, Lord, she thought, maybe he's Jewish.

"I would not spend another such a night were it to buy a world of happy days."

Gentian looked at him dubiously. She thought about asking outright and decided not to. The whole atmosphere of his conversation made such questions difficult, and he had snubbed at least one direct personal inquiry from her.

"Gentian," said Steph, appearing on her other side, "come and tell me if Becky would like one of these mugs."

"Steph," said Gentian, "this is Dominic Hardy. Dominic, this is my friend Stephanie Thornton."

"Every noble crown is of thorns," said Dominic.

There's no need to be ironic, thought Gentian. But Steph said, "Yes, I know, it's a silly name. My parents swear they didn't know. But they have a very strange sense of humor, really, and people in church look at them oddly sometimes when they hear my name. My middle name's Rosa, so that's no better, though it does raise fewer eyebrows in church."

"No rose that in a garden ever grew," said Dominic.

Just because she's got on a little makeup, thought Gentian indignantly. But Steph said, "Yes, it is nice to have a name with some resonance, with some history in it."

Gentian looked at her, amazed.

Dominic said, "History, that excitable and lying old lady."

"Don't you like your name, then?" said Steph.

"Chance may crown me without my stir."

"Let's see, Dominic means belonging to the Lord, doesn't it? Not that we all don't anyway."

Dominic, being pale already, could not really be said to have lost color in his face. But his hair and brows and eyes looked blacker somehow, and his lips redder. "I am the cat who walks by himself," he said, "and all places are alike to me."

"Your last name's all right, then."

"A mind not to be changed by place or time," said Dominic. He sounded so implacable that Gentian took Steph's arm.

"Sorry," said Steph. "We've got an awful lot of shopping to do, so I'm going to take Gentian away now. I hope yours goes well."

"Til it be done, whate'er my woes, my haps are yet begun."

"Nice to meet you," said Steph, and towed Gentian towards the racks of mugs.

"I'm sorry he was so rude," said Gentian.

"What? He was adorable. A little like a crossword puzzle, though."

"He said you were no rose that in a garden ever grew."

"Gentian. *Really.* That's a line from a poem by Millay. Becky loves it. It's about the effect of literature on life and love."

"Oh."

"Now, would Becky like this? I thought she could drink tea out of it while she composed her odes."

Becky had never composed an ode in her life, but the mug was beautiful, large and iridescent, with a handle you could actually get your fingers through. "I think she would," said Gentian.

They found presents for all the Giant Ants and for Gentian's mother, but not for the rest of her family. Gentian ran out of tolerance for the mall at about two o'clock and took the bus home, leaving Steph to wander happily for the rest of the day and meet her sister for dinner and a movie.

Saturday went on being cloudy. On Sunday there was a snowstorm in northeastern Minnesota, but in the city it just went on being cloudier. Gentian's entire family was home all weekend, which meant that using the computer or reading Junie's diary was impossible. They were all rather fractious, except for Rosemary, who was happily making paper chains for Christmas and leaving strips of paper and pasty bits all over everything. Gentian retreated upstairs and grimly tried to read a very dry book about celestial mechanics, wishing it had less to do with mathematics and more to do with repairing stars. Maria Mitchell had occasionally had trouble with calculations, but not with theory, merely with the fact that in the absence of a computer or even a calculator, some astronomical calculations were maddening and took forever.

When celestial mechanics palled, she tried to fathom what Dominic had been saying, or what Steph had thought he was saying. That remark about not being changed by place or time did not bode well for the time machine. And maybe it was just as well.

"He said," she remarked to Murr, who was sitting on her knee and occasionally chewing gently on the corner of the textbook, "that he was the cat who walked by himself. But he's nothing like you."

On Sunday night it snowed and snowed, which was pleasant in itself and also hopeful; and in fact Monday was almost viciously clear and sunny. Gentian ran home to make sure the telescope was still working, and cried, "Hell, hell, hell!" as the red side of the house next door slapped her in the eyes. She dived for the phone and called Becky.

"Come over here and make this telescope work!"

"I couldn't fix it last—"

"No, I mean, just *be* here and see if that helps."

"We never did test that out, did we?" said Becky thoughtfully. "I was too flummoxed by your session with the binoculars."

"Bring your homework if you want, and I'll find you something to eat. But I want to see Saturn; it won't be an evening star much longer."

Becky arrived at six o'clock, clutching the journal she had to keep for Creative Writing. Gentian shooed her up the stairs, handing her a peanut-butter sandwich on the way. Becky sat down and peered through the eyepiece of the telescope. "Looks fine to me." She got out of the way fast.

It was fine. In the south-southeast, Saturn burned and wavered amid the stars of Capricorn, its rings bulging it out on either side. She had missed the last time the rings were wide open; she had not had a telescope then. They would be edge-on in 1995 and almost impossible to see. The first time Galileo saw Saturn with its rings edge-on, after originally observing them in about the same position she saw now, he had asked whether Saturn had in fact, as in legend, devoured its own children. Gentian looked forward to seeing what Galileo had seen—and more, since she had a considerably better telescope. She went on looking until she saw a moon, and then another. Then she blinked. Saturn was usually fairly sedate, but just now the northern belts were oddly broken up and spotty. She would have to remember to see if *Sky and Telescope* said anything about this: if she had observed it, others had as well.

She said, "Becky, do you want to look at Saturn? You can see the rings and a moon or two, and it's a little more agitated than usual."

"Sure," said Becky, and took Gentian's place at the telescope. "That's a nice color," she said. "I like that rich yellow and the way it goes greener at the poles. Is that real or some kind of telescopic artifact?"

"Mostly real, I think. Do you see the moons?"

"No, but I see the rings—oh, wow, there, that must be a moon. You know, this is really extremely cool, but I couldn't stand all the finicky bits. And how in the world does anybody make any observations when it jumps around like that?"

"Well, you can look at stuff I've finicked up whenever you like. Move a minute and I'll find you Beta Cygni. It's called Albireo as a single star, but it's really a double." She found Deneb and moved down the Northern Cross to its foot. Albireo was a large brilliant gold star accompanied by a clear and vivid blue one, with behind them not blackness but the profound and myriad glitter of the Cygnus Star Cloud. A lot of the colors described in astronomy books were easier to imagine than to see, but Albireo was an abiding surprise; it was always brighter and more itself than she remembered. She focused the eyepiece and then scrupulously displaced the focus just a little, as recommended for the best color value, and gave her position at the telescope to Becky.

Becky sat quite still for so long that Gentian got fidgety, calmed herself, and took out her history homework.

"That is the most amazing thing," said Becky. "Here, take back your magical instrument. I have to write something down."

She made a dive at her journal and began scribbling vigorously. Gentian went back to the telescope and gloried in the Cygnus Star Cloud for a while; then she began ranging upwards until she came to Andromeda and M31, the Andromeda Galaxy, a ghostly canted oval with a splotch of companion galaxy above and another below it. It was 2.3 million light years away, the farthest object discernible by the naked eye. Gentian gazed and gazed at its millions of stars all crowded into a disk with, if you used averted vision, a few half seen, half imagined spirals of dark gas and dust for flourish, tracking it as the Earth moved, and wondered if anybody were looking back at her.

She sat away from the telescope, blinking. Becky was still writing, less furiously. It was getting late.

"Should I see if my father will take you home?"

"Oh, are you back?" said Becky. "No, I called my mom and she'll come get me. You need to stay here and see if the telescope goes on working as I recede from it."

"This is so absurd," said Gentian, "but I'll watch, and let you know."

"Thank you for the double star," said Becky.

"Can I see?"

"Not yet, it needs to compost a little. Maybe next week."

When Rosemary came up to say Becky's mother was there, Gentian found Orion and settled on Alpha Orionis, Betelgeuse, whose name amused her inordinately. It was said to be a corruption of the Arabic for "the armpit of the Giant." It was a fine deep orange, and if she got bored with it, the stars of Orion's belt and Rigel were close by for distraction.

She did not get bored. She was still looking at Betelgeuse when the telephone rang. She had put it into her lap, much to the annoyance of Maria Mitchell, and she answered it without taking her eyes from the star.

"Well?" said Becky.

"All systems go."

"Well, I guess really it's a relief."

"It's a mystery to me, but thanks."

Gentian stayed up stargazing until her eyes burned and ached and she could not keep them open. When she awoke clearly at eight the next morning, she was glad to be bleary: the day was gray and featureless and settled-looking. It was also warmer, but that was no consolation.

At least Steph had promised to unveil her Plan today at lunch. Gentian was mildly intrigued and mildly worried about it, and just as pleased not to be kept in suspense any longer.

Neither Erin nor Alma could afford even fast food this week, and nobody else could afford to treat them. They had all been Christmas shopping. So they pounced on a table for four in a corner of the school cafeteria, plunked down their brown bags, and snagged a fifth chair from the hallway.

Everybody looked expectantly at Steph, who was wearing a yellow ribbon in her hair and a loose yellow dress with a snowflake print. She said simply, "I want us to take over this year's Shakespeare production."

"Oh, well, that's easy," said Erin. "What, maybe four or five assassinations and a bit of brainwashing ought to do it."

"They're doing *Twelfth Night,*" said Steph, "and all the seniors want to work on Caitlin's adaptation of *The Giver.* So I think we all have a chance."

"Only if we can act," said Becky.

"You," said Steph, "can be Maria. Alma can be Olivia. Gentian can be Antonio. Erin can be Viola."

They gazed at her, except for Gentian, who looked at Becky. Gentian had not been able to finish *Twelfth Night,* but the notes and the remarks of her teacher had made it clear that Maria was a plum of a part; she thought up half the plot and was funny besides. Becky caught her eye and made a shrugging motion, as if Mrs. Clancy had complimented the one weak line in a poem of hers.

"I bet they just had a *plenitude* of black duchesses in Elizabethan England," said Alma.

"It's not set in—" said Steph.

"About as many as they had striking clocks in Rome," said Erin. "That wouldn't bother Shakespeare a bit. But Steph, has it occurred to you that however good a boy I make, I can't do the part unless I'm a twin separated at birth and you find the other one fast?"

"Just undergo meiosis," said Steph.

"Mitosis," said Erin, impatiently.

"Whatever."

"Steph," said Erin, "if I said Lancastrian and you said Yorkist and I said Whatever, you would never let me forget it."

"Yes, all right, I'm sorry," said Steph. "You can walk home with me this afternoon and pound it all into my head, though I doubt it's half as complicated as the Wars of the Roses. But right *now* I have a *plan.*"

"Who are you going to play?" said Alma.

"Malvolio," said Steph.

They all gazed at her. Gentian did try to catch Becky's eye, but Becky was looking at Steph judiciously, as she had looked at the telescope.

"Go on," said Erin. "Davy Boyajian's had that one sewn up since the day he was born."

"Davy Boyajian," said Steph, "is playing the lead in his own original play."

"Tyler Keough—"

"Is going out for wrestling out of pique at not getting the lead in *Fiorello.*"

"Huh," said Alma. "Maybe. Now, about Olivia."

"Olivia must have a nice voice," said Steph, "because Orsino loves music."

"It's not like having a black Portia, Alma," said Erin. "Nobody goes on and on and on about Olivia's golden hair."

"I've never even seen a blond Olivia," said Steph.

Since Steph's parents were Anglophiles who had been taking her to London for the theater every winter since she was ten, nobody could point out, as they might have had Gentian rashly made the same statement, how few Olivias of any sort she had as a sample.

"I did forget Shakespeare is so anachronistic," said Alma.

"How could you?" said Erin. "How could you ever forget Ms. Guitierre's telling us that the court of Henry V still spoke French, so that the whole English lesson with Katharine had absolutely no basis in fact? I thought Steph was going to die, and I didn't feel terribly good myself."

Alma shrugged. "I never could stand Hal," she said. "How dared he treat Falstaff like that?"

Steph opened her mouth. "Don't start," said Erin.

"All right," said Steph. "So I'll see you all at auditions on Tuesday."

Erin opened her lunch sack and removed a series of Tupperware containers. Becky took a bite of her hamburger. Alma stirred her spoon around in the cafeteria's version of chow mein and looked morose. Gentian, aware of Steph's eyes on her, abstracted her tuna-salad sandwich from the welter of apples and celery sticks and little packets of raisins her father always dumped into her lunch, and took a bite.

Steph put a spoon into her own container of strawberry yogurt and began eating tidily, like a cat.

After lunch Gentian went to the library and sat down on a

pile of cushions with a copy of *Twelfth Night*. It was easier going than it had been; maybe all that *Julius Caesar* was good for something after all.

It seemed to Gentian that Antonio had a very hard time of it. He rescued Sebastian from drowning, kept him company, gave him money, and ventured into a place where he was liable to be arrested for past offenses just to make sure Sebastian was all right. In return for these generosities, he encountered Sebastian's twin sister Viola dressed as a boy, mistook her for Sebastian, and thought as a result that Sebastian was refusing to let him have his own money back or even to acknowledge that they were acquainted. He was, in consequence of having appealed to Viola, in fact arrested. He seemed to be very fond of Sebastian indeed, but at the end Viola went off with Orsino and Olivia with Sebastian and Maria with Sir Toby, while Antonio, who had behaved nobly throughout, was left by himself. It was true that Malvolio suffered far more, but Malvolio was a bonehead.

Gentian wondered why Steph wanted to play him. The other parts Steph had assigned made sense to her, except possibly her own. She thought she might be better off playing Sebastian, since she was the nearest match for Erin they had available.

On Thursday it was sunny and warm, for December. There was not, as the astronomy books liked to put it, good seeing for planets, but Gentian had a pleasant time with Orion and went to bed early.

On Friday, the tenth of December, she got up an hour and a half before the sun. She had not slept very well, even with the electric blanket. It was extremely cold again, and she had turned the heat off when she went to bed rather than get up and do it later. She didn't like having her head under the covers, so her nose was cold and her breath had made frosty condensation on her pillow. Besides all that, Maria Mitchell, who also disliked having her head under the covers, had a tendency to wrap herself around Gentian's neck and growl if disturbed.

Gentian put several sweaters and a wool jacket on over her sweats, and crammed several pairs of socks and a set of down slippers onto her feet. She found her gloves, with fingers for this weather, and went to see how the sky was.

It was glorious. The southeastern sky, where today's spectacle was, was just beginning to curdle with faint light, but Jupiter and Spica glared out of it, abashing the crescent moon. Gentian named the larger stars of Libra: Zubeneschamali and Zubenelgenubi, rolling the syllables off her tongue with a relish that made Maria Mitchell come trotting up, in case she should have said something interesting. Gentian had a look at Jupiter through the telescope, but there was not, again, good seeing: the image wavered, wobbled, reformed, steadied just long enough for one to get one's bearings, and then broke up again, as if it were being seen underwater. Which, of course, effectually it was; that was the effect of Earth's atmosphere.

"Yes, I do think the moon," said Gentian to Maria Mitchell.

She went on looking at Jupiter for some time anyway; one was supposed to train oneself to ignore the irregularities and see what was there, and her *Sky Watcher's Handbook* said that observing the features of Jupiter was an area in which amateurs could still make a very considerable contribution. She had not yet concentrated on the tricky, delicate, finicky, boring routine of recording transits of various features, and she ought to get to that soon. Jupiter looked very roiled and spotty today, unless that was all the effect of the interference. She couldn't find the Great Red Spot, but the North Tropical and North Temperate zones were striped with belts that broke slowly up into spots and then flattened out again. She watched Jupiter's rapid rotation carry these halfway across its disk, and was late for school.

Becky collared her indignantly during second hour, when Gentian was in the library deciding which banned book to take home, as part of her program to remember to read more.

"Thanks for leaving me to Steph at assembly!" Becky said. She was pink and breathless and very solid-looking. Gentian decided not to point out that her socks and her belt were both purple.

"I'm sorry," said Gentian. "I didn't mean to. I was looking at Jupiter and then I had to make sure the room was heating up right so I could leave Murr in it, and then I had to take a bath, because I forgot three nights in a row."

"Well, obviously, she tried to talk me out of this seance."

"Where was Erin?"

"Being lectured by Alma."

"We're still doing it, aren't we?"

"Yes," said Becky grimly, "and Steph's going to pray for us."

"Well, they say it works for cancer patients."

"Gentian, you are callous."

"I am not. I'm sorry she's upset. She'll feel better when nothing awful happens." She was not all that sorry Steph was upset, but she was sorry for being flippant about cancer patients.

"She thinks something awful happened last time."

"Look. Alma is upset about something we can do something about, and Steph is upset about something we can't do anything about."

"We never used to have these kinds of problems," said Becky.

"Puberty," said Gentian.

Becky groaned.

She brought Becky and Erin home with her, fed them macaroni and cheese, and settled them down at the coffee table in the living room with the original ouija board and a planchette her mother had taken from the buffet in the dining room and handed to her when she saw the wreck of the old one. "There are bits of hundreds of old games in there," she told Gentian. "Your father won't throw anything away."

"I guess that's where Rosemary gets it from," said Gentian.

They had chosen this Friday because Rosemary was off with the Girl Scouts practicing, in the park, such staples of winter camping as building a fire in the snow, and Junie was at Sarah's. Her parents meekly agreed to sit in the television room as they had before, though her father did ask if they had to have the TV on.

"All right," said Gentian, feeling foolish, "shut your eyes, clear your minds, think sensible thoughts."

They set their fingertips lightly to the planchette. The wind tapped a branch against the big front window and made the porch swing creak a little. Her father laughed quietly in the other room. Pounce found a ping-pong ball and chased it under the dining-room radiator. Gentian realized that they had not spared anybody to write down whatever the planchette might spell. She raised an eyebrow at Erin, and mimed writing with her free hand. Erin looked blank, then pulled a pencil and her assignment notebook out of her pocket and laid them on the table. She put her left hand on the planchette and took the pencil in her right.

They settled back down. Gentian had trouble keeping her mind clear. Jupiter drifted in, and the perfidies of Mark Antony, and Dominic's ambiguous givings-out, and Steph in her bloomer costume and Alma bouncing Tiggerlike and Erin looking so much at home in Jane Goodall's guise, and Becky walking about in a tattered poem that talked about anguish.

The wind rose a little. The planchette began to move. That prickling, pressing, crowded sensation that Gentian had had on Halloween was not there. The big warm room, crowded with lamps and bookcases and armchairs and small sofas, felt suddenly vast, black, and empty, like the space between the galaxies. Things burned in it, but coldly. The planchette jerked on, faster and faster. She could hear Erin and Becky breathing, and the little scratch of Erin's pencil. She found herself tensing for the moment when the planchette broke.

The planchette glided to a halt and sat there.

They lifted their hands from it, rubbed their wrists and fingers, and looked at one another. "Did it make any sense?" asked Gentian.

"About as much as the last one," said Erin. "No rhyme this time, though—sorry, Becky. Here. Pauses supplied by the management. Hyracoid mind hoard icy mind. Man hid icy rod. Yon arc did him. Cardioid hymn."

"Cardioid him?" said Becky. "An esoteric curse?"

"H-Y-M-N."

"Oh."

Gentian got up, squeezing past three pot plants her mother had brought in for the winter to the nice wooden lectern with the unabridged dictionary on it, and opened the book. "Hydracoid?"

"No D. Hyracoid."

"There's a D on the end."

"Yes."

"Hyracoid. Resembling a hyrax. That's a lot of help. Oh, here. Hyrax. A genus of small rabbit-like quadrupeds, containing the DAMAN, cony, or rock-rabbit of Syria, an Abyssinian species or subspecies, and the Cape Hyrax or rock-badger of South Africa."

"And cardioid?"

Gentian looked. "I think it's a mathematical term—yes, here: 'heart-shaped, or, Math., a curve something like a heart in shape.' "

"You could publish it in *Tesseract* and hold a contest to decide what it means," said Erin.

"It's very promising," said Becky. "Too compressed, maybe."

"Do you think it will persuade Alma?" said Gentian.

"It should," said Erin. "It's a lot like the last one, just a bit less poetic."

"Well, assuming it will," said Becky, lying flat on her back on the hearth rug and putting her feet, in their striped socks, on the edge of the coffee table, "we just have to get Steph to forgive us."

"Forgiveness is her metier," said Erin. "What she'll do is mope."

Since Gentian was still standing by the dictionary, she stealthily looked up "metier." A trade or profession. Erin was sharp.

"Let's play Dictionary, since we've got it," said Becky.

"Are there enough of us?"

"Ask your parents and there will be."

"Should we call Steph first and say we have not been borne off to the netherworld by large fanged thingies?" said Gentian.

"I will call Steph myself and phrase it in a less insensitive way," said Erin, and stomped into the kitchen.

Gentian said to Becky, "That's twice she's called me callous or something like it. Am I?"

"No," said Becky. "Extremely downright and sometimes oblivious."

"Oh."

"After all, you're the one who remembered that Steph would be fretting and should be relieved."

"More to the point, really," said Gentian, pleased and herself relieved, "should somebody call Alma?"

"Steph is at her place," said Becky.

Erin came back in and said, "Be careful not to trip and fall downstairs; Steph has stopped praying for us—has stopped continually doing it, that is—so divine protection may suddenly have been removed."

"Now who's insensitive?" demanded Gentian.

"Sorry. I can't stand the tone of voice she talks about prayer in. Oh, and before I forget, Gen, she says do you want to go finish up your Christmas shopping next week?"

Gentian groaned and clutched her head theatrically; but their last expedition had reminded her that Steph was very good to go shopping with, having an extensive knowledge of little stores full of odd things and a great talent for suggesting good presents. It would help mend fences, too.

"I wish one of us were Jewish," said Gentian. "Or Wiccan. Or Roman," she added, thinking of *Julius Caesar* and the footrace at the Lupercalia. "I like to think I'm going Saturnalia shopping, but since I'm an atheist Steph goes on calling it Christmas. If I had a religion to offend she wouldn't, but I don't, so she does."

Becky sat up, looking incredulous, and threw a pretzel at her.

"We aren't as ecumenical as we might be," said Erin, laughing.

15

On Saturday after Erin and Becky had gone home, full of pancakes and camaraderie, Gentian called Steph and arranged to go shopping with her on Wednesday after school. Then she called Alma and arranged to go ice skating with her the next day. Having discharged her share of what Becky had been known to call Insectile Obligations, she wondered what to do with herself until the sun set and she could look at Saturn. Saturn would leave the evening sky near the end of February and would not be readily visible as a morning star until almost May.

It occurred to her that it was now after Thanksgiving, and that Juniper had supposedly had another date with The Light Prince on the same day Erin and Gentian went to the Planetarium and met Dominic afterwards.

She went into her father's office, moved Pounce from her father's chair to the cushion on the radiator specially provided for cats, and called the BBS. Her password was still good. Maybe I'm getting addicted to this, she thought. A very few minutes spent with the romance echo disabused her of this notion.

Mutant Boy had challenged Juniper and Crystal to answer Jason's accusation, and Crystal had answered that yes, Juniper was another alias of hers. Gentian giggled; Junie had a devious mind. Crystal had received two admiring messages and a storm of abuse. Gentian supposed that people had a right to be upset about being fooled, but they didn't have to be so malicious or so illiterate. She gave up on the romance echo and looked at the culture echo.

They were still going on about women in combat. The Light Prince was citing a lot of sociobiology, whatever exactly that was, and Juniper seemed a bit at a loss. Quote to him out of *The Mismeasure of Woman,* if he won't read it, thought Gentian irritably. Tell him about those studies NASA did that showed women would make better test pilots and astronauts than men, statistically. How can you want to go out with this creep?

She posted a short message recommending the NASA studies to Juniper's attention, and got out of there before she did something she would regret. Her debating skills were miles ahead of those of most of the posters, but The Light Prince was pretty smooth. Besides, it would irritate Junie. She put Pounce back on the chair and went upstairs, fuming. Juniper's room was empty. She might come back from Sarah's at any time. Gentian went into the sunroom anyway and extracted the diary.

Juniper had gone on that date, all right. If she and The Light Prince had talked about anything real, she didn't mention it: just a lot of sheeps' eyes and handholding and kissing and romantic compliments. Gentian thought about throwing up. She read on. In the outer room, a cat jumped from some high place.

Gentian slapped the book shut, thrust it into the cushion, zipped the cushion up so fast she caught her finger in it, and bolted into the bedroom. The black-and-white cat stopped rolling on the floor to hiss at her. Somebody was coming up the stairs, and it was Juniper. She came into the room in a billow of green velvet, windblown and flushed with cold. She flung her hat on the bed, said, "You are the best cat in all the universes," and saw Gentian.

She grew cold, still, and furious in an instant. It was almost like watching a shape-changer. "What the hell are you doing in my room?"

"I wanted to use the computer."

"Use Daddy's."

"I don't like the keyboard."

"Did you scare my cat?"

"Yes, of course I did, you know I just hate cats, I jumped up and down and shrieked at it."

The cat stood up and sniffed at Gentian's left foot. "You are an exceedingly fine beast," she said to it. "What's your name?"

"Yin-Yang," said Juniper. "I don't want you poking around in my room. If I so much as set foot on your whole floor you'd raise a stink that could be heard on the moon, so just stay out of here."

"What am I supposed to do when I want to use the computer?"

"What do you want it for anyway?"

"There are astronomy groups on the Internet," said Gentian. This was, of course, quite true, even though it was not an answer.

"Oh, God," said Juniper, flopping down onto her unmade bed. "Then they'd better get me a new computer and you can have the old one. If you start reading Internet newsgroups it'll be like having a roommate. I'd have to move out."

"Will you help me coax them, then?"

"Maybe. It's more than you deserve for invading my privacy."

Gentian felt simultaneously affronted because using Juniper's computer hardly constituted invading her privacy, and guilty because she had actually done far worse than that.

"Is it too late to ask for it as our Christmas present?" said Juniper.

"What do you mean, our? You'd be the one with the new computer; it'd be your present. I need those color filters for my telescope. I need a camera."

"Look, don't present this to me as a collaboration for our mutual benefit one moment and then say, it's all your present, it's nothing to do with me, the next. If they spend that much it has to be for more than one of us."

"Talk to Rosie, then. She lives on the same floor."

"Oh, no. I'm not having her in here. She leaves apple cores on the floor and spills stuff in the keyboard."

"Let me think about it," said Gentian. She wanted to leave

now, but Juniper's cat was sniffing earnestly up her leg, probably reading any messages Maria Mitchell had left there.

Juniper got up and ostentatiously hung her coat and hat in the closet, probably the first time she had done that in five years, or in her whole life.

"How's your sociological experiment going?" said Gentian.

"Fine. I'll thank you not to interfere with it."

Gentian opened her mouth and shut it again. Juniper was far more likely to say, "I'll kill you if you do" than "I'll thank you if you don't."

"I haven't truly, even though I was tempted," she said.

"Thanks for thinking of *The Mismeasure of Woman*," said Juniper. "I don't agree with a lot of it, but at least it would give those bozos something to chew on."

Juniper's cat finished with Gentian's left foot and started on the right. Gentian said, "Do you think The Light Prince is a bozo?"

Juniper's face darkened. She sat down on the bed again. "I don't know," she said. "He's contradictory. Anyway, he's the only literate person on there except all of me."

"I wondered about Hot Dud," said Gentian.

"I think he's dyslexic, so it's not his fault. And he's sharp. But he's not really interested in discussing things seriously. He likes to dart in, make a snide remark, and dart out again. Which is okay, but not for me."

Juniper's cat butted its head into Gentian's ankle. She reached down cautiously and petted it along the spine. It purred thunderously. Juniper looked thunderous herself.

"I'd better go," said Gentian. "I'll think about the computer."

"And stay out of my room when I'm not here."

Gentian left without answering. She went upstairs and thought about Steph's Plan. It would be fun, as anything theatrical was, as anything with the Giant Ants was. But it would take up a lot of time, including time in the evenings when she could be stargazing. She supposed she could do her astronomical work later and sleep in and just miss morning school.

But she was already committed to one project that would be

time-consuming. What if Dominic suddenly wanted to start
working on his project? She had said she would help; she had inquired after it several times.

She picked up the telephone quickly, before she could think
about it. She called Directory Assistance and asked for the
Hardys' number, giving the street address and adding that it was
a new listing. There was, she was informed, no such number.
Gentian put down the telephone, feeling stunned. She supposed
it might be unlisted; or perhaps they had no telephone at all.

If she wanted to get in touch with Dominic, then, she must either knock on the door of that house, or write him a letter. The
latter seemed far easier, until she actually sat down to do it.
Should she write it by hand, or use the computer, or borrow her
mother's typewriter? What should she say? I'm setting up my
schedule for the New Year and want to know if I should include
your crack-brained project?

She took out a sheet of the writing paper her father had designed on the computer for her twelfth birthday. Each sheet had
a different small image of some interesting astronomical object in
the upper right-hand corner, and along the bottom it said "Gentian B. Meriweather, Oak Street School of Astronomy, in the
Milky Way." The one she had taken out had the Crab Nebula on
it. She found a pen and sat biting the end.

She had not yet told Dominic that she was an astronomer. He
might have deduced that somebody in the house was, since the
telescope's dome was clearly visible, but he was more likely to
think, as many people did, that this was her father's hobby. He
did know, if he had been paying attention, that she was the one
who lived in the attic, but he might not have made the connection.

She dug about in the drawers of her desk, looking for other
writing paper. She had some with calico cats, and some with astronomical motifs that did not say she was an astronomer, and
some with dragons and unicorns, and some with Celtic knot-
work, and a vast number of sets, in all sizes and shapes and colors, with gentians on them. Anybody who was a loss as to what
to give her always produced stationery with gentians. Some of
them found jewelry or towels instead, but most of them found

stationery. Gentian chose one of the more botanical, less sickly, versions. He already knew her name, after all. She wrote out several rough drafts on the end page of her astronomical notebook, and finally produced the following:

Dear Dominic,

I have been asked to take part in a very time-consuming project at school starting in January, and don't know if I should agree, because I have a previous commitment to helping you with your science project. Could you please let me know when you plan to start it and how much work per week you think it will require?

Yours sincerely,
Gentian B. Meriweather.

She pondered this for some time. It was colorless, but it got the point across. It was probably best to sound businesslike. She sealed it inside a blue envelope and wrote Dominic's name across the front.

Then she looked for Saturn. Its northern belts were still unusually spotty. The seeing was not very good, but she practiced ignoring the ripples and wavers and wobbles and concentrating on whatever feature she was trying to observe. She found several moons, which always pleased her; one day she must figure out how to tell which was which. She wanted to know when she was looking at Titan, which was bigger than Mercury and had its own atmosphere.

When Saturn grew so wobbly that her eyes rebelled, she refreshed them by looking again at Orion. But she was aware all the time of a kind of itch at the back of her mind, and finally realized that her letter was bothering her. Not the thing itself, but how to deliver it. It would be silly to put a stamp on it and drop it in a mailbox, to go all the way to the local post office sixteen blocks away and all the way back again. She would just drop it into Dominic's letter box, or tuck it into some obtrusive spot on the front or back door, on her way to school.

The thought of meeting Dominic, or Mrs. Hardy, or the as-yet-unseen Mr. Hardy, made her nervous. She could go now. The house was dark as it could be; the night was cold; she could go quietly.

She put on her shoes and a sweater, got her flashlight, and went downstairs. Everybody was still up. Gentian said she wanted to go for a walk, received several offers of company, was obliged to say she wanted to be by herself, suffered expressions of scorn from Junie and commiseration from her parents, was made to put on a hat and jacket, and finally escaped out the back door.

The waning crescent moon had set at 3:12 that afternoon and would not rise again until 6:50 Sunday morning. It was very dark. The sky was high and remote, its glittering stars bright but seeming very small. The house next door, mean and low as it was by day, was a dark bulk. Gentian abandoned her plan of leaving the letter in the back door and went swiftly down the driveway. She had brought the flashlight from habit, but did not really want to turn it on; it might wake people up; they might think there were burglars. She went boldly up the Hardys' front sidewalk, took the one step to the small concrete stoop, reached to open the screen door, and realized there was none. Silly, in Minnesota, but it made things easier for her. She took the cold metal flap of the letter slot in her fingers and tried to lift it. It stuck. She tugged at it. The cold metal burned her fingers.

"Night and silence, who is here?" said Dominic's voice behind her.

Gentian did not scream, because she had clamped her mouth shut, but she made a short muffled sound that so infuriated her she forgot she was frightened.

"Don't sneak up like that!" she whispered, turning. It must be her day for being caught.

Dominic was a pale face, a gleam of eye, a bit of darker darkness in more or less the shape of a person. He did not answer her.

"What are you doing up?"

"Awful darkness and silence reign through the long long wintry nights," said Dominic. He spoke in his ordinary voice, and Gentian cast a wild glance at his house and then at hers.

It was terribly dark. The sky was still clear, but the large bright stars of winter seemed dim and far.

"Yes, that's a wonderful reason to wander around in the cold," said Gentian.

"Where are you going, my pretty maid?" said Dominic.

"I was trying to put something through your letter slot. I think it's frozen shut." She held out the letter to him. Dominic reached to take it and then drew his hand back abruptly.

"Letters should not be known," he said.

A breath of wind came through, and the darkness was less absolute. Gentian looked up, and her sky looked back at her. Castor, Pollux, Aldebaran, Betelgeuse, Orion's Belt, Rigel, the tight small splatter of the Pleiades.

"All right, I'll mail it."

"The mail from Tunis probably," said Dominic. As the sky regained itself, he seemed to look darker and larger.

"Good night," said Gentian, backing around him. He did not follow. She turned and went quickly over the smooth lawn, jumped off the top of the retaining wall, landed on the driveway with a force that made her feet smart, and ran up the driveway to her back door. She looked over her shoulder three times while she got out her key and put it into the lock. The new house loomed like the mouth of a tunnel. Nobody was there. She wrenched the door open, leapt inside, shut the door, and shot the bolt.

In the warm kitchen, her parents looked at her in amazement. They were making themselves whiskey sours, which probably meant they had had some kind of an argument with Juniper. Gentian hoped Junie had not brought up the idea of a new computer in some idiotic challenging alienating fashion.

"Genny, what on earth," said her mother.

"Did somebody bother you?" said her father.

"It's just colder than I realized," said Gentian; it took three breaths to get the words out.

The next morning she addressed and stamped the letter and took it to the mailbox on the corner.

On Monday the weather got warm and rather hazy. Gentian

did not really have time to notice, because Steph collected the
Giant Ants at her house to, she said, rehearse their strategy for
the auditions. She had chosen five fairly short scenes that would
show off each of the characters she wanted them to play, and she
drilled them through each scene four times before relenting and
letting them have their hot cider and popcorn. She wouldn't let
them just sit and read, either; she insisted on blocking the scenes
roughly and made people stand and move and make gestures.

In Steph's cream-colored room with its frieze of roses around
the top of the walls, its curtains of eyelet lace and framed prints
of Victorian fashions, they walked up and down on the powder-
blue carpet, grimacing, repeating lines six times in different tones
of voice, occasionally sitting down on the floor or flinging themselves across the rose-canopied bed in mock or real despair. Steph
stood in the middle of the room and exhorted them.

Gentian was, in the end, impressed with everybody except
herself. She did not think she had the stuff of a simple, affectionate sea captain in her. It wasn't as if he had anything to say
about navigation. Steph said she was just fine. Becky said, "I'll
practice with you again tomorrow, Gen."

On Tuesday it sleeted. Gentian and Becky met after assembly
in the library. They retreated to a well-cushioned corner by the
oversized books and opened their copies of *Twelfth Night*. Maria
and Antonio did not actually have any scenes together, which
meant that Gentian got to practice but Becky didn't.

"It's all right," said Becky. "I got a lot more chances than
you did last night, because I'm in three scenes and you're only
in one."

Steph had chosen the scene of Antonio's arrest for Gentian to
audition. Becky read Viola and the Officers, to let Gentian con-
centrate on Antonio.

When Antonio entered, Viola, in her boy's clothes, had just
been challenged by Sir Toby to fight with Sir Andrew. Viola said,
"I do assure you 'tis against my will."

Antonio said, "Put up your sword. If this young gentleman
have done offense, I take the fault on me. If you offend him, I for
him defy you."

"Wait," said Becky. "I think you should say, 'Put up your

sword' to Viola, not to Sir Andrew. Steph kept telling you to say it more gently, and I think that's why."

Gentian read it again.

Sir Toby asked who Antonio was.

"One, sir, that for his love dares yet do more than you have heard him brag to you he will."

"Slow down," said Becky. "Mrs. Morgan says monosyllables mean slow down."

"Should I be a little scornful with 'to you'?"

"Mmm, try it and see."

Fabian, Olivia's clown, came to tell them to stop fighting because the officers were coming. "Just like *The Three Musketeers,*" said Becky.

When the officers arrested him, Antonio said, "You do mistake me, sir."

"There," said Becky, "he's not quite as straightforward as you said."

Antonio said, "I must obey," and to Viola, "This comes with seeking you. But there's no remedy; I shall answer it. What will you do, now my necessity makes me to ask you for my purse? It grieves me much more for what I cannot do for you than what befalls myself. You stand amazed, but be of comfort."

Viola, bewildered, gave Antonio half of what money she had, since he had defended her. Antonio became upset; Viola repeated that she did not know him; the officers said it was time to go; Antonio told them that he had rescued Viola from the jaws of death; the officers asked what was that to them.

Antonio said, "But oh, how vild an idol proves this god! Thou hast, Sebastian, done good feature shame. In nature there's no blemish but the mind; none can be called deformed but the unkind. Virtue is beauty; but the beauteous evil are empty trunks, o'erflourished by the devil."

Gentian found this extraordinarily difficult to get through, given that she agreed with its basic sentiments. Becky told her to stop thinking of the last few lines as a philosophical speech and fling them straight at Viola, who had behaved very badly as far as Antonio knew.

"Don't you know any beauteous evil?" she said, exasperated.

"Well, Junie, I guess, but I don't expect better of her."

"Well, try it again. Pretend you're ranting at Junie if it helps."

It seemed to; at least, Becky consented to go to lunch. They went on to their afternoon's classes, and so back to the assembly hall for rehearsals.

The scene was chaotic in the extreme. Gentian did not like crowds. She let Steph charge about among the masses of people, interrogating teachers and senior assistants, and then followed her to a corner where Mrs. Morgan was conducting the auditions for *Twelfth Night*. Then Steph had to explain that they wanted to audition as a group and had chosen some scenes with which to do so. Mrs. Morgan said she reserved the right to choose only some of them, but that frankly, given how few students wanted to do Shakespeare, she would probably be glad to take everybody.

Gentian wished her scene were first so she could get it over with. But she did like Erin's Viola, who was irritable and despondent at the beginning rather than swooning about and whining; and she liked Erin's Viola's Cesario, who was very brisk and ironic, even when talking about being Patience on a monument smiling at grief. Becky was a fine Maria; she too was rather ironic, seeing through Sir Toby but liking him anyway.

Alma was an excellent Olivia, sighing and drooping, at first, quite as much as Orsino when he postured about how much in love he was. But she could be made to laugh, and to take charge of her household and an interest in Cesario; and her dry dismissal of Orsino's importunities made Gentian laugh outright.

Steph was quite amazing as Malvolio. It made Gentian uneasy. The footnotes and Mrs. Morgan had explained that Malvolio was in part a parody of the Puritans who had made so many playwrights' lives a misery in Shakespeare's time, and it seemed to Gentian that Steph sympathized with him greatly, not in his foolish excesses or gullibility, but in his position among people who did not share his beliefs and were inclined to make fun of them. Her Malvolio made Maria look bad; he made you wonder why, if she could put up with Sir Toby's foibles, she couldn't be more tolerant of Malvolio's.

Gentian disliked being made to think in these terms, but it would be intellectually dishonest to dismiss them. There was a break in their audition as Mrs. Morgan was called on to mediate some dispute elsewhere, and she used it, while the other Giant Ants chattered over the text, to ponder Sir Toby and Malvolio. Sir Toby was funny on purpose, and Malvolio accidentally; Sir Toby didn't take anything seriously, and Malvolio took himself very seriously indeed. Gentian didn't think she would like to live with Sir Toby, always having drunken revels when she was trying to do astronomy and probably breaking the telescope if she let him near it; but in the play he was far easier to take than Malvolio. Malvolio liked to lay down the law, that was his problem.

Mrs. Morgan came back, and gestured to Steph to begin her second scene as the law-layer. Becky assumed her Maria stance, becoming somehow much rounder and much less solemn, and said to Sir Toby, Sir Andrew, and Fabian, "Get ye all three into the box tree. Malvolio's coming down this walk. He has been yonder i' the sun practicing behavior to his own shadow this half hour."

Steph drew her tall, straight, thin self into a ponderous stoop and settled a look of judicious satisfaction over her face. " 'Tis but fortune," she said, in tones of busy persuasion, as if she were haranguing the Giant Ants into wearing makeup. "All is fortune. Maria once told me she did affect me—" She paused to smirk, and Gentian glanced over to see how Becky was taking Shakespeare's cavalier treatment of pronoun antecedents. The "she" in question wasn't Maria, but Olivia, for whom Malvolio worked and with whom he was in love, if you could call it that. Becky, however, was still being Maria, to whom such considerations were irrelevant.

"And," continued Steph, "*I* have heard herself come thus near, that should she fancy, it should be one of my complexion. Besides, she uses me with a more exalted respect than anyone else that follows her. What else should I think on't?"

You twit, thought Gentian. Just the kind of person who would get sued for sexual harrassment today. She watched Steph as Malvolio indulge in a daydream of being married to Olivia, Count Malvolio, leaving Olivia, who was perfectly capable of running her own household, sleeping while he called Toby before him and told him to amend his drunkenness. Toby and Andrew were infuriated by this display, and had to be restrained by Fabian's pointing out that if they leapt out of cover and beat Malvolio up, the sinews of their plot would be broken.

The plot was a letter written by Maria, whose handwriting was conveniently like Olivia's. The letter informed Malvolio that its anonymous author "could command where she adored," that is, was his employer; but, the letter went on, she simply asked instead that he do a number of things to demonstrate that he loved in return. The things he was asked to do, from wearing yellow stockings to being surly with the servants, were all calculated to irritate Olivia and get Malvolio in trouble. Steph read them out with a kind of greedy relish that ought not to have left much sympathy for Malvolio, but Gentian found herself getting more and more uneasy. After all, she thought, if you're the kind of bonehead who thinks like Malvolio, but you don't actually sexually harrass anybody, and then somebody writes you a letter like that, isn't anything you do as much their fault as yours? No, that was simplistic. There was something else making her uncomfortable.

They're encouraging Malvolio's faults, she thought. He has these faults and they're encouraging him to indulge them when so far he really hasn't, in the direction they're pointing him. I know their idea is that he'll come to grief through his own failings, but it seems dangerous to me. This is a comedy, so I guess nothing especially terrible will happen. But still. Maybe I just have no sense of humor?

The scene with Malvolio reading Maria's lying letter ended, and it was Gentian's turn. The other Giant Ants took Sir Toby and Fabian and the officers. Erin's Viola spoke faster than Becky's, which threw Gentian off her stride at first, but she managed to say, "You mistake me, sir," with the right air of innocent surprise, and to slow down with her monosyllables, and to deliver her rant with some genuine feeling. It was indeed a very strange sensation to look at Erin and think she knew her, but to find that Erin was really a stranger called Viola.

Gentian said to the officers, "Lead me on," in the tone of someone who has given up trying to account for the wickedness of the world, and sat down, faintly sweaty all over. Becky beamed at her. Steph nodded solemnly. Erin quirked her mouth. Alma jabbed her thumb up several times. I'll be revenged on the whole pack of you, thought Gentian in Malvolio's words, and then blinked. Steph had certainly succeeded in getting her to look at matters through Malvolio's eyes.

Mrs. Morgan meanwhile had thanked them and sat looking through her notes. When even Steph had started to look edgy and worried, Mrs. Morgan said, still shuffling notes, "I don't see any reason to keep you in suspense. I've already cast Sir Toby and Sir Andrew, and I think you all can take the roles you want. If you would like to find me a Sebastian and an Orsino, I'd be grateful. Otherwise, Gentian, you may have to be Sebastian and we'll find somebody less accomplished for Antonio."

"I'd rather not," said Gentian.

"We'll find a Sebastian," said Steph.

"I might still find one myself," said Mrs. Morgan, hurriedly. "But if you have any ideas, come and see me."

They filed sedately out into the corridor, after which Steph threw her purse into the air and yelled, "Yeeeeehaaaa!" Alma joined her, and they hugged each other.

"We didn't try out for *Paint Your Wagon*," said Erin. But she looked pleased too.

Becky smiled at Gentian. "You'll like it," she said. "Really. Maybe they'll give you boots and a sextant."

16

Gentian came home in a small glow of triumph and informed her family over dinner that she was going to be in the school production of *Twelfth Night*.

"What about your astronomy?" said her mother.

"How can you help with Dominic's project if you're rehearsing all the time?" said Rosemary.

"Who are you playing?" said her father.

"We don't need Genny to help with the project," said Juniper.

"Have I got an Electra complex," said Gentian bitterly, helping herself to salad, "or is Dad the only sensible person in this house?"

"Taking your career choice seriously isn't sensible?" said her mother.

"Well, all right," said Gentian, running her fork through the salad. She could tell that Rosemary had made it: it had no cucumber, no green pepper, no tomato, and a great many radishes. Her mother silently handed her a bowl of chopped tomato, green pepper, and red onion, and cocked one eyebrow to show she still wanted her original question answered.

"I figured I'd do astronomy after ten," said Gentian, "which is mostly a good time, and maybe miss school in the morning sometime."

"Mostly, I assume," said her mother dryly.

"The Giant Ants'll let me look at their notes."

"Well, as long as you don't start bringing home those oily communications from your counselor. I don't know how so fundamentally sensible a school can countenance so much psychobabble."

"Will you come see me in the play?"

"Yes, of course."

"Junie, weren't you going to try out for something too?" said her father.

Juniper took a deliberate bite of spaghetti, and chewed it with extreme thoroughness. All this got her, Gentian was pleased to see, was the complete attention of her entire family.

"I decided against it," said Juniper. "I think I'll have better things to do next semester."

Rosemary caught Gentian's eye and made a face of eloquent disgust. Their mother said, "Isn't it about time we met this young man?"

"In a while, Mom."

"Make it a short while, please," said their father. "This uncharacteristic concealment of what would generally be regarded as a triumph makes me wonder what exactly is the matter with him."

"He's got green hair," said Rosemary.

"He's covered in tattoos," said Gentian. "Inartistic ones," she added, since tattoos, like green hair, were probably insufficiently shocking to her parents. She thought it over. "He can't spell," she said. "No, wait, he won't spell. He says 'you know' after every phrase. He doesn't read."

Juniper said, with remarkable control, "I have to prepare him for my bratty sisters. He's an only child, lucky him."

"I don't see any need to meet him at all," said Rosemary, with dignity.

"No, you and Amber will just lurk outside the door and giggle instead."

"You needn't think that every time you hear us laughing we're even thinking of you."

Gentian tried to frame a neat phrase about how laughable Juniper was, but by the time she had it right Juniper had left the table and Rosemary was arguing with her mother about whether she could get a tattoo.

Gentian went upstairs feeling rather flattened. Her part was a small one, but the play would still take a great deal of work. It was, she supposed, as well to be in it, if she wanted to see much of the Giant Ants. She sat on the bed and rubbed Maria Mitchell under the chin, feeling dissatisfied. Maria Mitchell bit her gently on the wrist, and when she jumped, Murr bounded off the bed and galloped into the bathroom.

Gentian followed and fed her. "Where do you put all that food?" she asked, rinsing the water dish and refilling it. "Have you got a family of homeless cats in the attic? Are you in league with Daddy?" Murr, crunching steadily, paid no attention. "Or is it really that long since I fed you?" Maybe she should put another FEED CAT sign right beside the telescope, or on the seat of her adjustable stool, or inside the book of star maps.

She made three and put one in each spot. Murr returned and sat on the telescope stool to wash her face. Gentian decided to do her homework. Saturn would be up for a while yet.

When she finally looked at it, the seeing was still not good, and the northern belts were still spotty. Gentian made a few silly jokes to herself about acne, and moved on to Orion. Last time she had looked at Betelgeuse, a red supergiant and a very old star; now she looked at Rigel, a blue-white giant and quite young. It was not as striking a color as Betelgeuse, but it was brilliant and beautiful. Gentian spent a little time finding Rigel B, the giant's blue companion. Then she spent a long time trying to split the companion, since it was in fact a close binary. This had been confirmed by spectroscopic analysis, and seen by somebody with a six-inch telescope in 1878. But sometimes even huge modern telescopes could not split Rigel B. Gentian liked it for this, though she thought most astronomers must find it frustrating.

When she had given up on dividing Rigel B, she looked at M42, the Great Nebula in Orion. It spread out hazily from the middle of Orion's sword. Theta Orionis was a quadruple star, and even with Gentian's telescope she could see the main star and three tiny ones below it, forming an irregular polygon called the Trapezium. People had reported various colors for the four stars. Gentian could imagine nearly any she read about; her favorite was Admiral Smyth's "pale white, faint lilac, garnet, and reddish," but she knew any redness was a result of contrast with the vast filmy nebula itself, for that was a thin elusive green. She traced it out slowly into the darkness; the longer you looked, the further the whorls and filaments spread against the dark and the light, and the deeper the whole object seemed. She tracked it as it moved east for a while, and then let Theta Orionis drift out of view so that she could trace the fainter and fainter tatters of gas out and out and out, until the vast glittering track of the Milky Way blazed into her startled eyes.

It was late. She went to bed, still seeing against her closed lids the green wisps that were stars, coalescing.

Wednesday was not only sunny, but warm, like spring rather than almost-winter. Gentian got to school in time for lunch, and for the unwelcome reminder by Steph that they were finishing up their Christmas shopping this afternoon.

"Since it's so warm," Steph said, "we can just stay downtown. I want to go to the Museum Company."

"Okay," said Gentian, a little mollified. The Museum Company was pricey, but she could look at its reproductions for hours. Steph could go off to every other store on the block and try on clothes till they closed, and Gentian would still be happy at the Museum Company.

Gentian's study group met that afternoon and plodded painfully through a few scenes of Act IV of *Julius Caesar*. Gentian was so appalled by the goings-on of the play that she scarcely noticed how her fellow students were fumbling their lines. Act IV opened with Antony, who was now, along with Octavius and Lepidus, in charge of Rome, poring over a list of people and deciding which of them should die. They traded them off as though they were dividing up a box of candy. Lepidus said his brother could die if Antony would consent to having Antony's nephew killed too. Antony said, "With a spot I damn him." Gentian had plenty of time to read footnotes while her study group struggled, and she read with astonished revulsion one that said Antony's readiness to kill his nephew was supposed to contrast with Brutus's reluctance, earlier in the play, to kill Antony himself. Since killing Antony himself would have assured the success of the conspiracy to kill Caesar and take over Rome, Brutus's reluctance was seen by the commentator as a bad idea. Or, the note continued, maybe Shakespeare only wanted to show that Antony was a just and unsentimental man.

Gentian almost choked on her tongue. If that's unsentimental, she thought, give me the gooiest, rosiest sonnet Edna St. Vincent Millay ever wrote. What is wrong with these scholars? I'll believe Shakespeare was that dimwitted when I get to the end of the play.

After they had decided who should die, Lepidus went away, and Antony promptly said that Lepidus was a slight unmeritable man who had no business ruling a third of the world.

Octavius said Antony had been ready enough to let Lepidus tell him who should die. Antony said he was older than Octavius, and explained that he was going to blame some of the nastier things they would be doing on Lepidus and then turn him out to pasture.

Octavius said Lepidus was a tried and valiant soldier.

Antony said that his horse was, too, and that he would treat Lepidus like a horse, adding that Lepidus had no new ideas. He then said that Brutus and Cassius were levying armies, and that they had better decide what to do about it.

Octavius said they were bayed about with many enemies, and he feared that many that smiled had in their hearts millions of mischiefs.

No shit! thought Gentian. What do you expect, you bonehead? Give me Brutus any day. Yeah, right, Brutus who stabbed his friend in the back. I'd trade the whole bunch of them for one paragraph of Jane Austen. She sat fuming and ignoring the rest of the reading, and finally escaped to her math class with an alacrity she did not often expend on that subject.

By the time she met Steph on the front steps of the school, she was extremely sleepy. "I've got to have some tea," she said. "I'm just dead."

"Too much astronomy?" said Steph. "We can stop at the bagel place."

Gentian got a large cup of tea with milk and sugar and a poppyseed bagel with chive cream cheese and a cup of vegetable soup, to fortify her for shopping. Steph had a cup of tea, black. Steph was worrying about the production of *Twelfth Night* and began talking about it while they were still standing in line. "I hope we didn't overreach ourselves," she said. "I didn't realize the competition would be so thin. We need to find a Sebastian we like the look of. I wish you'd just agree to play him. We can find lots of Antonios."

"I'm not good enough."

"It's not really a much bigger part than Antonio."

"Well, maybe not, but it's harder. Especially with Erin playing Viola. I think she's perfect, and I think Sebastian would need to walk and talk like her. You'd need a good actor, and, I don't know, somebody with not much ego, or a funny kind of ego, who'd take pride in looking like Erin instead of working everything out from scratch."

"But would you do it if we absolutely couldn't find anybody?"

"I don't know, Steph. Let me think about it."

They paid for their food and found a minute round table in a corner.

"Well, think quickly," said Steph.

Gentian mumbled something around a mouthful of bagel.

Steph took a paperback of the play out of her purse and began ruffling through it, frowning.

"If music be the food of love, play on," said Dominic behind Gentian.

Gentian swallowed her mouthful carefully. Dominic came around her left side and smiled faintly at her. He was wearing black. He stood very straight. He had a vaguely ironic look. He said, mellifluously, "Give me excess of it, that surfeiting, the appetite may sicken and so die."

Gentian considered him. He might make a good Orsino. If Mrs. Morgan truly couldn't find anybody else, it might not matter that he didn't go to their school, though his own school, always supposing he had one, might have something to say about it.

Steph put her book down and said, "Oh, hello. Sit down if you like, though we're about to rush off to go shopping."

Dominic pulled out a chair and sat down, gracefully. He looked from Gentian's laden plate to Steph's cup and said, "Dost thou think because thou art virtuous there shall be no more cakes and ale?"

Gentian felt piggish and irate. She took a larger bite of bagel. Steph laughed. "I'm not virtuous, I just have a nervous stomach."

"An army marches on its stomach," said Dominic, thoughtfully.

"Yes, but luckily a shopper doesn't."

"I cannot eat but little meat," Dominic told her. "My stomach is not good."

"Oh, I hope you're not getting the flu. It's going around."

"Here, have some of this soup," said Gentian, seized by mischief. "I'll get you some. I'll get you some tea." She leapt up, almost spilling her own tea, and went back to the counter. If he was a vampire, let him get out of this.

When she came back to the table with the new tray, Steph and Dominic were laughing. She put the tray down in front of him and said, "That should settle things."

Dominic gave her a level, limpid gaze, and then he smiled. "To taste," said he, "think not I shall be nice." And he put a spoonful of soup into his mouth, and swallowed it.

Well, thought Gentian, as he went on eating, and then drank his tea, I guess that's that. I hope Rosie isn't too disappointed. Well, unless he's going to excuse himself now and go get rid of it all.

"We'd better go," said Steph. "I've still got lots of shopping to do. We're going to the Museum Company, Dominic, if you're interested."

Dominic came along with them, his hands in the pockets of his leather jacket, looking remote and austere but hardly uncomfortable. They went into the Museum Company and dispersed, Gentian heading for the reproductions of Egyptian cat statues and gargoyles and Steph making for the jewelry. Dominic went along with Steph, and she could from time to time hear them laughing. Gentian decided to get her father a small cat statue; he would be short a cat since Junie had adopted his latest find. She was still looking for something for Rosie. A store with camping equipment might be a better choice than here.

There was a great burst of laughter from Steph and Dominic. Gentian looked around, and saw them coming towards her, picking their way past stacks of jigsaw puzzles of famous paintings and pyramids of replica ship's bells and hourglasses.

"Genny," said Steph, "you're saved."

"Oh, good. What from?"

"Playing Sebastian. Dominic can do it. He even stands like Erin."

Gentian looked at him. He did. He had the slight tilt of the chin right too, and the way Erin raised a sardonic eyebrow at very little provocation. He had not used to have Erin's mannerisms. She wanted to tell him to stop it at once. And what would Erin think of this dark mirror?

"But you don't go to our school," she said.

"I have knowledge never learned in schools."

"Who doesn't?" said Steph. "Anyway, I thought I'd tell her he was my cousin, or something, come to stay with us."

"His coloring isn't really right, you know."

"We'd just need to lighten it a bit, or darken Erin's. She went gray for Jane Goodall, I bet she'd go dark for this."

"I don't know," said Gentian. "I'd do a lot more for Jane Goodall than I would for Viola."

"Well, we can ask, anyway."

"Sure." Why am I protesting, she thought. I'd see Dominic all the time; we'd have a project in common. But I'll have to share him with all the Giant Ants. Especially Steph. Steph was not, however, being flirtatious in the least; she seemed more sisterly, talking to Dominic in very much the same way as she talked to Gentian. Having him in the play might, in fact, be better than trying to do a science project with him and Juniper, who certainly would flirt with him. Then she remembered her bet with Erin, and Alma's saying, "There's something the matter with him."

When they had found Rosie a compass and a flashlight and

said good-bye to Dominic and boarded a bus for home, Gentian said to Steph, "You know, Alma can't stand Dominic and Erin doesn't think much of him either."

"I think Alma misunderstood him."

"Well, Erin didn't, and she doesn't like him."

"Theater is about learning to work with lots of different people," said Steph, stubbornly. "Gentian, doesn't he live next door to you?"

"Yes."

"Why didn't he take this bus, then?"

"I have no idea. Steph, really, Alma and Erin can't stand him. It'll be very awkward."

"We need a Sebastian," said Steph, "and not somebody Mrs. Morgan digs out of the woodwork because she thinks it'll be good for him to be in a play. We need somebody good. You said yourself we need somebody who can imitate Erin."

Gentian looked at her. Against the dark window of the bus her profile was unyielding. Steph seldom dug her heels in like this, but when she did, direct argument was not the way to budge her. Gentian sighed, and said nothing until she bid Steph good night and got off the bus.

She trudged through puddles just beginning to skin over with ice, amid the wreck of all the snowdrifts, under a slightly hazy sky. When she let herself in the front door, she saw a blue envelope lying on the hall table. It was her letter to Dominic, stamped, "No Such Address." Gentian stood holding it. She went back out onto the porch and looked at Dominic's house. It was there. It had numbers on the door. Gentian was as ready as anybody to complain about the post office, but she was not at all sure they had really had anything to do with it.

She put the letter into her pocket and went back inside. Her family was just finishing supper and had not left her any. "We thought you and Steph would eat downtown," said her mother. Since she and Steph had done just that, there was nothing much to say. Gentian made herself a tuna-and-olive sandwich, grumbling, and stomped upstairs and called Becky.

"Steph has become as stone," she said.

"Oh-oh. What about?"

"She thinks Dominic should play Sebastian."

"Oh. Well. I asked Micky if he would, but we could give him Orsino, if he's allowed to clown."

"That might work. Orsino takes himself seriously, but I think he's pretty funny. But Becky, look, Alma and Erin have met Dominic and they don't like him."

"Oh, great. So he's going to play the beloved of one and the twin of the other."

"Well, Steph wants him to. Nobody's asked Mrs. Morgan yet."

"Steph's got a lot of credit with her after rounding us up and drilling us like that. She'll probably say yes."

"I suppose it's good theatrical practice," said Becky.

"That's what Steph said, but I think it's a very bad idea."

"Is she going to talk to Alma and Erin, or just spring it on them?"

"Oh, gosh, I don't know. She was vastly unyielding."

"I'd trust them to talk her out of it, I think."

"I don't know. She's very set."

"So you keep saying. You know, Gen, I hate to say it about a friend of yours, but Dominic causes a lot of trouble."

"He's not a friend of mine, and he didn't do anything; Steph just took one look at him and decided he looked enough like Erin."

"I never put no bullet in the furnace," said Becky, laughing, "and stop talking about my mother."

"What?"

"Sorry. Never mind. My parents have been playing their Bill Cosby records again. Well, at least I'll get to meet Dominic."

"You'll probably hate him too. Though he does talk very poetically. Let's not talk about him, all right? Tell me about Micky."

For the next week Gentian devoted herself to astronomy. It was the only thing besides Maria Mitchell that did not irritate her. She was annoyed with Steph for being stubborn; and with Dominic for dropping his science project without a second thought to cavort in Shakespeare, just because Steph asked him;

with Mrs. Morgan for saying Dominic could do the cavorting; with Alma and Erin for failing to talk Steph out of it and refusing to quit the play themselves, or even to threaten Steph with quitting. The three of them had had a long solemn conversation in which Gentian tried to remind them how much they disliked Dominic and they explained to her that letting Steph down would be worse than putting up with Dominic in the play. Gentian didn't think saving somebody from her own foolishness and stubborness constituted letting her down, but neither Alma nor Erin would agree with her.

She was annoyed with her family for going on and on idiotically about a commercial holiday based remotely on a religious event none of them believed in. She was annoyed with all her teachers, with bus drivers, mail carriers, pigeons, squirrels, and two out of the three cats in the house.

Only the telescope, despite earlier freaks, did not betray her. She considered Capella, Procyon, and Sirius; she stared into the dark winding depths of the Horsehead Nebula; she considered the Crab Nebula, which was the tattered and still-glowing shells of a supernova whose light had reached Earth in 1054 A.D. The Chinese had called it a guest star. There was a pulsar in the middle of it, the collapsed and tight-clenched fist of what matter the original star had not blown away from itself.

Her telescope did not show her much detail, and most of the interesting aspects of the Crab Nebula were looked at by radio astronomy and spectroscopy. But she liked thinking about it. She liked looking at it when she herself felt crabby. She felt tempted to do the equivalent of its spectacular act, to burn everything around her with a huge explosion and then curl up into a sphere so perfect that nothing could get in or out. But she was not a star, and while she had the energy for the explosion, she did not have the mass for collapsing afterwards. If she blew up, she would have to take the consequences.

Maria Mitchell sat on her lap, or at her feet, or on the bed in the middle of the electric blanket when the room was coldest, and made an occasional interrogatory sound, and purred thunderously when, at three or four or five in the morning, Gentian fell stiff and dry-eyed into bed.

On the twentieth of December the warm spell ended, and on the twenty-first it snowed. Gentian had to go to bed early when the clouds came in, so she was up by ten, and on her way to school by ten-thirty.

The whole outside sparkled dimly, in the diffuse cloudy light, with fine powdery snow. At least, if they had to have Christmas, it would come with the right weather. All the Giant Ants had family commitments on the day itself, but maybe they could go sledding the day after. Gentian scuffed through new snow and old ice, down all the steps to the sidewalk. Nobody in Gentian's family had shoveled any snow before rushing off to their day's occupation, but the Hardys' walk was bare and dry.

"Merry meet again," said Dominic.

Gentian jumped, which added another drop to the large pool of her annoyance. He had come down the driveway without making a sound.

"Hello," she said resignedly.

"I hoped to catch you before you went."

Gentian stared. He had said a rational English sentence, without poetic reference, that conveyed information. "Well, here I am," she said.

"I would like to begin my science project."

"What, now?"

"Yes."

"Well, I was going to school." She looked at him. He was as pale and beautiful as ever, but he did have on a red shirt with his black pants and boots and jacket. It might be as well to encourage his rationality and initiative. Besides, if he got involved in the science project, maybe he would change his mind about the play. "I guess I can miss a day," she said. She had no specific appointments with any of the Giant Ants, and it might be a relief to just not see any of them for a day. They were terribly excited about the play and had already learned most of their lines, which they recited with abandon at every opportunity, until they were almost as annoying to talk to as Dominic in his usual mode.

"Sure," she said. "Come on in."

"In a moment. I have equipment to bring."

"Can I help you?"

"I shall bring it inside and you carry it upstairs."

"So much for chivalry," said Gentian, but quietly.

The equipment appeared to be arranged in chronological order. Dominic first brought two leather trunks full of thick glassware and scrolls tied up with ribbon and brass instruments; then a series of wooden boxes with more glassware and more brass instruments and leather-bound printed books; then wooden boxes of vacuum tubes and wires and strange small heavy metal boxes, and an old black Royal typewriter; then a series of unboxed greasy objects that looked as if they had once been part of a car; then cardboard boxes of cables and cards and keyboards, and computer manuals; and finally one more large cardboard box heaped with a tangle of headphones, binoculars, CDs, tapes, small speakers, and floppy disks.

Gentian hauled all these to the second floor, gasping. Then she ran down to the basement and borrowed a couple of her mother's trouble lights, abstracting as well two desk lamps used to illuminate the laundry room and the workbench. Her parents didn't like overhead lights. She lugged them upstairs, dumped them on the hall floor, and unlocked the padlocked door. She considered the bulk of the things Dominic was bringing, and decided they would have to work in the main attic. She plugged in the lights, turned them on, shooed Maria Mitchell out again, and went downstairs to get Dominic's equipment.

After she had toiled upstairs with all of it, she went into the kitchen and got herself a Coke. She didn't like soft drinks as a rule, but right now a nasty jolt of sugar and caffeine seemed exactly right. She went back to the front porch and found a few more cardboard boxes and a large pile of lumber interspersed with tapestry cushions and an entire box of old calendars. Gentian sat on the porch swing, enjoying the winter air on her overheated self, waiting for Dominic.

He came up the porch steps about five minutes later, a towering pile of boxes, with legs. He put them down lightly, and emerged neither flushed nor breathless.

"Is that all?" said Gentian.

"A woman waits for me, she contains all," said Dominic, "nothing is lacking."

Gentian sighed. He was back to normal, and now she was stuck with him.

17

D ominic left after they had brought everything upstairs; he said, "I will return when I may," and walked out of the attic and down the stairs, leaving every door open. By the time Gentian had got over her surprise and anger and gone after him, he was nowhere to be seen. She shut the front door and went back upstairs, shutting other doors as she went. She looked into the main attic to see if everything was really there. Yes, in piles and stacks, all over. There seemed to be more than either of them had carried up—where had that strange stark ergonomic office chair come from, or that tattered tapestry, or this enormous wooden radio from, what, the 1920s? They might have been there already and she had failed to notice them; but she and her mother had cleared this attic out thoroughly when they did the wiring, and she had inspected it herself not very long ago. She would have to ask her parents if they had been storing things up here.

She went into her own room. Maria Mitchell hissed at her and vanished into the closet. Gentian checked the food bowl, but it was only half empty. She topped it off and changed the water for fresh, but no cat appeared. She stuck her head into the closet and coaxed, but Murr only bundled herself into the very back under some old notebooks, and hissed. She might be sick;

or she might have sneaked downstairs, engaged in battle with Pounce or Yin-Yang, and ended up with an abscess. Gentian's father would have to come look at her when he got home from wherever he was.

"How will I practice astronomy with no cat in my lap?" she asked.

Murr growled. It was in any case still cloudy. Gentian read some history and solved some algebra problems, periodically putting her head into the closet and speaking to her cat, who hissed and growled at her.

Gentian went downstairs to see if her father was home. He wasn't, but Rosemary had come in and was making herself some cocoa. "What's that box on the porch?" she asked.

Gentian went out and looked. One more small wooden chest banded with leather and padlocked shut. She picked it up, grunting—it was extremely heavy—and lugged it to the foot of the stairs.

"It's part of Dominic's time machine," she said. "We must have missed it when we took everything upstairs."

"Oh, let me see!"

"It's not built yet, but you can look at what we brought. Are you going to help?"

"Well, if I have time after Girl Scouts."

They carried the trunk up to the attic. Rosemary, having walked all around Dominic's building materials and said, "Huh," several times, went back downstairs and built a fire in the fireplace. Gentian had some cocoa too, and curled up on the couch with the newest copy of *Sky and Telescope*, which she had not yet brought upstairs. It said nothing about the spots she had seen on Saturn. She would have to look again when the weather cleared.

Juniper came home next. She went immediately upstairs without saying anything, but she came back down in about twenty minutes in her green flannel nightgown, with her cat under her arm. When Junie came home and put her nightgown on, it meant she had had a very bad day. It was therefore less than sensible for Rosemary to tell her, before she had even had a cup of tea, that the materials for Dominic's science project were up in the attic.

"When did that happen?" she snapped. "And who let him in?"

"This morning," said Gentian. "I did."

"Why weren't you in school?"

"I was up late doing astronomy and he caught me just as I left the house."

"I thought you were doing the play instead."

"Well, so did I, but there he was."

"That's really stupid, Gentian."

"You don't have to help if you don't want to."

"You needn't think you can elbow me out."

"Much luck I'd have if I tried."

"I'll help you," said Rosemary, flourishing her elbows.

"Neither one of you has a chance in hell," said Juniper, and she took her cat and her teacup into the television room and turned the television up very loud.

Rosemary got up and shut the door.

"I hope she gets bored," she said, returning to her armchair.

"It won't help if she does, she'll just make us miserable."

Their father got home next, with two canvas bags full of library books. He looked harassed. While he was hanging his coat up and putting the books away in his office, Gentian went into the kitchen and made him some cocoa.

"Maybe you do have an Electra complex," he said, when he came into the kitchen and she handed him the mug. "You want to watch that. I'd hate to find myself bringing home Cassandra."

"You wouldn't, unless she was a stray dog."

"Well, in fact, your mother's more likely to consider that a matter for murder than she would my bringing home a mistress."

"Only if it were another pregnant stray dog."

"I don't think Cassandra was pregnant."

They wandered into the living room and sat down. Rosie put another log on the fire. "Junie's sulking," she said.

"It sounds more like conducting aerial warfare to me," said their father, eyeing the door to the sunroom.

"Dad, does Mom even know that Yin-Yang's here?"

"Oh, yes, but as long as Junie's taking care of him, she doesn't mind."

"Oh, I almost forgot—Murr is hiding in the closet and hissing and growling at me. Can you come look at her?"

"I should have been a veterinarian," said her father, pushing himself out of his armchair. "Then I'd get paid for these visits. And I wouldn't have to deal with publishers."

They went upstairs.

"It's freezing in here," said her father. "It'd be enough to make me hide in the closet."

"I want to look at Saturn later on."

"As long as he's not bathing."

"That was Diana. I don't think anybody ever got punished for watching a god bathe."

"Very good," said her father.

Gentian rolled her eyes.

Gentian sat on the bed while her father inserted his upper half into the closet, talking soothingly. After a moment he said, "She's purring, but that doesn't mean there isn't something wrong." After a few more moments he said, "I can't find a sore spot, and I don't think she has a fever."

He backed out of the closet. Gentian took his place. Murr, dimly visible, puffed herself up like a nebula and hissed ferociously.

"I think she's mad at *me*," said Gentian, removing herself hastily. "I can't think what I did."

"Forgot to feed her, I assume."

"No, I checked that. Oh. Maybe she's annoyed that we brought all that stuff into the attic."

"What stuff? Or do I want to know?"

"It's just the stuff for Dominic's science project."

"Oh, he came through, did he? And how do you propose to work on his science project and be in a play and do astronomy and go to school?"

"I'm not the only one working on it. We all said we'd help. And it's his project. Let him work on it."

Her father contemplated her with his head on one side for a moment, rather as Murr might look at a piece of carpet fuzz to see if it was worth pouncing on.

"Do I sense some disillusion?" he said.

"I wasn't illusioned to start with."

"I wouldn't believe Juniper if she said that, but maybe you weren't. What about Rosie?"

"She thought he was a drug dealer, but he was just quoting Keats."

"Well, the Devil can cite Scripture to his purpose."

"I guess, but he wasn't trying to sell her anything."

"You're sure that science project isn't to do with making some vile New Age extract of animal tranquilizer?"

"I told you, it's a physics project, not chemistry."

"So it won't work, but it won't blow up either. That's all right, then."

He wandered out, leaving Gentian to wonder what a conversation between him and Dominic would sound like.

She had to go on wondering. Dominic was in evidence quite a lot for the next few days. But he only showed up when her father was gone, and usually when everybody else was gone as well. He brought in a few more boxes and a set of tools, and then set to hammering and sawing in the attic. Gentian, who had in her time built everything from a treehouse that was still safe five years later to bookcases to a couple of replacements for the cherry steps up to her telescope, offered to help.

"Very learned women are to be found," said Dominic, "in the same manner as female warriors, but they are seldom or never inventors."

It would be a terrific pain to drag all that stuff out of the attic again. Gentian took a deep breath. "I don't think I can work on this project if you're going to go on talking like that, Dominic."

"Talk is cheap."

"Well, good, because I sure wouldn't pay you for it."

Dominic seemed to make an effort, and finally said, "I must do the preliminary work myself; no man may aid me either."

"Well, all right. Let me know when you're ready."

Maria Mitchell came stretching through the open door, ostentatiously ignored Gentian, and brushed her variegated tail against Dominic's leg. He looked down at her, but made no move to pet her. "A harmless necessary cat," he said. He sounded hopeful.

"She's one of your female warriors," said Gentian.

When he left, Murr climbed into her lap, but did not purr.

He did not, naturally, show up on Christmas, though Gentian was secretly entertained by the thought of his doing so. Her family seemed pleased with their presents, even though this had not been an inspired year for her. She felt she fared better than they did: they had given her not only the color filters she asked for, but a talking clock intended for blind people. She could press a bar on it, without looking away from the telescope, and in an abrupt computerized voice it would tell her the time. She had not yet done any systematic record-keeping, let alone timed anything's transits, but now she had the wherewithal. They had also given her Carl Sagan's *Comet* and both the *Astronomical Calendar* and the *Observer's Handbook* for 1994. The latter was particularly valuable, being produced by Canadians who knew there were latitudes north of the fortieth.

They had a large and varied dinner, at which Junie only snapped at Rosemary once and Gentian was nobly amiable to everybody; they read aloud from "A Christmas Carol" and then, for contrast, from *A Child's Christmas in Wales*. They trimmed the tree, telling stories about all the ornaments. Gentian had found a telescope ornament in her stocking: as it turned out, Steph had called her mother and told her about it. Juniper got one of the little papier-mâché books, and Rosemary a sailing ship.

They sat around the fire afterwards, drinking cider and eating cookies. Pounce sat on Gentian's father's lap, and Yin-Yang perched precariously on Juniper's knee and made the occasional threatening noise. Gentian had brought Maria Mitchell down when she came to breakfast, but Murr was as usual hiding under the sofa. She would probably come out when things were quieter.

"So is Dominic ever going to start his project?" said Rosemary.

"Probably after New Year's," said Gentian.

"I'll believe it when I see it."

"That's probably a good attitude."

Rosemary looked vaguely thwarted, but did not pursue the point.

Gentian was so full of food that she went to bed at ten and didn't waken until eight the next morning. It was nine below zero, and sunny. That boded well for astronomy, if not for the astronomer. She went sledding in Memorial Park with the Giant Ants, and brought Becky home with her afterwards to bestow another blessing on the telescope.

"I thought it had been working fine," said Becky.

"It has, but I don't want to take any chances. It was about time for you to come over anyway."

"It's about time for me to stop coming over until spring, actually."

"You can sit on the electric blanket with Maria Mitchell."

"Somehow, it's still cold when I do that."

"Just let me look at Saturn a bit and then a couple of large obvious stars, and I'll quit and turn the heat on."

"If you'll show me something especially fine, all right."

Gentian found Saturn. The seeing was, for no reason, spectacularly good: Saturn was rock-steady, like a photograph, a fine creamy yellow with dark rusty stripes, still broken up into spots and blotches in the north. She touched her clock, which told her she had been looking for about twenty minutes, and reluctantly set about thinking of something especially fine to show Becky. Sirius was impressive, but perhaps not sufficient. After a moment she decided to show her Castor and Pollux.

She found Castor first; it was an aggressive and definite white against the edge of the Milky Way. She followed it until she could split it into Castor A and B. There was a third star, a dim red dwarf, also associated with them, but she had never actually found it, though other people with six-inch telescopes had. They hadn't lived in the middle of a modern city.

"Hey, Becky, come look at Castor, and then I'll find Pollux."

"Oh, the Heavenly Twins."

"It's more than that. Castor is three visible stars, if you're lucky, and each one of them is a spectroscopic binary, so where we see one star with the naked eye, there are actually six altogether."

"What am I going to see?"

"Just Castor A and B, probably, unless you get to see C, that's the red dwarf. I wish you would."

"I just see the one—oh, all right. That's *white*, isn't it, very assertive."

Gentian reclaimed the telescope after a while and found Pollux. It was brighter than Castor, a fine pale gold, and was itself only, with no elusive companions splitting and splitting again. She showed Becky.

"What's all that behind them both?"

"The edge of the Milky Way."

"You know, nothing you've shown me has really had a black, dark sky behind it."

"Well, there are a lot of stars. It's the same with just binoculars: you point them at something bright that looks all alone, and a whole bunch of little stars jump out all around it."

Becky was silent for a while, looking. Finally she spoke.

"They aren't really much like twins, are they, either in color or in number?"

"No, not at all, but to the naked eye that's how they've looked. Every civilization that named them called them twins—well, every one I know about, anyway."

"There's something in this more than natural, if philosophy could find it out." Becky relinquished the telescope to Gentian, looking, in the red light, vaguely glazed.

"Weren't you going to write a poem about Betelgeuse?"

"Yes, I've been working on it. The actual description is all right, I guess, but I can't make it mean more than that."

"So you don't know when I can see it."

"No, sorry."

"Maybe if you put Castor and Pollux in, it will all come together?"

"Maybe."

Becky climbed back under the electric blanket. Gentian decided, as long as the telescope was aimed in that direction, to take a look at M35. She found the orange star near its center, and looked with approval at the curves of bright uniform stars, like lights seen from an airplane at night, winding out on a background of fainter stars. She looked long enough to see the orange and yellow giants amongst the bright white stars, and then with great reluctance put the telescope to bed, shut the windows, turned on the heat, and turned on the plain white lights.

Becky blinked at her. Maria Mitchell came out of the closet and jumped onto the bed. Gentian joined them, feeling a little out of focus. "Are you going to entertain me splendidly now?" she said.

"Well, I wanted to talk to you; I'm not sure if it's entertaining," said Becky, giving a scornful twist to the last word.

"What, what?"

"I think I'm in love."

Gentian forgot the telescope. She felt as if somebody had slammed her solidly in the chest, as Alma had once tackled her playing touch football. She sat trying to get her breath. "Micky?"

"No, I've met somebody new and not told you."

"You sound like Erin."

"Well, really, who else would it be?"

"I was just trying to adjust. Tell me everything."

"I hate to. It's so stupid and embarrassing. I have no idea how he feels, but I'm obsessed. I think about him all the time. He keeps popping up in my poems whether he belongs there or not. I fantasize about arguments we might have and about his calling me and about all sorts of things I don't even think I'm old enough to do."

"But what do you do about it?"

"Writing and fantasizing is doing, don't you tell me it's not."

"Yes, all right, sorry, but, well—"

"I thought you might feel the same way about Dominic."

"No," said Gentian, slowly, "I don't think so. I think about him, and I plot ways to see him, but he's so unpredictable he's exhausting, and we never really get anywhere. There isn't any— what's that theatrical term Mrs. Morgan is always going on about?—there isn't any continuity. It's like starting over at the beginning every time. It's exciting, but I really can't get up an obsession. Besides, he's a sexist."

"So's Micky. He thinks he isn't, but he is."

"But he'll argue with you, he takes your opinions seriously—doesn't he?"

"Sure. He's—he's kind of a historical sexist. He thinks I'm okay, but he doesn't really think women have ever done anything worth making a fuss over in the entire history of the world."

"You know," said Gentian, thinking it over, "that's disgusting, but it's kind of romantic too, if he makes you an exception."

"It's very alluring," said Becky, almost growling, "but it's awful just the same."

"So what things don't you think you're old enough to do?"

"Never mind," said Becky, turning pink. "If you haven't thought of them too, never mind."

Gentian wasn't at all sure she wanted to hear, but she was hurt that Becky wouldn't tell her.

"Let's play Scrabble," said Becky.

"All right, but wait a minute. Does he call you?"

"Once or twice."

"Maybe he feels the same way but he has no idea how you feel."

"Oh, probably, but who wants to risk looking like an idiot?"

"It'd make a good poem."

"Maybe if I run out of other subjects. Let's play Scrabble."

Dominic continued not to appear for the whole of Christmas vacation, and the telescope continued to work. Gentian went on looking at Saturn, and was finally driven by its continual exhibition of unusual spots to make drawings of them. All the handbooks recommended soft pencils and charcoal, and she worked over the drawings for hours and ended up very smudgy, while Maria Mitchell, who could not be dissuaded from supervising her, took on the appearance of a calico cat with gray feet and chin.

She also made a thorough study of the whole constellation of Gemini, returning often to Castor, splitting it as far as she could and thinking of how much further it split. She went back to Orion and looked again at the Trapezium, because closer study of her books had shown her that it was another set of stars of the same kind. It looked like one star to the naked eye, surrounded by a fuzziness that was the Orion Nebula. In a small telescope it was four large stars in a trapezius with two smaller ones, one a little above and to the right of the trapezius, the other just outside it on the left. Two of the trapezium stars, in their turn, were eclipsing binaries. Gentian had her suspicions of all the others as well. The revelation of multiplicity in unity interested her deeply, although when she tried to write down why, the result sounded so trite she tore up her efforts and burned them in the family's nightly fire.

The Giant Ants always had a New Year's Eve party. It was at Alma's house this year. Becky called Gentian three days before, sounding panicked.

"I want to ask Alma if I can invite Micky," she said.

Since all Alma's siblings would be there, Gentian felt less strongly about this than she might have.

"I know it isn't fair," said Becky, "since Alma doesn't like Dominic."

"I couldn't invite him anyway," said Gentian. "He hasn't got a phone."

"Maybe Erin could invite Brent."

"There's no point in trying to make it all come out even. We are not all double stars in this constellation."

"I'd have said you and I were a double star," said Becky, disconsolately.

"Sure. Micky's just a comet you've captured and Dominic is, oh, a comet I haven't captured, but he's come under my gravitational influence for the time being."

Becky laughed, as if in spite of herself. "I'll call Alma and ask if it's okay."

Gentian hung up the phone and sat there, thinking. She herself had been behaving just as usual, so Becky's disconsolation must stem from something in Becky's feelings; she must be finding that thoughts of Micky somehow crowded Gentian out of her mind. What does that mean, in the long run? she thought. Will she not sit by me at the party, or not talk to me, or what? Maybe it won't matter. I get very concentrated on Dominic sometimes too, but it's just temporary. It wouldn't interfere with anything important. She almost called Becky up and told her so, except that the line would be busy while Becky was talking to Alma. Besides, another thought was intruding. She sat absently rubbing Murr's belly for a while, and then went downstairs and found her father in his office.

He called, "Come in!" when she knocked. He was sitting at his computer, playing solitaire.

"Daddy," said Gentian, not apologizing for the interruption, since he obviously was not working, "remember you said Mom would be more upset if you brought home another dog than if you brought home a mistress?"

"Ah," said her father. "I wondered when that would go in."

"Well, are you planning to?"

"Bring home another dog? No. I don't plan them. They just happen."

"Dad."

"I don't think I could," said her father reflectively. "We haven't got a bedroom to spare. You couldn't put a mistress in the sewing room, could you?"

"*Dad.*"

"No, Gentian, I am not planning to bring home a mistress. I will even go so far as to say that I do not have a mistress, although I'm not sure it would be any of your business if I did, unless I were planning to bring her home."

"Would it be Mom's business? Even if you weren't planning to bring her home?"

"Yes, of course."

"Well, that's something."

"What about you? Are you planning to bring somebody home? We'll look as respectable as we ever do, I assure you. No unaccounted-for adults cluttering up the place. Just the usual ration."

"Just the usual double-star system," said Gentian, slowly.

"Are they usual?"

"Well, multiple-star systems are, I'm pretty sure. I'm not sure about doubles as opposed to triples or whatever."

"You can bring two people home if you like," said her father, equably. "Just warn us so we can put some water in the soup."

He was in a skittish mood; there wasn't much point in talking to him any longer.

"Thanks," said Gentian, and went out.

"Are you turning into a teenager?" her father shouted after her.

Gentian did not deign to answer.

18

The day of New Year's Eve was warm, seventeen degrees above the average high, which meant it was just below freezing. Gentian set off for the party, therefore, without a great deal of astronomical regret; the seeing would probably not be good until the weather settled more.

She was the first one there, and Alma was still getting dressed. She was informed of these facts by Alma's brother Duane, who was ten; he was the one who owned the hamsters. She consented to go see them, and to let them climb up her arm and burrow inside her sweater, and to exercise them by letting them walk from one hand into the other and then putting the first hand in front of them so that they walked onto that, all without going anywhere.

"I feel that way sometimes too," she said to the one she was holding. It climbed busily onto her other hand, nose working, whiskers twitching. Gentian wondered why Lewis Carroll had not had a hamster rather than a Red Queen.

Alma came and fetched her presently and took her down to the basement recreation room where Alma entertained her friends. She was wearing a brilliant red caftan, red ballet shoes, and red earrings. Gentian resigned herself to feeling like a sartorial barbarian for the rest of the evening. She had completely forgotten that she had a new white silk shirt and a red jumper in her closet. Well, her jeans were clean and she had washed her hair.

Becky arrived next, and took off her jacket to reveal a vivid orange skirt, a dark green sweater, a yellow scarf around her waist, red socks, and, once she had taken her boots off, purple slippers.

"Becky, we clash," said Alma.

"Good," said Becky. "You look very elegant."

Alma told them to keep one another company, and went to supervise whatever was happening in the kitchen. Her brothers tagged along, despite threats on her part to kill them if they touched anything before everyone else arrived. Becky took a folded piece of paper out of the pocket of her skirt and handed it to Gentian.

"Read this before the rest of them get here," she said.

It was a poem in three verses, called "Betelgeuse on a Winter's Night." The verses were sonnets. The first was about how Becky had felt waiting for Gentian to come back, the night she suggested Gentian try the binoculars. The second was about the time Gentian showed her the double star Albireo through the telescope, and the third was about all the arguments she and Micky had had. When she had read them, Gentian turned the paper over, to see what the conclusion might be, but the three verses were all there was. She read them again. They all had certain things in them: the colors of Gentian's room, of Albireo's stars, of the sky and the sun when she was walking with Micky; the cold of the balcony and of Gentian's room when she was stargazing and of the park where Becky had walked with Micky. They had recurring phrases. But she could not fit them together. She thought they were all good, especially the one about Albireo, but she could not see how they made a whole.

She said so, reluctantly.

"I know," said Becky. "I might fiddle with them some more or I might just let them alone. They're as connected as I can make them. I wrote about five different last verses and they just didn't work."

"You know you're always sorry when you try to finish things before they're ready."

"Yes, I know."

"Maybe you're too nervous because Micky is coming."

"I am fairly nervous. How am I supposed to act? Who am I supposed to sit by? What if everybody hates him? He's going to argue with them, he always does. He argued with my mother about how to make chocolate pudding."

"What did she think?"

"That he was cute. And how nice that a boy should take an interest in cooking."

"Maybe the Giant Ants will think he's cute too."

Becky made a grimace, eloquent of exactly what Gentian could not tell, and Erin came in with Steph. Erin was wearing leggings and a very large sweater, which made her look remarkably like Viola dressed as a boy. Steph had a broomstick skirt made in tiers of different materials, over black leggings and a black leotard. She looked extremely pretty, but then she always did.

"Where's Micky?" said Erin to Becky. "Did you leave him to make his way here all alone?"

Becky stuck out her tongue. "Where's Brent?"

"Visiting his grandmother, as usual on New Year's." Erin sat down on the floor. "Well, at least now I know that. He looked completely blank when I asked him."

"Is Dominic coming?" said Steph to Gentian.

Gentian refrained from sticking her own tongue out, and said, "He hasn't got a telephone and I haven't seen him."

"You could have dropped him a note."

"He doesn't get letters," said Gentian.

Alma came in with a huge tray of fresh fruit and vegetables, and Steph sprang up to help her. Erin gave Gentian an odd look but said nothing. Becky said quietly to Gentian, "What does that mean?"

"The post office thinks the house isn't there."

"Maybe they should talk to your telescope next time."

Gentian giggled.

"Are you saying," said Steph, returning, "that Micky is going to be the only boy here?"

"He's used to it," said Becky. "He's got three sisters."

The doorbell rang. Alma ran upstairs and could be heard arguing with Duane in the upstairs hallway. Becky sat where she was, but her eyes got big.

"Some of Duane and Peter's friends are coming, too," said Erin quietly. "Alma says she'll put them in the living room."

Footsteps sounded on the basement steps, and Alma came down with Micky. He had grown since Gentian last paid him any mind, but he was basically the same, a very nice study in shades of brown, with his dark curly hair and big brown eyes and pale brown skin. He was thin and sharp-featured and restless-looking. At the moment he also looked apprehensive, like Becky. His eyes glanced off everybody else; then he found her and grinned. Becky didn't grin back, but she did stand up and go to meet him. They were just the same height, but Becky could have beat him at wrestling. Alma vanished upstairs again, and Becky brought Micky over to where Gentian and Erin and Steph were sitting.

"I think you've all met before," said Becky, "but it was a long time ago. Micky Adomaitis, Gentian Meriweather, Erin Kerr, Steph Thornton."

"Erin's in my study group," said Micky.

Trust Erin to say nothing whatsoever about that to anybody.

"And I think I remember the rest of you from the butterfly incident."

"Except Steph," said Erin. "They sent her to the wrong school that year."

"It was actually a good school," said Micky. "My baby sister liked it."

"It was okay," said Steph, "but I didn't know anybody."

"It wasn't as good as the open school, anyway," said Gentian. "Awfully regimented."

"I didn't mind much," said Steph. "At the time I wanted to join the Navy, so I liked being terribly rule-bound."

"Regimentation is better for most people," said Micky. "Especially kids, who tend to be flighty."

"Your sisters are flighty," said Becky. "Don't overgeneralize." She sounded just as she might when chiding Gentian or Erin for something they had been doing since the second grade. How does that happen so fast, thought Gentian.

"I'm a scientist," said Micky. "I have to generalize. You're a poet; you have to be specific."

There was a brief confounded pause as every one of the Giant Ants present gathered herself to contradict him. Becky, who after all had had more practice, got in first.

"I have to be specific because that's the kind of poet I am," she said. "It's nothing to do with poetry. Lots of poets generalize. Look at Alexander Pope."

"And science has to be specific," said Erin. "It's made up of specifics."

"The whole purpose of science is to discover general rules," said Micky.

"Yes," said Gentian, "but not by making them up out of too few examples."

"What do you mean, yes?" said Erin. "That is not the whole purpose of science; science is too big to have a whole purpose."

"Now you know how I feel," said Steph, "when one of you starts going on about how the whole purpose of religion is this or that."

"The whole purpose of religion is to keep people from thinking for themselves," said Micky.

"You might just as well say that's the whole purpose of science," said Steph. "It comes to exactly the same thing. Religion really does say it knows general rules and tells you what they are."

"Not—" began Erin.

"Don't start on Eastern mysticism. Refusing to have a general rule is just as much a general rule as having one."

Gentian looked at Becky, to see how she was taking this. Becky did not look overly alarmed. Gentian thought she herself might be more alarmed than Becky. She did not want to talk about science with a stranger, and was a little surprised that Steph would so readily engage in a discussion of religion, which was her science, with somebody she hardly knew.

Then again, Steph had odd notions of what privacy was.

"That's logically true," said Micky, "but—"

Alma burst upon them with her arms full of CDs, and made Micky and Steph help her choose five to put in the changer.

"Was that a rescue?" said Gentian to Becky.

"I don't know; the rescuer and the rescuee may be one and the same. Alma hates arguments."

"Rescuee?"

"Sorry. I'm all about in my head."

"What else is anybody all about?"

"What's got into you?"

"Just taking up the slack you're leaving."

"Hoist with my own petard," said Becky.

"Are you sorry he came?"

"I don't know yet."

"Well, at least nobody will be able to tease you about him. Or me about Dominic."

"How is Dominic?"

"I have no idea. He came and put huge quantities of stuff in the attic, to build the time machine out of, but he hasn't been back. I wonder if they're away for the holidays. There's no way to tell, the house looks as if nobody lives in it anyway."

"But the lawn's always cut and there's no snow on the sidewalk, and there aren't those little newspapers that always pile up when people go away."

"No, that's true. It doesn't look neglected, but it doesn't look lived in, either."

"Gentian. Did you say 'time machine'?"

"Mommy, that man said 'time machine' to himself," said Gentian.

Becky acknowledged the joke with a smile, but kept on looking expectant.

"Well, yes. That's his science project. He wants to build a time machine."

"Is that scientifically feasible?"

"I don't really know; I haven't taken physics yet. What I think is that it might be theoretically possible but for a couple of kids to build it in an attic is very unlikely."

"Like all those books about building a moon rocket in your

back yard," said Becky. "So, if it's not scientifically interesting, why are you helping?"

"Well, because Dominic is scientifically interesting. I think helping him on something like this will tell me what I want to know about him." And give me a chance to make an impression on him, she added silently.

"You're an astronomer, not a psychologist," said Becky.

"Well, I have to live with people, don't I?"

"Do you?"

"Well, not really. Maria Mitchell didn't have to live with many of them, and she didn't get along with any of the bone-heads at all. But I have to live with me, anyway, and I seem to be fascinated by Dominic."

"Flawlessly logical," said Becky.

Alma came twirling up to them. "Why aren't you guys dancing?"

They looked at her. Neither of them could dance and they had made a private pact that they would never learn. They had also agreed never to get married and never to wear high heels or makeup, but they had not told the Giant Ants about that part.

"You know we don't," said Becky.

"Well, I thought since Micky's here."

"If I won't dance with just you guys around, I certainly won't dance if there's somebody else in the room."

Alma looked as sad as her bone structure would allow. "Poets need to develop their sense of rhythm," she said wistfully.

Gentian felt guilty, but it was evident at once that Becky was not moved. "Has anybody ever done a study," she demanded bitterly, "of whether people who make their career choices early are bullied and categorized and labeled by everybody in sight? I can't tell you that anthropologists shouldn't interfere with the normal workings of society, or marathon runners should be vegetarians, or veterinarians ought to have a pet of their own, because you haven't settled on one yet."

Alma laughed delightedly, which made her look much more like herself. "You're so funny when you're mad," she said, "but I do apologize. Can I dance with your boyfriend, then?"

"He's not my boyfriend, and you can run away to Mexico with him if you think he'd like it."

"What did I invite him for, if he's not your boyfriend?"

Becky cast a wild glance over Alma's shoulder. Gentian looked too. Micky and Steph were apparently arguing more or less amiably about music: each was making a stack of CDs, and there was a very small stack between them, which they would add to and take away from as their conversation dictated. They could not be heard over the music Alma had put on, which Gentian thought might be a Tori Amos album Juniper also owned, so probably they could not hear what Becky and Alma were saying either.

"It was very good of you to invite him," said Becky, in somewhat strained tones, "but how do you suppose somebody would get to be my boyfriend in the first place? If he didn't like the Giant Ants or you didn't like him, it would hardly be worth the trouble."

Alma immediately became serious, and sat down on the floor at their feet in a billow of red. "That makes me feel a lot better," she said.

"I thought it went without saying," said Becky, much more naturally, "or I'd have said something."

"I guess it should, but everything's changing so much. I don't even know how tall I am or what size bra I wear, and when I had that cold last week I got out a Goosebumps book to read, and it was so bad I wondered if somebody had taken the inside away and substituted a different one."

Becky gurgled. "Changeling books! Oh, that's nice."

"Changeling everything," said Alma. "And it's not nice."

Gentian thought of Dominic's saying to Steph, "A mind not to be changed by place or time."

"Not everything," said Becky.

"Look, Alma," said Gentian, "it's not any given book that matters as much as reading the same things and talking about them. Erin lent me some extremely weird ones called *Witch Baby* and *Weetzie Bat*. I'll bring them over next week if you want. I think they're the Giant Ants books of the future. And I read *Alice in Wonderland* the day after Christmas and it was just as good as ever."

"In the meantime," said Becky, "go and dance with my boyfriend so I can see if he's any good at it."

Alma stood up, but she looked dubious and unreassured. Gentian waited for Becky to cope with this, but Becky seemed at a loss. "You know she's always been like that," Gentian said to Alma. "Ever since kindergarten. Don't you remember, we were so jealous of our little group and didn't want to add anybody and she was always trying to bring people in because she thought we were so neat she wanted to share us around?"

Alma laughed until she had to sit down. She snorted so much that Becky patted her on the back and looked reproachfully at Gentian.

"Oh," said Alma eventually, sitting up and wiping her eyes. "I forgot. She did use to do that. Oh, Lord, my sides hurt."

"So go dance with her boyfriend."

"Yes, all right," said Alma, leaping up again. "I'll make him show you his paces."

"Good grief," said Becky.

They watched Alma bound across the room to Steph and Micky and engage in another argument. Steph stopped the music and they argued some more and then started digging through their piles of CDs again.

Alma finally went upstairs and came down with another handful; Micky selected one and put it into the player.

"That's that collection of Hungarian dances her father got when they first bought the CD player and there were hardly any CDs except classical music," said Becky. "She played it over and over and over."

"I think your boyfriend is a folk dancer," said Gentian, watching Micky demonstrate steps to Steph and Alma.

"Please don't call him that. It's only funny once or twice."

"Sorry."

Erin had been sitting on the floor by the CD player, following the discussion and demonstrations with a slight sardonic smile. She got up suddenly and came over to Gentian and Becky.

"Micky says he wants to do a circle dance. he says it hasn't got partners or gender roles and it doesn't require any skill, just energy."

"How's that for a romantic invitation?" said Becky to Gentian. "Sure." She got up.

"Becky!"

"Oh," said Becky. "Just a minute, Erin."

Erin went back across the room, and Becky said, "Is this dancing within the meaning of the act?"

"Maybe not, but what if it's a slippery slope?"

"I'll probably hate it," said Becky, "but just allow me to observe that this is probably as close to a sport as you'll ever get me."

"Huh. Well. All right. But this is an exception. It is not a precedent."

"Strike hands and a bargain," said Becky, and they smacked their right hands together smartly and went to join the others.

Micky taught them a series of hand and foot movements and then had them go around in a circle executing them in whatever order he called them out. When one song ended he just went on calling out moves into the next. Three songs in, Becky said, "What are you, the cruise director? Get in here," and he joined them in the circle, between Becky and Steph.

Gentian found the steps easy to learn, and having done so, performed them efficiently and watched everybody else. Becky had a much harder time learning and a much harder time staying in rhythm with everybody else, and she turned very pink and got out of breath long before anybody else. But she seemed pleased. Alma danced in a Tiggerlike fashion, with bounces, beaming and turning, all red and brown with an occasional silver flash from her earrings. Steph was also smiling and laughing and whirling around to make her skirt fly out around her. She was precise and delicate in her movements; she reminded Gentian of somebody she had once seen in a kitchen store demonstrating a Japanese tea ceremony. Erin was expressionless, but she seemed to move with no effort at all, as if there were no gravity in her part of the room, like Maria Mitchell running across the tops of all Gentian's bookcases.

I wish we had a mirror, she thought, like they have in dance studios. I'd like to see all of us. I hope I'm not spoiling the effect. I know Becky isn't. Maybe it's all the bright colors, but she goes with the music.

Micky stamped his way into the middle of the circle and executed a series of turns with each Giant Ant; then, just as Gentian was being made very uneasy by this spectacle, he nodded at her and moved back beside Becky. She turned sedately into the middle, since the music had become suddenly much slower, and held out her right hand to Alma. They went around in a smaller circle of their own while still moving in the big one, a double planet orbiting some unseen center; and she managed to put in three of the clapping patterns Micky had taught them and two kicks before the music made her move on to Erin. Erin had watched her with Alma, and imitated the sequence of steps precisely. When she let go of Gentian's hand at the end, she actually smiled. Steph threw Gentian off her stride momentarily by making a curtsy, but they recovered at once and made a much brisker round, because the music had changed again. This is actually better than most sports, thought Gentian; there's something about the music. And it's more collaborative. I wonder if sex is like this.

Micky was next, which made Gentian feel shy and prickly at once. He did say, "You could have used that double kick," but she knew already that he would always have some comment or other, and he was good enough to stick to her routine and not interpolate anything.

She came to Becky last. Becky was completely out of breath, but when Gentian raised an eyebrow at her and tilted her chin at the CD player, Becky shook her head. They made their round within a round, and then Gentian fell back into her place, and while Erin was thinking out what to do, the music ended.

Becky sat down on the floor immediately, gasping. Alma ran upstairs, two steps at a time, and came down a few minutes later with a tray of ice and soda and fruit juice. By the time everybody had drunk a glass or two or three, Micky and Erin were arguing about the space program. Gentian began to wonder, listening, if this were merely his method of extracting information he didn't have, without putting him to the bother of actually asking.

By the time Becky had gone from bright red back to pink, she and Micky were arguing about Edna St. Vincent Millay, with Steph putting in an occasional sentence; and by the time she was her normal pale self, Alma had hauled out a pile of board games, which they played amiably, though not peacefully, until a little before midnight. Micky consistently sat by Becky, but since that left Becky's other side for Gentian, she did not find this especially unsettling. Becky made just as many asides to her as usual. Near midnight, Alma passed out noisemakers; then she went into the bathroom and opened two bottles of nonalcoholic champagne, emerging triumphant with no spillage at all. Last year Steph had lost most of one bottle down the kitchen sink, and the year before Becky had broken a lamp with an escaping cork. Before that somebody's parent had usually opened the bottles, or else they had had something less volatile, like lemonade.

Alma poured champagne for everybody; the old clock on the wall struck midnight, rustily; everybody made a lot of noise and cheering. Then there was an uneasy pause. They usually all hugged one another, but who knew, thought Gentian, whether Micky wanted to hug any of them, even Becky, or whether any of them wanted to hug him? She didn't, particularly, herself; he was perfectly fine company, but the acquaintance was much too short.

Becky hugged Gentian and then hugged Micky, which gave the rest of the Giant Ants a chance to hurriedly hug one another. Gentian then asked Micky, more or less at random, what he liked to read, and during the long dissertation on science fiction writers, all male, that followed—he'd enjoy talking to her father, probably—Becky went around and hugged the rest of the Giant Ants.

Then they had to sit on the floor in a circle and make toasts until the champagne was all drunk up. The origins of this ritual were in an Irish custom that Steph's sister Caitlin had found out about and introduced them to at one of Steph's birthday parties, but the Giant Ants had changed it a fair amount in the intervening years. You were supposed to toast a dead hero in the first round, a living one in the second, and an unborn one in the third. If anybody had not heard of your dead or living hero, you could give a brief biographical sketch. Becky explained this to Micky in an undertone, and then immediately offered her first toast, so that they would go around the circle widdershins as usual, and Micky's turn would be last.

"John Keats," said Becky. Gentian was quite startled; Becky almost always said Emily Dickinson.

"John Keats," said everybody in a ragged chorus, and drank.

"Maria Mitchell," said Gentian, as always.

"Maria Mitchell," everybody said, and drank.

Micky looked inquiring.

"She's often called the first woman astronomer, though actually Caroline Herschel did a lot of work before her. But Caroline just helped her brother. Maria Mitchell discovered the first telescopic comet and taught astronomy at Vassar for years." Gentian felt this was pitifully inadequate; she knew Maria Mitchell from her strict Quaker upbringing to her last days in the tiny Lick Observatory in Lynn, Massachusetts, whence she had sent her love to "the whole catalogue" at Vassar College, and remarked, "Well, if this is dying, there is nothing very unpleasant about it." She had said, "I believe in women even more than I believe in astronomy." She had defied all the Baptist trustees of Vassar; she had run through the corridors of the dormitory in the middle of the night, rousing her students to come see whatever astronomical sights were going. No nutshell or capsule would hold her.

Erin was next. "Gus Grissom," she said. She was working her way through dead astronauts, and usually said she was sorry to have so many left to go. This year she said the name alone.

"Gus Grissom," they echoed her.

Micky did not require to have Gus Grissom explained to him.

Steph was next. "King Arthur," she said.

"King Arthur!"

Micky looked skeptical. Becky said something in his ear, and he shut his mouth. Gentian smiled to herself. Steph probably knew more about the historical Arthur, and whether there had been one, than Arthur had known himself.

Alma was next. "Edith Cavell," she said.

Micky looked inquiring.

"She was an English nurse during World War I who helped about two hundred prisoners to escape. The Germans arrested her and had her shot."

It was Micky's turn. "I don't know if I'll be PC enough for you guys," he said.

Becky put her hand firmly on Gentian's arm, so Gentian merely simmered while Erin said calmly, "It's your toast, it's your hero. I suppose there are people we'd refuse to drink to, but we'll worry about that if it happens."

Micky raised his glass, looking perplexed. "There are so many," he said.

"Yes, we know," said Becky, "but the ones you leave out won't have their feelings hurt. Just say whoever you're thinking of at the moment."

"Well, all right," said Micky. "Robert A. Heinlein."

"Robert A. Heinlein," they said.

They went around again. "Eva Hoffman," said Becky. She must already have told Micky about Eva Hoffman, for he made no inquiry. "Vera Rubin," said Gentian. Micky did look puzzled, so she said, "She's an astronomer too. She discovered that the galaxies aren't distributed evenly, but tend to clump up, and that a lot of local ones are moving in a particular direction; and she discovered dark matter, by studying the rotation of spiral galaxies." Micky did not look impressed, but he raised his glass and drank with the others.

"Jane Goodall," said Erin.

"Mother Teresa," said Steph.

Over a gathering chorus, Erin said clearly, "No, really, Steph, I just can't."

"She's as much a hero as any of the rest of them."

"She's done a lot of good, but she's done a lot of damage."

"You aren't a hero if you haven't."

"What damage did Edith Cavell do?"

"Ask the Germans."

"What damage did Maria Mitchell do, then?" said Gentian.

"The trustees of Vassar sure didn't like her."

"Oh, right," said Erin. "A bunch of male egos just begging to be punctured. Mother Teresa has Stone Age ideas about birth control and lots of people to listen to her."

"If I could drink to Heinlein, who is *completely* immoral—"

"He is not."

"You *guys,*" said Alma. Gentian saw with some satisfaction that Micky's eyes were enormous.

"Drink to the good bits, Erin," said Becky. "Just have a sip."

"Oh, all right," said Erin.

"Mother Teresa," they murmured, and drank.

"Maya Angelou," said Alma, defiantly.

"Now look," said Steph.

"She is heroic, you can't deny it."

"Just a sip," said Becky.

"Maya Angelou," they said; Gentian watched, and Steph did take a sip.

"Stephen Jay Gould," said Micky, warily.

But they knew who he was because of Erin, and neither Steph nor Alma was a creationist, so that went over all right.

"Now the unborn heroes," said Alma, "and let's just all drink at the end to whichever ones we like, all right?"

Becky said, "Whoever writes the first really American epic poem."

Gentian said, "Whoever detects the first signal from extraterrestrial life."

Erin said, "Whoever puts gender in its proper place."

Steph said, "Whoever makes abstinence fashionable."

Alma said, very quickly, "Whoever makes tolerance fashionable."

Micky said, "The first man who sets foot on Mars. And everybody who worked to make it happen."

They all drank. Gentian's father was coming in fifteen minutes to take everybody home, so they started to stand up. Gentian felt awkward, and could see that nobody was very comfortable. Erin cleared her throat. "I'm sorry, Steph," she said. "I know everybody is good and evil mixed. I just—"

Steph flew at her and hugged her, saying something incoherent. Gentian felt better, but she didn't think it had been the most inspired round of toasts they had ever had. As with their Halloween costumes, they were running out of standard responses and had not yet figured out new ones. She wondered what Micky thought. She wondered if his phrasing of his unborn-hero toast had been deliberate or just clueless. She knew Becky would have noticed: Becky always noticed words.

After they had delivered everybody safely home, and were driving the six blocks from Alma's house, Gentian's father said, "Junie and her date are in the living room, so try to restrain your sisterly scorn."

"Who is it? The one from the chat echo?"

"Yes," said her father, in a slightly odd voice, "but I think you may recognize him."

"Somebody from school?"

"No," said her father, pulling the van into the driveway.

They went in through the back door. Gentian's mother was sitting in the kitchen eating garlic toast.

"Well, I'd better tell her it's time he went home," said her father. Gentian trailed him into the living room, consumed with curiosity. Juniper and her date were standing in front of the fireplace, looking into the deep orange bed of coals.

She had gone out for New Year's Eve with Dominic. Dominic, then, was the Light Prince. As he had retained Gentian's interest while being a racist and a sexist and a very indifferent conversationalist, so he had retained Junie's while being those things and insulting her intellect into the bargain. he did not look notably triumphant. Gentian wondered if anybody had ever said No to him.

"Merry meet again," said Dominic to Gentian.

"Happy New Year," said Gentian.

"We made a resolution," said Juniper, who did look triumphant, "that we'd start work on Dominic's science project tomorrow afternoon. He says he tends to be dilatory, so we must be diligent."

"Sisters three," said Dominic.

Gentian stood looking at him. I could say No to him, she

thought. But she was tired; she would not properly appreciate the reaction. It would have more effect if she said it later; she could choose her time; and anyway, she was curious about just how he proposed to build a time machine. And this was not Junie's forte: she was neither mechanically inclined nor methodical nor patient nor perservering. It might be that Juniper would say No and later on Gentian would say it too. Or not.

"I'll be there," said Gentian.

Then she said good night to her father and went upstairs, where she sat until 5:00 A.M. with Maria Mitchell on her lap, looking at the Pleiades and considering the structure of open clusters.

19

When Gentian woke up at one in the afternoon, with Maria Mitchell sitting on her chest and suggesting that she might want to get up now and throw this damp catnip mouse around the room, or possibly move her feet under the covers to be chased, or maybe just get up and let the cat out to find her own entertainment, she could hear voices and thumpings in the front part of the attic.

She sat up, rubbing her eyes. She could feel her hair sticking straight up all over her head. She wondered how long she would have to grow it before it would stop doing that. She reached to pet Maria Mitchell, but Murr jumped off the bed and made for the door, complaining. Gentian went to let her out, and encountered Rosemary, in paint-stained jeans and T-shirt, toiling up the last few steps with a huge box in her arms.

"What's in there?" said Gentian.

"Rocks," said Rosemary, puffing, and let the box fall to the hallway floor with a resounding crash.

"Very funny."

"It is rocks. It's fossils. Dominic says we have to get the oldest things we can find and start with those, and then we have to have something from any historical period we want to visit, so the time machine will have something to resonate with."

"What if something's a forgery?" Gentian grinned. "You could have a sideline testing stuff; it'd be better than carbon-14 dating."

"Aren't you helping, then?"

"Yes, I am, but I reserve the right to make fun of anything that strikes me that way." Gentian's mother had said this when she helped Juniper paint her sunroom purple.

"I don't think Dominic likes being laughed at. Junie laughed at him for wearing that big black silk shirt when he was going to be doing carpentry in a rustic attic, and he said, 'Nature never wears a mean appearance,' in a very snotty way." She rubbed at an especially involved paint spot on her shirt, and looked morose.

"Never mind, Rosie," said Gentian. "I'll wear an appearance as mean as yours, as soon as I've had a bath."

Rosemary picked up her box again and staggered past the bathroom. Gentian opened the attic door for her, shut it smartly before Maria Mitchell could slip in, and went into the bathroom, with Murr managing to be both before and behind her, purring and demanding furiously.

Gentian filled up her food bowl, turned on both of the bathtub faucets, and started to drag her sweatshirt over her head. She stopped with one arm entangled and hastily shut the door. She was not accustomed to having people wandering around the attic without her permission. Come to think of it, hadn't Dominic said she could have control over when anybody was there working on the time machine? She would have to talk to him.

Maria Mitchell emerged from her corner, stalked to the door with her tail erect, and pawed at it.

"I'm sorry," said Gentian. "You can stay in, or you can go out."

Murr lay down against the bottom of the door, the tip of her tail flopping about as if, her father always said, it possessed independent life, and heaved a long weary-sounding sigh.

Gentian removed the ping-pong ball from the rapidly rising water in the tub, dried it on her sweatpants, and tossed it at Maria Mitchell, but Maria Mitchell only turned her head in the other direction with great deliberation, and then looked meaningfully at the doorknob.

"You're going to hate this project, aren't you?" said Gentian, grabbing her lavender soap from the sink and climbing into the bathtub.

Maria Mitchell leapt onto the curved slippery side of the tub and balanced there delicately, looking censorious. "Maybe if you were to sleep quietly in a corner, or only play with the things we give you, you could watch," said Gentian, scrubbing her feet vigorously. Bathing was actually nice once you got to it, but it took such a lot of time, and you had to do it either in the morning when you were rushed and sleepy or else during stargazing time. They should let you have your bath at school, during study period; but they wouldn't, they'd only let you shower after Gym, and the showers were fairly disgusting. Most people avoided them altogether.

Gentian jerked the plug out of the drain and climbed out of the tub. Maria Mitchell leapt into the sink and began biting at that plug. Gentian decided not to notice. She wrapped herself in her large towel with the solar system on it, reached for the doorknob, and stopped. She was accustomed to just walking across the hall to her room in a towel, but now not only her sisters but Dominic were flitting around out there. She looked dubiously at her discarded sweats. She couldn't remember how many nights she'd slept in them, but it was probably about a month's worth; these were the green ones, and she was pretty sure that she hadn't had the purple ones on since well before Christmas. There was no point in wasting being clean by putting them back on.

She put her ear to the door and listened, but Maria Mitchell set up such a complaint that a herd of rhinos could have gone by in the hallway and you wouldn't have heard them.

"Well," said Gentian, "maybe he'll be more embarrassed than I am."

The hall was empty, and from the front attic came the sounds of hammering. Gentian walked sedately across the hall to her doorway. Murr immediately lay down in it, so that she could not shut the door. Gentian shut it most of the way and got dressed in a hurry, choosing her most raggedy jeans and the shirt in which she had helped her mother stain and varnish the banisters of the main stairway. She brushed her hair until it more or less lay down, put on her old sneakers with the holes, and marched into the front attic. Maria Mitchell ran ahead of her and disappeared into the finished room where she had found the old catnip mouse.

Dominic and Rosemary and Juniper were in the other finished room. They had already built a structure out of two-by-sixes, rather like an openwork bookcase, that covered two walls. Rosemary was handing Dominic rocks from her box, and he was examining them and placing them on the shelves. Juniper was sitting on the floor, in a large denim skirt and a T-shirt of surpassing whiteness and tightness, her hair bound up in a green scarf, measuring bits of wood with a tape measure and scowling.

They were all absorbed. The shelves looked makeshift, the fossils shabby; it was more like children playing museum than a scientific project. And how scientific was it, truly, to say that the time machine had to resonate with various objects from different periods of history? Gentian thought of her telescope just a room away; the new color filters and eyepiece; her resolution to learn more mathematics, to time transits of features on Jupiter and Saturn. She shifted her feet. She was in a play already, too.

Dominic looked up, and smiled right into her eyes. "Ah," he said. "The star for which all evening waits."

Rosemary looked resigned; Juniper shot Gentian a glance of immense vitriol. Oh, fine, thought Gentian, glaring back at her, you don't like the way Dominic is behaving, so you get mad at me.

Dominic stood up and came across the room to her, holding out his left hand. Gentian found herself reacting just as Maria Mitchell would to the advances of a stranger: she moved a little out of the way and created a diversion. Murr would usually pounce on something invisible; Gentian said, "So what's the plan?"

Dominic, for no reason Gentian could see, looked at Juniper, who said impatiently, "This is the prehistoric room; we have to set up this stuff and label it all. Then we'll set up a timeline for history, and when that's all done we start building the time machine."

"What does it do, travel around on a little track until it comes to the age it wants to resonate with?"

Rosemary giggled. Juniper looked at Dominic. Dominic contemplated her for several seconds in what looked to Gentian like mutual commiseration; then he said to Gentian, "Time, which is the author of authors, bears away all things. Time the destroyer is time the preserver. Physical space and time are the absolute stupidity of the universe. For a moment of night we have a glimpse of ourselves and of our world islanded in its stream of stars— pilgrims of mortality, voyaging between horizons across the eternal seas of space and time."

"You know," said Gentian, though he might only have paused for breath, "I really don't think you can explain how to build a time machine just by being poetic."

"The way is the way," said Dominic.

"Yes," said Gentian, forging ahead grimly, and feeling as if she were spitting tobacco juice over the edge of a box at the opera, "and one of the things we said about the way we'd do this was that I got to decide when people were up here working. I have to live and work right next door, and you woke me up this morning."

"It was afternoon already," said Rosemary, who was still sorting rocks.

"That isn't the point. Did we or did we not agree that I got to decide?"

"Dominic said you would," said Juniper, "but I don't remember agreeing."

"I wouldn't have said you could use the attic if he hadn't said I could decide when. So. Check the schedule with me in the future, all right?"

Rosemary giggled. "We can't do that until the time machine is built, can we?"

Gentian suppressed a sharp reply; Rosie's silly jokes ought to be encouraged, and she wasn't the one who had been duplicitous.

She smiled at Rosemary briefly and then looked back at Dominic. "All right?"

"To do a great right, do a little wrong," said Dominic, amiably.

"If you don't give me a straight answer, we can all just pack
up this stuff and take it back to your house."

Dominic looked first taken aback and then very much as if he
were angry, but while he was ruffling through whatever box of
quotations it was that he kept in his mind, Juniper jumped up
and stamped over to them. "For heaven's sake!" she said. "What
a spoiled brat. All right, we'll consult you; we'll make out a
schedule and follow it until Doomsday. All right?"

"The moist star," said Dominic, favoring Gentian with a
charming smile, "upon whose influence Neptune's empire stands,
was sick almost to Doomsday with eclipse."

"All *right?*" said Juniper, dangerously.

"Felicity or doom?" said Dominic.

"Oh, felicity, for heaven's sake. Gentian, are you satisfied?"

"For the moment," said Gentian, borrowing a line from their
mother.

"Eternity was in that moment," said Dominic.

"These," said Juniper, quoting *Hamlet* with great impatience,
"are but wild and whirling words, my lord."

"Oh, fine, now you're doing it," said Gentian.

Dominic, however, did not quote the next line and apologize,
which Gentian thought he very well ought to have. He said,
"These words are not mine."

"So we've gathered," said Gentian, borrowing another line
from her mother. What she was going to say next was rude, but
she said it anyway. "Look, Junie, he can hardly come up here unless one of us lets him in, so as long as you and Rosie agree to
consult me, it should be all right."

"Yes, I suppose so," said Juniper. "Well, then, Your Majesty,
may we work here until suppertime?"

Gentian bit the inside of her cheek until she could simply
reply, "Sure. What should I do?"

"Ask Dominic," said Juniper, and she went back to her measuring tape.

Gentian was so fed up with asking Dominic anything that she
almost gave up right there. But then she looked at Rosemary,
who seemed to be enjoying herself; and at Juniper, who was stiff
and bristly with annoyance, and thought, I won't quit before she
does. She looked at Dominic, who had been leaning against the
doorframe with his hands in his pockets ever since Junie told
him he was speaking wild and whirling words.

"What should I do?" she said.

"Here you and I stand in our degree," said Dominic. "What
do you mean to do?"

Black your eye? thought Gentian, but that was just exasper-
ation. She was never tempted to hit people; she was tempted to
make cutting remarks or to go off quietly and just show them
what idiots they were. Was Dominic an idiot? What was he?
What did she mean to do? He was looking at her unblinkingly,
and whatever her father might have said about black hair and
blue eyes and lips as red as wine, his eyes were quite black
enough already.

What did she mean to do? To fare boldly forth into physics
and mathematics. To live on the moon and look at the stars. To
look out and away, as far as she could, as far as there was to
look, to the place where space curved back on itself and there
was no farther. To tell Becky everything about it, in case she
wanted to make it into poetry. To read all of Becky's poetry, so
that she would give the subjective as well as the objective its due.

What, then, was she doing in this attic? One-upping Juniper,
taking care of Rosemary, trying to pluck out the heart of Dominic's mystery, to make him look straight at her and say something he had thought up himself? To flirt with him in whatever
way she might find to do that? To find out what was in his head?
All right, she thought, yes, all of that. But still: what if he wanted
to build a model railroad? Would you be up here helping? No.
It's the time machine. What if he can build one? What if we help
him do it?

How could he? He was a boy, her own age, possibly a genius

of some kind but just as possibly so far out on the curve of eccentricity that he might be mentally ill; what could he know, how could he have learned enough to do this? Then again, look at what Maria Mitchell the astronomer had done with almost no formal education and a two-inch telescope. Gentian walked past Dominic to the shelves of fossils, and picked up the first one. Rosemary had labeled them in her round, careful printing. She was in the habit of dotting her i's with little hearts—Gentian had used stars at the same age—but she did not do it here.

The fossils were exceptionally delicate, complete, and clear, and the rock they were embedded in was crystalline, full of depths, colored green and purple and orange and red and yellow. If the Museum Company were selling these, they would make them into bookends and charge hundreds of dollars for them. The one she had picked up was a fernlike frond in clear greenish rock; it looked like an underwater plant, almost as if it were moving in small currents. "Carboniferous," said Rosemary's writing. "Three hundred million years."

The one after that she did not recognize. "Sea lily (Crinoidea)," said the label. Embedded in translucent orange, it had a cluster of thin rootlike tendrils at the bottom, a long leafless segmented stalk, like an earthworm, and a bulging head rather more like a lily bulb than the lily itself. Gentian thought it was probably a sessile animal, but it might be a plant. "Cambrian—570 to 500 million years."

Gentian laid the lily down and picked up a flat dark-red oblong with a trilobite in it. It looked three-dimensional, as if the entire creature were embedded there like a fly in amber. The trilobite, freed from its rocky nest, would have huddled into the palm of her hand like Duane's hamsters. "Paleozoic—570 to 280 million years" said Rosemary's label.

The next one was an ammonite, in pale blue stone. Gentian's eye followed its spiral inwards, tighter and tighter, further and further, as she would follow the structure of a galaxy outwards.

"Those were once called snake-stones," said Dominic.

"Devonian to Cretaceous, 395 to 136 million years" said Rosemary's note. When the ammonite was alive, the light now reaching earth from the Coma Galaxy Cluster was just starting on its journey.

The next one was yellow, too yellow to be amber. "Opabinia," said the label. "Cambrian—530 million years." The animal was about two inches long. It was segmented, and the segments of its body turned down, like overlapping kernels of corn, but the three segments of its tail stuck rakishly upward. It had five eyes, two in front and three behind, on a head like an overgrown corn segment. And most delightfully of all, it had a long trunk or nozzle with a claw on the end, so that for just a moment it looked like somebody in mirror shades smoking a cigar.

The last one was white, a long oval enclosing a huddled featherless bird—no, not a bird, for it had a long curled tail like a lizard. "Embryonic dinosaur (hypsilophondontid) near hatching age. Cretaceous, 145 million to 60 million years." We could go there, thought Gentian, we could see them hatch. This one never had, but when its mother laid that egg, the light from the Ringtail Galaxy, in the Corona Borealis, was a third of its way to Earth.

It was the other end of the telescope. There was astronomy in everything.

"Show me the next piece of work," she said to Dominic.

And Dominic took her into the other finished room and taught her how to solder. Maria Mitchell crouched in the corner until he left and then hissed and growled and batted at Gentian's arm until she had to be picked up and put back into Gentian's bedroom lest she be soldered herself. Gentian could still hear her making long, threatening wails from time to time. The solder must smell awful to her.

"My cat hates this," she said.

"She'll love you more when all is said and done," said Dominic.

"When the soldering's done, more like," said Gentian.

Dominic left at sunset, having provided enough instructions that he probably would not need to come back for a week. Gentian wondered if he planned to stay away and let them do all the work. She didn't intend to, unless it turned out to be unexpectedly interesting, and she doubted Juniper would either. Rosemary was very dogged, but she probably wouldn't continue all by herself.

At dinner, their father asked how the project was coming.

"We got a lot done," said Rosemary, rapidly picking the cucumber and green pepper out of her salad and piling it at the side of her plate. "But I don't think Dominic is a very good manager. He doesn't explain things very well and then he gets mad if you don't do them right."

"He's a wimp," said Juniper, scowling. "He snapped at me for saying—"

"Don't say it again, or somebody else will snap at you," said her mother.

"It wasn't anything you can't hear at school every single day. Even Rosie wasn't embarrassed."

"Well, honey," said her father, "they say the devil's a gentleman, you know."

"They say sticks and stones may break your bones but words will never hurt you, too," said Juniper.

"They say red sky at morning, sailor's warning," said Rosemary.

"Well, Gentian?" said her father. "Would you like to add a non sequitur? We all know your mother doesn't approve of them."

"Birds in their little nests agree," said Gentian's mother, passing him the butter.

They were being romantic again. Gentian supposed it was better than fighting like Steph's parents or apparently ignoring one another like Becky's, but they did not have to look quite so pleased with themselves.

"There's glory for you," she said, helping herself to the rejected vegetables from Rosemary's salad.

"I don't want a nice knockdown argument," said Juniper. "I just want to be able to talk however I like in my own house."

"You can't do that anyway," said her mother.

"I can with my peers, at least. Dominic is stuffy and overbearing."

"You don't have to invite him back," said her father. "Though it sounds like a job removing all those objects from the attic. I can help, if you like."

Rosemary's head came up. She looked at Juniper, and so did Gentian.

"You don't have to work on the time machine if you don't want to, Junie," said Rosemary.

Gentian said, "You've been dating this guy for how long, and you only just discovered he's stuffy and overbearing?" This was, in fact, not at all the way Gentian would have described Dominic; whatever was exercising Juniper and Rosemary must have happened before she got up.

"He wasn't that way on the teen echoes. And he isn't when he's being romantic," said Juniper. "He is when he's working."

"It's just as well to have found out," said their mother. "Most relationships are about fifteen percent romance and the rest work."

Their father looked at her.

"Your father and I," she added, "have gotten the romance up to almost twenty percent by conspiring to baffle our children with quotations."

"Oh, God, they're being cute again," said Juniper, against a chorus of groans from Gentian and Rosemary.

The three of them had not even had to look at one another. Are we romantic, too, then? thought Gentian, and immediately giggled. Her parents laughed too, her father got up to clear the table, and in the resulting discussion of dessert, Dominic was relegated to the sidelines, where, Gentian thought, it would be better to leave him.

It was cloudy that evening, with light snow predicted, so she went back into the attic and practiced her soldering.

20

There was a great deal of soldering to do; there was a great deal of carpentry and much arranging of historical items; there was a lot of wiring and fitting together of various objects. The time machine consisted of at least three parts. First, there were the historical objects, what Gentian still liked to call the track and Dominic called the guidance system. Gentian's father, dragged upstairs one day by Rosemary and Juniper to admire their work, suggested that they put up a sign saying "Quick Museum—Six Hundred Million Years of History in One Hundred Square Feet" and charge admission.

Next, there was a vast tangle of electronic objects crammed into the other finished room. This morass came to include three or four computers, an oscilloscope, a shortwave radio, the old radio Gentian had not carried upstairs, a small home copying machine like the one her father had in his office, and a flatbed scanner. Dominic called the contents of this room the control system. Gentian did most of the work on it, though he directed her. She did not ask anybody up to admire it.

Finally, there was the time machine itself. This was simply a small, light, heavily wired object that fitted over the head; Gentian thought it might originally have been a bicycle helmet. Dominic worked on this himself and did not answer questions about

it, in a manner somewhat different from his usual way of not answering anything you said to him. He called the helmet the trans-
porter, and when Juniper and Rosemary made "Star Trek" jokes
he looked at them blankly. Once he said, "Such tricks hath strong
imagination," and Rosemary and Juniper fell over laughing. He
did not admit that this small thing was the real time machine, the
object that would move the person wearing it about in time.

It came to Gentian one cold day as she struggled to fit a second shortwave radio—"That one's for the past," Dominic told
her when she pointed out that they already had one; "this one
will be for the future"—into the little room, that Dominic's de-
sign meant that, whatever the time machine did, only one person
could use it to actually go anywhere—or rather, anytime. She
did not say anything, but the same idea occurred to Juniper a little while later.

The four of them were together in the cold unfinished attic
between their museum room and their control room, working on
their separate tasks. There was no longer space to work in either
finished room, and finding somewhere to put the various addi-
tional objects that Dominic kept providing or having them build
was beginning to consume more time than the work itself.

"Hadn't you better make three or four of those things?" Juniper said to Dominic. "So we can all go?"

"He travels the fastest who travels alone," said Dominic.
He was putting yet more wires on his helmet, and did not even
look up.

"So what?" said Juniper. She spoke calmly, but Gentian could
see that she was angry already, and expected to be angrier. "If
there's any point to a time machine at all, surely it's that you
have all the time there is?"

"Well, that's one theory," said Gentian, who last summer had
read every time-travel book and story her parents possessed and
had emerged a perfect agnostic on the entire subject. "What's
your theory of time, Dominic?"

"Time is what keeps everything from happening at once."

"I should never give you anything to read," said Juniper. "Be
serious for once in your life."

Gentian looked at her with interest. Dominic was being serious; he had no more sense of humor than Malvolio. It was
strange that Juniper couldn't see this. Did she think all his eva-
sions and quotations were just jokes?

Dominic went on working.

"Dominic," said Gentian. "Why do you want to build a time
machine?"

"Ye Gods," said Dominic, mildly, "annihilate both space and
time, and make two lovers happy."

Rosemary looked vaguely nauseated. Gentian felt her face
grow hot; she looked at Juniper, and saw that Juniper had turned
pink herself. He must mean her, thought Gentian, there's no reason in the world to think he means me.

"Dominic," said Juniper, still pink but not at all softened as
far as Gentian could see, "who is going to get to use that thing?
Who is going to do the actual traveling, all fast and alone?"

"I am," said Dominic.

"I think you'd better reconsider that."

"Consideration like an angel came," said Dominic, and then
seemed to bring himself up short and start over. He looked away
from his helmet and did, in fact, consider Juniper. He said at
last, "Words are women, deeds are men."

"Oh, certainly," said Juniper. "When you talk more than all
three of us put together and we're doing most of the work."

"What are ideas, then?" said Gentian, unable to resist.
"Both? Neither?"

"Look," said Rosemary, nervously, "I don't want to travel in
time, I just want to hear what happens."

"You would," said Juniper. "Well, I assume somebody has to
stay here and monitor things. You can do that."

Rosemary looked alarmed.

Dominic said, "The time on either side of *now* stands fast."

They all looked at him. He seemed to make a considerable effort, and said, "The invention is mine; it must be I who test it."

"Well, it's nice you don't mean to use us as guinea pigs," said
Juniper, "but suppose it does work, what then?"

"All who will may come."

"Why in the world didn't you say so before?"

"I thought you would sit by the fire and spin."

Rosemary chortled, "Crosspatch, draw the latch! He's got you, Junie!"

"That remains to be seen," said Juniper; and they all went back to work.

"The trouble with Dom," said Rosemary, at dinner not long after, "is that he wants to have all the fun."

"That's said to be nine-tenths of the law of chivalry," said their father, in a satisfied tone.

"What is?" said Juniper.

"The desire to have all the fun."

"Are you calling him a gentleman again?" said Gentian.

"Very good," said her father.

"Gentlemen don't ask riddles all the time," said Rosemary.

"Ask him why he asks them; riddle him that," said their father.

"He says because he can't remember the answers."

Their father sat up straight and looked delighted. Their mother said dryly, "Can't he look them up?"

"He says that's cheating," said Juniper.

"I told you he was a gentlemen," said their father.

"If you mean he abides by a strict set of arbitrary rules of no use to him or anybody else, you're right," said their mother.

Juniper and Rosemary laughed. Gentian sat wondering when they had asked Dominic about his riddles, and how they had gotten answers anything like as straight as those sounded.

The weather continued cloudy. Gentian had plenty to do; she wanted to get the time machine as far along as possible before rehearsals for the play started. It was lucky that school didn't start again until the eighth of January; most kids had to go back the day after New Year's. She kept meaning to call Steph and ask her what the play schedule was, but she was too busy filling up the room in her charge with boards and keyboards and computer terminals all wired together just so, in tight bundles of color like a galactic center. She could just as well ask when she saw Steph at school again.

There were a few phone messages from Alma or Erin or Becky, about ice skating or sledding or cookie-baking parties, but she decided she must forgo these usual winter pleasures. Socializing now would, in the end, mean neglecting astronomy later, because there would not be time for the play, the time machine, and astronomy, and astronomy did not include people to whom she had promised help. It was odd to be spending so much time with her sisters and one boy who hardly seemed to notice her at all, instead of her friends who appreciated her, but it was only for a little while. Juniper continued impatient, scornful, and abrasive, as well as taking up as much of Dominic's attention as she could manage. Rosemary, however, was quiet, cheerful, and hard-working, aside from a tendency to make silly jokes and giggle. Dominic treated them both exactly the same; you could not tell whom he was speaking to unless you could see the conversation.

This was good for Rosemary, Gentian decided. She was being permitted to help with something important and intriguing and grown-up, with her skills appreciated as much as Juniper's or Gentian's, and she must be comfortable if she was making those jokes. It was good experience for a shy person, and she wouldn't get hurt because she had no romantic interest in Dominic and he had none in her.

Junie, on the other hand, could not be having a great deal of fun. Dominic had seemed to have a romantic interest in her, which she had certainly returned, and now he behaved as if she were just another eleven-year-old Girl Scout.

Gentian began to think, after a while, that his manner to her was a little different. He looked at her when he spoke to her, and he often said "Well done," when he inspected her work. Since she heard Juniper berating him for being unappreciative about once a day, this seemed to mean something. She dwelt on this for a little while, but then she remembered the deluded Malvolio's saying that Olivia used him with a more exalted respect than anybody else who followed her, and decided to stop thinking about it.

The weather continued cloudy. The attic was cold, but she was used to working in the cold, because of her astronomy. Dominic had rigged up bright lights everywhere, so that the short days and long nights of a Minnesota winter did not slow them down. Gentian was underslept, and her mother kept commenting on it. She did not seem able to understand Gentian's reassurances that this was temporary, that as soon as vacation was over, Gentian would get more sleep. Her father quoted the poem about burning the candle at both ends. He even asked her if she would like him to speak to Dominic about easing the pace of their project, so that Gentian could blame paternal interference for everything.

They were for some reason sitting on the attic stairs when he said this, and Gentian looked at him in amazement. "I thought you believed in noninterference," she said.

Her father's expression moved from sardonic, which their mother said was his default, to rueful. "If I didn't, wouldn't I simply speak to Dominic without asking you if you'd like me to first?"

"I guess you would."

"I could do that if it would be easier."

"Dad!"

"I'm just trying to match Dominic's deviousness."

"Are you trying to warn me about something?"

"I'm trying to find out what you want."

"So you can give it to me, or so you can take it away?"

"That would depend on what it was, wouldn't it?"

"I want to help Dominic build his time machine."

"How likely do you think it is that he actually can build one that works?"

"It's not just him."

"How likely do you think it is that an eleven-year-old, a fourteen-year-old, a sixteen-year-old, and Dominic actually can build one that works?"

"Maria Mitchell discovered the first telescopic comet when she was—"

"True for you. And," her father said thoughtfully, looking over her head at one of the gouges in the plaster they had made bringing Gentian's desk up long ago, "it's a truism in the history of science that many of the most innovative discoveries, especially in mathematics and physics, are made by people in their twenties. Newton and Einstein are commonly cited. But they still had ten or so years on you four."

"I don't really know enough about it to be able to tell," said Gentian. "And Dominic doesn't talk about it. I'm not necessarily expecting it to work. So I'm not courting disappointment," she concluded; this was something both parents were always worried their daughters would do.

"I wonder if that's true," said her father, vaguely. "Courtship being what it is."

"I really won't mind if it doesn't work," said Gentian, sticking firmly to the time machine and refusing to discuss courtship. "I'll just be very interested in everybody's reactions."

This caused her father to stop looking vague. "What about your sisters? Do they expect it to work?"

"I think Rosie must, because otherwise she wouldn't work so hard. She doesn't like Dominic."

"And why are you and Junie working so hard?"

"Junie does like him."

"And?"

"I think he might like me."

"And?"

"I think a very good way to get to know somebody is to work on a complicated project with him."

"I advise less complication and more sleep," said her father, and, to her relief, stood up.

Gentian did slip out once or twice to peer through gaps in the clouds at anything that offered itself. The only really notable thing she saw in these excursions was a bit of the constellation of Serpens, including R Serpentis, one of the few long-period red variable stars that one could make anything of in a small telescope. It showed somewhat redder than usual that night, so she lingered over it. When the clouds thinned and broke up, she looked for and found M16, a widely scattered star cluster enveloped by a diffuse nebula. In Gentian's telescope it looked like an open cluster of twenty or so stars. Gentian ritually found the little double star at the edge, just to make sure that she was where she thought she was, and then settled in to see the nebulosity. It revealed itself gradually as a faint light behind the stars; she could not, tonight, see folds or whorls, just that faint shining. She liked it because it was a young cluster, full to bursting of O- and B-type giant stars and dotted with the dark globules of still-condensing gasses. Photographs showed it to be far more spectacular than her telescope could, but one day she would look at it with a 200-inch telescope, and then she would know it. Gentian looked until the wind got up and blew a new set of clouds across the sky.

"I've been looking at the Serpent's Head," she said to Dominic when she returned.

"The serpent, subtlest beast of all the field."

"M16's not very subtle, as globular clusters go."

The weather continued cloudy. Day or night, the attic was brighter than the outdoors. The tight and intricate tangle in Gentian's finished room grew and spilled outward into the unfinished part of the attic, like the arms of a spiral nebula reaching far into the darkness. Dominic would periodically come in and power up more of what she had built, until the room filled with a pervasive hum. It masked his conversations with her sisters, and even their footsteps and the pounding and hammering they were still doing. But one day, lying underneath a stack of boards to make another connection Dominic thought was needed, she could hear somebody yelling.

It was Rosemary, resurrecting the skills she had had as a three-year-old. "I am going winter camping. I am going winter camping. I am going winter camping. And I'm not coming back up here, ever."

Gentian wriggled backwards out of her cave and stood up as far as she could and proceeded towards the door, stepping carefully over half-assembled circuits and yet another keyboard. As she came into the unfinished part of the attic, where dust motes circled in the blaze of artificial light, Dominic said, "A sad tale's best for winter."

"A lot you know about the Girl Scouts," snarled Rosemary.

"Good heavens," said Juniper, appearing in the doorway of the museum room, "let the child go camping if she wants to."

"I am not a child."

"You put soft pillows under my head," said Dominic.

"How many times do I have to tell you, I did *not!*" cried Rosemary. "You're just like a broken record. You never change."

"Change lobsters, and retire in the same order."

"I am retiring," said Rosemary. "No, I'm not. I'm going on strike. Juniper, Gentian, you come too."

Gentian looked at Juniper.

"He's a jerk!" cried Rosemary. "He's an idiot. He won't let us do anything but drudge."

"You go winter camping," said Gentian carefully, "and we'll talk about it when you get back."

"You," said Rosemary, "are full of hormones. I'm never going to grow up, no matter what I have to do."

She ripped the bandanna from her head, flung it in Dominic's direction, and marched out of the attic, shutting the door behind her with a bang that shivered the dust motes sideways and made something slide, tinkling a little, in the museum room.

"You know, Gentian," said Juniper after a moment, "Dominic and I can manage on our own."

Gentian looked at Dominic. "Many hands make light work," he said.

Gentian went back into her room and crawled under the table again. She was pleased with herself for not having stuck out her tongue at Juniper.

The weather continued cloudy. The control system oozed through the attic until there was only a narrow corridor to walk along. The museum room also overflowed, but not to such an extent. Gentian found this odd, but she did not have much time to think about it. She was getting worried about finishing before school started, and it occurred to her that she could call on the Giant Ants to spend the last day of their vacation all working together.

"I need to call Becky," she told Dominic.

"Need must, when the devil drives."

Gentian thought of the Laurie Anderson song about the devil's being a rusty truck with only twenty mile, and giggled, and went to her room and called Becky. It must be about time that

Becky came over to spend the night, anyway. Gentian would not be able to spend hours and hours with her, talking the sun down the sky, as her father liked to say, because of the work she had to get done, but Becky could read. Gentian dialed the number, and got Becky's mother.

"Who? Gentian? Well, this is a surprise. Just a minute, I'll see if she can be disturbed."

Becky did not take many telephone calls when she was writing poetry, but her mother had been told that she would always take Gentian's.

Becky's voice erupted from the telephone. "Gentian! What do you have to say for yourself?"

"I just wanted to ask you how time worked."

"Gentian *Betony* Meriweather, how can you disappear for months and let Steph down and then call me with a culinary question?"

"It's not a culinary question and I haven't disappeared anywhere."

"Yes, I'm sure you always know right where you are. Well, we don't. I've left you a hundred and fifty phone messages."

"Rosie or Juniper must have forgotten."

"I left them with your parents."

"I never got them."

"I came over and we couldn't find you."

"I've been right here. I haven't gone anywhere all week."

"Gentian, you sound awfully strange. Did they take you to that therapist after all and put you on drugs?"

"What therapist?"

"The one your mother said maybe they'd better take you to after I told her you'd dropped out of the play."

"What play?"

"Oh, God, I knew those drugs were a bad idea. They've crunched up your memory. I mean *Twelfth Night*."

"I'm not taking any drugs and my memory is fine. Who told you I'd dropped out of the play?"

"Dominic. And how could you, how could you send messages by that viper?"

"I didn't. I'm not dropping out. You haven't found another Antonio yet, have you?"

There was a long pause. Gentian was glad she had brought a tricky bit of wiring with her. She tucked the telephone under her chin and went to work on it.

"I guess you didn't know," said Becky, slowly. "What day do you think it is?"

"Friday?"

"Well, it is at that. What month, then?"

"January," said Gentian, more firmly.

"Gentian. It's the first day of April. The play's over. Steph is by turns furious and devastated, depending on, as far as I can tell, the phase of the moon."

"That's not funny. Just because I got confused once last fall—"

"Ask anybody who is not working on that infernal device of yours. Turn on the radio. Turn on the television. Look outside, for God's sake, at your precious stars."

"Oh. Well. Yes. I could do that. Unless they play jokes on April Fools' Day too. You wrote a poem about that."

"Well, sort of," said Becky, but she sounded considerably mollified, or perhaps relieved. "Look, promise me. Promise me you'll do some stargazing tonight. And I think you should tell your mother you want to go to that therapist."

"My mother hates therapists. She hates psychobabble."

"Promise me you'll do some stargazing."

"All right. I just have to get this bit wired."

"What's a good stargazing time in April?"

Gentian concentrated. She put her bit of plywood with its wires and lines of solder down on the bed. "Um. Well, you know, it depends on what you want to look at, but if you want, say, the Coma Berenices, ten in the evening is about right. If you want a last look at Orion before it gets too far west, more like eight."

"All right, look, which do you like better?"

"Well, the Coma Berenices is just bursting with deep-sky objects."

"All right. Look at it, then, at ten o'clock. I'll call to remind you, all right?"

"Are you doing a paper or something?"

"Something," said Becky. "Definitely something."

"Are you writing an astronomical poem?"

"Not just at the moment."

"What are you writing, then? You haven't shown me anything in forever."

"I haven't seen you in forever. What in the world is going on over there?"

"Well, we're helping Dominic build his time machine. You know, I wonder if it's working already somehow and he didn't tell us, or he doesn't know."

"That's an explanation," said Becky, slowly. "Is it the best one?"

"I guess it might multiply entities unnecessarily."

"Well, or not. You know what entities *I* think are unnecessary?"

"What?" said Gentian, fascinated. It sounded like a Becky poem in the making.

"That you'd change so much you'd let Steph down, and me, and all of us."

"You shouldn't have believed Dominic."

"You believe him."

"I don't believe him about people."

"Good point," said Becky, still slowly. "Look, you promise me you'll look at the Coma Berenices."

"I did already."

"Turn the heat down now, so the temperature will be equalized by ten."

"You don't have to tell me how to do this," said Gentian, irritated.

"Good. Do it, then. I'll call you at ten." She hung up, rather loudly.

Gentian hung up too, and went to turn off the radiator. It was stone cold. That would explain why she hadn't seen Maria Mitchell much. Murr would be in the bathroom where it was

warm. Gentian started across the hall to find her, and was almo
bowled over by Juniper, who came charging up the stairs and ran
for the door to the attic.

"Watch where you're going!" said Gentian.

"Where's Dominic?"

"In the attic, I guess."

"I'm going to kill him."

"What's he done now?"

"He told Sarah I didn't want to see her any more."

"Why'd she believe him?"

"Why shouldn't she? I haven't called her for months." Juniper wrenched open the door to the attic, banged it against the
wall so hard bits of plaster fell down, and bounded into the blar-
ing light. She immediately fell over Gentian's latest addition to
the control system and landed with a resounding crash. "Jesus
Christ!" said Juniper. "God-damned mother-fucking son of a
bitch!"

Dominic came out of the museum room. He had cobwebs in
his hair. "Bear your body more seemly," he said to her.

"Fuck you!"

"High thoughts must have high language."

"My thoughts," said Juniper, struggling to her feet and walking up to within an inch of him, "are not high. They can't be.
They're of you. How dare you lie to Sarah about me?" She bristled all over, like a furious cat; her red hair, even tied back for
dusty work, sprang around her head brighter than all the copper
wires in the time machine. Her green T-shirt and blue jeans hurt
Gentian's eyes like spring. Dominic, eye to eye with her, was like
a faded black-and-white photograph.

"You let me in," he said, "and barred the door with a silver pin."

"I'll be happy to let you out again," said Juniper.

"You lied to Becky about me, too," said Gentian.

"What is a lie," said Dominic, "but truth in masquerade."

"You are coming with me," said Juniper, "to tell Sarah you
lied."

"That way madness lies."

Juniper took several steps back, and Gentian saw the flush of
anger leave her face. Gentian came forward. "And then," she
said, "you can tell Becky you lied to her. And Steph—you can tell
Steph you lied about me and the play."

"There's no remedy save this," said Dominic. And he darted
his hand about in the air, over the attic and the time machine.

Juniper made a derisory sound through her nose. "I assume
you lied about that, too, you—you walking *Bartlett's*. I can't
make you do anything," she said, shoving past Gentian, "but
there are people in this house who can. I'm telling Mom and
Dad," she said to Gentian, and went out. Her furious footsteps
diminished; the door at the bottom of the attic stairs slammed.

Gentian did not know what she felt. Before she could think,
Dominic said, "She will forget."

"Are you kidding? Junie never forgets a grudge."

"She will forget to tell your parents. She won't forget that she
hates me, but—" he shrugged, one of the few gestures Gentian
had ever seen him make, "—we have just enough religion to
make us hate, but not enough to make us love one another."

Gentian tried for a moment to make this remark apply to
Dominic and Juniper, but then she realized that his voice had
changed. With that remark, he had begun quoting again, rather
than speaking as himself. She said, still at a loss, "Junie's not religious."

"I don't mean by religion what you mean."

Gentian looked at him.

Dominic, whom she had never seen sweaty, or out of breath,
or affronted more than once or twice, seemed to be making some
enormous effort. "The myths she partakes of helped her to love,
and then to know, and thus to hate," he said. He sat down
abruptly on a small leather trunk that had strayed out of the museum room. Gentian's eye found and automatically read Rosemary's label: "Victorian traveling trunk, ca. 1867; U.S."

"Your verbs haven't got any object," she said after a moment.

"My object is always myself."

"Well, that explains a lot."

Gentian had no idea what to do. Marching out in a fury was not the way she operated; even knowing what he had done, even remembering, more clearly, it seemed, than she had known it while it was happening, his earlier behavior with Alma, she was as curious as she was outraged. And her conscience prickled a little too; Becky's mention of a therapist had been nagging at her. Gentian was perfectly well aware that she didn't need a therapist; but maybe Dominic did. Diseases desperate grown by desperate appliance are relieved. Oh, great, now she was quoting too. And what a quotation: that was the way those conspirators in *Julius Caesar* had thought, and look where it had gotten them.

"Even if Juniper does forget," she said, "I don't think my mother will forget that she's thinking of sending me to a therapist." She hardly knew if she was comforting herself and threatening him, or the other way around.

"No," said Dominic, "but it will be as a new thought to her, each day."

"What? What the hell are you doing?"

"The time machine isn't finished, but certain outliers can be accomplished. Come and see." He stood up, and moving slowly and with great care, as a cousin of Gentian's who had arthritis used to move on a bad day, he went into the control room. Gentian followed. She expected Juniper and her father to come frothing upstairs at any second, but she might as well see what she could before then.

Dominic never seemed to have as much trouble navigating the crowded room as Gentian did; he was standing beside a collection of four monitors while she was still negotiating the first few feet of the room, with its thick ropes of colored wires tied up with duct tape and occasionally anchored to floor or wall or table. He did not do anything until she was standing beside him; then he waved his hand, and all the monitors lit up. Gentian was familiar with motion-sensing lights, but she had not installed one here, and in any case she had never heard of a motion-sensing monitor.

"See, then," said Dominic.

In the upper left-hand monitor, Juniper was sitting at the

computer in her bedroom, typing furiously. She had on the same green T-shirt and blue jeans as she had been wearing when she was in the attic a few minutes ago, and the same green scrunchie, one Rosemary had given her for her birthday, to keep her hair out of her eyes. She must be sending E-mail to Sarah. Either that, or informing the entire teen chat echo of The Light Prince's perfidy. She seemed to have just come from the attic, and yet she was not talking to her parents. They must not be at home.

"When did you put a camera in Junie's room?" demanded Gentian. It was monstrous. And good grief, how long had it been there? Did he know she read Juniper's diary? She swallowed her intended remarks; she was not in a good position to make speeches about the odiousness of spying. But she's my sister, she thought, that makes it different. And I didn't put in a *camera;* I never watched her most private moments.

"No camera but time," said Dominic.

Gentian looked away from Juniper, violently. In the upper right-hand monitor, the entire family, including Gentian, was sitting at dinner. Oh, that's interesting, thought Gentian, does my hair always mat and stick up that way in the back? No wonder Maria Mitchell grew hers long and braided it. And I don't slouch like that, really, do I? It doesn't feel that way from inside. Everyone else looked as usual, so she must too. They were having an argument. Gentian craned forward, and Dominic touched the side of the monitor. Talk burst over the quiet hum of the control room. It did not sound just as usual; Gentian was not talking but watching, and the person who slouched, who was wearing Gentian's Planetary Society T-shirt and Gentian's blue jeans patched with red corduroy, was saying what she would say, but not in her voice, not precisely.

What she said, while helping herself to salad—and spilling lettuce on the tablecloth quite obliviously—was, "Have I got an Electra complex, or is Dad the only sensible person in this house?"

"Taking your career choice seriously isn't sensible?" said her mother.

"Well, all right," said Gentian, running her fork through the

salad. She looked awfully clumsy; no, not that exactly: inatten-
tive. Her mother silently handed her a bowl of chopped tomato,
green pepper, and red onion, and cocked one eyebrow to show
she still wanted her original question answered.

"I figured I'd do astronomy after ten," said Gentian, "which
is mostly a good time, and maybe miss school in the morning
sometimes." Gentian, watching, was pleased. She liked sounding
matter-of-fact, and uninvolved, and this tone was just as she had
hoped.

"Mostly, I assume," said her mother dryly.

"The Giant Ants'll let me look at their notes." Oops, there
was a bit of pleading in that sentence.

"Well, as long as you don't start bringing home those oily
communications from your counselor. I don't know how so fundamentally sensible a school can countenance so much psychobabble."

The sound faded out; the picture continued. "Now," said Dominic, still with an obvious effort, "How fares your mother after
that talk?"

"Um, reassured but wary?"

"Precisely. A state she thinks good for the mother of such as
you. So, then, when she hears report of your failures, this is run
through her, and she feels she has made an investigation and will
be continuing to pay attention."

"Get away from her!" cried Gentian. "Stay out of her head!"

"I am here," said Dominic, simply.

And what did he mean by failures? Gentian looked at the
third screen, the lower left one. It was divided into nine windows; and even in her fury, perplexity, and annoyance, she almost
laughed, to see that they really were windows, the windows of
the house. Then she saw what they meant, and stopped smiling.
The view outside every one of them showed a cloudy sky, bare
trees encrusted with snow, snowy bits of lawn and street and
roof. This was why she thought it was January, when it was
April. Gentian turned on him. "You presumptuous, intolerable
bastard."

Dominic looked, if anything, pleased. He inclined his head at the monitors, so Gentian looked at the fourth and last one. Rose-mary and Amber were sitting in Rosemary's room, eating straw-berry ice cream with chocolate sauce on it and giggling. Rose-mary's voice faded in, "So he's a jerk. He tried to make me miss winter camping and he's trying to make Genny miss her school play, but my father says he'll take care of it." I guess he does say that, thought Gentian, over and over and over. She was glad there was no monitor to show him doing it.

Gentian almost said, "Becky's not here, or Steph, or Sarah," but she didn't want to give him ideas he hadn't already had. She remembered then that he had been obliged to lie to Becky and Steph and Sarah; he had not been able to trap them in time and send them scrambling like hamsters over and over the same space, held in the two palms of his hands. For whatever reason, they had not let him in. No, nor put soft cushions under his head, either. She felt glad that Rosemary was out of it, and then looked again at the monitor and felt cold. Not quite out of it.

It would be better to go through with finishing the time ma-chine, and use it to clear things up. If Dominic had what he wanted, whatever that was, whatever he needed the time ma-chine for, then he would go away. At least, she hoped he would.

"What do you want the time machine for, anyway?" she said to him.

"For the same reason you do," he said. "There is something to be done over."

Gentian saw no particular reason to believe one thing he said more than another, but he was at least speaking in his own per-son, and it did make sense. "All right," she said, briskly. "What do we need to do next?"

"We must construct another helmet," said Dominic, blandly.

Gentian raised her eyebrows at him. So he was capable of learning from experience.

"We need but two more objects," said Dominic, "to anchor us to the present, so that we may return at need."

"Won't the house itself do?"

"The house is old. Let it be your telescope."

Gentian's breath stopped. "Why?"

"Theirs not to reason why," said Dominic, placidly, "theirs but to do or die."

"This isn't the army and I am not under your orders." He's doing it too, she thought, just like my father, just like Jamie. He's laying down the law. Well, I won't have it. Not to reason why, good grief, and about a science project.

"A mind not to be changed by place or time," said Dominic.

"You're not a place or a time, and I'm not handing you the most valuable thing I possess without a very good reason."

"Oh, reason not the need."

There he went again. Reason not. "Look," she said, "I'm your assistant, I'm not your servant. Tell me why you want my telescope."

"I have said. To anchor us in time."

"Use something of yours, then. Or I'll be happy to go buy a brand-new toaster or something."

"Something too much of this," said Dominic.

Some time later it occurred to her that she had neither looked at the Coma Berenices nor called Becky back. It would all be fixed in the end, would be as if it had never happened; only Becky was angry and worried and feeling deserted now, this moment, this day, this week, this month, whatever it was. Could you really undo such things altogether?

"I need to call Becky," she said to Dominic.

"Need must, when the devil drives."

Gentian thought of the Laurie Anderson song about the devil's being a rusty truck with only twenty mile, and giggled.

The weather continued cloudy, but she knew that meant nothing. One gray day she said to Dominic, "Since we have all the time in the world, is there any reason I can't have a bit of it off? I'd like to catch up on my astronomy."

"Better not," said Dominic, painting silver lines on yet another circuit board. "The means whereby I keep us undisturbed are tedious to me."

"Well, I get bored too; that's why I want some time off."

"Tedious," said Dominic. "Difficult."

"Oh. You mean you can't keep them up forever?"

"Yes."

"It's only after the point where the time machine works that we can start being profligate of time?"

Dominic raised his head for a moment; she thought he was going to quote something, but he only said, again, "Yes."

Sometimes, since there was nobody else to talk to, she found herself talking to him of whatever she happened to be thinking. Now that Rosemary and Juniper had quit, she had work to do in the museum room as well. The objects there, which Dominic was always wanting arranged in a different order, continually reminded her of something or other; had it not been for discoveries made there she would probably have fled screaming with boredom long ago. It was not as good as astronomy; it was the wrong end of the telescope, not just the other end. Earthward the trouble lies, she thought, turning a small heavy Egyptian cat statue over in her hand.

"I miss my cat," she said to Dominic, who had just come in with another box of fossils.

"Shoot at tax collectors and miss."

"You're not all here today, are you? I want to go see my cat."

"Cats and monkeys, monkeys and cats—all human life is there."

Why was she asking permission, and in her own house? "I'm going to go see my cat," she said, putting the statue down and getting to her feet. "I'll be back in a little while."

"A little while will see the end of all."

Gentian started for the door.

"She'll love you better when all's said and done."

"When the soldering's done, more like," said Gentian.

She worked on soldering for some time, reminding herself that patience was required for astronomy too, and she could consider this as practice. She tried to think of it as sweeping for comets; she thought of Caroline Herschel's register, ruled into squares representing a quarter of a degree, and how she had checked off, night after night, each tiny piece of the sky as her brother, at the telescope, did the actual sweeping.

"But I am not going to discover any comets in here," she said aloud.

"When beggars die, there are no comets seen; the heavens themselves blaze forth the death of princes."

"I thought they were supposed to blaze forth the birth of princes," said Gentian idly; most of her attention was on a tricky bit of three-dimensional jigsaw work. Dominic had a bad habit of deciding that things should be added after a space was mostly full. "The Star of Bethlehem and all that. Though I guess the leading theory about that is that it was a supernova, only they can't find it in the Chinese records."

Dominic said nothing. This was not unusual. Gentian finished what she was doing and squirmed backwards out of the cave she had first made some weeks ago, or months. Dominic was still kneeling where he had been, a fossil in one hand and a pair of needle-nosed pliers in the other.

"Is anything the matter?"

"From the table of my memory I'll wipe away all trivial fond records."

"Be my guest," said Gentian. "I think I'll take a break and see what's to be seen through the telescope."

"The serpent, subtlest beast of all the field."

"M16's not very subtle, for a globular cluster," said Gentian.

There were clouds and snow outside, but the lights and all the humming, blinking, and chiming equipment made the attic hotter and hotter.

"We still have no present anchor," said Dominic. "We need a poem of your fair friend Becky's. It will be fresh, abundantly of the very present."

"I don't know," said Gentian, slowly. "I'd have to ask her. And she's mad at me."

"Fair use," said Dominic.

"Use all gently," retorted Gentian, and realized that she was quoting instead of answering him.

"The law allows it."

"I don't care about the law. I can't show you a poem of hers without asking her, and I can't ask her until this confusticated device is done, because she's mad at me, and with good cause."

"If she is not to be angry with you forever, we must have the poem."

"Which poem?"

"The last one she gave you."

"How the hell do you know about that?"

"Which doesn't matter, just that it be the newest."

"Oh." That would be the three-sonnet one about Betelgeuse, which was a weird one. It wasn't one of her favorites; but it was about her and Becky, which very few of Becky's poems were. "Well, you still can't have it."

"Poetry is not a career, but a mug's game. Poets seek honor; this is one."

"No." Gentian thought about it anyway. No, he really could not have that one. But how could he tell which was the newest? She could give him a failure, maybe; the "Garbage In, Garbage Out" one Becky disliked so much. It would anchor them to the near past rather than the present, though; that might be a problem. Why, after all, was she thinking of handing over a copy of a poem as some kind of sacrifice, as if she would not have it after, as if Becky would not have her own copies?

"Would you have to read it?" she said.

"It would be our invocation."

So much for the idea of using a bad poem. "No."

"This is the crowning touch; it honors her. The subject matter of poetry is not that 'collection of solid, static objects extended in space' but the life that is lived in the scene that it composes, and so reality is not that external scene but the life that is lived in it. Reality is things as they are."

"No." The time machine was too chancy. For all she knew, it would consume its invocation. And what was a science project doing with an invocation, anyway, as if it were a religious ritual? "I don't mean by religion what you mean," Dominic had said.

"You can't have anything," said Gentian, with renewed energy, "unless you tell me why."

"Tell me why the stars do shine."

"Nuclear fusion," snapped Gentian. "You can't riddle your way out of this. Tell me why or go away."

"Away, and mock the time with fairest show."

"You can't compliment your way out of this, either."

"The way is the way, and there's an end on't."

"Fine. The end is on it, then."

"If you would repair your rift with Becky, you will give me that poem; and if you would bid time return and make all as it was, untroubling yourself, you will give me your telescope."

"That's just blackmail. How dare you?" She sounded exactly like Juniper. Was this how Juniper felt much of the time?

"I dare do all that may become a man," said Dominic.

"What did you ask us to help you for, then?"

"Since there's no help, come, let us kiss and part."

Gentian, knowing he was quoting and thinking he was being metaphorical, contented herself with rolling her eyes. Dare do all that may become a man, indeed. But Dominic walked up to her, took her by the waist, and kissed her on the mouth.

His own mouth was soft and sweet. He was so uninsistent that it took her a moment, or several, to think that she still wanted to make him stop. Then she thought, but this is my first kiss, and given what a mess this has all been I'm not at all sure I plan to kiss anybody else ever again. It's awfully interesting, though—it's like living in your body instead of in your head. She was thinking whether she should kiss him back, so as to have gotten both sides of the experience, when he flung his hands away from her and stepped back so violently that he knocked one of the shortwave radios—the future one, she thought—onto the floor.

Gentian put a hand backwards and steadied herself on one of the monitors. I can see it's better to be the one who stops, she thought. Dominic was pale and sweaty and looked remarkably sick. Could kissing somebody be as much effort for him as using his own words?

"I am sick," he said, "and full of burning."

Gentian knew it was inane, but she said it anyway. "Did you eat something that disagreed with you?"

Dominic's head came up. "*Gentian,*" he said.

"Yes, what?" Gentian was becoming alarmed; should she think of calling an ambulance?

"Juniper. Gentian. Rosemary."

"Should I applaud?"

"Hear the world applaud the hollow ghost," said Dominic. "Juniper, that hung by the door will keep out the witch unless he count every needle of it. Rosemary, herb of remembrance, whose vigorous growth means a woman rules the household, whose sprigs, laid under the sleeper's pillow, ward off evil dreams and the visitation of demons. And Gentian. Bitterwort, felwort, wild symbol of ingratitude that dies under cultivation. I know my enemies, but not in such guise. What is worse nor woman was?"

It was the question he always asked, with everything he said and did.

"Is that a riddle?" said Gentian, out of a white-hot and pure fury. "I'll answer you. You are. You're worse than all of us put together, you, yourself, alone and nameless."

Dominic, with a blank face worse than an angry one would have been, stepped towards her. Gentian backed away, reminding herself that there was a hammer lying in the narrow corridor just outside the door. She moved more quickly, jumped through the door, and grabbed it. She put her back against the door into the house; that was better than being trapped in the attic, and she might have time to get it open.

Dominic came out of the control room, but did not follow her farther. In the overbright light all his colors were exaggerated: black hair, black eyes, white face, red lips. He grew bright himself, and brighter, and blazed up, without flames, into such a white cold, blue-white, colder light, brighter than Rigel or the blue giants of the Orion Nebula, that the tears ran out of Gentian's eyes. He turned and walked away from her, growing brighter still, and larger even as he moved away. She could see nothing, but she heard the drag of the door to the balcony opening, and then the brightness went out.

Gentian sprang forward, retaining the hammer, and went as fast as she could to the front of the house, and so out onto the balcony. It was whitened with ash, or with light. She craned over the railing, not touching it; the cold of the shingled floor was already burning through her shoes. The air was crisp but not so cold as that; the front steps and walk were covered with red leaves. She looked down and to her right, to the Hardys' house.

There was no house. There were no gardens, no miraculous restoration; there was no lawn, nor any gaping foundation. There was a flat white expanse, like concrete under heavy frost; but other lawns were green, or red and yellow with leaves. A white mist rose from it, like the clouds that billowed out when you opened the freezer on a warm day.

She had used a quotation against Dominic at the last, she realized. She had quoted Tolkien at him, Tom Bombadil's question to Frodo. "Who are you, alone, yourself, and nameless?" It was still a good question.

She turned back into the attic. The huge bright Sirius lights were out. The forty-watt bulb shone dustily on the heaps and tangles of the time machine. Gentian wandered among them for a little while. All the lights were out, all the monitors and other equipment silent. It was as if Dominic had taken all the power when he went. Feeling that only system would save her, she found her flashlight where she had left it in the Museum Room, and went to check connections.

There were none. She did not ever catch anything in the act of disappearing, but whenever she looked closely at something, she saw less of it than there had appeared to be from further off. It was as though a deep-sky object should show as a rich spiral galaxy, blazing with the individual jewels of its blue and white giant stars, flinging its long spirals of stars and dust across half the field of view, to the naked eye, but then shrink and dwindle and fall together into a single hazy point of light as you used larger and larger telescopes to look at it.

Gentian poked into corners and crawled under things that were not there when she stood up again, and in a very short time found herself standing in the control room, surrounded only by the original objects she and her sisters had carried up to the attic and put there, on the first day of the new year. She walked across the empty, dusty, echoing boards to the museum room. There were two boxes of fossils. She found her fern, a mere etching on gray rock; the ammonite, whitish against gray; the trilobite, rusty brown on brown; a rough oval that might have been the dinosaur egg, or merely a roundish rock.

"Fairy gold," said Gentian. "Changeling technology."

21

entian pushed the short wide door open, slowly, and entered her part of the attic. The hall rug was gray with dust. Dust balls lay in the corners. She opened the door to her own room. It was dusty too, and in the bright sunlight that came through all the southern and western windows, she saw loops and whorls of cobweb. Her bed was unmade. The room was cold, colder than the outdoors. They must be having a warm spell after a frosty one, not uncommon in the fall, and the house had not yet warmed up again.

Maria Mitchell wouldn't like that much. Gentian went into the bathroom to see if she was hiding under the radiator in there. No cat. The water bowl was dry. The food bowl was empty. Gentian stood in the cold bathroom and felt her heart freeze. She tried to open her mouth to call, but she could not move.

When had she last gone to see her cat? She remembered talking to Dominic about it, but not finding and petting Maria Mitchell, let alone feeding her. The last thing she remembered was Murr's rising wails from the bedroom, as Gentian sat in the attic with Dominic learning to solder.

Gentian ran down her stairs, calling. She looked in the second-floor bathroom, where Murr would sometimes sleep in the laundry hamper. No cat. She looked in the sewing room, where Murr would sometimes sit to watch the birds in the crabapple tree. She looked in Rosemary's room, in her parents', in her parents' bathroom.

The doors to all these had been standing open. The door to Juniper's room was shut. Gentian put her mouth to the crack between door and frame and called again. The thought of going into Juniper's room was a sore one, as if there were a bruise in her mind. The sun was setting, it was fall, maybe Juniper was home. Gentian knocked. She called, "Juniper!" She called Murr again. She opened the door.

The light of the setting sun dazzled her eyes. In a heap on Juniper's bed, in the last patch of sunlight, was a mass of cat fur, legs, tails, ears, noses. Black, white; it was Yin-Yang, or rather, Yin-Hang and Pounce. Gentian walked over automatically to pet them, and saw a checkerboard pattern of black and orange, and one orange ear rimmed with white.

"Murr," said Gentian, and rubbed the top of her head.

Maria Mitchell sprang out of the cat-heap, scattering Yin-Yang and Pounce to opposite ends of the bed. She flattened her ears and hissed at Gentian. Pounce curled up and went back to sleep. Yin-Yang crouched, tail puffed up, making a sound somewhere between a growl and a wail. Gentian reached out a hand to Murr and got a deep scratch for her trouble. Murr vanished under Juniper's bed.

Gentian sat down on the floor and cried. My cat's not dead but she hates me. And she's Juniper's cat now. And it serves me right, she thought. After a while she got up and took several tissues from the box on Juniper's bedside table. While she was wiping her face and blowing her nose, Murr came ostentatiously out from under the bed and sat with her back to Gentian, staring up at the computer as if it were the only object in the room.

"I'm sorry, Murr," said Gentian.

Maria Mitchell growled.

"All right. I'll come see you again later."

Maria Mitchell whipped her tail once, and went on staring at the computer. An old reflex stirred sluggishly in Gentian. She was in Juniper's room; she could look at the teen echoes, or look at Junie's diary. It would fill in the gaps in her memory, it would tell her what her family thought had been happening. She thought of Dominic's monitors and their repeating loops. She left Juniper's door ajar, and went downstairs.

The kitchen was alight, but empty. Gentian moved around it slowly, as if she had never seen it before. The compost bucket was crammed with orange strings and large pale seeds, and under them triangular pieces of pumpkin rind. There were a scattering of sequins, a needle threaded with black, a heap of lipsticks, and six jars of face paint on the table. If it were Halloween, as it seemed, her parents would be on the porch. Gentian went softly down the hall and put her head around the door to the living room. Nobody was there. The sunroom beyond was dark. She craned further, to see through the archway into the dining room. There were a teapot and mugs and a plate of brownies on the table, but no people. A gray-and-black tabby she had never seen was asleep in a curl like an ammonite in the middle of the hearth rug, and did not stir. Gentian went back through the kitchen, through the empty breakfast room, and looked thoughtfully at the door to her father's office for a moment. She opened it and stepped inside.

Her father was putting a book away in the bottom bookcase, which meant that for the same instant he did not see her and she did not see him. He stood up; Gentian jumped and uttered a squeak that dismayed her; her father, to her great satisfaction, said, "Argh!"

"Sorry," said Gentian. "I didn't know you were here."

"Honey," said her father, in an extremely odd voice, and stopped. "Well, I am here," he said, more firmly. He looked at her with more attention than she found comfortable. "Did you want the computer for your arcane project?"

"No. I want to know why you named us what you named us."

"Ah," said her father. He sat down in his desk chair and gestured to her to come in. Gentian shut the door and perched on the filing cabinet; it put her on a slightly higher level than her father and she felt she could use the advantage. He was still looking odd, though his voice was back to normal.

"You're back with us, then," he said.

"I didn't think you noticed I was away," said Gentian, feeling boggled in her turn. She felt as if she had seen him quite recently, more often than she might during one of the periods when a book of his was late and he never emerged from the office. He might think he had not seen her since January.

"I wasn't supposed to, I'm sure," said her father, in the tone he used when he was about to lay down the law. "Was that your idea?"

"What? No! I only found out about it later. What made you realize what was going on?"

"I have my methods," said her father.

"How could you think I'd do that?"

"Well, isn't that every adolescent's dream? Freedom from parental supervision, and no need to pay in arguments or worry?"

"I am not every adolescent. And even if I would like that," said Gentian, and paused. Before her time with Dominic she certainly would have liked that, though actually freedom from Junie's opinions was almost as nice. "Even if I would have, I wouldn't achieve it that way."

"What way?"

Gentian felt better. "It was like he got inside everybody's head and put in an infinite loop so every time any of you wondered about me, the same conversation went by you and you thought you'd just been reassured, or just decided to do something about it."

"Interesting. That's not how it felt."

"Does Mom have her methods too?"

"She hasn't, but when I saw what was going on, I told her. It's immoral to go on letting people be deluded that way."

That's right, thought Gentian, lay down the law. "Why have *you* got methods?"

"For the same reason we named you what we named you."

"Well, *what,* then?"

"I think, in my classes, they called it Prophylactic Nomenclature. Rosemary used to call it Preventive Naming of Parts. No, no, not your sister."

"Mrs. Zimmerman!"

"Yes, she was one of my professors in college."

"Did Mom know her too?"

"No."

"Oh, that was the college you went to before you transferred to Blackstock and met Mom."

"Yes."

"That still doesn't explain anything."

"I know this is going to upset you, but it's magic."

Gentian eyed him warily. *Somebody* in this house certainly needed a therapist. And if he quoted Horatio at her about how there were more things in heaven and earth than were dreamt of in her philosophy—but she knew that already. She knew that from Dominic. *I wish I'd had a thermometer up there,* she thought, *to see if he really did make it cold as he vanished.*

"I'm a failed magician," said her father. "Now I write fiction."

"Fiction isn't failed magic," said Gentian automatically. She added to herself, *and I'm not sure that's a very good reason for writing it. I should ask Becky. If she ever speaks to me again.* She said quickly, "What about Mrs. Zimmerman?"

"She's a successful magician. She helped me do the name-magic, and to pick the flowers."

"You mean, to choose them," said Gentian, automatically doing as Becky would, since Becky wasn't here.

"Well, yes, I do, but we had to pick them as well."

"So this works how?" *Changeling technology again;* she might as well find out about it. *Though given what Dominic had said about juniper, gentian, and rosemary, she supposed she knew.*

"Well," said her father, "it wards off harmful influences, however exactly you want to describe them; the manuals say these plants keep away evil spirits, and witches, though since you can certainly describe Mrs. Zimmerman as a witch, it isn't that simple. We assumed that by a witch they meant somebody with evil intentions, which is consistent enough. When the harmful influence is a person, that person is afflicted with whatever effects the herb has. I assume Dominic made advances to you, and it made him feel sick."

"Well, yeah, I guess you could say that, but—but—look, Daddy, he was making advances for *months,* with that time machine, not to mention lying his head off whenever he thought he could get away with it, but your preventive stuff only worked when he tried to kiss me." And succeeded, she thought, and a shiver, neither pleasant nor unpleasant, went up her back. "That was probably the *best* thing he did, not the worst." Or was it? How captivating might kissing have been, if Dominic had not stopped it? Might she have stopped it herself?

"Where is he, by the way?"

"He went out to the balcony and disappeared." She added, as her father looked expectant, "Well, he swelled up and turned into a very cold blue light, like a type B star, and then he disappeared."

"I wouldn't have thought the effect would be that powerful. It would just give you time to think, we thought, and keep you from being persuaded against your will. We'd hoped, too, you might be protected from the basic cultural harassment girls are subject to; I think that part worked all right."

Gentian extracted from this rambling speech the part she found relevant, and answered it. "Well, it wasn't just the kiss. He said, 'What is worse nor woman was,' and I said that he was. That was what made him leave."

"Ah," said her father. "The devil is worse nor woman was. That's the answer to his riddle."

"Oh, *fine.* Talk about damning half the human race with faint praise."

"The devil is not known for his evenhandedness."

"Dad. You don't even believe in the devil."

"I don't believe in the overall system he's usually said to be a part of. But there are more things in heaven and—"

Gentian groaned, theatrically, and he stopped, smiling.

"What did you mean by 'we'?" said Gentian after a moment. "When you said you hoped this or that? You and Mrs. Zimmerman? What about Mom?"

"Well, your mother and I had agreed that I would get to name the girls we had and she would get to name the boys, but there didn't turn out to be any boys."

"Huh. Don't boys need protection too?"

"That's what Rosemary said. Mrs. Zimmerman. She wanted me to tell Kate what we were doing, and I agreed, finally, to do so if we had a boy."

"I think you should have asked us."

"Since this is not a society in which people choose their own names at some age of reason, there wasn't a way to do that. Besides, the teenage years are times of crisis, but you needed protection earlier just as much."

"I think it was wrong."

"Gentian, all parents protect their children. I just had a little extra ammunition."

"And I just got a little extra supernatural weirdo."

"I guess this is what comes of trying to protect you from ordinary garden-variety sexuality. I suppose we upset the ecological balance, in some way. Only the top predator was left."

"You know," Gentian burst out suddenly, "I keep getting really mad at you, and then I get interested in how this all worked and I'm not mad any more. Is that another effect?"

"I doubt it. It'll be nature or nurture. Your mother is like that. And that makes my point in another way. Parents influence their children, in a multitude of ways."

"I don't want," said Gentian, sticking to the one thing she was sure of, "to go through life making people sick."

"You won't make everybody sick. Just amnesiac gentlemen with improbable ambitions who make sexual advances."

"But what if I *like* amnesiac gentlemen with improbable ambitions?" It was just like parents, to give you a name that protected you from what you wanted.

"Learn all the riddles you can, until your taste matures," said her father, dryly. He sounded like her mother. He rubbed his forehead. "Amnesiac gentlemen are really nothing to the purpose—they could kiss you till the cows come home and feel entirely splendid if they don't wish you any harm."

"But who *decides* what's harm?" cried Gentian. "What have you got, some kind of computer program?"

"I'd put it in another way; I'd say you have an instinct for harmful intentions."

"If I did, wouldn't I be the one feeling sick?"

"Yes, all right, but I don't see why you should suffer instead of the person who means harm."

"But I don't have any control over it!"

"Well, you could, when you're older. Rosemary and I could teach you."

"I'm a scientist, not a magician."

"You can't be scientific about feelings," said her father, wearily.

"You can be scientific about *anything.*"

"Well, then you can be scientific about magic."

Gentian was silent. She had walked right into that one. It might even be true, not just a rhetorical point. "How old is older?" she said.

"Oh, the default is eighteen, among the children of magicians; but given how you've acquitted yourself, maybe earlier. I'd have to consult your mother. I didn't expect to have to think about this."

"How many magicians *are* there? Is it heritable?"

"I don't know and sometimes. It's not a separate talent, it's part of the same complex as lots of creative endeavors."

Gentian dragged herself back to the point, and said, "But you won't show how me to control this, this instinct right now."

"You didn't acquit yourself that well."

Gentian was so furious she could not speak.

"What have you done with his time machine?" said her father.

"It's—it's kind of shriveled up," said Gentian, intrigued all over again, in spite of herself. "It was an illusion, I guess. Or it was supernatural too, and he was the power for it."

"It's probably just as well," said her father, but he looked wistful.

"If he hadn't kissed me," said Gentian. Why had he? Because

he liked her? No. Because he had tried every other form of persuasion. Because he wanted his own way.

"If kissing you could make him sick," said her father, "then I wouldn't care to trust him with a time machine."

"What, you mean this spell or whatever you call it doesn't just look at whether somebody wants to hurt me? That it'll only let in people you could trust with a time machine? How the hell does it decide that?"

"Well, you do. It's just an aid."

"But I didn't. I let in Dominic. And you got it all backwards, anyway—he could kiss me until the *cows* came *home* and it wouldn't do any harm, but you let him lie and cheat and upset Alma and Steph and Erin and make me neglect them all and lose a whole nine months of astronomy and—"

"Neither I nor any spell could keep Dominic from lying to anybody or you from mislaying your priorities."

"I really don't get this. What's the use of this thing if it lets me be deceived and gets all upset when I get kissed?"

"There's a difference between dreaming and doing. That time in the attic, all your thoughts of Dominic, that was dreaming. When it came to doing, you found out what he was."

Was that true? When had she found out what he was? It wasn't a discrete moment, like the pinpoint of bright Castor to the naked eye; it was a complicated dance of spectroscopic and eclipsing binaries that only tended to a point when you were far enough away. She wasn't far enough away yet.

"He kissed *Junie,*" said Gentian, jarred into memory. "Months and months ago, when they went out to a movie. And *she* didn't make him sick."

"That must have been dreaming for her, not doing. Did she ever make him sick?"

Gentian considered this. "Not that I know of—well, you know, in fact, when she told him off and stomped out of the project because she found out he'd lied to Sarah, he looked as if he felt awful. That is, as if he'd eaten something he was allergic to, not as if his feelings were hurt. I can't think what might hurt his feelings."

"They're permanently hurt," said her father.

Gentian thought it over. "I think," she said, "I'd rather have been left alone to figure things out for myself."

"Well, it's as well you weren't, under the circumstances."

"And if you were *going* to interfere, why did you let it go *on* so long?"

"Well, that was your mother's idea."

"Where is she?"

"Attending to the trick-or-treaters."

Gentian got up without a word, and when through the bright kitchen and the hallway, and into the front hall. She opened the door on the cool, leaf-smelling autumn night. Her mother had just sent a group of five very small children on their way; Gentian could see a couple of older kids waiting for them at the bottom of the stairs.

"Mom," said Gentian. "I need to talk to you."

Her mother turned without hurry or surprise, but when she saw Gentian she closed her eyes for a moment, as Gentian had once seen her do when a cat that had seemed about to be hit by a car reappeared unharmed on the other side of the street. "Oh, good," she said. "I was beginning to think you would be immured in your tower forever, spinning cobwebs. Just a minute." She pulled from under the porch swing a piece of cardboard on which was printed in block letters, "TWO PIECES OF CANDY PER CUSTOMER; SORRY WE CAN'T ADMIRE YOU," and propped it up against her basket of candy.

Gentian went back into the house and made her way to her father's office again. She heard her mother shut the front door, and the jingle of hangers as her mother hung up her coat. Her mother came into the office through the door into the dining room, the pan of brownies in one hand and the teapot in the other, three mugs hooked by their handles over her thumb.

"Welcome back," she said to Gentian. "I was getting worried."

Gentian's father took the teapot and mugs from her, put them all on the filing cabinet, and started pouring tea. It was strong black tea flavored with cinnamon and orange rind, and as the steam of it filled the air it seemed to Gentian the first real thing she had smelled since last Halloween's wood smoke. Her father touched his little CD player to life, and Laurie Anderson started singing about how in heaven everything is made of light, and the days keep going by. The song about the lawn-mowing angels would follow. Everything seemed the same as ever. But it's not, she thought. I've lost three-quarters of a year, and maybe my cat, and maybe all my friends; my parents didn't take care of me, they didn't trust me to take care of myself; and I've lost—. She said, "Why didn't you get worried back in January?"

"I did, of course. But I'm a financial analyst, not a witch. Juniper and Rosemary, who are in many ways far weaker characters than you are, had had enough of Dominic in a month. If you were still there, there might be a reason."

"Dad says that was all dreaming, not doing."

"You won't have the second without the first."

"Platitudes Unlimited," said Gentian.

"It's true just the same."

"You put a spell on me because you didn't trust me to take care of myself, and then when I couldn't, you didn't rescue me."

Gentian's mother looked at her for a long moment, but when she spoke she said only, "You didn't need rescuing."

"I did need it. I'd have gone on forever if it hadn't been for that spell."

"It's not a spell," said her father, "it's a property of—"

"I don't care what the technical term is."

"You rescued yourself, Genny. You answered Dominic's riddle. From your experience and your heart. You named him what he was."

"That's just legalistic. It sounds good but it's not true. I hate you." That was legalistic, too, but there was no other way to say what she felt.

Her parents glanced at one another, in that way they had, looking sober but far from devastated. She waited to be told to go to her room; as an outcome with a slightly higher probability, she waited to be told it was all her fault and she had brought this on herself.

Her last remark was not a bad exit line, and would forestall whatever they were going to say. But she still had to live here; exiting did not really seem reasonable. They all sat there, Gentian on the floor, her father in the desk chair, her mother on the filing cabinet. Gentian felt thirsty, and drank her cooled tea. Her mother handed her a brownie on a discarded sheet of legal paper. Gentian ate it; why not. Laurie Anderson had gone through the lawn mowing angels, and a song called called "Coolsville," that Gentian always skipped, and the brain song, and was almost finished with "Beautiful Red Dress."

Next would be "The Day the Devil." Gentian decided to walk out on its first line. She might have to live here, but she could not think of anything to say, and she didn't want to think of the time she had played those songs for Becky, when everything was all right.

"Well," said Laurie Anderson reflectively, "I could just go on and on and on, But tonight, I've got a headache."

So have I, thought Gentian. She put her mug on the bookcase, occluding several of the works of Dickens. From the speakers came, not "The Day the Devil," but the next song, which Gentian always skipped; it was about how Hansel and Gretel were alive and well and living in Berlin, and it made her furious. Gretel had been the smart one when she and Hansel were kids, so why, when they were grown up, did she ask questions like "What is history" and let him hold forth interminably?

Gentian's mother handed her another brownie, which she took without thinking; so she had to stay and listen. The drama of her exit was ruined both by the absence of the Devil song and by the fact that it is hard to make a tragic exit with a large gooey brownie in your hand. She bit into it instead. Laurie Anderson sang:

"And he said: History is an angel
Being blown backwards into the future
He said: History is a pile of debris
And the angel wants to go back and fix things
But there is a storm blowing from Paradise

And the storm keeps blowing the angel
Backwards into the future
And this storm, this storm
Is called Progress."

Gentian did not believe in Progress; she believed in evolution. She had used to believe in, at least, social progress, but Erin had shaken this faith badly by reading her bits of Susan Faludi's *Backlash*. Steph's contention that a lot of the figures in that book were wrong only made her gloomier. That journalists were always getting statistics wrong and Susan Faludi might have done so said nothing good about social progress either.

The illusions of progress aside, she wondered if Laurie Anderson had met Dominic too. *He knows the way to your house, he's got the keys to your car. And when he sells you his time machine, you say, funny, that's my size.* Gentian finished her brownie, licked her fingers, and said, "What if I apologize to you and then you apologize to me?"

"Fair enough," said her father. "I apologize for using magic on you when I wasn't good enough to pull it off."

"I'm sorry I couldn't rescue you from yourself," said her mother, dryly.

"I'm sorry I tried to have it both ways, autonomy and rescue." Gentian stood up. "Well," she said, "I've got an awful lot to do. Good night."

She gave them each a hug, which they returned with considerable force. Then she ran up the stairs as fast as she could. It was not time to try coaxing Murr yet, but she left the door to the attic stairway ajar.

In her dusty, crumpled room, she picked up the telephone, and then paused. It was Halloween; either Becky was not home, or everyone was there, having a Giant Ants party without her. She could not possibly face them all at once; this would have to be done one at a time. How much truth can I tell, she thought. To Becky, everything. But what on earth will I say to Steph and Alma—or to Erin, either? They'll all be revolted, for different reasons. I guess I could say I had a mental breakdown. If Becky thinks that's a poetic kind of truth rather than a lie, maybe I'll try it. It'd be awful to have them think that. I guess I could tell them the truth. That might be more awful, but I wouldn't have to act a part and remember my lies. I don't think they've ever lied to me.

She looked around her room, feeling helpless. It was in a mess very different from the sort she put it into when she was living in it. Her bed, which she always kept clear, was piled with a wild assortment of objects. She supposed she had better clear it off, just in case she actually felt like sleeping tonight. Where had she been sleeping, anyway? I don't think I want to know, she thought. She walked over to the bed. It was more orderly than it had looked from a distance. About a third of it was covered with clean laundry, folded T-shirts and jeans, neatly rolled socks, underwear all sorted into a pile. The top item on each pile was perhaps a little grimy with dust, but she decided to ignore that, and put them all away, smoothing and laying them neatly in their places. Her father or Juniper had done all her laundry.

The next third of the bed held paper: catalogs, junk mail, a scattering of hand-addressed letters on the orange stationery Becky was trying to use up, and a large stack of *Sky and Telescope*. The subscription would have run out in May, on her birthday. She sorted through. No, her mother must have renewed it. They were all here, January through April 1994 and then on without a break, May, June, July, August—Gentian stopped, the magazines under August sliding out of her hand and landing on the floor with a slithering thud that would have brought Maria Mitchell running, if she had been there. Tucked among the magazines were newspaper clippings, computer printouts, Xeroxes of other articles.

Something had hit Jupiter. While she was toiling on an illusion, soldering nonexistent circuits, working for somebody who did not and never would love her, a comet called Shoemaker-Levy 9 had slammed into what was then the far side of Jupiter, with such violence that amateurs, watching through telescopes like hers, or smaller, had seen the bright flash of impact. She sorted feverishly through it all. Not something, some things.

Shoemaker-Levy 9 was in pieces; it had looked like a string of pearls to the first few astronomers who discovered it in March of 1993; they called it a comet train, not just a comet. It had hit Jupiter over and over, with fragments lettered from A to W. The Hubble Space Telescope had sent images that were uploaded to the Internet; the Galileo space probe had sent images; astronomers all over the world had watched the impacts and then tracked the spots left on Jupiter. It did not in fact look as though Gentian, or much of anybody else in North America, would have been able to witness any of the impacts. But she could have looked at the spots. She could have seen Heidi Hammel and other astronomers being paid respectful attention by television reporters. She had missed the most spectacular astronomical event of the century.

She looked over at the telescope, and turned out her reading lamp. If she remembered correctly, Jupiter would be hard to see this month, too close to the sun, and would have set by now anyway. She did not check her memory. She would not look at the new Jupiter just yet.

She sat, waiting for her eyes to adapt a little to the dark. The fixed, eternal stars were neither. Comets hit planets; stars blew up. The entire universe was expanding, at a rate astronomers had not yet calculated precisely, but that they thought was somewhere between fifty and a hundred kilometers per second for each megaparsec of distance between the distant galaxies and the sun. Stars and clusters and galaxies had their own local motions as well, as names like the Ursa Major Moving Cluster demonstrated. Thuban, not Polaris, had once been the Pole Star; the Big Dipper had once had a longer handle and a much less dipper-shaped cup, and in another hundred thousand years would look more like a shoe tree or a Dustbuster than a dipper.

But compared to events here, earthward where the trouble lay, industrious man tossing his ribald stones all over, the stars were indeed, as they had once been called, the firmament. Gentian took her red-hooded flashlight from its drawer, and examining matters with it, saw with relief that she had taken care of the telescope, she had not left the dome open to weather, or forgotten to put the lens caps back, or done any of the other terrible things she might have, in her idiot state, to damage it. Her room was still colder than the night outside, the best condition for stargazing.

It was October 31, at eight o'clock in the evening. Overhead were Pegasus, the Great Square, Andromeda, Casseiopeia, Cepheus, Cygnus. Orion was not there; it would not rise until between three and four in the morning. The last thing she had looked at was Serpens Caput, the head of the serpent constellation split by Ophiuchus, once Aescalepius, the Healer, now called Serpent-Charmer and Serpent-Bearer. Serpens was the only constellation that came in two parts. The second part was called Serpens Cauda, the tail of the serpent.

That wily old serpent the devil, Gentian thought. He's turned tail and run—in fact, he's kaput. She smiled grimly at her joke. What shall I look at, then, in the tail of the serpent? Oh, yes, of course. She would find M5, an extremely fine globular cluster in the same constellation. It was finer in photographs, or in a larger telescope, but even in Gentian's it was very bright, and seemed to grow larger while she contemplated it, as slowly its fainter outlying stars showed themselves. It looked like a luminous pile of spilled sugar, a concentrated heap of bright white in the center thinning out to granular edges, with smaller fainter grains the further out you looked. She used averted vision on it, automatically, letting the edges of her eyes gather light, as was their function. The sugary dusting grew denser.

I should have tried this on Dominic. I looked at him with the wrong part of my eye. I wonder what his faint companions, his mother, that woman with the mirror, that house, would have looked like then.

I wonder if my yellow flag iris will come up in the spring.

"The serpent, subtlest beast of all the field," she said, repeating what Dominic had said to her when she came back from viewing M16. "Then I am a beast of the house, and I am subtler yet. What else shall I look at?"

Ophiuchus was the reason Serpens was split into two parts; Ophiuchus, the Serpent-Charmer. She had not charmed Dominic;

it was the other way around. But Ophiuchus had the Serpent in
his grip, and she would look at him. He was right above the
western horizon, not the best place, but she would look at him
anyway. She would look at that portion of the Milky Way that
lay in Ophiuchus, with its dark rifts and lanes, the equatorial dust
band beyond which was the nucleus of the galaxy. She looked for
a long time, because when she stopped, she would have to read
Becky's letters.

She could not quite bear, especially with no cat on her lap, to
read all of them. She sat on her bed under the electric blanket
with the rest of the mail weighing her feet down, and skimmed
the letters in orange envelopes, putting each aside as it became
unbearable. She had a hard time opening the very last one. It was
much thinner than the others, and probably said something like,
"Go to hell, then." She opened it at last, ripping the envelope in
half, and pulled out one folded sheet of paper. It was a poem.

Some say we picture lovers face to face
Entwined, intent each on the other alone,
While friends are side by side intent, and gaze
Upon some truth each thought himself to own
Sole, strange, and lonely: Friendship is that wood
In which run rank all flowers we thought rare,
In which at first aghast we stared and stood
To see two phoenix dazzle the dim air.
But when I think of you in terms of these
Symbolical fine patterns, full of grace,
We are not side by side but back to back,
Intent upon two mirrors where we gaze:
But I see your face multiplied in glass,
And you see mine, through those infinities.

Gentian turned the lamp off again and sat in the dark for a
little, clutching the paper. She went back to the telescope, and
found Albireo.

She gathered the telephone into her lap, and still looking
steadfastly at the double star, she dialed Becky's number.